BY FIRE AND FLOOD

SONGS OF GALARMOS
BOOK 1

SAGE KAFSKY

Tellicoee
Publishing

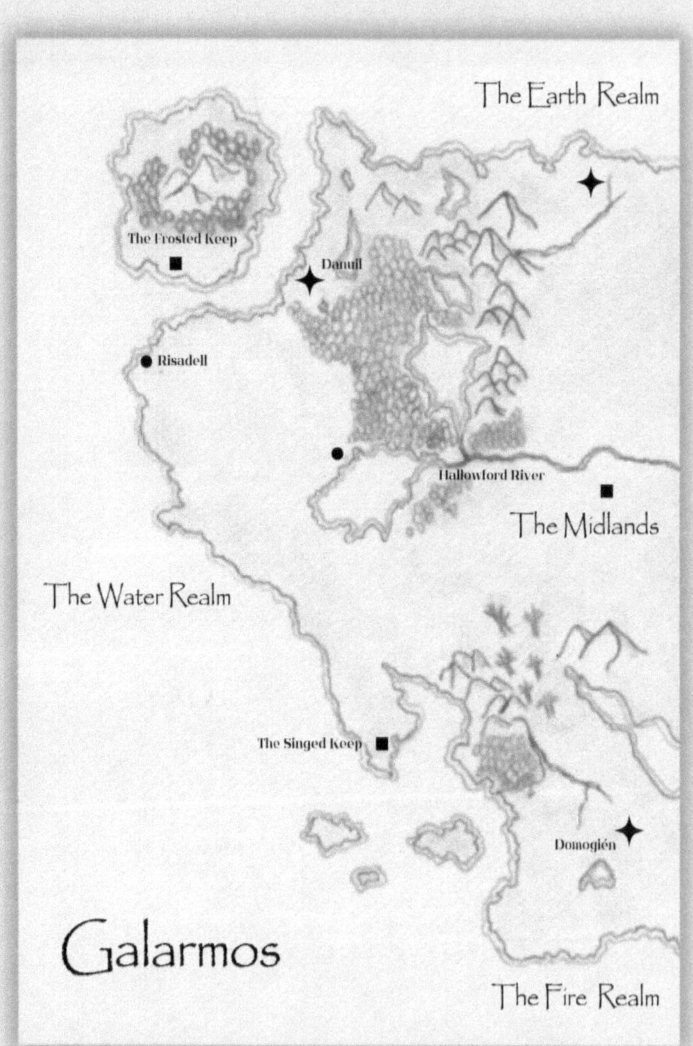

The Earth Realm
The Frosted Keep
Danuil
Risadell
Hallowford River
The Midlands
The Water Realm
The Singed Keep
Domogién
Galarmos
The Fire Realm

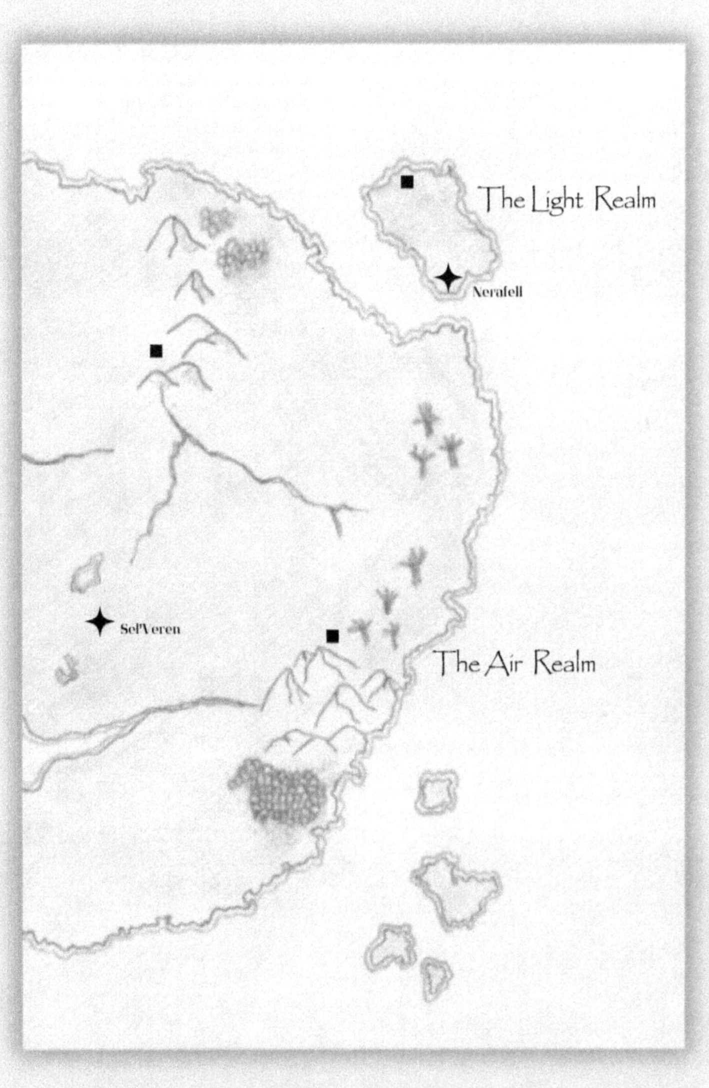

The Light Realm
Nerafell
Sel'Veren
The Air Realm

For the life-changers, the cycle-breakers, and those who refuse to stop fighting for the life they deserve.

This one's for you.

1

———————

restful night of sleep is an apology in advance from the gods. Nissa groaned at the knocking at her door, which turned into heavy pounding before she could pull the pillow over her head to drown it out. *What time is it?* She turned her head, cracking one eye open a slit to survey the color of the light piercing her room through the window on the far wall. It was faint enough to tell her that she still had an hour or two before dawn wreaked its havoc on her day.

"Nissa! Wake *up*." An annoyed, muffled voice reached her through the wood of her door, and she groaned. *Training... Right.* She took a breath and heaved herself from beneath her heavy bed covers, and goosebumps erupted across her skin at the sudden cold. She shivered involuntarily as she shuffled across the room and grasped the garments she'd picked out the night before. She jumped as a particularly aggressive thud shook the door on its hinges.

"I'm coming!" she called grumpily. "Give me a second." Moments later, she pulled open the doors to reveal the sleep-mussed, brown hair and scowling face of her best friend.

"Took you long enough." Faris stepped back, arms crossed as he surveyed her. Nissa stifled a yawn.

"Sorry. I was sleeping. Some of us do that, you know."

"I thought this was *your* idea." He rolled his eyes good-naturedly, nudging her with one shoulder. She dodged the blow and shoved him back with a quiet laugh.

"I'm more awake than you," she teased. Faris shook his head, sending strands of brown hair dancing haphazardly around his head with the motion, before he let out a long-suffering sigh.

"I guess we'll see." Nissa bit back a returning jab as a shuffle around the corner made her freeze in horror. She tossed her eyes from one end of the hall to the other, wondering which of the presumably locked doors she should wrench open in search of a hiding place. In the next moment, the sounds of movement shifted in the opposite direction, and she let herself relax. Daughter of the Water Realm's governing lord she might be, but that hardly gave her the freedom to do as she pleased. Worry had darkened Faris's expression by the time her eyes found his face again.

"Are you sure you want to do this?" he asked. She forced herself to scoff as she looked away.

"We wouldn't have made this much progress if I'd turned back every time I thought some busybody was lurking around the corner." It was a bravado that she didn't feel.

"I just want to make sure. You know that if your father—"

"My father has enough poor opinions of me. I doubt this would tip the scale." There was no hiding the acid in her tone now.

"I just don't want to be the reason that things get worse." His voice was soft now, and when she looked up again, she found that he was studying her carefully. He'd seen too much of her over the years for her to pretend that she could fool him now. Her father had never approved of her doing anything that didn't further their House's power, and they were both long past the point of being too naive to consider the consequences.

"You know my father," she said with a humorless laugh. "Things will always get worse regardless." When he didn't respond, she forced herself to brighten. "At least this way, I can kick *someone's* ass when he finally ships me off to marry some lord." Faris shook his head with another sigh, taking a step back as his expression darkened further.

"Come on," he muttered. "We're burning daylight." Nissa swallowed nervously at his change in mood, but she didn't argue as they trudged on in silence.

The tension in her body loosened instantly as they reached a familiar door. Faris pushed ahead of her to push it open, and when he shut it behind them after they entered, it was as though he'd shut the world out with it. There were plenty of rooms in her father's house that nobody visited; her home in Danuil was old enough that the stones spoke to a time when the House of Chantara spread its branches across the continent. The smaller remains of the once-widespread family that clung to a residence here reveled in the power that had been passed through the bloodline, but they certainly didn't need all of the old bedrooms that came with it. She flipped her hair over and gathered it into a bun, tying it off before she straightened again.

"What are we working on today?" she asked Faris, turning to him as she bounced on the balls of her feet. He looked her up and down thoughtfully, his lips twitching as he considered. Finally, he jerked his chin to where three discarded blades rested on a dusty side table.

"Pick a target and throw those. I want to make sure that your form is—" Before the words had left his mouth, a trio of thuds drowned out his voice as, one after another, the tips of the knives sank into a plank of old wood that leaned against a far wall.

"You were saying?" she asked brightly. His mouth curved in a bemused smile. He cracked his knuckles.

"Alright, then. Warm-up's over. Let's see what you can do today."

Nissa's muscles were burning, deliciously on fire when she finally returned to her rooms. Light was streaking through the window now, pale yellow against the frost that bloomed on the glass; she would have time to wash up from the exercise but not for much else. The same could not be said for Faris; he would have to rush across the grounds to make his morning guard shift.

Her knees wobbled as she crossed the room to the tub that stood partially concealed behind folding panel of darkened wood. She grimaced as she turned a knob and cool water spilled out. *Better enjoy the warmth while you can.* She slipped from her exercise clothes, shivering in anticipation, before she settled herself in the tub. Her body stiffened as the water's chill rose to caress her, and she lifted a hand to let the stream from the faucet pool in her palm. She amused herself with manipulating the water into different whirls for a few moments, wishing that her water wielding also allowed her to heat the water, but that was beyond the scope of her abilities. Nissa curved her palm around the stream and coaxed it to flow faster into the tub; if she was going to be cold, she might as well get the worst part of submersion over with. She was just becoming used to the coolness of the tub when another knock at the door signaled that it was time for her to get dressed.

"Lady Nissa, are you awake yet?" A feminine voice called out to her, and she rose shakily, spilling over the edge of the tub as she fumbled for her robe. When the fabric was securely belted around her waist, she stumbled out from behind the privacy panel.

"Oh, yes, I was just getting ready!" she called in reply, glancing frantically around for her clothes from earlier. She kicked them so that they were fully concealed behind the wooden panel before she sprang over to the basin that stood near her bed. She winced at the protest in her quads. Faris's workouts had put her through her paces, and she knew she would be sore before evening.

"May I come in?"

She glanced up at the mirror that hung over the basin, wrinkling her nose at the way that her hair hung in tangled strings around her cheeks. With a hasty sweep of her arm, she tossed her hair so that the dripping ends hung above the basin and screwed up her eyes, pleading with her magic to wring the water from it for her.

"Of course, Phaedra." The last of the water was nearly gone from her hair when the door creaked open. A slight, pale young woman slipped through the door and shut it neatly behind her. As she turned, the gleam of her dark hair, pulled tightly into an unforgiving bun, caught the light and shone.

"Please forgive the intrusion, my lady," Phaedra said quietly, keeping her eyes lowered respectfully. "They sent us early to strip the beds." Something unpleasant curled in Nissa's stomach. When it came to her father's household, deviations in schedule—however slight—were never a good sign. They were usually a sign of an impending complication.

"Oh, it's no trouble." She kept her voice light as she turned back to face her reflection in the mirror. She schooled her expression into careful neutrality as she picked at a few ends of her hair before letting them fall limply back in place. *At least today won't call for anything too special.* She pulled it back into a tail low on her head, tying off the ribbon with a flourish before she stepped toward her wardrobe in search of the day's dress. She dressed hastily once the maid had left the room, stepping quickly down the hall with steps that felt too loud against the aged stone.

2

The voice of her tutor took on a droning quality, and Nissa occupied herself with the journey of an iridescently winged insect as it climbed across the wall behind him. A loose thread sprang from her skirt, and she twirled it absently between her fingers. The day had, despite the change in her chambermaid's routine, gone on as expected. She'd taken breakfast in silence with her mother and younger brother. After breakfast, she'd attended a fitting for a new cloak, a gaudy number lined with enough fur that she was amazed she hadn't suffocated, and then she'd gone for a brief walk in the gardens—supervised, of course— before the chill of the wintery air had driven her back inside. Lunch had been a solitary affair, as her brothers and her mother had been summoned to a meeting with her father—one that Nissa wasn't sorry to miss. Finally, as expected, she had arrived at her afternoon lessons precisely on-schedule, during which her tutor, a wiry man nearing middle age, had continued to the next in his series of lectures on the cultural traditions that each region of her realm held most dear.

"Lady Nissa, are you listening?" he asked, breaking

through her trance impatiently. Her hand stilled as her eyes jerked to his usually mild face. His brow was creased with annoyance, and his brown eyes, normally gentle, snapped with irritation.

"I'm sorry, Master Blake. You were saying?" She forced a bland smile onto her face, the very same she'd seen her mother give over the years. He wasn't fazed.

"This is important," he insisted. She sighed softly, dropping her eyes to her lap. She knew that she should be thankful for the monotony of her day. In her experience, deviations meant some unpleasant idea of her father's. At this moment in time, though, she wanted to be anywhere else.

"I understand, sir. The Realms each have uniquely rich, cultural histories." It was a phrase he'd repeated to her innumerable times, but from his scowl, he didn't appreciate her parroting it now.

"You'll be expected to take the Oath yourself one day, Nissa. You would do well to pay attention now." She winced at the exasperation in his voice.

"I don't see why." She'd had only rudimentary lessons on the significance of the Water Realm's sacred Blood Oath, but from she knew that it required her to share her power with another. From what she also knew of her father's less-than-favorable opinion of her abilities, she couldn't imagine why he would ever want her to weaken herself further.

"It's a tradition, and it will make you stronger," Master Blake insisted. "Your parents took the Oath, and so will you. It's how our strongest bloodlines have continued to thrive."

"By dividing their power further?" she shot back. He shook his head.

"You really haven't been paying attention." She blinked at him, taken aback at his tone. "The Oath isn't about division. It binds the swearers together. In taking it, your abilities are married to each other so completely that they become indistinguishable from each other. In that way, you become a greater whole." Her stomach sank.

"I don't want to do that." She barely registered her own whisper as it slipped from between her lips. A flicker of sympathy broke through Master Blake's exasperation, but it was gone before she could seize it. He dropped his gaze, shuffling some papers in front of him before he cleared his throat.

"The Oath is made by blood and confirmed and sealed with an oath of fealty. In your parent's case, they swore the second part of this when they married each other. I expect that yours will be the same." She shuddered at the thought of binding her blood to some malevolent stranger hand-selected by her father.

What would he sell her for? Would he exchange her hand for greater control of one of their realm's far-reaching regions? What goods or services would be worth plopping her in front of the highest bidder? She wondered if he would even bother vetting the person he selected, or if she would be thrown to someone who was a stranger to them all.

"Surely we aren't there yet," she said in a small voice. Master Blake took a deep breath, his thin chest expanding more than she would have thought possible.

"I can't speak for Lord Alvar," he said, before dropping his voice with a wary look around them, "but it's important that you pay attention, Lady Nissa. It's important that you know these things so that you can prepare yourself." The non-answer left her with more questions, but before she could pose them, he moved on.

She rubbed the space between her brows roughly, struggling to focus as he shifted his discussion to a different region of the realm. He was right; she needed to prepare herself for whatever was to come. *Take the crumbs you're given*, had been the advice Faris had given her years ago, after she'd spent the better part of a half-hour ranting about a lesson devoted to the different ways to curtsy to those of varying ranks. She was the daughter of Governing Lord Alvar Chantara; she didn't expect she'd have to curtsy to anyone. At the time, Faris's advice had stung, had felt dismissive, but once her temper had cooled, she'd seen what he'd meant. Knowledge was a privilege in her world. She might never be heir to their realm like her older brother or have the chance to be an emissary, as her younger brother was expected to become, but knowledge could be power in its own way. The thing that mattered most was how one chose to wield it.

Nissa was absorbed in Master Blake's description of a particularly unique harvest tradition, adopted by one of their realm's most prominent fishing towns to honor the high season, when a knock at the door interrupted him mid-sentence. She cut her eyes at the door, annoyed at the distraction, when Master Blake cleared his throat.

"You may enter." She stifled a smile at his imperious tone. A young man—more of a boy really—entered meekly, dipping his head to them both.

"My apologies, sir," he said, bobbing his head as his face reddened.

"To what do I owe this intrusion?" Master Blake arched an eyebrow.

"Lady Marin, sir, she wants to see Lady Nissa at once…" He trailed off, turning to Nissa with an apologetic nod as his flush deepened. "Something about a cloak, my lady." Irritation sparked in her blood, but she pressed her mouth into a neutral line.

"Of course. I'll come at once," she said flatly. *Naturally, she'd summon me when I'm actually doing something I'm interested in.* Her lip threatened to curl at the memory of that thick, hot fur, and she forced it down as she turned toward Master Blake.

"I suppose that concludes our day," he said disapprovingly. She inclined her head.

"Thank you for the lesson, Master." *And the reminder*, she

finished silently. Nissa rose to her feet wearily, wincing as the stiffness zinged through her legs. To her relief, the boy servant didn't attempt to make conversation as he lumbered along beside her. There was no need; Nissa knew where they were going. She'd spent countless hours in her mother's preferred fitting room, being prodded one way or another, pinched by corsets or stuck with pins. It was second nature to venture down that hallway.

She was only half-present as the seamstress on duty guided her onto the pedestal in the center of the room, clucking about fabrics and the color of frost as she turned her this way and that. Nissa felt a bit like a doll being spun on an axis, and she didn't bother asking what occasion this particular garment would grace. Half of the gowns that were made never saw the light of day due to her father's changing whims. She'd stopped wondering. For her mother's part, Lady Marin sat quietly in the shadows, barely moving, never speaking. She'd maintained a soft, nearly silent vigil for years, and any memory of her as lively or spirited existed, in Nissa's mind, as a memory so distant that it could have been a dream.

There had been a time when she'd aspired to something more. She'd hoped to be a powerful wielder, like the women in both sides of her ancestral line. As a child born into the union of two powerful Water Realm families, one who boasted the powers of ice, and the other who held the might of flowing water, she'd had the chance at greatness. She knew that there had even been whispers that she—or one of her brothers— might be gods-blessed with the powers of both. When the first flickers of power had revealed themselves when she turned 16 and had only allowed her to manipulate water in its liquid form —and even then, in simple ways— Nissa had solidified her role as a disappointment in her father's eyes. When her powers matured at 18 and she had still shown no sign of greatness, the disappointment had hardened into distaste. Now, at 23, her father's ambitions were unchanged. He'd been making noises for years about allying with other powerful families. It was only a matter of time before one of his ideas took hold, and Nissa had seen enough of the world and her father's hunger to rise that she knew that such alliances meant marriage. *Anything to rid himself of the family disappointment,* she thought sourly.

She returned her attention to her reflection, watching motionlessly as women scurried around her, bending and scraping and pulling delicately on the silvery fabric that swathed her body. It was a lovely garment, to be sure, but it, like so much of her life, felt colorless. Nissa didn't think she was imagining the hollowness that had started to sneak into her hazel eyes. Her eyes darted to the space where her mother's figure was reflected, wreathed in too many shadows to make out any of her more defining features.

3

———————

"Nissa, wake up!" She jerked abruptly as the sound of her name pierced through the veil of sleepy fog. Her eyes flew open, locking on Faris's gray eyes, widened with concern. She clutched her covers to her chest as he ran a hand through his already tousled brown hair, shaking her head to clear the last cobwebs of slumber.

"What are you doing in here?" A glance at the window told her that the first, peach light of dawn had crept above the horizon. Frosty tendrils had crept up the glass, shining gold against the light. Day was breaking, but it was still far too early for any male to be seen in her rooms alone.

"Lord Alvar called a meeting, and he wants you there. He didn't sound happy," Faris said. Nissa winced; her father was rarely happy, but for Faris to risk being discovered in her room at this scandalous hour, she knew that his displeasure must have been more obvious than usual. Iron-clad rules governed where members of her father's guard could roam. Despite their friendship, her bedroom at dawn didn't fit within those parameters.

"A meeting... *Now*?" She blinked at her friend. Dawn meetings never boded well when her father was in a mood, and it seemed as though he was always in some sort of mood these days, for all manner of reasons. Her mouth twisted sourly as she recalled the tone of their most recent confrontations.

"Nissa? Did you hear me?" Faris broke her from her thoughts, and as she focused her gaze on him again, a small line of distress creased the space between his brows. He scratched behind one arched ear, and she smoothed her scowl.

"Sorry, what was that?" She forced a small smile onto her face, trying to ignore the spiral of thoughts that threatened to drag her down.

"He's sending Murdoch up to escort you. I thought you might want to be ready." Nissa scowled. Murdoch was a hulking, brutish man, who wore a leering smile and the constant stench of unwashed sweat. He was also her father's favorite henchman. She avoided his company whenever possible.

"Thanks. I'm up. You should probably go before someone finds you here." Nissa swung her legs out of the bed and prepared to stand, still clutching the blankets to her to shield her nightclothes. His face reddened, as though he was recognizing her state of undress for the first time, and he averted his eyes.

"I know," he said quietly. "Nissa," he paused for a second, eyes searching her face for a moment before they clouded. "Good luck today. And be careful. I don't know what's going on, but... Be on your guard."

"I always am." She answered with a confidence that she did not feel. He nodded shortly, the worry not altogether gone from his face, and in the next moment, he was gone. Nissa inhaled, forcing her ribs expand and allowing the pressure to quiet her thundering heart. There were only a handful of reasons that her father would deign to speak to her, and she was under no illusion that the most likely reason was the prospect of a new alliance. He'd been pressing her on the subject for years, and she knew that—in his eyes—she had long outlived her time at home; it was time to face the consequences of her birth and her lack of power.

She had just slipped into a day dress of frosty gray when a pounding at her door signaled Murdoch's arrival. Nissa ignored it for a moment as she twisted two, soft brown strands of her hair back, clipping them in place before threading glittering, diamond teardrops through the lobes of her delicately pointed ears. She studied the contrast that the cool stones cast against her hazel eyes before she took another steely breath and opened her door.

"My Lady," Murdoch greeted, the steely gray crown of his head revealing a balding patch as he inclined his head in mocking respect. Nissa was almost pleasantly surprised at the lack of odor wafting off of him. *Did he wash his uniform?* Murdoch was wearing Chantara colors, a tunic that sported intertwining vines of frosted blue and gray over silver pants. His boots, black and shining, gave off the strong tang of a fresh polish, and his hands were as clean as Nissa had ever seen them where they rested on the hilt of his sheathed sword. He'd even trimmed the grizzled tufts of hair that normally protruded from his ears. Only the unsettling grin was unchanged. *We must have a guest.* She nodded coolly in response.

"Murdoch," she greeted, "what does he want?" Murdoch's smile faded as his lips tightened.

"I suppose His Lordship will be the one to tell you that," he answered. Nissa forced a close-lipped smile on her face.

"Off we go, then. It wouldn't do to keep Lord Alvar waiting," she said. He nodded sharply, gesturing with one hand for Nissa to lead the way. She tried not to recoil as she swept past him, even more so when he matched his pace to hers. Thankfully, he followed the example of determined silence that Nissa set, and when they arrived at what Nissa privately referred to as her father's throne room, she was thankful to be rid of him at last.

There were no named kings in the Realms of Galarmos, at least not in the traditional sense, although in Nissa's opinion, their system of governance was much the same as if there were. Generations ago, far beyond living memory, particular heads in families of power had been given the title of Governing Lord. For now, the titles of Lord and Lady amongst the wielders of the Water Realm belonged to Nissa's family, what remained of the House of Chantara. Her father was determined that the continuity of their line remained unbroken—at least, he had repeated the sentiment often enough over the years that Nissa assumed his blind fervor was unchanged. The strength of their line manifested itself in this high-ceilinged room in the Water Realm's capital city of Danuil—no doubt named after one obscure relative or another— where beams of warm-toned wood lay at odds with walls of pewter stone.

On a dais against the far wall sat her father's throne of choice, a high-backed chair crafted of twisting tendrils of black elm. It was carved with intricate designs that spoke of an age long forgotten, and it was undeniably a seat of power. Nissa's father, Lord Alvar Chantara, tall, lean, and angular, lounged in his chair, his piercing blue eyes peering out from beneath his jet-black hair and high forehead. Next to him, Lady Marin, Nissa's mother, sat delicately in her chair carved of warm-toned wood, decorated with whimsical whirls that had always reminded Nissa of the sea. Her mother's blonde hair was braided into a coronet, with delicate strands freed and curling to frame her face. Her eyes, once a vibrant, stormy gray, stared placidly across the room without even a flicker of acknowledgement at her arrival. At Marin's side stood Nissa's younger brother, Lorcan. He let loose a toothy grin as he made eye contact with his Nissa. Nissa felt herself smile despite her nerves. Nothing phased Lor's ten-year-old innocence. She found herself studying his ears, still rounded with youth. How long would that innocence last once his power came to be? She adjusted a piece of her hair and flinched as her fingers brushed the slight point of her own. It was a visible reminder that her magic hadn't sharpened according to the family standard.

As she crossed the room with Murdoch at her heels, Nissa's smile dripped from her face as she met her father's cold eyes. There was no welcome in his frosty expression, but then, there usually wasn't. They made a contrasting picture on the dais, her father lounging in casual power, her mother seated expressionlessly at his side, and Nissa's brother cast as the sole light in the room. Something was missing to complete the picture. Her eyes tugged over to the empty space at her father's other side, where her older brother normally stood, and Nissa felt a flicker of gratitude at his absence. Her elder brother, Ward, had a way of making tense situations worse. If this meeting was what Nissa thought it would be, she was glad that he wasn't there to witness it. The silence roared as she came to a halt in front of the dais and locked eyes with her father again.

"Nissa," he said after a lengthy pause, "welcome." She might have been a guest, rather than a member of his family.

"Father," Nissa answered pointedly, keeping her chin high. Let her mother duck her head in submissive weakness; Nissa had promised herself a long time ago that she never would. "Where's Ward?" she asked, jerking her chin toward her older brother's usual place. Nissa felt a surge of satisfaction as her father's mouth twisted with displeasure.

"Out," he answered. She tried to repress a grimace in response. *Out* for Ward usually meant scandals, which always meant a problem for her father to cover up. Such instances rarely did much to brighten Alvar's mood. Still, it rarely amounted to more than a minor inconvenience for him. Lord Alvar was powerful, and Ward was his heir. If he ran into barriers, they were few and far between.

"Why am I here?" she asked coolly, not bothering to mask her displeasure at the summons.

"It's time that you contributed to our family legacy," he said, matching Nissa's tone. Her heart thundered in her ears. She had expected this, of course, and she knew what this meant. That fact did not make the reality of it any easier. Nissa's eyes bored into her mother, who still had not moved.

"Ah," she said noncommittally.

"We've come to a decision." The words rang in her ears. That, she hadn't expected. She'd anticipated more cold promises, more cutting reminders of her duty to her House. She hadn't expected any kind of formal decision.

"Who?" she forced her voice to match his icy indifference.

"This shouldn't come as a surprise, Nissa. We've been planning this for years." Her heart galloped in her chest again, but only for a moment. It stilled as her hands and feet ran cold, and she felt strangely disembodied from herself.

"If you're going to use me as a broodmare, can I at least know who you're selling me to?" Nissa asked, unable to keep the edge from her voice. Her father's eyes flashed a warning that she barely noticed.

"You will be *married,*" he emphasized, "into the House of Pallinor." Nissa's heart raced again, and she squeezed her eyes shut. The Pallinors, distant cousins from somewhere in her father's line, had been given an island off the coast of the territory. They ruled from the Frosted Keep, and they were a powerful family of ice-wielders. Her father maintained a tentative peace with the head of their House, mostly because he had largely yielded control of the island to him. Of that portion of the realm, Lord Alvar governed in name only.

"Will you be shackling me to Torian or Lamaris?" she asked, her voice ringing strangely in her ears. *This can't be real. This isn't real.*

"You will *marry,*" he emphasized again, a note of warning in his voice this time, "Torian Pallinor. He is as powerful as his father. Given your," he looked down his nose at Nissa, his eyes flickering to the tips of her ears, "deficiencies, we hope that mingling our bloodlines will be mutually beneficial." She scowled, barely resisting the urge to drop her hair as a shield against him.

"What makes you think that our bloodline will be any different? You wield ice, and mother wields water. Your children have yet to manifest more than one power each," she spat. Her father's mouth twisted again.

"Lorcan may very well hold both," he answered. Her little brother flinched, and the movement was too adult in his child's body. The remains of her self-control snapped as her blood boiled in her veins.

"But there are no guarantees. You're really going to sell your daughter on a *maybe?*" She rounded on her mother as her heart raced once more. "And *you!* You're okay with this? Trading your daughter like an animal?" Her mother's distant stare did not change, and she clenched her fist, feeling a slippery, whiplike tendril of water stutter to life and then die. She cursed under her breath; magic rarely turned against others of the same blood, but if there was ever a time for an exception, Nissa thought that surely this would warrant it. Lorcan made a sound of distress, glancing toward their father with a plea in his round, blue eyes.

"Don't speak to your mother that way," her father barked. When Nissa looked back, he had risen to his feet, the tips of his leather-encased fingers frosting over as the only sign of his rising temper.

"This isn't fair." In any other circumstance, the words would have made Nissa feel like a petulant child.

"Torian Pallinor is a good man. His family is powerful, and he isn't cruel. The other realms are growing more powerful by the day; we can't afford to wait," he said. "The island around the Frosted Keep is beautiful. You'll be well taken care of," her father added shortly, as though Nissa was a dog that he was rehoming. She ignored him, staring daggers at her mother again.

"Will you just *look at me?* How can you let him do this?" Her voice broke at end of her question. Marin's gray eyes snapped to meet hers, and she saw a flurry of emotions that she couldn't entirely place—panic, grief, anger in quick succession—before her mother's expression smoothed into that far-off gaze once more.

"Take her back to her room," Lord Alvar ordered Murdoch, and strands of Nissa's long, brown hair ripped from her clip and whipped across her face as she twisted away from his outstretched arm and took a step back.

"Don't touch me," Nissa slashed her arm through the air, a whip of water lengthening in her hand with the motion. Murdoch side-stepped the blow before it could crack against him. As she raised her arm again, it froze in place, the strand of water suddenly leaden and burning with cold fire in her grip. Nissa yelped as the frigid ice seared against her skin, dropping the frozen chunk with a thud as she shook her hand furiously. It shattered on impact with the stone floor. She reached automatically for her power again, blind with desperation as she whirled around again.

"Enough," her father ordered. She froze in spite of herself, only her eyes moving as they darted to where he had risen from his chair, stone-faced, jaw clenched, and arm extended.

"You *will* marry Torian Pallinor. You *will* do your duty by your family. There will be *no* further discussions." He turned to Murdoch again. "Take her back to her rooms, and make sure she doesn't leave." Murdoch moved to grab Nissa, and she wrenched away from his grip, the spell broken.

"I can walk," she hissed.

"Then walk, my lady," he said rudely. Nissa turned back to her father once more.

"I'll never forgive you," she said, hating the way that she nearly choked on the words.

"Forgiveness doesn't build dynasties," he answered, staring past her as though she wasn't even in the room. Nissa turned on her heel, ignoring her mother and brother, and left the room on her own terms. She held back most of the tears of rage that gathered in her eyes, hating herself as much as her parents as one spilled over and trailed down her cheek. The door to the throne room thudded shut on Nissa's past, and she was determined not to look back.

4

Night fell again, and then Nissa was alone, left with nothing to do but stare at the winking stars that taunted her through the window. After a long day of solitude, they seemed to taunt her with their freedom, unencumbered by the weighted decisions of those more powerful than them. Nissa pressed her forehead against the cold glass, the sensation soothing against the pounding ache behind her eyes. She pulled her knees to her chest, the soft fabric of her pants stretching over her legs as her breath sighed a fog against the glass of the window. The solitude wasn't altogether unwelcome; Nissa supposed that she could only hope for that same courtesy when she was shipped off to the Pallinors. The thought ripped from her in a shaky laugh before a pounding echoed through the room, and she leapt from the cushion that benched the sill of the window. Fear vibrated through Nissa as she felt the tingling of power in her palms. She wasn't planning to go yet, and she wasn't ready to leave without a fight.

A key jingled in the lock, and the needling in her hands became almost painful as she withheld the power there, but when the door swung open and Nissa raised her hands to do battle, it was her mother who swept into the room. Lady Marin's golden-blonde hair shone in the candlelight, braided loosely down her back. She held up her palms in truce, and the loose, silken sleeves of her robe fell back to bare the crisscross of scars that laced her forearms as she fixed Nissa with a steely look. Gone was the deadened expression that had taken up residence on her face for so many years. For the first time in a long time, her mother looked *alive*. Still, Nissa didn't trust it.

"Lady Marin. What are you doing here?" Nissa asked. Her mother frowned at the formality as she cast a glance behind her, and the door swung shut with a neat click.

"Faris let me in when the guard switched. I couldn't risk this getting back to your father," she said, loosing a breathless laugh. Nissa edged forward, lowering her hands to her sides.

"Why?" she demanded, not bothering to be polite. Her mother blinked at her before she swept an errant strand of hair out of her eyes.

"This can't happen."

"What?"

"All of this," she said, gesturing wildly with one hand. "You, Torian, the bloodline. This can't keep happening."

"And what caused this sudden epiphany?" Nissa asked coldly. Lady Marin shook her head, impatient in every part of the movement.

"Your grandmother warned me when my marriage was arranged that this pursuit of power wouldn't lead to anything but heartbreak. It's an eons-old story, but I loved your father, and I loved the life that he promised. So, I took the Oath and bound my fate to his." She looked at the window, at the stars twinkling beyond the frosty glass. "I loved a dream."

"More like a nightmare," Nissa muttered. The frown on her mother's face twisted into a scowl.

"He thinks he's doing what's right."

"He's delusional."

"Do you want my help, or not?" she hissed, and the question made Nissa pause.

"Help?"

"You shouldn't have to be punished for the mistake that I made." Her mother looked at the ground, her gray eyes as dark as the sea in a storm. Nissa felt herself soften, feeling the tension seep from her shoulders.

"How do we get out of this? How do we stop it?" she whispered. Something in Lady Marin's spine stiffened, and when she fixed Nissa with her eyes, the storms had cleared to reveal a simmering rage.

"You have to run," she said. When Nissa stayed silent, she gestured behind her to reveal a knapsack, bulging at the seams, but presumably filled with supplies for a journey.

"And where am I supposed to go that he won't find me?" Nissa asked softly.

"Anywhere. Get out of the Water Realm if you have to. Go south. The Fire Realm will be the easiest border to cross, but you could lose a tail in the mountains on the Earth Realm border." Nissa's thoughts whirled as she considered her options, and her mother's hands forced the surprisingly light pack into hers.

"But—" Her mother held up a hand to stop her.

"It's probably best that I don't know, Nissa. The Oath—you know that it means I can't lie for you... not to him," she said. Of course. Nissa's parents had sealed their union with an ancient rite, a blood oath, when they had married. That oath's magic demanded a loyalty that Marin couldn't escape, one that Nissa hoped she would never have to understand. She knew only a little about the tradition, but what she had been taught had done nothing to endear her to the practice. Nissa opened her mouth to tell her mother that she understood the need for secrecy, but before she could speak, a shout came from beyond the door.

"What are you doing here? You're not scheduled to be on duty!" The voice was muffled, but it was undeniably angry. *Faris.* What had he risked helping her escape?

"You have to go," her mother whispered frantically, her eyes darting from side to side.

"If you've stirred up trouble, there will be hell to pay, boy," the voice beyond roared. Her mother flinched as the undeniable thud of fists on flesh joined the angry shout. Marin spun to face her, and Nissa froze as her mother's hand encircled her wrist in a vice-like grip. Terror had replaced the defiance on her face, and the heartbeat that Marin held her in place, Nissa was sure she had changed her mind. Then, in a matter of heartbeats that felt like a lifetime, Marin dropped her arm and backed up several paces, hugging her arms around her as she quivered. *She's fighting it. Whatever devilry is in that oath, she's finally fighting it.*

"Go. Out the window. Climb down the trellis. I'll handle things here," she whispered. Nissa did not give her time to change her mind. She stumbled across the room, where her little-used traveling cloak hung on a hook. Her fingers fisted the thick fabric before she pulled it around herself. She turned to face her mother one more time.

"I—" Nissa swallowed the words she was going to say and just nodded once. She glanced back once as she pried open the window, shuddering involuntarily against the chill of the breeze. Her mother had her back turned, her shoulders square, and Nissa realized that this was how she wanted to remember her: strong, confident, defiant, and—if the escape went as planned—triumphant. As Nissa swung her leg out of the window and began her descent on the trellis, her hand nearly slipped when she heard the door burst open. Her mother unleashed an otherworldly scream.

"She's gone!" she wailed. "I came in and she was just *gone.*" A chill swept down Nissa's spine as she realized that Lady

Marin had just thrown Faris to the wolves. As she leapt from the trellis onto solid ground, Nissa swayed on the balls of her feet as she looked upward again, torn. Faris would be punished —and badly—for the crime of giving her a chance at freedom.

"You can't help him if you're shipped off and shackled to a Pallinor," Nissa muttered, her decision final. *I'll come back for you, Faris,* she vowed silently, pressing herself into the vines climbing the trellis as a shadowed figure peered over the edge of the windowsill.

"She's long gone by now." The wind carried the voice away, so that all that reached Nissa was the faintest of whispers, but she let out a breath. If they thought she was already far gone, that would give her little time to run. She turned to face the open night in front of her, glancing to the northeast, where the faint ridge of mountains rose, a behemoth that separated Nissa from freedom in the Earth Realm. She then glanced south, where a longer journey awaited, but no mountains stood in her way. She stiffened as an idea seized her. The Fire Realm was a dangerous place for someone like Nissa, and it was a longer journey. As aloof as the Earth Realm was, after the way that her father had ranted and raved about the bloodlust of the Fire Realm's families of power, they would never dream that such a "defective" wielder would dare trespass upon their territory. That made it the only choice. Nissa took a deep breath as she faced south; her decision was made.

She had never spent much time in the southern part of their realm, despite the fact that her mother had hailed from the region, but Nissa knew from her studies of geography as a child that her chosen route allowed her two options that would keep her close to the water. She didn't dare consider an alternative that would keep her from a source to aid her power.

She could follow the coast, the longer route, but it would take her close to the channel that separated the mainland from the Pallinor's island. The alternative was for Nissa to cut through the dense forest on the eastern side of the realm, where she could have access to the Hallowford River once she reached it. The prospect of being separated from a source for her powers for even a short journey was a daunting one, but not nearly as much as the thought of getting any closer to the Pallinor stronghold. Another gust of wind cut across Nissa's face like a blade, and she shivered, thankful that her chosen path would at least allow her the shelter of the trees. Her cloak was warm, but its shelter would only go so far. She glanced back up the walls of the fortress that she had called home, thankful that she did not see any watchful eyes. *It's now or never.* She took in the shadowy silhouettes of the trees in the distance, hefted her pack to her shoulder, and ran.

The snow-covered boughs of the forest cradled Nissa against the wind as she broke through the first lines of wooded defense. Where there had been a howling gale, there was now only a muffled whooshing sound from the world around her, and the only gusts came from her lungs as she struggled to catch her breath. Her foggy breaths rose to join the blanket of white that coated the branches above her, and despite the snow, Nissa was quite warm out of the wind. Under the protection of the canopy, she dropped her pack to the earth and hunched over with her hands on her knees as she allowed her breathing to stutter and slow into a steady, even pace. When Nissa straightened again, she squared her shoulders, turned her back on her father's house and the city that laid beyond it, and set off again. She had stalled for long enough.

Her boots crunched against the frosty leaves, and Nissa was thankful that—through whatever strange trick of her father's had caused it—that the snow above had not coated the ground below. She hadn't inherited her father's abilities to manipulate snow and ice, which meant that any footprints that she would have left behind would have been a giveaway as to her direction. *I guess that's* something *I can thank him for,* Nissa thought wryly. She glanced uneasily behind her, feeling a prickle of worry up her spine that thinking of Lord Alvar would summon him to her, but the sensation passed. She shook her head again; *I needed to get moving.*

It would not take long for him to demand that her mother scry her for him, one of the additional powers that came with her gift, and while Nissa knew that her mother would stall for as long as she could, she wanted to be far away from home before that happened. After a lifetime of submission and an oath-bound compulsion not to work against him, Nissa also knew that Lady Marin would not resist him for long.

Focus. She forced herself to concentrate on the meter of her breath and each foggy exhale as she trudged through the forest, glancing up every so often when the sky peeked from between the trees to check her direction against the stars.

Nissa's shoulders were screaming from the weight of the pack by the time the first tendrils of peach dawn slithered between the branches, shading the snow with varying shades of pink. She had stopped once or twice for a sip of water before the cold seeped into her bones in spite of the sheltered canopy, and she realized quickly that she needed to keep moving to stay warm. Fatigue and cold were a brutal cocktail when it came to aching joints, and in Nissa's case, they had made it a double. Still, the only way out was to keep moving, and so she did, each footstep feeling heavier than the last.

She walked until mid-day, and when her legs buckled under her, she decided that it was time to see if her mother had packed her any food for the journey. Saliva flooded Nissa's mouth as her frantic search yielded a couple of cranberry tarts and a small loaf of bread. Her stomach growled at the sight of the bounty. She re-wrapped the loaf in its cloth and settled for two of the smaller tarts; for all that Nissa wanted to gobble the feast, she knew that she still had at least a few of days of journeying ahead before she reached the Fire Realm border, and she would need her wits about her if she had a prayer of surviving the infiltration. The realms were not enemies, per se, but the Fire Realm had few outright allies and even fewer friends. Nissa's father had always been especially suspicious of their governing family, the powerful House of Brandell, for reasons he'd never seen fit to share with her, and the last thing that Nissa wanted to do was be caught on their side of the border, weakened and unaware.

You're already weak by their standards. Nissa huffed at the snide thought, scowling down at her slender arms. For the general population of the realm, her father was very supportive of training women as warriors. Unfortunately, the public facade had not extended to his wife or daughter, and nobody in his court had felt led to defy him. *Except Faris.* He had given Nissa exercises in recent months that had kept her muscles toned, but they had done little to build up her strength. Still, some chance at self-defense was better than none. Nissa felt a new surge of regret as she wondered what had happened to him, what price he'd had to pay for helping her to escape. *You could find out.* The snide voice had returned, but Nissa shook her head against the temptation. She may have taken after her mother in the magical sense, but she was still too close to risk scrying home. Her father's intuition—a fortunate, or in Nissa's case, unfortunate secondary gift that came along with ice-wielding—would sense the scry before Faris's image had even materialized, and it wouldn't do at all for her friend's sacrifice, whatever it had been, to have been in vain.

The thought of her proximity to her home and her father's temper rocketed Nissa to her feet. A breeze twisted through the shelter of the trees, and she shivered again; she had dawdled enough, and she needed to keep moving. Nissa squinted up to where the sunshine snapped through the trees, thankful that at least she was no longer traveling in the dark as she hefted her pack, ignoring the protest of her upper back, and set off again.

At least you won't have to worry about being cold once you cross the border. Not all of the Water Realm was coated in this frosted layer, but in the Fire Realm, far to the South of her family's home, she knew that the concept of cold would seem nothing but a distant memory. *Not that you'll be able to stay there forever.* The promise of warmer days spurred her into a faster pace, and Nissa had gained considerable ground by the time the sun had started to set once more.

The shadows seemed to dance around the tangled roots of nearby trees, and Nissa knew that she needed to sleep. It was better for her to do that under the cover of darkness than to keep pushing through until morning, when anyone could stumble across her. Thankfully, the landscape had changed, ridged with shallow ravines brought about by the centuries of erosion before the forest had sprouted, and she had no shortage of options for a hiding place. Nissa settled for a narrow dip in the earth, where she could rest comfortably without the fear of being seen immediately should someone venture by. Her joints popped as she dropped her pack and rolled her neck from side to side, and she twisted her torso to extend the stretch to her spine. Once Nissa settled herself against the earth, she reached into her pack, groping for the thin blanket that she had felt earlier. Nissa wrapped it around herself as she pressed her body into the mercifully dry soil, and that was the last thing she remembered before sleep claimed her.

5

S unlight knifed against her eyelids, and Nissa woke cursing as a drooping root knocked against her forehead. Clearly, she had needed the rest, but as she rubbed the sore spot irritably, she huffed. *An apology in advance from the gods indeed.* She snorted. This wasn't the time to catch up on her beauty rest anyway.

She gritted teeth against the eminent cold as she threw the blanket off her body, bundling it into a haphazard lump before stuffing it in her pack. Her stomach clenched as her hands brushed against the food bundles, and after a moment's deliberation, she curbed her appetite with one of the cranberry tarts. After chasing the last crumbs with a swig of water, she repacked her canteen and rose, hefting the pack onto her protesting shoulders. She had been in one place for too long; she needed to move.

Nissa blinked at the shallow rise in the earth as she raised her hand to shield her eyes from the light. *Nothing like starting your day on an uphill climb.* At least it would not be a steep one. Unfortunately, the same could not be said of those to come. As she alternated half-sliding down steep dips and picking her way up the other side, Nissa's calves and thighs screamed in protest with every step. She panted as she crested the top of the steepest climb yet, wishing for all the world that Faris's exercises had focused more on building stamina. When Nissa stopped at the top to catch her breath, she allowed herself another swig of water, and she noticed that her supply of water was already dwindling.

I wonder... she took a deep breath, focusing her energy on the moisture in the air around her, pulling it toward her upraised hand. She smiled with closed-lip satisfaction as the water collected around her palm, and she directed a tiny trickle into her canteen. *Nice to know I can stay prepared with that.* What Nissa was not prepared for was the sudden drain on her energy, and she had to steady herself with a widened stance as her fatigued body rebelled. She hadn't tried to use her powers often so far away from a water source or her family home before now —not that she'd had a reason to. *I guess I should have trained more there too.* Then again, she had never expected her sudden flight. Still, she cursed her stupidity; the drain on her body had been senseless, and she couldn't afford to stop and rest.

You needed water, though. She couldn't have afforded to wander further east, where most of the Water Realm's water stemmed from, and she couldn't very well journey further toward the Fire Realm without drinking water. *A necessary sacrifice, then.* Still, Nissa knew she should have anticipated the energy loss, and she shook her head. It was one of the first lessons they were taught when their powers manifested: they had to know their limitations and build their strength gradually. Under Alvar's watchful eye, she hadn't been given the opportunity to practice much beyond his tests of her power, and she needed to be even more aware of her limits, since she still wasn't sure of them. She scowled; it was just another way her father had sabotaged her. At this point, though, the resentments of the past were unhelpful, and she pushed the thoughts from her mind, looking at the downhill trek that awaited. Thankfully, she didn't see any more hills to climb in the distance, and she realized with a strange thrill that this meant she was drawing closer to the river that marked the border.

The clear smell of running water complimented the newfound coolness in the air when she set up camp for the night. She couldn't hear the river, not yet, but Nissa could feel in her bones that she was close. With the prospect of leaving her bubble of solitude within her native realm looming over her, the full weight of Nissa's situation pressed on her shoulders. She was about to disappear from the Water Realm, to risk crossing into rival lands to flee the fate her father had planned for her. Once she did that, there was no looking back. She would be considered, at best, a captive to misguided fortunes and, at worst, a traitor. Lord Alvar wouldn't let speculation shadow Nissa's absence for long before shedding light— however artificial—on the subject. She was leaving one kind of danger and flirting with the realm that housed another. The House of Brandell, the governing family of the Fire Realm, was not to be underestimated.

They were a notorious family, the Brandells, none more so than their heir, Tryamon, and one thing that was never left to unfounded speculation was reputation as a powerful family. If there were rumors, there was a reason behind it. Nissa had only seen them once, at a summit between realms when the governing families came to acknowledge the manifestation of her abilities. It was a generations-old courtesy to acknowledge manifestations of power within the governing families, but for Nissa, it had been one of the only times she had seen the lands beyond her own. If she closed her eyes, she could still picture the Brandell family, proud and appraising. Edris Brandell, the pale-skinned, red-haired Lord of the Fire Realm, came from a powerful line of merciless fire-wielders that traced their lineage to long before the Realms of Galarmos had been divided. His wife, Lady Aithne, darker-featured and beautiful, was just as powerful, and it was even rumored that one of her ancestors had gone beyond basic fire and had wielded lightning. As such, the other realms were also wary of their son, Lord Tryamon. He kept himself out of the public eye—she remembered her father blustering that Tryamon had even refused to be acknowledged when he came of age and his power had manifested— but with such powerful bloodlines, rumors of his potential were already widespread. Rivals of the House of Brandell had everything to fear. So, while Nissa knew that her father would hardly publicize her escape himself, since it would be seen as a weakness to the other realms, he would have to confront it eventually, and it would be a bad day for her to be a Chantara daughter if she was caught and identified in Brandell lands. Still, it was worth all of that to escape a forced marriage to someone she didn't know and couldn't love. It was worth it not to be reduced to a bloodline and a prayer. It was worth it for the chance of being free.

With the specter of the Brandells looming over her, it was hard for Nissa to settle enough to sleep when she finally came to rest that evening. She tossed and turned on the cold ground as the contents of her stomach churned, and the blanket wrapped around her did nothing to warm her against the grip of icy dread she was feeling for what was to come. Sometime long after the crescent moon had reached the summit of its nightly ascent, she slipped away into blissfully dreamless slumber, ignoring the niggling feeling that she would regret her restlessness in the morning.

It was, as expected, a brutal awakening when the morning light smacked her in the face. Nissa groaned as she pushed herself into a sitting position, shaking her head slightly to clear the sleep from her hazel eyes. She was close; she was so close to escaping her father's reach, and all she had to do was spend one more day in flight. She could figure out the rest after she crossed the river, although unless she woke more fully, getting that far would prove to be a task. *You won't be taken back to the Water Realm because you were too tired to function. Move.* The thought sobered her. So far, Nissa had been lucky enough not to run into any of her father's guard. That kind of luck wouldn't hold forever, and she needed to be on her guard for whenever it ran out. With that in mind, Nissa pressed against her protesting joints to rise, grabbed her pack, and started again, ignoring the objections of her stomach.

The day passed quickly, and she hardly noticed the sun tracing its path in the sky. Before she knew it, the scent of the moving water had turned into something audible, and in what seemed like a handful of minutes she could see the faint glimmer of its source materialize through the trees in the distance.

Nissa froze as the sound of a sneeze resonated through the trees behind her. Spinning around wildly, she tossed her eyes through the trees, her eyes darting from trunk to trunk as she finally located the source of the noise. The frosted blue and silver of the Chantara colors stuck out against the russet trunks, and Nissa blinked at it for several seconds, rooted to the spot before she recovered her senses. As though struck by an arrow, she turned on her heel and fled toward the river.

Shouts followed Nissa as she forced herself to lengthen her stride. *Away, away, away,* she willed each step to carry her further, faster than the one that had come before it. *Can't go back. Can't go back.* The thoughts thundered against her skull in tempo with her pounding heart, punctuated by the strides of the guardsmen in pursuit. She zigzagged between trunks, dodging around every obstacle that she could find before two fallen trunks, stacked with only a thin gap in between, loomed in her path. Nissa shot forward, flinging her body horizontally as she dove into the space between them with her eyes clenched shut. Her teeth gritted, waiting for the impact of rough bark across her skin, but as she sailed through the air, her eyes opened just in time for her to stumble and crash to the earth on the other side of the collapsed trees. She pushed herself upward, staggering a bit from the impact as she resumed her pace with stinging palms and her pack thumped against her back. As Nissa burst through the final tangle of trees and underbrush, the river yawned ahead of her. It was wider than she had expected. She glanced helplessly around, looking for something—anything—that she could use as a makeshift raft, but as the guardsmen thundered at her heels, Nissa knew that she was out of time. She whipped her pack off, twisting the strap so that it fit across the front of her body before she plunged into the river itself, praying that this time, her powers would be enough.

"Grab her," a voice roared behind her, and Nissa recognized Murdoch's call before the current swept her away. The current carved between rocks and bubbled over ledges, pouring into her gaping mouth as she fought to swim against it diagonally. *A drowned nymph. How poetic.* The snide voice in her head was back, and Nissa shoved it angrily away as she thrashed and fought to tread the water. The current shifted under her, pulling her slowly, painfully back toward the shore that she had just left. *Magic.*

"No!" The cry ripped from Nissa like flayed skin as she twisted harder. Panic threatened to drown her as much as the river as she clawed for the thrumming power that always lay in her veins, calling it to her palms, where it tingled and hummed with untapped potential. Nissa screwed up her eyes and held her breath as she extended her arms and pressed her hands down into the river that held her. Like rabid dogs, cords of current snapped at the bonds reeling Nissa back to shore. Piles of foam frothed and churned around her as it pushed her away, away, *away.* Calls to action turned to cries of surprise, but she kept her eyes clenched against the wind in her face as the forces of the river propelled her onward.

Nissa's teeth cracked against each other as she crashed face-first into the soggy, squelching mud of the bank. She gasped for air, spluttering as the mingled water and muck fought with the air around her for residence in her lungs. She coughed against the invading sludge, eyes and nose streaming as she got her bearings. She blinked against the tears that had congregated in her eyes from the force of the wind, and when Nissa finally dared to peer back toward the Water Realm's bank, it was empty; the only sign that she hadn't imagined the whole thing was the waterline that left a mark several feet higher than the present level of the river and the boot prints that marred the landscape. *Where did they go?* She supposed it didn't matter; she knew that her father would never give them orders to cross into Fire Realm territory.

She let herself breathe for a moment before she crawled down the shore of the riverbed to more stable ground. She certainly couldn't travel covered in muck—not comfortably, at least. Thankfully, drier, sturdier shore was not far from her. Once she reached it, Nissa scrubbed at the ground-in grime on her clothes and body as well as she could without stripping completely. When Nissa had finished ringing out her long, brown hair, which hung in gnarled clumps down her back, she twisted it into a tangled braid and tied it in place before examining what was left of her pack. Nissa had expected the bread to have disintegrated in the water, but to her dismay, she had also lost the remaining tarts. Her canteen still clung to her pack where she'd tied it the night before, and the blanket was still tucked in place, as was the extra set of clothing her mother had packed. It was in no better shape than the ones she was wearing though, so she left them stuffed where they were. *At least you still have a way to carry water.* Food, she could *maybe* forage along the way. She could even venture into some towns if she passed them; it wasn't likely that Nissa would be recognized here. But with no access to coin, her situation was more dire. With all of her remaining belongings accounted for, Nissa crept along the riverside to the reeded bank that led to her land, careful to look over her shoulder as she turned her back on the only home she had ever known.

6

Nissa slowly stretched upward to look over the thick reeds lining the riverbed, toward the foreboding, auburn forest that lay between her and the mainstays of the Fire Realm. It was a risky gamble. Her father had always told his children that fire melts ice, and so they mustn't ever get too comfortable being around them. Her father also reminded her often that she was her mother's daughter, born with flowing water in her veins. The Brandells might still be dangerous, but they wouldn't nullify Nissa's powers—at least, not in the way that they might have if she had favored her father. Still, the silence roared around her, broken only by the gurgle of the river behind her, so Nissa rose, stepping through the reeds that swished around her as she picked a delicate path, trying her hardest to leave little trace of her presence.

To Nissa's surprise, the trees on the Fire Realm side of the river were not all that different from those on the Water Realm side. Both boasted thick trunks that spoke to their age. Both held large boughs, twisted with age but strong enough to withstand the most enraged tempest. Both held roots that dug through the soil, reaching for a stronghold beneath the layers of grime, and both made her feel less exposed than she would have if she had chosen the route on the coast. She was not sure what she had been expecting, but from the way that her father had described the Brandells, she had expected a more ominous change. In truth, she was surprised to see that the Fire Realm didn't seem so different from home at all. *I guess you can't really call it home anymore.* Nissa winced. *A woman without a country.* The thought felt lonely, somehow, even though it was only stating the obvious. *A woman without a prison*, Nissa corrected grimly. After all, that's what she was fleeing: a prison.

Birds tittered in the trees, and leaves rustled on the forest floor as small, squirrel-like creatures darted around the roots when she passed by. For all that the House of Brandell had a reputation for ruthless ambition, the borderlands they occupied were lovely. Of course, Nissa knew that she was only seeing one small part, but the thought that there was beauty here was a soothing one.

The problem was that Nissa had little idea of where she needed to go next. Her goal had been to escape the Water Realm, and she had made it over the border. Now, she was at a loss. She couldn't stay in the Fire Realm; Nissa knew that much. From her knowledge of basic geography, she knew that the Air Realm lay on the other side of the Fire Realm, and to the north of the Air Realm was the Light Realm. There were islands far off the coast of the Air Realm if she needed to put distance between herself and the rest of continental Galarmos. *Then there's an ocean between me and the Pallinors, at least. An ocean and a continent.* The irony that she could be trading one island for another was not lost on her. Now, there was just the matter of how to get to wherever she decided to go. The Brandells were notoriously secretive about the specifics of their Realm, and what Nissa's parents knew of it had never been part of her education; that had been something they had shared only with Ward. She had no clue how far she was from any town or hope of supplies. She could follow the river, but it veered northward, toward Light Realm territory. If her goal was the islands to the south, that would be counterproductive. Nissa remembered vaguely that there was a forest to the southeast, ominously called The Dead Wood. It was a pinch point in the territory, a funnel into the deeper parts, as it was bordered on both sides by foreboding mountains. She had heard about it when she had overheard a snippet of conversation between her father and one of his strategic advisors. He had noticed her listening and ordered her from that wing of the castle. The alternative was to hug the coast, which—if it was anything like the coast in the Water Realm—was highly exposed.

"Into The Dead Wood it is." Nissa didn't like the idea of feeling trapped between the mountains, but the forest would offer her more shelter and a more direct route. In a strange land in which she knew next to nothing, going for a known set of variables felt smarter than heading for the unknown void. She took a deep breath as she surveyed the trees around her warily. After all, she was in rival lands; danger could be lurking behind every proud trunk. Sensing none, though, Nissa shook the last of the squelching muck from her shoes and set off once more.

It didn't take long for the chaffing to set in. Soft as her pants might have been when dry, they grated against the sensitive skin of Nissa's inner thighs, and she clenched her teeth against the roughness with every step. She could not afford to delay her travels until her clothes dried out properly; time was a luxury that Nissa did not have, especially now that members of her father's guard had seen her at the border. She tightened down on her resolve and continued making her way through the woods.

It was undeniably warmer here. With simply a cross of the river and a couple miles of walking, the air seemed to have shifted, growing moist and thick the further she traversed further south. Her normally smooth brown hair was growing bushier with every step, a combination of the snarled knots and newfound humidity doing its best to disguise her as she traipsed along. There was only one explanation for the swift change of climate: *magic*. It was true that their powers came from the earth, and as a result, the land was impacted by the magic that manifested and the wielders who held it. In a way, the blanketing warmth of the air was refreshing and reminded Nissa of what could have been had her home not been held clenched within her father's icy fist.

There's no stopping that now. My father holds power, and Ward will be next. Nothing will change. She frowned at the thought of her brother, whose primary concerns recently consisted of sleeping his way through the women of the realm, as the holder of any sort of real power. He shared their father's hunger for power without understanding any of the nuance required to wield it, and that made him very, very dangerous. *Just another reason to be well rid of it all. It's not your problem anymore.* She sighed. *Just the problem of any of the women who cross his path.* Nissa grimaced at the thought. Her brother didn't like to take no for an answer, whether with his birthright, diplomatic dealings, or in romantic pursuits. For someone in Nissa's position, however, there was not much she could do to change it—not without getting herself killed at least. If she was a woman without a country, he was more certainly a man without a conscience. Nissa shuddered to think of what the Water Realm would look like when he took power. *Careful now, keep thinking backward too much, and you might turn back altogether. Then they all win.* For once, her snide inner voice said something helpful.

Thankfully, the reminiscing and ruminating had distracted Nissa from the raw patches forming where her thighs scraped together beneath her pants. The fabric was drying astonishingly slowly; Nissa attributed this to the moisture that dampened the air. The theory did nothing to ease her discomfort or to soothe the headache that was slowly building behind her eyes.

She lost track of the hours as the sun tracked overhead, mourning the loss of her rations when she stopped to fill her aching stomach with sips of water. Nissa was tired, and she was hungry. The last thing she needed was to be dehydrated, and she was only getting further away from the nearest water source that she knew of. Unless she got very lucky further on in her journey, Nissa needed to ration what she had for as long as possible. She'd been very careful to take regular, measured swigs from her canteen, but still, the pressure continued building behind her forehead, and now it had spread behind her eyes, wrapping like a band to encapsulate her temples and join itself together around the back of her skull.

"I did *not* come all this way to let a headache get in my way," Nissa muttered, screwing her eyes shut against the pressure. She cracked them open again when she realized that the twittering conversations between the birds of the wood had ceased. Nissa glanced around warily, her eyes roving over the rough-barked trunks of the nearest trees. She blinked against her hazy vision as she sought to focus between the rays of dappled light that penetrated the cocoon of the canopy above her, and still, there was only silence. The snap of a twig had Nissa crouching into a defensive position behind the nearest tree, every muscle taut, although she had no way of knowing what she needed to prepare for. *Pathetic. You don't even have a weapon.* The power in her palms tingled in response, and she clenched her fists shut. She was too exhausted, too inexperienced to risk using her powers without the crutch of a replenishing source unless she had to.

"Well, well, well... What do we have here?" Nissa's skin crawled as she whipped around. She held up a hand to block the light as a broad-shouldered silhouette in black leathers stepped forward with a sneer.

"I don't want any trouble," she managed, the pressure in her head building as she took in his long, dark hair and the malicious glint in his narrowed, green eyes.

"You seem lost. Where's your flock, little lamb?" The words sent a shiver down her spine.

"I'm not lost," Nissa cleared her throat as the words rasped, "and I'd like to be on my way. If you'll excuse me..." She moved to sidestep the man, whose sneer only widened with delight as his hand gripped her forearm roughly and held her in place. The calluses on his palm scratched at Nissa's skin; this was not a man to be trifled with.

"Oh, I don't think so." His eyes dropped from Nissa's face to appraise her body, and she forced herself to stand still and keep from shuddering. "Lost lambs need tending." At the implication in his words, Nissa's control wavered, and she spat in his face, finding some satisfaction as the saliva hit its mark. A sharp sting smarted across her cheek as his free hand hit its mark as well.

"Perhaps, but not from you." A voice rang out from behind her assailant's shoulder, and Nissa noted the way that the sneer on his face dropped into a scowl.

"Sir?"

"We didn't come here to assault traveling women, Cyril. Let her go." With a final squeeze that made Nissa's jaw clench, Cyril complied, stepping back.

"We came to patrol the border. She was at the border," Cyril said rudely.

"That doesn't mean you can do what you want with her. You're still under my command. You don't breathe unless I allow it." The pressure in Nissa's head thundered in her ears now, drowning out whatever was said next.

"...take her with us..." The roaring in her ears screamed

across the rest. Nissa blinked at the two men as she swayed in place, neither of them so much as glancing her way. The other man—not Cyril, turned to face her, strands of his shoulder-length, dark hair blowing across his face as his amber eyes widened in concern at whatever he saw on her face. He took a hasty step toward Nissa with one arm extended as the forest floor spun up to meet her, and the world went dark.

7

Nissa was flying. That was the only way that she could describe the almost-euphoric sensation as she sped back across the river and hurtled through the ice-crusted forest from which she had come. A branch whipped toward her face with impossible speed, and Nissa clamped her eyes shut and braced for impact as she tried to duck. Then... *nothing.* There was no impact, not even from the pinpricks of snowflakes as she raced past at an ever-increasing speed that should have disturbed the branches where the piles of snow clung. When she snapped her eyes open again, Nissa was hanging above the walls of her former home as though suspended by a thread.

This shouldn't be possible. Nissa fought the force holding her in place, all but screaming at her body to fight the force that held her as she plummeted back toward her home. Her traitorous limbs did nothing. She braced again for impact as she fell toward the manor's walls, but again...nothing. When she blinked again, she was in a room she didn't recognize. *My father's study?* It must have been; of Nissa and her brothers, only Ward had ever been allowed in. Lord Alvar—for she needed to stop thinking of him as her father—stooped over his desk with his hands supporting him, his back turned to where Nissa's mother stood over a basin of water, eyes closed serenely as she held her palms over the silvery pool. Nissa hovered there, unseen and wraithlike, as the rippling surface clouded and then revealed a wooded scene. With a gasp that no one else in the room seemed to hear, she recognized her own prone form in the image that materialized, flanked by Cyril and a hazy, unfocused figure that had to be his commander, who crouched by her side, face twisted in confusion. *She's scrying...me?*

"She is in the Fire Realm," her mother said placidly. Nissa's father turned suddenly, storming over to the pool as his brow furrowed. Nissa watched, fascinated as the figure of the commander rose and turned his face away at her father's approach. It was as though he had sensed the need to conceal his identity.

"The guards already told us that," he snapped. *But how could they have told him so quickly?* Nissa nearly missed his next demand. "What's happening? What's wrong with her?"

"She seems to have collapsed," her mother replied, and Nissa caught a spark of annoyance in her eyes as she turned her face away from Alvar.

"But *why?*" he growled, stalking to the other side of the basin. "And why is the Fire Realm guard with her?"

"Perhaps they've chosen to defile her to send a message to you, dear father," a droll voice suggested from the shadows. "You always knew they would become our enemies one day." Nissa tensed as Ward stepped out to join their parents, at his casual implication that she would be molested in her vulnerable state. He might have been discussing the dinner menu.

"Ward, watch your mouth. Your mother is here," said Alvar. Ward looked down his thin nose at their much-shorter mother.

"Sorry, Mother," he said lazily, flicking his ice-grey eyes

back to the scene in the pool. "You shouldn't have warned her about the Pallinors."

"Would you have dragged her to the altar?" Lord Alvar's shoulders tensed dangerously, and Ward held up his hands in mock-surrender.

"Perhaps not." He crossed his arms. "Perhaps I can drag her back here, though." Marin's eyes flicked up to Ward in startlement before she dropped them demurely again.

"You shouldn't talk about dragging your sister anywhere," her father chided.

"Even after she ran off?" Ward raised an eyebrow.

"To invade Brandell lands with any kind of armed force would send the wrong message." Lord Alvar paced around the pool, staring at the scene as both men crouched to the earth, temporarily blocking the view of Nissa's prone form.

"To let them keep her is to send a message of weakness," Ward pointed out.

"What do you suggest?" Alvar's eyes flashed dangerously as he stared at Nissa's brother, his long-fingered hands clenching into fists.

"Perhaps I can negotiate." At Ward's words, Alvar relaxed his hands.

"We don't even know if Edris knows his men have her," he said.

"And would they take better care of her once he knows that they do?" Ward asked silkily. Nissa watched as her father considered for a moment, shifting from foot to foot.

"Very well. You can take the horses and a *small*," he narrowed his eyes at his son, "diplomatic band if you wish. The fewer who know about this, the better." The corners of Ward's mouth twitched upward in a smirk, and he nodded, turning on his heel to make his departure.

"I'll collect her, and I can do it alone," he said confidently.

As he made to stride away from the basin, Alvar grabbed his arm roughly.

"Do not," he snarled, "mess this up. This is not just some mission; this is your sister and the honor of our family. I will *not* have you make it into a theater again." Ward's face drained of expression.

"Sir," Ward answered coldly.

"Am I understood?"

"Yes, sir."

"Then go. Be done with it." He dropped Ward's arm, and Nissa's brother stalked away. The heavy, walnut door slammed shut behind him.

"You're sure he can bring her home peacefully?" her mother asked, her voice as serene as Nissa had ever heard it. Alvar scowled as the image in the basin fogged over.

"She's your daughter, more than she ever has been mine. Would you go quietly?" To that, she had no answer. As the image dissipated, Nissa felt a sensation hook near her naval, and she was flying once again, careening out of her father's house and above the walls before streaking through the forest once more.

She crashed back into her body with all the force of a tidal wave. Nissa came back to consciousness, gasping for air as she jerked up into a sitting position. Cyril, thankfully, was several paces away, but his commander was still hovering over her, his face etched in troubled lines. He was younger than she'd had originally thought; in fact, he looked to be around Nissa's age, a realization which instantly made her shoulders tense. What kind of monster was he, that he could command respect from an unapologetic brute like Cyril at their age? Still, with his soft, black hair brushing across his shoulders, the smooth tan skin stretched taught across his cheekbones, and his shockingly amber eyes still wide with concern, he didn't look as much like the monster anymore. *Looks can be deceiving.* Sure enough, a mask of haughty annoyance descended on his face. Nissa shifted, wincing slightly as she got to her feet.

"Are we that frightening?" the commander asked. She tossed a scowl at him.

"No," Nissa said shortly, mind whirring as she tried to reconcile what had just happened to her mind with what was happening around her now.

"You're a long way from any towns in the Water Realm," the commander said quietly.

"That's my business."

"You're in the Fire Realm now, girl. That makes it our business," the commander said more forcefully. She whipped her head around to glare at him, but he had her there.

"I'm just passing through," she said.

"That's for us to decide."

"Enough of this talk. We've wasted enough time out here." Cyril spoke again, and to Nissa's amazement, the commander fell silent. She turned her pleading eyes upon him then, hating every moment that she had to beg.

"Please. I don't want trouble. I'm just passing through, like I said," Nissa said softly, searching for any trace of the humanity she had thought she had seen only moments before.

"And what reason would a woman from the Water Realm have to pass through this part of the border?" he replied with a raised eyebrow. Nissa pressed her lips together tightly.

"I can't answer that." She shook her head, and her matted hair pulled at her scalp with the motion.

"We can't let her go," Cyril interjected again.

"It's my call," the commander snapped.

"Your mother might disagree. She sent you to lead a border patrol, not to waste the opportunity for political leverage." *His mother? Political leverage?* Nissa eyed the commander again as suspicions dawned on her.

"She trusted my judgment," he said stiffly.

"She trusted you with a patrol, *Tryamon*. She'll want to have the final say on this." Horror replaced the suspicion, and Nissa looked upon her captor with new eyes as she realized that she had run headfirst into the Prince of Flames himself.

"Thank you, *cousin*," Tryamon said pointedly, the slightest hint of a snarl in his voice. He considered Nissa thoughtfully again. "We'll take her to the Keep. I'll decide whether or not to send word to my parents from there." A chill ran through Nissa as she realized that they were talking about the Singed Keep. *No.* The Singed Keep was notorious at home for keeping high-level prisoners under the watchful eye of a very brutal guard force. Nissa hardly warranted that kind treatment. Her palms tingled as she willed the water in the air to gather in her grasp. Her lips dried, cracking in protest as she unwittingly drew from herself. She fought to adjust the pull of magic.

As Tryamon stepped toward Nissa again, she whipped her arm, snapping forward with a strand of fluid that threw him off-balance as he dodged. When he stumbled backward into Cyril, Nissa turned on her heel and did the only thing that she knew might give her half of a chance: she ran.

8

———

Nissa was still close enough to the river that the drain on her powers wasn't debilitating, but her footsteps were clumsy as she tore through the trees. She let out a cry of frustration as her foot hooked on a root and sent her sprawling before, cursing under her breath, she leaped to her feet and took off again. Her breathing grew ragged, both from the exertion and the tight fist of panic that clenched around her lungs when the footsteps behind her grew louder and heavier. She gritted her teeth against a wail of desperation as she willed her legs and arms to pump harder and faster.

A moment later, she was flying again, although this time, Nissa remained one with her body. Arms hooked around her waist as she crashed toward the earth, and her fall was cushioned by another as they skidded to a halt, inches away from running face-first into the base of a tree. The arms bound her in place as she came to and resumed her struggle, and another yell of frustration ripped from her chest before Nissa let herself fall limp.

"Are you done?" Tryamon's breath was hot in her ear, and she felt her lip curl with disgust.

"Get off of me," she snarled. To Nissa's surprise, the arms loosened, and she wasted no time as she shot to her feet.

"I wouldn't try that again if I were you," he said casually, "or I'll let Cyril take a turn." He rose and brushed the earth from his uniform. Nissa narrowed her eyes at him, biting back the retort that burned on her tongue.

"What would be the point?" she replied gruffly. Tryamon raised his eyebrows at her, but he didn't otherwise indicate that he had heard her.

"She's quick," Cyril called, emerging from the direction they had come. She glowered at the ground.

"Not quick enough," Nissa muttered. The corner of Tryamon's mouth twitched.

"Did you get the horses?" he asked Cyril, who shook his head.

"No, I was trying to make sure you had backup in case she was too much for you to handle." Nissa repressed a shudder as his eyes looked up and down her body with a new hunger, and she had to resist the urge to step backward. Tryamon, for his part, looked sharply at his companion, shaking his head ever so slightly, before putting his fingers to his mouth and letting loose a shrill whistle. Nissa winced at the pitch, but moments later, the sound of clopping hooves gave way as the forest revealed two saddled geldings, one black, one roan, approaching.

"Guess they weren't far," Tryamon said nonchalantly. He looked at Nissa for a second before glancing back at his cousin. "You'll ride with me." It wasn't a suggestion. She huffed, eying the horse skeptically. Nissa was a fair rider, but either position would end up with either Tryamon pressed up against her from behind or with Nissa having to wrap her arms around him. Neither was preferable, but she wasn't about to argue that point if Cyril was the alternative.

"You aren't going to let her decide?" Cyril asked with a leer. The other man ignored him.

"Get on," he ordered in a voice that left no room for argument. Seeing no way out, Nissa complied. The gelding stirred underneath me, and she stroked his neck gently, admiring the way that the colors of his mottled hairs mimicked soot and ash. It was a fitting mount for the Prince of Flames. Nissa stiffened as the man himself swung his leg over the horse and settled in behind her, and she shifted as far forward as she could manage. The saddle was constructed in a way that easily accommodated both riders, and Nissa wondered fleetingly how often the poor horse bore tandem riders.

"Steady there, Hagan," he leaned across her to murmur at the gelding as he danced on his hooves. Nissa kept her shoulders stiff as she leaned away to make room, watching as Cyril swung himself onto his own mount. Her body felt as though it was still detached from her mind—although not in the same way that it had before—as she processed what was happening. She had made it over the border, and she had been accosted by members of the Fire Realm's governing family. Her worst-case scenario had happened. In all likelihood, she was about to be imprisoned at a Brandell stronghold or returned to her father's house, which was a prison all of its own. Despite the detailed summary of events looping endlessly in her mind, Nissa felt surprisingly steady. After only few cycles of the reality of her situation, Nissa was thinking less about her future fate and more about what had happened to her when her mother was scrying her.

Nissa knew that her father's intuition allowed him to sense when someone was scrying him; it was an ability that he claimed with pride. She had never heard of him—or anyone—collapsing when they were being watched, though. *And why was I able to see them?* The thought turned over in her mind like a leaf on the wind, and she clung to it like a lifeline. Panic bubbled into her throat when she didn't find an answer. *Control yourself,* she ordered sternly.

She remained resolutely silent as they journeyed, bouncing back and forth between theories and thankful that Tryamon did not try to make conversation. When Nissa blinked, returning to the present, she was surprised to realize that they had broken out of the forest and were heading toward an open expanse of grass, and the sun was setting behind them. The shadows of their bodies inched longer as it made its descent.

"There's a copse of trees up ahead. We'll camp there for the night." Tryamon said quietly, seeming to sense her return to the land of the living. Nissa nodded once, still determined to maintain her stoic silence. It hit her that, while they knew that she was from the Water Realm, they hadn't immediately known who she was. Concealing her identity for as long as possible could be her only advantage, especially if her father kept her disappearance to himself. If they didn't think she mattered; maybe, they would let her go. If they released her, Nissa's change in location would still be a setback, but it didn't have to be the end of her journey. *Being the forgotten daughter has its perks. No one expects a pawn to be of any kind of value.*

They reached the trees before Nissa had fully fleshed out her plan, but she knew that she was out of time when Tryamon pulled Hagan to a halt and swung off his back. He landed softly and took Hagan's reins in one hand, reaching up to offer her the other. She eyed his extended hand skeptically for a moment, and her eyes darted to the side to see his eyebrows creeping up his forehead. She set her mouth in a stubborn line, and with a gentle pat of Hagan's neck, Nissa swung her leg over and dismounted on her own in a descent that was just as graceful as the Brandell's prodigal son. He lowered his hand, one corner of his mouth twitching up briefly, but he did not say anything to her. Instead, he turned his head to Cyril.

"We'll take turns keeping watch. I'll take the first one." Cyril narrowed his eyes at the implied order, but he nodded. Given her interactions with Cyril so far, Nissa couldn't repress the flicker of gratitude that arose at the words. She didn't have a reason to trust Tryamon, but at least he hadn't been looking at her like a piece of meat. The males unpacked their saddlebags while she shifted her feet uselessly from side to side. *You're their prisoner. Why do you feel like you should be helping them?* To the snide voice in her head, Nissa had no response. She focused instead on the surroundings, with wondering how this little collection of trees had withstood the wind and gales that she was sure ripped through the open plain. So lost in thought was she that Nissa did not see Cyril's looming figure approach, and she recoiled as he moved to lean close to her face.

"You dropped this." The odor of his breath stained the air, and Nissa edged further back as he pressed a bundle into her hands. She blinked down in surprise at the pack that she had dropped when she had fled. She glanced back up at him, trying to ignore the crawling sensation under her skin

"Thanks."

"A little brave—or foolish— of you to travel without weapons," Tryamon interjected. Nissa glanced around Cyril to see Tryamon's shadowed figure observing them with crossed arms. To her relief, Cyril stepped back at the sound of his cousin's voice. Of course they'd searched her things; she only wondered when they'd found the time.

"It was a spur-of-the-moment trip, and I'm hardly undefended," she replied with a bravado that she didn't feel.

"Well, as your things haven't had time to dry out properly, you can have my set-up for the night." Nissa opened her mouth to protest, narrowing her eyes as suspicion clouded over her. She shut it again a moment later; she was in no position to really refuse what was a very generous offer, given her current status as prisoner.

"Thanks," she answered gruffly.

"Hang your things on one of those branches so they don't stink." Nissa squinted to the gloom to see a low-hanging branch just beyond the makeshift camp.

"Seems like if you're taking prisoners, you should be prepared to face the stench." She narrowed her eyes frostily.

"Is that an invitation to take a whiff, little lamb?" Nissa cringed as Cyril called to her from across the copse.

"Cyril," Tryamon crossed to stand between them, fixing the man with a firm look. "You will not touch her."

"Sir," Cyril sneered, giving a mocking bow. Tryamon grabbed his cousin by the arm and jerked him around, his eyes flashing.

"Am I understood? You will *not* touch her. You're under my command. What happens to her is my business, and you will not touch what is mine." Cyril's face hardened, but he did not argue. Nissa took a step back, half-bristling at the implication that she belonged to *either* man, but she was in no position to contradict him... not when Cyril was the alternative.

"I understand." He ripped his arm from Tryamon's grasp and stalked back toward where his own bedroll lay waiting. It was several paces away from where Nissa would be sleeping, but the thought of him so close while she was lying in a vulnerable position sent a shudder through her. *And the alternative...* She swallowed as her blood chilled with the knowledge that even if Cyril left her alone, there was no guarantee that Tryamon would.

"He'll leave you alone. You should sleep." His voice was softer than it had been, so Nissa swallowed her discomfort and settled for a nod instead. As she turned her back on him to head for her designated sleeping space, he cleared his throat behind her.

"How are we going to let your family know that you've been found? You haven't told us your name, and we'll need to know that to begin negotiations." Nissa bristled.

"You don't need my name," she answered quickly. *Too quickly.*

"Certainly not," Tryamon said with a lazy smile. "But it'll make things go faster. I'm sure your family will want to know where you are." Nissa debated for a moment before she answered, and she forced her reply to be as casual as possible as she tossed it over her shoulder.

"You don't need my name, and you won't need to find them. They already know I'm here," Nissa answered shortly. Leaving him with that tidbit to consider, Nissa strode the rest of the way over to Tryamon's bedroll and curled up in a tight ball beneath the thin but surprisingly warm blanket that rested atop it. Before she could consider the wisdom of the decision, she was fast asleep, the burn of Tryamon Brandell's curious gaze still hot upon her.

9

I t was a fitful sleep, and Nissa woke feeling as exhausted as she would have had she not slept at all. As she tossed and turned, Nissa kept expecting to feel Cyril's hot breath and wayward hands on her, but true to Tryamon's word, she spent the night untouched and undisturbed by anything other than her own thoughts. By the time she finally woke for good in the morning, Tryamon had already risen for the day, and the reality of her circumstances crashed anew against Nissa's mind. She was a prisoner. She was at their mercy. She had traded one form of domineering lordship for another. Escape was her only hope again, and this time, she had no friends or family to help her. Nissa sighed heavily as she pushed herself into a seated position, flinching at the way the still-filthy crust of her hair scraped against her neck.

"Good morning," Tryamon said politely, and she nodded her response. For whatever reason, he was playing nice; she could play along.

"Sleep well, little lamb?" Cyril jeered, and Nissa cut her eyes at him. It would have been impossible for him not to notice her state of restlessness during the night.

"I'll sleep better when I'm far away from you two," she muttered. Cyril opened his mouth to respond again, but Tryamon cleared his throat. She shuddered involuntarily, but to her relief, both men had turned away from her. She had no doubt that they were still aware of their surroundings, though. Wherever they were going, there was no guarantee of her getting away any time soon.

"We'll reach the Keep today," Tryamon said. "We'll figure out what to do with you from there."

"I could think of several things," Cyril said quietly, and when she took a step away, he threw his head back in a laugh. Tryamon rounded on the other man, who took several steps back himself.

"You will keep your filthy thoughts *to yourself*," he snarled. Cyril's amusement rose to delight before he narrowed his eyes thoughtfully.

"Yes, cousin," he said, but there was no respect in his voice. Nissa raised her eyebrows at the title.

"It is not your place to think of what will happen to her, and it's not your place to make decisions. It's mine." Tryamon's eyes had darkened into a stormy amber as he towered over Cyril, who scowled.

"Sir," Cyril answered, the mockery in his tone lingering in the air. *Perhaps the Brandell line is not as clearcut as it seems.* Nissa seemed to have plopped directly into the path of another power struggle. Cyril mercifully did not test Tryamon again, and as the trio rode on, Tryamon stewing in silence on the horse behind her, Nissa watched with a sense of foreboding as the blackened walls of the Singed Keep rose in the distance.

It was widespread knowledge that each governing house maintained a secondary residence to deal with the more unpleasant matters of politics within their realms, but it was a rare occasion when visitors from other realms were introduced to such places. Nissa's father had left the Frosted Keep in the

hands of the Pallinor line to keep the peace between their families, so while she had visited, Nissa had been there sparingly
and never as a prisoner—thanks to her fortuitous escape from
marriage. The endless white walls, while beautiful and shining
upon first sight, were a colorless void upon closer inspection.
The Singed Keep, as they made their approach, appeared to be
its opposite in every way. The blackened tops of the walls faded
into a gradient of silvery-grey stone at the base of the building,
and Nissa realized very quickly how the Singed Keep had
gotten its name.

Whomever was on guard must have been anticipating their
approach, because they were met by two gangly young men at
the gate, a tangled mass of shining steel, who wordlessly took
their horses after their dismount without so much as a backward glance at their prince's new acquisition.

"I hope they rub down the horses properly this time," Cyril
muttered, watching the retreating figures through slitted eyes.

"Follow them and make sure they do," Tryamon said.

"And the girl?" Cyril asked.

"I think I can handle her in my own home," he said.

"Don't forget to share, cousin." With a sound in his throat
that was nearly a growl, Cyril looked her up and down before
spinning wildly to stalk away after the horses before Tryamon
could respond. He watched Cyril go with naked rage upon his
face, but that wasn't what had caught Nissa's attention.

"You live here?" She couldn't keep the surprise out of her
voice.

"Yes." There was a note of finality in his voice, but she
ignored it.

"But what about your parents? Don't they need you with
them?" She asked in surprise. Her own parents, while they
allowed Ward a loose leash, were always adamant that—as heir
—he maintained his main residence in the family home. He

had responsibilities there, they said, and for the sake of those duties, they wanted him close at hand.

"My parents are none of your concern," he snapped, his eyes darkening again. Nissa took a step backward.

"I'm sorry," she began in spite of herself, "I didn't mean…"

"You won't even tell me your name. You are a trespasser. So far, I haven't pushed you while I've figured out what to do with you, and I've kept Cyril on his leash. Don't make the mistake of thinking that gives you the right to question me." His voice was low and dangerous, and Nissa knew that she was barely treading water.

"I understand," she said levelly, swallowing the lump that rose in her throat. *And I need to get away from here as soon as possible.* Tryamon turned and pushed on the large, double doors with both hands. She watched, amazed, as they swung inward. *They must be very confident in their other defenses for their doors to open that direction.* If one little push had made them open, she could only imagine what a battering ram might do in a full assault. *What other defenses are they hiding?* The Keep was still and silent as she followed Tryamon when he stepped inside. The inner walls held the same gradient quality as the exterior, and the low-hanging chandeliers of the spacious entry hall cast ominous shadows on the wall and the unlit torches that hung in place along it. The center of the hall was overtaken by a large, sweeping staircase, with a walnut banister that shone and reflected the lights in the chandeliers. The stairs narrowed to a platform before splitting into two winding offshoots that wrapped to join the floors above. She blinked in surprise as Tryamon led her to the stairs. *Up, not down.* Her breath hitched at the thought of a holding so massive that they needed to keep prisoners above *and* below, and Tryamon turned, one eyebrow raised.

"Something wrong?" he asked, his voice more even now.

Remembering his dark mood only moments before, she shook her head.

"Not beyond being held against my will, no." He turned without saying anything further, and Nissa might have imagined the ghost of a smile that dashed across his lips.

She found the lack of staff disconcerting. The Keep was clean, almost meticulously so, but where the Frosted Keep might have held a bustle of servants, scurrying to and fro as they fought to maintain their standards of cleanliness, the Singed Keep remained silent and empty. It was not a gloomy place, but the stormy air of isolation permeated the room. This was not a place that saw many visitors, and Nissa imagined that those that did left intimidated and cowed. She took a deep breath as she looked at the yawning stairs above, and she followed Tryamon as he began the climb.

To her surprise, the aura of the Keep lightened as she moved upward. What was a gradient of smoke and darkness below faded into a gentle gray, and the light changed so that the shadows cast were the softer ones cast on an overcast day. From the appearance of the exterior walls, she would have expected the opposite. When they approached the long hallway of the third floor, Nissa blinked at the contrast. If the floor below was a scorched earth, this was the warm embrace of candlelight. This hall, too, was silent, aside from their footsteps as they thudded gently on the long, orange-and-gold tapestry rug. *High décor for a prison.* She nearly smacked into Tryamon's back as he lurched to a stop directly in front of her.

"These will be your accommodations," he said without further introduction, gesturing to one in a line of walnut doors. Nissa scrutinized the intricate carvings on the door, which depicted a phoenix, flame-tail trailing as it soared over a forest. *Carvings on a cell?* She was confused. With a huff that could have been annoyance, Tryamon brushed past her, seizing the handle himself and pushing the door open. Nissa braced herself, expecting shackles bolted to the walls and a shaky, creaking bed frame. What the door revealed, as it swung open, was hardly a prison. A wide, four-poster bed with deep, russet curtains claimed one wall; the other was taken over by a writing desk that overlooked a large, bay window. A rug that boasted designs similar to the one in the hallway blanketed a stone floor that was anything but cold, courtesy of the roaring fire that occupied the hearth to the far side of the room.

"Are you sure?" The words left Nissa's mouth before she realized she had spoken, and she edged backward.

"As I said, I haven't figured out what to do with you yet. Until I do, you'll be treated as a guest." Nissa blinked at his response, her thoughts whirring as she processed this new information.

"But... You said I was trespassing, and..." she trailed off.

"And you weren't harming the Fire Realm, which means that for now, you are no enemy of mine, just an inconvenience. Make yourself comfortable. Your dinner will be brought to you in two hours," he said mildly, gesturing for her to enter the room. She took tentative steps inside, casting her gaze warily from side to side. Tryamon watched her closely, seeming almost eager to see her reaction, but Nissa kept her face carefully neutral as she turned to face him again.

"Thank you for your hospitality, Lord Tryamon," she said stiffly. He winced.

"My name will suffice. Lord is my father's title." This wasn't true, strictly speaking, as the titles of Governing Lords required a degree of respect to all in their immediate family's address, but she wasn't going to argue that point with her host.

"Tryamon, then," she amended smoothly. The hint of a smile curved the corners of his mouth. It didn't reach his eyes.

"It's a mouthful. Call me Trey," he suggested. Nissa studied him for a moment, looking for any signs of jest.

"If you'd prefer."

"Don't try to break the glass," he said, gesturing to the large window. "It's warded not to shatter, and I would hate to have to replace the furniture because you broke it trying to throw something through the window." Her smile dropped, and she opened her mouth to retort. Before she could, he spoke again. "Same with the door." He stepped back, shut the door, and in the next breath, he was gone.

10

———

We trust that our daughter will remain unharmed in your presence until our son arrives to retrieve her.

The note was unaddressed and unsigned, but he didn't need a signature to know who it was from. Trey swore as he released the heavy, dove-gray scrap of paper, watching it flutter to the already-crowded desk. He curled his lip against the sour taste that threatened to overwhelm his mouth as he studied the faint outline of the family crest in one corner. He'd had his suspicions about the cause of her collapse earlier, and her reaction to Cyril's suggestion about using her for political leverage had been evidence enough to her identity. Nissa Chantara, daughter of Alvar and Marin—the governing family of the Water Realm—was sitting in a room in his Keep. Without any real intention of taking one, he now possessed a political prisoner. Somehow, she had been right; they knew where she was and who she was with.

"The Water Realm has seers," his father had once warned,

after his parents had given him the authority to conduct patrols along the border. "Be on your guard when you approach their border." It seemed as though he had not been guarded enough if they had been able to see into his territory. He lifted a hand to finger the pendant that hung at his throat, a chunk of obsidian cradled in a wire net. It was meant to protect him from such abilities. *Of all the times to have not been wearing it.* He'd left it behind for what was meant to be a short patrol.

One thing was certain, though: he would not send word to his parents in Domogién. He had escaped out from under Edris and Aithne's thumb when he had been given leave to move away from the city, and he wasn't going to involve them in this. He knew Cyril had been right when he'd said that Trey's mother would leap at the opportunity to use the woman for political leverage. From a rival realm or otherwise, he didn't think that Nissa had done anything to deserve the punishment of becoming a pawn in one of his mother's games. She was an inconvenience, and he wanted rid of her, but not so she could become his mother's newest plaything.

"How do I even respond to this?" he grumbled. Nissa had left her home and everything she knew to take the chance of entering a rival realm. Families of power didn't leave their realms, not without an invitation. She was running from something. *But what?* If it had been serious enough for her to sneak away like a thief in the night, he doubted that Nissa would be very willing to share her motives with a stranger, let alone the heir of a rival realm. *And for her brother to come for her so quickly, without waiting for an invitation...*

"She's not my responsibility," he reminded himself. He could easily just send her home with her brother and wash his hands of the whole situation. Trey had his own problems to worry about without getting wrapped up in someone else's. He rubbed wearily at his temples, massaging them to try and release some of the tension that had built behind them. He thought of his own family, of his own parents and the cost to be given control of the Singed Keep. It was the loosest definition of freedom, but it still kept him out of their direct control—for the most part at least. He couldn't imagine having someone—let alone a stranger—take that away from him so carelessly. He stayed out of inter-realm politics as much as possible, but if there was one thing that he knew, it was that Ward Chantara was trouble. Ignoring the missive was just as likely to cause problems though. It had been hand-delivered to him by a member of the guard who had met their messenger at the border. The guard had ridden straight through to deliver it; excusing his nonresponse as the message having been lost wouldn't work either— unless he killed the guard, of course, but he hadn't yet sunk to that level of conspiracy.

He was making a lot of assumptions though. It was just as likely that she'd gotten into a fight with her parents and left in a bout of temper. Ward's reputation preceded him, and with him as her brother, it wasn't a stretch to think that Nissa could be just as volatile. Her behavior on their journey to the Keep could have easily been a front; after all, she had been outnumbered and held against her will by total strangers. It was possible that she had been concealing her true nature until she found a moment of weakness to exploit. Trey sighed, a hand through his shoulder-length hair and wincing as his fingers snagged on a tangle. His conscience had trapped him between two hard decisions. *This was what you wanted though, remember? The power to make your own decisions?* He shoved the thought away angrily as he tied back his hair at the nape of his neck. He could deal with his personal grooming later. The thoughts tangled in his mind, snagging together and tearing at him like thorny vines. He let out a huff as he realized that the only way to get the answers he needed so that he could make a decision was to ask Nissa himself and hope that she played nicely.

He leaned back in his chair, lifting his face toward the

ceiling as he put his hands over it. He was too tired for this; his family kept him on a loose tether these days, but it was still a leash, and he had enough to worry about as it was. The last thing he needed was to get wrapped up in some Chantara mess that wasn't even his business.

You made it your business when you brought her here, a snide voice in his head crept in, and he glowered at the floor. He'd laid a claim to her as much to keep Cyril from pawing at her. He should have known better than to bring Alvar Chantara's skulking, spoiled daughter into his home. He should have just looked the other way or sent her back home. He groaned at the ceiling. It was too late for regrets now; he had made his choice in dirtying his hands, and he needed to stand by them and decide what to do with whatever fate had dealt them—that *Trey* had dealt them.

"Gods, Cyril is never going to let me live this down," he groaned again from beneath his hands. That was the worst part of it all; his cousin would be present to witness every misstep. He took a breath before dropping his hands and pushing out of his chair. Delaying his conversation with Nissa was only delaying the inevitable, and he needed to see that this situation was handled.

11

———

Nissa expected dinner to be a lonely affair after their argument. As such, she jumped to her feet, slightly startled, when she received a knock at her door. She glanced down as she smoothed the slight wrinkles in her skirts before she stepped across the room and opened it to reveal a somber faced but pretty young woman who looked to be around her age. The woman's olive skin was pale, as though she didn't often venture outside, and her hands shook slightly as she held out a tray. *I guess the Keep isn't totally devoid of servants.*

"Thank you." Nissa reached out to take the tray and once it had transferred into her hands, the woman took several steps back, eyes narrowed in scrutiny.

"The Brandells do not often have guests, especially Lord Tryamon," she ventured boldly, barely concealing the quiver in her voice. *She's familiar with the family, then.* Nissa pressed her lips together in a firm line.

"I'm hardly that," she answered dully. The woman's face drained of color as she turned on her heel without reply and disappeared up the hallway. Nissa watched her go, half-lifting her foot to take a step to follow her. As she tried to complete the swing of her foot over the threshold, however, her heel was suddenly leaden, and she was unable to move forward. *Ah, there were the shackles I was missing.* Nissa jerked her foot for good measure, and the pressure was suddenly white-hot. A gasp hissed from between her teeth as she allowed herself to be pulled back into her gilded cage.

Nissa let the tray clatter onto the desk, her appetite buried by her frustration. She had traded one cage for another, and this one had magically reinforced bars.

Abandoning her tray as her appetite had abandoned her, she found herself standing at the window, staring through the enchanted glass at the landscape beyond. Her window faced away from the direction they had come, and Nissa stared out into the beyond, across the edge of a cliff, and out to the sea. Somehow, it felt different than the oceans of home; she could sense a different kind of tension bubbling beneath the surface. To match it, a thrumming pressure began thudding against the inside of Nissa's skull, and dread in her gut rose to join it.

No, not here. She fought to steady her breaths as she recognized the sensation that she had felt the last time her mother had scried her. If they were scrying her again, there was no telling what Trey's wards would do to her if the magic tried to sneak between them. Nissa clenched her teeth as the sensation reached the rumbling level of thunder. Between the wards and the thought of being rendered prone in an enemy stronghold, this was the last thing that she needed. The room spun, and Nissa felt her head grow lighter as the dizziness set in. A murmuring noise joined it, as though she was listening to someone speak from beneath the surface of a lake, and her stomach turned as the pressure in her head locked tighter. Something that sounded faintly like her name clawed down the inside of her skull like talons, and Nissa realized what was happening. *They're scrying me again.*

"Get out of my *head*," she hissed at no one as she felt the first flutters of flight make her knees wobble. *How am I feeling this?* The point of scrying was that the subject was caught unaware. That was the beauty of the power. The thundering booms in her mind were punctuated as a clatter reached her from the room, sounding distant in the haze. Nissa swayed slightly as she turned to see the door to the room had been flung open and a hazy figure strode across the room toward her.

"What's wrong with her?" the voice, Trey's voice, barked behind him. She did not hear the reply, which sounded nonsensical as the staccato beat in against her skull drowned it out. Trey knelt beside her, pulling her into a seated position on the floor as the room spun on its axis once before tilting on a new point and whirling again.

"Out of... my head," she said, the words sounding garbled even to herself as they left her lips. The details of the room blurred around Nissa as she fought to focus on something, anything.

"Nissa." The sound of her own name snapped her attention to Trey's eyes, a glowing amber that penetrated the haze like a torch in the night. She focused on them, holding onto the sight like a lifeline.

"Leave us," he barked behind him, and Nissa was vaguely aware that the door clicked respectfully shut as whomever had arrived with him followed the order. She grasped for any thread that would lead her to it as the room around her darkened, leaving only the piercing amber of Trey's eyes before they too vanished into the mist.

It could have been only moments or an eternity that passed before the room rematerialized around Nissa again. She blinked her eyes open slowly as the details of the room returned into focus before her gaze settled on Trey, sitting several feet away and watching her warily. Strands of her hair whirled around her from an unseen draft, the scent of salt coloring the air. Nissa tilted her face toward the window and realized that the glass has shattered. When she glanced back, he had crossed the room, his expression inscrutable as he bent to examine her.

"Did I do that?" she rasped, clearing her throat before asking more clearly. "I mean, did I do—" She felt something sharp cut into her palm, and she glanced down to see that her fingers had wrapped around the pendant dangling from a chain around his neck. She uncurled her fingers hastily, leaving the black stone swinging back in place. He leaned backward, seeming ruffled.

"The wards would have killed you. I broke the glass," Trey answered shortly. Through the gap, the wind howled as it ripped across the planes of stone that made up the Keep's walls, and Nissa could hear the waves crashing angrily against the shore.

"But how..." Nissa trailed off. Trey rose roughly to his feet, stalking several steps across the room before turning and pacing back.

"I told you that the room was warded, Nissa. Why would you try to use your power here?" he demanded.

"I didn't," she protested, "and how do you know my name? I never said—" He interrupted her again.

"Your family has been in touch," he said darkly. His eyes clouded as he looked away. "As you said, they know you're here." *Who have they sent for me? My father? My brother?* She shuddered visibly at the thought of Ward being sent to collect her. "What?" Trey demanded.

"I didn't contact them," she said, sensing the accusation as he folded his arms across his chest.

"Then how would they know you were here?" he asked. Nissa opened her mouth to reply before shutting it again. The ability to scry came secondarily to the physical manifestation of their powers; in short, the logistics of it were a closely guarded secret of both her family and her realm. Nissa may have left the Water Realm, but she was not about to hand over one of its most closely guarded secrets to the heir of their rivals.

"They just did," she said unhelpfully.

"How?" he asked again, more bluntly this time.

"How did *you* know who I was?" Nissa fired back. His eyes danced dangerously, but they didn't meet hers.

"As I said, your family has been in touch."

"I don't know why they would be. My mother helped me leave." It was a half-lie.

"And why would she do that?" The suspicion dripped from his voice.

"Maybe she didn't want me to be trapped by a *male* who assumes that he has all the answers before he asks questions," she snapped. "A shame it all came to nothing."

"Cyril didn't trap you. You're my guest," he replied. Her eyes shot from the floor to stare daggers into his. He was being purposefully obtuse.

"You have a strange version of hospitality," she spat, rolling her eyes. His brows lowered into a glare before smoothing into chips of coal that she could not read.

"Maybe I'll invite Cyril up to speak with you then. Perhaps you'd prefer his version," he answered dangerously. Nissa opened her mouth to protest in spite of herself as an arrow of fear shot into her chest, but she held the response stubbornly behind clenched teeth. She stared in silence as he turned and left the room without a backward glance, slamming the door behind him.

Nissa waited for what seemed like hours to see Cyril's swaggering form lurching across her threshold. Each time footsteps padded in front of her closed door, Nissa's heart thundered in her chest, but the latch never clicked. When she finally deemed it safe to uncover her tray and attempt a meal, the food had gone cold.

"THAT WAS BADLY DONE," Trey muttered to himself as he stormed away from Nissa's room, his temper roiling against his remorse like opposing storms on the sea. Threatening her with Cyril's presence had been a low blow— one that he had known would petrify her.

He had been ready to believe her innocence, had been ready to listen to whatever reason she could provide to give him justification to keep her out of her family's clutches, but the sight of her in her room, collapsed on the floor in whatever trance she had succumbed to on the very day he received word from her parents, had been enough to spike his temper. It was all too convenient. Her family knew that she was with him, and then as soon as they send word to him, suddenly she's succumbed to the same type of twisted communication from within the Keep. He shuddered at the memory of her prone form, twitching as the magic that reached to her grappled with the strength of the wards of the room. She was lucky he had come to her room when he had. The pull of the magic would have snapped her spirit from her body against shields that strong. He'd seen it happen only once, and the experience had branded him for life. Shattering the wards had been an easy decision, and apparently an effective one, since the trance had dissipated as soon as the barrier was gone. *What strange magic is this?* His theories defied everything he'd been taught about her realm.

He pinched the bridge of his nose and took a deep breath as he considered her other accusation. He hadn't meant to trap her; the warded doors and windows were as much for her protection as they were for his; this way, none the fire wielders could enter without express permission, and anyone who came into her rooms had to be invited into the Keep itself. To be compared to—*no, diminished beneath*—the moral compass of someone like Cyril was just... He took another deep breath, rolling his shoulders as the crackle of his temper lightened to a few errant sparks.

The gentle sound of footsteps made him straighten, blinking open his eyes as a familiar figure approached. Her pale-faced expression was sympathetic, her blonde-brown hair loosely arranged so that it was out of her face. She was a new hire, and in the chaos, he hadn't learned her name yet. As his eyes washed over her pretty face, he wished that he had taken the time to learn; his inattention reminded him too much of his parents.

"This just came for you, sir." She extended a pale hand, and he took the folded letter automatically, his stomach churning as the light glinted against the seal pressed into the black wax. Word from Domogién was never a good sign— nothing involving his parents was.

"Can I get you anything, my lord?" she asked in a soft voice, looking down at the ground between their feet as the color rose in her cheeks. Trey forced his jaw to unclench as she raised his eyes to meet his before flickering them away again.

"No," he said gruffly, and her expression dropped into disappointment, "thank you, though," he finished with a less abrasive tone. Whatever her name was, it wasn't her fault that he was in this mess. The ghost of a smile hinted at her lips as they curved, and she nodded before turning to tread softly up the hall again.

12

———

Nissa did not see Tryamon again the next day or the next. In fact—aside from two, silent men who replaced the glass in her window the next morning — she saw nobody at all, except for the young woman who had delivered her tray of food on the first night. By the end of the third day, Nissa had resorted to pacing around the room in a prowl, cursing at the air any time she heard the whisper of footsteps in the hall. *Let them think me angry or let them think me mad. As long as they let me go.* To her relief, Nissa did not feel the pull of her mother's magic again, although she wondered what that meant for her and for them. Tryamon had said that her family knew that she was at the Singed Keep; Nissa didn't know if that meant that they would come for her or if she was to be dumped haphazardly back at the border. A faint glimmer of hope whispered that perhaps they would leave her alone, but it faded as quickly as it materialized. By the fourth day, she had leashed her unsettled feelings and was sitting well-composed on the chair near the writing desk, staring at the fog that gathered over the sea beyond the window when a knock rapped against her door.

"Enter," Nissa said with as much dignity as she could muster. Before the word had fully left her lips, the door swung open and the Prince of Flames stepped inside, his eyes wary. Nissa lifted her chin, staring hard at him, challenging him to speak first.

"Since I didn't get to the point of my visit to your rooms before, I thought I would tell you that your brother is coming." A roaring in her ears that had nothing to do with scrying filled Nissa's head. She fought back the feeling and forced her lips together in a smirk.

"How fortunate for you," she answered lightly. Trey's brows furrowed darkly above narrowed eyes.

"I didn't invite him." She shrugged against his words, staring hard at the window as she forced her fear to retreat.

"And who would usurp the authority of the mighty Prince of Flames?" Nissa asked loftily, forcing the edge of mockery into her voice even as her heart pounded to match the roaring in her head.

"My parents," he spat. Her blood froze in my veins. If all the Brandells knew of her presence here, then Nissa was to be a bargaining chip. She might have stayed home and achieved the same effect. She squinted at him.

"And how would they know I was here?" she demanded sharply before reigning in her temper with a breath. "It wouldn't have mattered if you did; it's the same result either way," she finished, examining her fingernails with feigned indifference.

"I didn't mean that—I wasn't talking about..." He closed his eyes, and his chest rose with a deep breath. "Forget I said that; it's not relevant to this," he finished.

"Then who do I have to thank for this uninvited guest?" she said, edging her voice dangerously.

"I'm just telling you what I know." he said gruffly. Nissa's jaw clenched to iron, fingers curling as she fought the urge to summon her abilities. But the window was back, and it would be a death wish.

"How brilliant of you to realize that I didn't ask for help from the place I escaped." Nissa could have bitten her own tongue out for divulging even that much about the circumstances from which she had fled. His eyes flared with interest.

"Escaped? You said your mother helped you leave," he said sharply.

"And so, she did. I said nothing about the rest," she answered, lifting her chin stubbornly. To her surprise—and against what Nissa would have assumed was against his common sense— Tryamon crept closer to her.

"What are you running from, Nissa?" he asked, his voice soft as he studied her face with a careful kind of curiosity. Nissa had never felt more like a display piece as she leaped to her feet and whirled away from him, away from the window and the false promise of freedom that lurked beyond the spelled glass. When she had wrestled the last vestige of her self-control into submission, she faced him again.

"I suppose you'll find out soon if Ward is already on his way," she answered flatly. Frustration and impatience warred as they wove into the intrigue that had been on his face, but to Nissa's surprise, he did not rise to the threat. Instead, he stood studying her for another moment before striding over the repaired window. He bent at the waist, looking closely at where the glass met the wall behind a braid of inlaid stones. He ran a hand against the seam, as though testing the edge, and the barrier glimmered with an unnatural iridescence. Nissa swallowed the bile that rose in her throat at the visual reminder that she was trapped again. When Tryamon turned back to face her, his face was a careful mask, those spectacular eyes suddenly hard and unyielding.

"I hope you can escape whatever it is that made you run. And whatever comes for you after," he said. Nissa blinked at him, bristling slightly at the implied threat, but before she could snap at him again, Tryamon had swept from the room and the door had thundered shut behind him. Nissa glanced back toward the window, at the storm clouds that gathered at the edge of the horizon, wondering what kind of storm was coming for her and how she would survive this one when it did. Bile rose in her throat, choking, thick, and rancid on her tongue.

In her heart, she knew that she wouldn't escape. Nissa tasted the word as it pressed past her throat, pushing against her teeth, as though the very word itself knew that it needed to get out and breathe. There would be no chance, not once Ward arrived. She flung her body toward the door that had just closed behind Trey, wrenching at the handle until the joints of her fingers screamed in protest. It was no use; the latch had clicked shut behind him, effectively closing the coffin on her chances of escape. *As if the wards hadn't done that already.* A scream of rage worked its way up from her chest, choking Nissa as it gargled to rip past her lips with violent ferocity. She reached within the well of herself, trying to summon any tendril of water to her, gasping as she felt the sudden hot moisture on her face. Nissa's eyes flew open, her vision blurred as they darted around the room. There was no power, there was no escape; there were only more tears and continued helplessness.

Come scry me again, Mother. Let the window shatter me instead. She willed with all of her might that she would feel that pull into nothingness, that she would shatter against the spelled glass like a champagne flute rather than be dragged back to their family home in disgrace. Whatever thread of connection she'd felt with her parents seemed to have slipped away, and after another moment of silent challenge, Nissa slumped to the floor, utterly spent. She had failed. She would be dragged to her father's house and then bred for her magic. It was over; she had wasted her mother's efforts, and she had wasted her own magic on a fool's errand. After all, wasn't that always what unfounded hope ended up being? *Perhaps I deserve what's coming my way.*

TREY BIT back his mingled guilt and frustration as he stalked back up the hallway. He wasn't mad at Nissa, not really. The letter from his mother, berating him in the usual vein of disappointment, set his teeth on edge. The detailed instructions for how to handle his incoming guest had grated on him all the more. *I anticipate your timely return to Domogién once your guests have departed*, it had finished. His jaw worked furiously as he played the words over in his mind.

He didn't even know how she'd found out about Nissa's presence in the Keep. Had Cyril—*no, he wouldn't defy a direct order.* He shook his head frustratedly. He'd been feeling too comfortable; he was due for a reminder of how his fate was set. He could play at independence in the Singed Keep and have control over his own forces. He could patrol the border and give orders. At the end of the day, though, his mother still pulled the strings in the realm. His lip curled. Lady Aithne prided herself on always being one step ahead of everything and everyone; now, she was reminding him that as the de facto queen of the realm, she was still the one who held the power. Trey had spent months weeding out her eyes and ears in the Keep, and it still hadn't been enough. Now, he had to prepare to deal with Ward Chantara, and then he had to prepare to face life in the capitol once more.

He'd only met Ward once, at one of the few inter-realm summits he'd attended in the Midlands. Ward's ice-chip eyes had been cold and calculating, even when they were boys, and his mother had whispered to him that he, a child, would be the biggest threat to the Fire Realm's strength when it was Tryamon's turn to govern.

"Play nicely," she had ordered ominously, "and learn what you can." What Tryamon had learned from the experience, he recalled with a disgusted curl of his lip, was that Ward was a bully, who talked down to anyone he saw as beneath him—which was everyone. The Water Realm's heir had lost interest in Trey when he learned that his interest in harassing the servants at the summit was not shared. From what Trey had heard, Ward hadn't changed much over the years, although he had moved beyond harassing servants as a child to harassing women as conquests, and that insight had done nothing to improve Trey's opinion of him. This was the male who was about to invade Trey's personal sanctuary. He spat out a window as he passed by, rounding a corner.

"Trouble in paradise, cousin?" Cyril leaned against the wall, his arms crossed and his dark eyebrows raised in wicked delight. Trey scowled at him.

"I don't want to talk to you," he said.

"That's a shame. I hear we'll have another guest." Cyril sneered, and Trey balled one hand into a fist at his side.

"Were you the reason for his invitation?" he asked evenly, forcing a bored expression onto his face. His stomach burned as his cousin's sneer deepened.

"I would *never* overstep my role like that," Cyril said. Trey shook his head, forcing down the rage that boiled his insides. His cousin was trying to goad him, and he wouldn't give him the satisfaction.

"I hear Ward Chantara has a way with women," Cyril continued. "At least *I'll* have something in common with him." Trey shook his head and pushed past his cousin.

"I'm proud to have *nothing* in common with someone like Ward," he growled as he passed. Cyril barked a laugh as he pushed off the wall, sending his dark hair dancing around his face with the movement, and the sound set Trey's teeth on edge.

"That won't make for very interesting dinner conversation." His cousin followed him, and a muscle feathered in Trey's jaw.

"I won't be having dinner with him," he said darkly.

"And risk offending a guest from a neighboring realm? What will your mother say?" Cyril mocked. Tryamon whirled around, gripping his cousin by the shirt as he forced him against the wall.

"If you're the reason he's coming here, I swear on all that is —" Trey's growled threat was cut off as Cyril laughed again, his deep, green eyes glittering coldly.

"As I said, *cousin*," his mouth twisted sardonically as he drew out the word, "I know my role here. My aunt has her own way of doing things." Trey's fingers loosened, and Cyril shoved him roughly away before stalking back up the hallway. With another growl of frustration, Trey rounded on his heel and stalked in the opposite direction. It had been a mistake to let Cyril know he'd gotten under his skin. He scratched at the back of his neck as he fought down the temper still boiling in his gut.

13

When Nissa stirred from where she had collapsed on the floor, the stiff, salty tracks on her face were the only real reminder that she had finished weeping hours before. Nissa rose carefully, shaking the stiffness from her joints as footsteps sounded and then stopped outside of her door.

"She's here," someone growled. Nissa's lip curled as she recognized Cyril's voice.

"You don't have to leave." Another familiar voice slipped silkily through the air, and she felt frost drip down her spine. *Ward.*

"It's not possible," she whispered, nearly missing Cyril's response. *He can't be here so soon.*

"I have orders." *Trey's orders to leave me alone,* she realized with a start.

"As you wish," Ward replied, and Nissa forced her body to unfreeze as the lock turned. By the time the door clicked open, she had arranged herself into a figure of indifference in the chair at the writing desk.

"Hello, brother; do come in," she said disinterestedly, forcing herself to meet his eyes as he cut across the threshold. The blue eyes of her younger brother, Lorcan, were hardened chips of ice against the harsh-cut lines of cruelty that etched Ward's tanned face.

"Ah, little sister. You've caused a stir at home. Who would have thought that you would be here, intruding on the Brandell's—" his eyes roved over her curiously for a moment as he chose his next word, "hospitality." Nissa kept her face carefully neutral. Whatever leverage Ward was searching for in her, she wouldn't make it easy for him to find.

"I would not have intruded for as long had they let me leave in peace. Or didn't Lord Tryamon tell you that part?" Nissa answered coldly.

"Tryamon is not the one who invited me here," Ward raised his dark blond brows. "Aithne Brandell sent her regards to our father once I departed." *So, it* was *his parents.* "My escort was very helpful in providing us with the details of your stay."

"I wouldn't trust much of Cyril's bravado, brother. He has his own motives," she answered, examining her cuticles.

"And what of young Tryamon's motives? Has he made those clear to you?" Ward's eyes darkened in accusation as he looked down at her again. She resisted the urge to scoff; Ward was only a few years older.

"The Prince of Flames has not honored me with his presence often," she managed flippantly. A knowing glint replaced the accusation.

"And when he did? What type of honor did he bestow upon you?" Nissa snorted in reply, and as fear and anger warred within her, she chose one to let rise.

"None that would compare to the *honor,*" she spat the word, "that you bestow on every woman you stumble across." The slap across Nissa's face came so hard and so fast that she heard it echo through the room before she felt its sting against her cheek. She reeled for a moment; he'd never struck her before.

"One of us has to make sure that the family line is continued," Ward said quietly, dangerously. Rage thundered in her ears at the accusation.

"Excuse me?" Nissa demanded, feeling the swelling across her cheekbone from where her brother's blow had landed.

"Spreading your legs for a rival realm's heir... I wouldn't have expected it of you, Nissa, although it explains why Tryamon kept you to himself. Thankfully, his discretion has meant that the Pallinors haven't heard of your little dalliance. And they won't, not until you are safely married to our dear cousin." The leer on his face was nothing short of wolfish. Despite the pain in her cheek, Nissa sneered in reply.

"Why? Would thinking I slept with Tryamon Brandell damage our little would-be union?" she asked innocently. A sound that could only be described as a growl rumbled in Ward's throat, and Nissa braced herself as he stalked toward her again, his shadow looming over her as he gripped her jaw.

"Listen here, you little wretch. You have one purpose for our family, and if you do *anything* to mess it up, breeding your power will be the least of your concerns," he spat.

"Am I interrupting something?" Ward shoved Nissa's face away roughly, and as her neck twisted to slow the momentum, she caught sight of Tryamon leaning up against the door frame, his arms crossed and his eyes flickering dangerously between them. Ward straightened, a catlike smile curling onto his lips.

"Of course not, Lord Tryamon. Just scolding my sister for the inconvenience she's caused your family," he answered smoothly. Trey's eyes snapped from Ward to Nissa, and she felt herself warm with embarrassment as he appraised the blooming welt on her face. She dropped her eyes to study the stone floor, jaw tightening as she clenched her teeth. *Helpless again.*

"It was no inconvenience, Ward." Her brother bristled, and Nissa's eyes darted up to meet Trey's, which were fixed on her face as though her brother was no longer present. "I do wish you'd have given me the chance to bring you here myself... or let me arrange a more formal welcome." The displeasure dripped from his words.

"Apology accepted, although it's unnecessary. Cyril was welcome enough for me, and your parents sent their regards already," Ward's lips curled in another smirk as Trey's eyes snapped back to him.

"Why don't we give your sister some privacy to freshen up for dinner while we discuss your travel arrangements?" Nissa blinked at the sudden change of subject.

"Our travel is arranged," Ward retorted.

"Good. I'd love to know when you'll be out of my house," Trey's voice sharpened. "Until then, I'll show you to *your* accommodations, and we can see your sister at dinner." To that end, Ward seemed to have no argument, and he stalked across the room, pushing past Tryamon as though he was part of the wall décor. Nissa met Trey's eyes once more, watched as his lips tightened into a grimace as his gaze flicked between her and the spelled window. Her lips parted, although she wasn't sure what thanks she could give that wouldn't be an admission of weakness. Before she could figure it out, Trey turned, and the door snapped shut behind him. Nissa allowed herself to slump into her chair again, face still throbbing, as the sound of their footsteps retreated.

Dinner with Tryamon Brandell, she mused on the subject as she pressed around the outskirts of the forming welt, gaging its size. Nissa glanced down at her worn—although, thanks to the staff, mercifully clean—clothes, and she wrinkled her nose. She turned with appraising eyes to study the wardrobe that stood against one wall. She hadn't taken the liberty of dressing up since coming to the Keep. Perhaps this was an occasion to make a statement. With newfound resolve, Nissa forced herself to ignore the throbbing in her cheek and step across the room to the closeted possibilities.

14

―――――

Nissa took a deep breath as she surveyed herself in the dark, rain-flecked glass of the window as she stood outside of the Keep's Great Hall. Her hair was braided down her back, the twists revealing the lighter highlights in the flickering candlelight. The pull of the hair away from her face accented the sharpness in her cheekbones, drawing attention up to where her eyes looked stormy beneath her brows, just as she had planned it. Nissa had gone back and forth about whether or not to cover the bruise that colored her cheek, but she ultimately decided against it. Its ugly shadow was the only thing that marred her otherwise unbothered-looking face. She smoothed her palms over the shimmering charcoal of the dress she had chosen. She wasn't sure where it–or many of the articles of clothing she'd come across in her search–had come from, but that was the least of her concerns. In the dress she wore, Nissa felt for all the world like a tendril of smoke curling her way toward her destination.

With another fortifying breath, she turned from her reflection and faced the door, and in a few short strides, Nissa had entered the room unannounced. Ward and Trey were already seated at the table, the tension in their shoulders the only indi-cation of their mutual dislike, and to her displeasure, Cyril was seated to Tryamon's left. Nissa's displeasure sank into dread as she took in the man on Ward's right: Murdoch. She sucked in a breath before fixing a placid expression on her face.

"Murdoch," she greeted, "I didn't realize we would have the displeasure of your company as well." Her father's man blinked at her as his harsh mouth twisted into a scowl. She'd thought that Ward would come alone. *Maybe our father doesn't allow him as loose a leash as it seems.*

"Lady Nissa," he replied quietly, his voice as sharp as a razor's edge. His eyes glittered as he took in the bruise on Nissa's cheek, and she narrowed her own in response. Warning flashed in Ward's face, and Nissa fought the urge to shrink back as she met his eyes evenly. Her brother gestured to the seat on his left. Instead, she took the seat squarely in the center of the table, ignoring a snort from Trey as she settled in place.

"What's for dinner? I'm starving." She pasted a tight-lipped smile on her face as she glanced to Trey's side of the table, unnerved to find the Prince of Flames leaning forward, elbows on the table as he looked on at her performance with interest. *Please play along.* Trey cleared his throat and tossed a glance to the door behind him. As if on cue, five servants filed out, each bearing a silver-topped tray. With an impressive sense of decorum that would rival the most somber of military parades, the servants settled behind the group, one for each of them, and then in unison set the trays in front of them with a uniform clang. As the lids were removed, the scent of spices wafted into Nissa's nose, and her mouth watered.

"I hope you aren't opposed to blackened Tashfish; it was the best we could prepare on short notice." Trey's voice was light enough, but the barbed expression of dislike that he shot toward Ward with his eyes spoke volumes.

"Will there be anything else, sir?" Nissa blinked at the soft voice that emanated from behind Trey, recognizing the girl who had brought her meals.

"No, Shae, that will be all for now. Thank you." It was a clear dismissal. *Shae. At least now you know her name.* She did not miss the suspicious glance that Shae cast between Nissa and her brother as she hesitated before nodding and trailing the men who had served them as they left the room.

"Looks delicious," she said nonchalantly, staring at the perfectly charred Tashfish. It was a regional fish, native to the Fire Realm and the southernmost reaches of the Water Realm. She'd never had the chance to try it. Conscious that no one else had moved, Nissa picked up her fork and stabbed an asparagus spear, segmenting it neatly with her knife before taking the first, citrus-infused bite. She chewed carefully as she watched Ward and Trey stare daggers at one another, still bristling. She swallowed before she cleared her throat.

"Am I the only one who's hungry here? Seems a pity to waste the food." Nissa shrugged before spearing another piece of asparagus on her fork. Ward's head whipped around as he glowered at her, and she knew that her bravado meant she was treading on dangerous ground. Still, he waited until Tryamon dug his fork into his fish before taking a bite himself.

"We leave at dawn. Be ready, or I'll drag you out myself," he growled, turning his cold eyes on Nissa. Trey's fork clattered to the table.

"You will watch your tone at my table. I give the orders here," he said with a warning edge to his voice.

"Are you going soft, Lord Tryamon? Or is she that good in the sack? Her fiancé will be pleased to know if it's the latter. You might even be paid extra for the revelation." Nissa stiffened, her appetite suddenly evaporating. From beside Trey, Cyril smirked knowingly in her direction. *As if there was anything either one of them would know about me in that regard.* She resisted the urge to spit as she plastered a pleasant smile on her face, noticing that Murdoch had gone suddenly still.

"Not all of us have your predisposition to rutting like an animal, Ward," she forced herself to answer lightly, but she couldn't contain the savage rage that speared through her tone.

"He's in for a lifetime shackled to you. He may as well get to enjoy some of it," Ward sneered. Her hands trembled then, but not with fear; it was rage flowing through her veins now. She stared hard at the sheen on the glass that made up the windows of the hall. *Spelled too, no doubt.* It wasn't worth killing herself to find out.

"I suggest you refrain from saying another word, Chantara, if you want to leave this Keep in one piece," Trey said in a voice that was quietly lethal. Murdoch leaned forward, but Ward lifted his palms toward the Fire Realm's heir in mock-surrender.

"As you wish it. I'd hate to spoil your man's cooking." As though the verbal sparring had ignited her brother's appetite, he dug in. Nissa stared hard at what remained of her meal, picking apart the fish with her fork. *I have to get out. I won't be dragged back to that life.* She sat silently for the remainder of the dinner, mind whirring as she walked herself through the different means of escape that would become available as soon as she was beyond this spelled prison. Each plan led to the same place; Ward's icy shackles holding her in place for the remainder of the journey home. Still, it would not do to let her despair show; Nissa would not weaken her realm in the eyes of its rival. She forced an expression of careful neutrality onto her face as she clung to the repeating keen in her mind that told her that Faris's sacrifice, whatever it had been, had been in vain.

She fought the thoughts that threatened to spiral her down into despair for the rest of the ominously quiet dinner, and when Nissa made her exit, it was with only the barest of farewells. Was there any point to formalities when she knew what the future held? A shudder wracked through her as she reached the door to her room, and a part of Nissa was proud that she had found it without an escort. She barked out a harsh laugh as she realized that her lack of escort probably correlated to their perception of her threat level, and the despair washed over her again. *Helpless. Useless, helpless, a vessel.* She stared hard at the door as fear, shame, and self-loathing washed over her. *I could make a run for it. I could at least try to leave.* Nissa shook herself and lurched into the room; she stood a better chance on the road, away from this hall of spelled glass and unknown threats lurking around the corners. She swung the door hard behind her, part of her reveling in the violence of the motion, but to Nissa's surprise, it did not slam.

She whirled around, braced for impact or attack or harsh words, but as she balled her fists at her sides, Nissa saw that the broad hand that had caught the door was Tryamon's. She looked him coolly up and down before spinning away with a mask of indifference on her face.

"You disappearing from dinner after me will do nothing to convince my brother that I haven't defiled myself." Her voice was strangely detached. To her own ears, it sounded nothing like her own.

"He excused himself shortly after you did." She twisted back around to face the Prince of Flames, and Trey shrugged.

"What do you want?" Nissa asked flatly.

"Mostly to make sure you found your way back here. The place is a labyrinth." To her annoyance, Trey stepped over the threshold and let the door click shut behind him. His face was a tan mask, and try as she might, Nissa couldn't read what motives lurked beneath the surface.

"As you can see." She swept her hands around to gesture to the room around her.

"Has he always been so...." Trey trailed off. *Abrasive? Insulting? Abusive?* There were countless words to describe her brother, but the family loyalty ran deep, so Nissa chose none of them.

"No," she said without further explanation. She didn't feel like explaining the sudden change that had come over her brother over the past months. To her relief, he didn't press it.

"And your family just lets him?" He cocked his head, a dark eyebrow arching incredulously.

"He's their heir," she shrugged. "We all have a part to play, and some things get overlooked." Nissa hated the casual way she excused the monster her brother had become, the way that her family had normalized his behavior and looked the other way, but divulging her family's deepest darkest secrets would get her nowhere. Trey fell silent for a moment then, staring at the window as the wind howled against it and thunder rumbled into the ocean beyond. His gold eyes snapped to Nissa's face again, a determined set to his mouth.

"Nice night for a walk," he said suddenly. Her eyes narrowed.

"Is it?" she asked.

"Such a shame you didn't get to explore the Keep fully before you had to go. There are all sorts of twists and turns in here. You could disappear for hours exploring them all." She stared hard at him then, as the amber in his eyes sparked a reckless gold. "Care for a walk before you go?" He extended one hand and Nissa stared at it dumbly as another peal of thunder rattled from beyond the wall. *If this is a trick, it could have very serious consequences.* She gritted her teeth as she considered the alternative.

"Yes," she said carefully, "a walk would be lovely." She stared hard at the hand he extended before he lowered it slowly. Despite the snub, a smirk worked its way onto his face.

"After you, Lady Nissa." He used the same hand to gesture toward the door, and Nissa nodded once, staring hard at him for a moment more before brushing past. Their arms brushed as she slipped past him toward the door, and Nissa froze as a bolt of lightning cracked beyond the glass. She watched, transfixed on the window as another roar of thunder shook the air. She looked hard at Tryamon again, piercing into those amber eyes with a fierceness of her own.

"Why are you helping me?" She asked, the mask slipping. *And what game are you playing?* Trey looked at her for a moment, seeming to debate with himself before answering.

"We all deserve to be more than prisoners of someone else's plot." She focused on the lines of his face once more, looking for any trace that he was trying to trap her too. Finding none, Nissa relaxed her shoulders and looked thoughtfully toward the door. *Known evil or the unknown potential for it: choose.*

"It *is* a nice night for a walk," she acquiesced, and the answering smile that curved Tryamon's lips told her that he had meant every word.

15

———

The hallway was dark, not that she had really expected it to be otherwise at night, but somehow, Nissa felt at ease. It was easy to let herself fade and meld into the shadows that the moonlight cast on the walls. She let Trey slip in front of her, and then she became his shadow as well, focused on keeping her footsteps soundless. Nissa was so focused that she almost slammed into his back as he lurched to a stop in front of a large painting. He glanced over his shoulder at her, seeming to consider for a moment, before pressing his hand into the bottom of the frame. The painting cracked outward, as though hinged, and Nissa blinked into the yawning mouth of a tunnel.

"Secret passageways, huh?" she whispered to Trey, but he ignored her as he stepped forward. Nissa felt a flicker of unease as the darkness swallowed him whole. *This could be a trap,* something in her mind hissed a warning. She knew that no trap could be worse than the one her family had waiting for her back in Danuil. She took a breath, shaking off her nerves as she followed him into the void.

A torch materialized when they rounded a bend, and she

wondered at the way it spontaneously lit. *You're walking with the Prince of Flames,* Nissa chided herself. The lighting should be self-explanatory. As though sensing her reflection, Tryamon turned his head, and the faint light cast a shadow across his smirk. In the faint light, his dark hair melded with the depth of the tunnel.

"I hope you're not afraid of the dark," he said.

"There are worse things to fear," she retorted, and his shoulders stiffened as he ripped the torch from where it was held in place on the wall. The sudden cast of light revealed dingy stone that was a world away from the chiseled polish of the main hall.

Nissa lost track of their movements as the tunnel split into several and wound around in an impossible spiral. The air felt ancient and stale, as though nothing and nobody had stirred within the depths for the last century. From the confidence with which Trey navigated them, however, she knew that this couldn't be the case. It was unsettling in a way, but the solitude was refreshingly honest.

She smelled the air before she felt it on her face, cool and sticky in the storm. Salt flooded her nostrils, the scent of the sea heavy in the air, and hope flared in her chest, as changeable as the flickering flame of the torch casting shadows on the wall. Nissa inhaled deeply. *Home.* The ocean was as much a part of her as the air in her lungs. She didn't know how she had missed the taste of it on her tongue on the way in. She blinked away time as the salty spray sprinkled against her face seasoning the night air. The moon was a cat's claw in the velvet backdrop of the sky, with stars sprinkling across it like silver paint flecks against canvas.

"Do you know where you'll go?" She spun back around toward the Fire Realm's heir to see him quietly studying her, his amber eyes darkened in the gloom. She held her breath for a beat, at war with herself before she answered.

"Anywhere but home," she answered vaguely. Her time at

the Keep had done nothing to expand her knowledge of the Fire Realm. She had been taught a few major cities so as not to embarrass herself if her family ever had any visitors from the other realms, but the details had never been deemed important—rather, she had never been deemed important enough to know them.

"Domogién is your best bet, I think," Trey said thoughtfully. Nissa started at the name of a city she recognized.

"Isn't that your capital?" she asked suspiciously. However loose her plans were, traveling through the biggest stronghold of potential enemies hadn't been among them.

"It's a stronghold of my family," he corrected, "and it's somewhere they would never expect you to go. Not if my parents were the ones who invited your brother to cart you home. Not if they all know you're trying to flee."

"It's mad," she said, "but it might work." *If you aren't caught again.*

"Domogién hosts visitors from many realms, and it's not hard to find. There's a main road that's easy to find if you go straight east, and once you're on that, you can follow it straight there. It shouldn't take you more than a few days if you're able to stay on course." She blinked at the influx of information, but she didn't dare to interrupt. "When you find yourself in the city, it'll be easy to become someone else, someone who won't attract attention. When time has passed and they stopped looking so closely, you can move on to wherever you want to be." There was a wistfulness in his voice as he finished, and Nissa wondered for the first time just who it was that Tryamon Brandell *wanted* to be. The night would not last forever, though, and there was not time for her to ask, nor was there any reason for him to answer. She reached forward and grasped one of his broad hands in her own, clutching it as she looked up into his face to meet his eyes. A guarded look shuttered over them as he tensed, clearly unsettled by the movement.

"Thank you, Trey. Truly. I am in your debt." She wondered if she would regret the words, but Tryamon's eyes clouded over as he pulled his hand back. The calluses of his palm scraped against her fingers with the motion.

"No, you're not," he said quietly. He shifted, hesitating for a moment, before he spoke again. "There's one other thing," he reached into his pocket, fishing for a moment before he pulled out a chunk of dark stone. She recognized it as the one he'd been wearing the last time she'd collapsed, although it was on a more delicate chain. The stone flashed in the moonlight as the clouds spun around to expose it. In the next moment, the light dimmed behind its misty shroud.

"What is it?" Nissa asked warily.

"Obsidian. It comes from one of the volcanoes to the islands south of the Keep. It—it protects us from being seen by those who would do us harm..." he hesitated. "And from the eyes of Seers." Nissa blinked at him for a moment before the realization hit her. The Fire Realm's aptitude for secrecy finally made sense. *He knew what scrying was all along.*

"This stone," she said carefully, "will keep them from scrying me?" He looked at her for a moment as though conflicted before he spoke again.

"Go be free, Nissa," he said finally, turning away. It was the best gift she could have asked for. He hesitated a moment, turning back and fixing her with his amber eyes once more. "I left a weak point in the window of your room. Find it with your power and break the glass. Then run the other way." *With my power?* There seemed to be no question in his mind of whether or not she could; in Trey's mind, it was a given, so it would have to be done. She watched his retreating form until the darkness of the tunnel swallowed him whole. As the echo of his footsteps disappeared to join him in the shadows, Nissa turned away, raising her face toward the sky and breathing in the salty scent of the ocean and her salvation. She allowed herself one moment to soak in the magnitude of what Trey had done before she opened her eyes again, slanting them toward the Keep. This close to the sea, she could feel the power thrumming through her veins, all but begging to be used. Nissa closed her eyes, allowing her consciousness to ebb and flow with the waves as it washed over the mighty stone walls of the keep. *A point of weakness, find the point of weakness.* The mantra hummed in her mind in harmony with the power that flowed through her, and Nissa's lips curved into a smile as they found the chink in the otherwise impenetrable shield around the building. It was further than she would have liked, but so close to the sea, where Nissa could anchor her abilities, she felt her power gathering outside of it, spinning between the magical wards and the glass itself like a spider spinning a web as she allowed the moisture to fill it. *If I could just—* Nissa gave a mental push.

The splintering sound cracked through the night, and she thought that she could hear the tinkle of the glass that fell inward as the water soaked through its weak points and the window collapsed. Her lips parted to bare her teeth as she turned back toward the sea with savage triumph. No doubt, someone would come running at the sound; Nissa was under no delusions that she was in the clear. She looked down at her clenched fist, at the fingers wrapped tightly around the silver chain as she stared down at the shining black pendant that Trey had left with her. She tucked it in the folds of her dress. The idea of the extra weight hanging around her throat while she wielded was unsettling.

She had chosen to take a land route last time, against the pull of her abilities, and she knew that they would expect Nissa to keep her vicinity to the source of so much raw power, but this time, she decided, she wouldn't care. *A keep this close to the coast surely has*—Nissa smiled again as lightning split the sky, revealing a dock down the shore with three dinghies bobbing against the swells of the water. It could be a fool's errand, braving the tempest, but no more so than anything else she had done. Decision made, Nissa crept down the rocks that separated her from the shore, blinking at the rain that zinged against her face without really feeling it.

She made short work of the ropes that bound the boats to the dock as she untied all three boats, holding closely to the rope of the one furthest from the shore. *No need to make it easy for them.* Nissa took a deep breath as she let another wave of power wash over her. She allowed the waves to crash against the boat nearest to the shore as it carried it to where treacherous rock lay in wait as she focused in on the second of the freed boats. *You might regret this later,* Nissa chided herself as she felt the sudden drain that always came with a heavy use of her abilities. She gritted her teeth against her own warning as she fought with the dragging, sucking current to create a stream that carried the second boat in a new direction. To her satisfaction, the boat bobbed out with the tide's recession, only bobbing slightly backward with each swell until it was finally out of sight. *Work with the waves, not against.* Nissa's mother had told her that once, on a rare trip to her family's home. It seemed a lifetime ago now.

"Hurry, hurry," Nissa muttered to herself as she walked the final dinghy to the edge of the dock. She froze as she heard the shout of distant voices. It would have to be now, before they finished searching the perimeter. She looked skeptically at the oars of the dinghy and then out at the storm breaking against the coast. *Choose your odds.* With one swift step, Nissa was in the boat and had pushed off the dock and into the churning water. She grasped the oars and pushed her mind into the rhythm of the sea. *Rise, crest, break, retreat.* Over and over, Nissa matched her breath to the tempo, gently nudging the currents beneath the boat to pull her away, away, *away,* as she pushed and pulled the oars. *East,* she reminded herself. *You have to go East.*

She was not sure how long she kept repeating the directions over and over in her mind, her heart beating in time to the rhythm of the waves as they were punctuated by the thunderclaps, but when she finally looked up, the sky was clear and full of stars, the only hint that the storm had ever existed a shadow of thunderheads on the western horizon behind her. Nissa smiled again.

"East," she murmured, putting one hand out and letting her fingertips brush against the water. "Take me East." And with the stars winking at her overhead, she closed her eyes again.

16

———

Somehow, it was not the blinding rays of light that roused Nissa from her slumber. Instead, it was the scrape of wood against earth that had her leaping to her feet, plunging calf-deep into the brine. She squinted into the mid-morning glare as she fought to get her bearings. She had drifted all night, and she had wound up—*where?* To the west lay the waters Nissa had crossed overnight, and to the north, she was able to make out the hazy rise of mountains. She clenched her eyes shut, picturing the last map she had seen of the realms. This far to the south, there were only two ranges of such mountains, and she would have had to drift a lot further than overnight to reach the second. Nissa let out a sigh of relief; she was still on track.

Raising her arm, Nissa cupped her palm to block out the sun as she made out an expanse of trees up ahead. *A Live Wood instead of the Dead Wood.* A small smile played on her lips before she grew somber again. She felt drained; her ability to wield had apparently continued to work long after she had drifted off to sleep. That had helped her reach the shore, but it made her a vulnerable target. She hadn't expected the magic to continue after she had fallen into slumber, not when she'd had to work so hard to maintain any flow of power back in Danuil. Perhaps, when she was locked in a fortress of ice, her power had remained as frozen as everything around it.

Nissa dipped her hand into the folds of her dress, feeling through the fabric to where the shard of obsidian rested with its chain coiled around it. She took a deep breath as she pulled it from its hidden pocket and looped it around her neck, brushing her fingertips over the stone when it came to rest beneath her collarbones. She was free, where no one could find her if she played her cards correctly, and all she had to do was get to Domogién and lay low for a while. *Easy enough, right?* If she was where she thought she was and her sense of direction held true, Nissa could reach the Brandell stronghold with another day or two of travel. She looked toward the trees, toward the still-climbing sun. *East.* She started walking.

It wasn't long before she reached the tree line that formed the forest. It took even less time for the thick humidity of the air to make her clothes stick to her skin as sweat beaded and dripped from her body. *Shocking: the Fire Realm is* hot. She snorted at the thought. Nissa found her hand grasping for the chunk of obsidian again. It didn't make sense, Trey helping her, not when he was heir to a rival realm. Then again, he lived apart from his parents and away from their family stronghold. Perhaps he was not as interested in the role as his family had led the rest of the world to believe. It was brave, what he had done, as brave as Faris had been when he had helped her escape that first time.

Nissa shivered despite the heat as she allowed herself to think, for the first time in days, of what might have become of her friend from helping her. Her mother would have shielded him to the best of her ability, as Nissa had reassured herself the last time these thoughts had crept into her mind, but Marin's influence was limited against Alvar's rage. Against his and

Ward's…. Nissa shuddered again. *I'll get him out,* she soothed herself. *Once things are settled, maybe I can send for him.* The thought sounded hollow. *If they let him live.* She shook her head roughly. No, they wouldn't have killed him, not for that. Her father was many things, but he was not a murderer. He would not have gone that far. *But Ward…* Nissa shoved the thoughts away roughly, angrily. Erratic as her brother was, such thinking would do nothing but distract her. Nissa's journey to safety, to a place where she could start thinking of helping Faris, was not over yet, and it was her responsibility to make sure that his sacrifice, whatever it had been after her first escape, would not be in vain. *I owe him that much.*

Somewhere in the trees beyond, leaves rustled, boughs brushing against one another, and Nissa stiffened. When the movement stilled, she slipped behind the nearest trunk and dropped into a crouch, cursing her own distractibility. *I need to focus, I need to pay attention, I need to…* The sound stuttered through again, and this time, Nissa felt the kiss of breeze on her face. *It was just the wind.* She dropped the tension from her shoulders as she rose from her position and stepped forward again, casting her eyes side to side warily as she went. There was nothing moving beyond the gnarled trunks, left swaying against the roots that fisted into the sandy, coastal soil like a lifeline when the breeze ruffled their frond-like leaves again.

The sun arced across the sky as she continued her forward trudge, and as she rationed the drinking water she carried with her, Nissa became more and more aware of the cotton dryness on her tongue and of the weight of the light pack she carried scrubbing against her spine from where she had bound it across her back. The canopy of trees provided some measure of protection from the heat of the day as late morning blistered into afternoon, but it did nothing to alleviate the thick, suffocating humidity that came from being this far south and this close to the sea. When she could take it no longer, Nissa twisted the haphazard braid she had worn since the previous evening and knotted it above the base of her neck. It was not a complete relief, but it helped some. *East, East, East.* The direction thudded into her brain in time with her footsteps as she pressed forward into her further purpose: continuing onward.

When her bladder couldn't take the pressure anymore, Nissa veered off-course to find a secure place to relieve it. *Not that you've come across anyone in the woods.* Then again, it would have been just Nissa's luck to have her solitude run its course with her in such a vulnerable position. As she crouched and the thought made her snort, the hunk of obsidian she wore at her neck scratched beneath the bodice of her shirt and she was reminded of a crucial fact: Trey had known about the scrying.

Nissa wondered what other secrets the Fire Realm had withheld from its neighbors, both of other realms' and their own. If he had known about scrying, how much did he know about how it worked? Did he know why Nissa had episodes when her mother tried to see her? *If so, that's more than I know about myself.* She pursed her lips in agitation. *More to the point, why would he give this to me?* A stone like obsidian, if it possessed the properties that the Prince of Flames claimed, would be incredibly valuable as a protective charm. What did it mean that he gave it to her? *That he's hiding something else?* She held the chain out from her body, watching the sheen of the stone play in the light as she rose and stepped back toward her path. *What else can it do?* How vulnerable was she if she continued to wear it? There was always the chance that Tryamon had been lying and that wearing the stone would expose her to further attacks. Her stomach twisted knots at the thought.

Not sure what he would gain from stalking an outlaw, she reasoned, just as she provided her own rebuttal: *leverage.* Still, Nissa could not bring her to cast away the stone. She hadn't had any further episodes while wearing it, and Ward had surely noticed her absence by now and sent word home. There was always the chance that the news hadn't reached her parents yet, but given the speed of Ward's initial arrival, Nissa wasn't convinced.

There was no reason to trust Tryamon, but as Nissa thought back to the urgency in his amber eyes, to the sincerity of what had appeared to be carefully chosen words, she found no reason to distrust him either—at least no more than anyone else. *At this point, there's not much more to lose anyway.* In any case, he would have little to gain from helping her escape just to drag her back later, especially if her brother was under the impression that she was, as he had so eloquently put it, *defiled.* Bile rose in Nissa's throat at the reminder that, in the eyes of so many in her realm, those like her could be reduced to body parts and bloodlines. Power crackled in her chest, and she felt the air around her suddenly thicken. Nissa fought against it as panic flooded her system and it grew harder to breathe. She forced herself to drag in several deep breaths until the sensation dissipated. *Well, there's a new party trick,* she mused. Control was key. When it came to her power; she could either control it or be consumed by it.

17

———

Trey shuffled through the papers that littered his desk, trying to find a rhyme or reason to them. He had placed them hastily before he and Cyril had left to patrol the border, and now, the disarray made them impossible to make sense of. His eyes snagged on the message he'd received from the Chantaras before Ward had arrived, and he paused. Had Nissa made it to the other coast yet? Had she gotten lost on the way to Domogién? He lifted a hand to brush over the empty space where his pendant normally rested against his skin. Had the charm worked for her?

Tryamon had no way of knowing if it had even worked for him; if he had ever been scried, he'd had no symptoms of it. He wasn't sure why it affected Nissa so profoundly to be the subject of a scry; he'd never heard of anyone collapsing when they became a vision for someone else. He sighed, shaking his head. In all likelihood, he would never see her again, and that was probably for the best. He smiled grimly as he thought back to Ward's reaction at waking the morning after her timely disappearance to find her missing. If nothing else, it had been worth getting involved just to see the look on his face.

"Where is she?" He had thundered into Trey's study, ripping him from his chair and slamming him against the wall. Trey winced at the memory as he shifted and felt the bruise against his back. He had stared back at Danuil's heir blankly.

"I have no idea what you're talking about?" he'd replied coolly. Ward had slammed him against the wall again, and the ghost of a temper had flickered in his eyes. "I suggest you let go of me."

"Or what?" Ward had sneered at him, and in the next moment, Trey had ducked beneath his arm, shoving Ward face-first into the patch of wall he had just vacated, twisting Ward's arm at a dangerous angle where he held it pinned behind his back.

"I told you to mind your manners in my house." Trey had growled, reveling in the way that the other man squirmed against his grip.

"Where is my sister?" he'd demanded, the sound muffled by the pressure of his face against the stone.

"Dangerous habit, losing important women. I wonder why that is," Trey had taunted, shoving Ward hard against the wall again before releasing him and taking a tense step back. Ward rounded on him, stalking forward again. Trey's eyes flared, the light of battle crackling through his blood as he prepared to fend him off again.

"You know something," Ward narrowed his eyes threateningly. Trey shrugged.

"You'll have quite a time proving it." He'd answered with a dagger-sharp smile. "Get out of my house." Ward had all but flown from the Keep in a rage, cape billowing in the wind as he launched his horse into a gallop. *Good riddance.* Trey's smile had faded as the man's silhouette had disappeared, wondering what the consequence would be for his interference.

As the memory dissipated, he looked down at the pages in

front of him, knowing that as long as she made it out of Ward's clutches, it would have been worth it. *That's two times you've gotten involved in situations that weren't your responsibility.* Trey's jaws tightened at the reminder. There were a lot of things he'd done that he wasn't proud of; letting a monster like Ward treat women that way wouldn't be one of them.

His eyes snapped up as Cyril sauntered into the room, a lazy smile on his tan face. *Speaking of treating women poorly.* Trey's lips tightened as his cousin waved a piece of paper in the air, holding it aloft when he approached. Trey glared up at him, unamused.

"A letter from home. How special," Cyril crowed. Trey rolled his eyes and snatched it from his grip.

"You can leave," he said.

"And miss out on what mommy dearest has to say to her favorite boy? I think not." Trey huffed as he glanced at the message, which was indeed addressed in his mother's hand-writing. He scowled. Some battles weren't worth fighting.

"I don't know why you care." He gritted his teeth as Cyril plopped down in one of the chairs by the window, kicking his feet up onto the sill irreverently as he smirked.

"Where's the pretty little Chantara girl? Are you finished with her already? You might have let me have a turn before she left." Anger flared in his chest.

"You're foul," he said coldly, without looking up.

"A shame Ward had to go so soon too. I hear he has quite the way with women. We could have exchanged strategies." Trey slammed his palm on the desk and fixed his cousin with a hot stare.

"As I told Ward, you will watch your mouth in my house," he snarled. "If you admire him so much, you're welcome to ride after him. The Fire Realm would be well rid of you." Cyril raised an eyebrow, looking unbothered.

"Your mother disagrees. Who would look after you for her if I left?" The fingers of the hand on the desk curled, and he was overcome with the sudden urge to blast his cousin into oblivion. He turned roughly away, seething, and focused back on the now-crumpled message in his hands. His hands shook slightly with rage as he broke the Brandell Seal, edged sharply in crimson wax, and began to read:

TRYAMON,

I am disappointed to hear of your actions as they pertain to your former guests. It should be no surprise to you that the cost of your indiscretions will be severe. As you can no longer be trusted to maintain peace and civility at the border, consider this your indefinite dismissal from the Singed Keep. I expect you to return to Domogién immediately. Your replacement is already on the way.

LADY AITHNE of House Brandell

HIS FIST CLOSED over the paper, wadding it into a crumpled ball before he tossed it against the wall opposite of Cyril. His cousin tilted his head to survey him with a patronizing stare. Trey forced his temper down into the depths of his core. This was not the time to let himself be goaded.

"What news of home?" Cyril asked with a smirk. Trey closed his eyes as he took a deep breath.

"I'm sure you already know. We're leaving," he answered shortly. Cyril kicked his boots off of the windowsill and rose, facing Trey with an exaggerated bow before swaggering toward the door. He shook his head, fuming, as he stood and tossed the crumpled ball of the note away. *Summoned like a child.* His teeth ached as they ground against each other. Dread sank like an iron ball in his stomach. Being called back home never boded well for him, and given the tone of this most recent message, he was not looking forward to finding out what his mother had in mind.

18

W*ater!* The sound of flowing water tickled her ears as it babbled through the woods. Nissa's tongue was thick in her mouth, the last drops of her own supply drained just before she had collapsed into sleep. Now, the scent of running water hung against the air. How had she missed the promise of a resupply last night? She rose, casting her eyes warily around her as she studied the surroundings that she had taken no precautions in selecting before exhaustion had claimed her.

She stretched, reveling in the momentary ecstasy the sensation poured into her tired muscles. She said a silent prayer that the water she was hearing would be drinkable as she pressed her cotton-like tongue to the roof of her mouth. Then, she perched on her elbows and half crawled out of the hole, peering carefully over the lip of the embankment that separated her from her query. *There!* A spring glistened as it bubbled over the stones that contained it. Sparing a glance around her, Nissa allowed the rest of her body to follow her head as she rose, dusted off her clothes the best she could, and stepped toward the stream.

The water tasted like an elixir of life as she cupped her hands into the spring and brought them to her mouth again and again. Nissa pulled her waterskin from her bag and filled it to bursting, thanking her lucky stars to have found a clean water source in such a private and protected space. The odds finally seemed to have smiled in her favor, however briefly it might last. When she had at last had her fill of water, Nissa placed the waterskin back in her now-dingy pack and rolled her neck to stretch again before looking to the sky for the placement of the sun.

She blinked into the rays of light that peeked through the trees and realized that it was still early. She could still cover some ground before she needed to worry about being intercepted as she got closer to the city. *Domogién can't be far.* Trey had assured her that, if she stayed on track, the journey couldn't take more than a few days. Still, for someone with only the vaguest senses of direction, the thought of finding the city felt a bit like finding a dewdrop in a rainstorm.

Standing in one place isn't going to help you get any closer, Nissa reasoned to herself with a sigh. To her relief, the stream seemed to be meandering southeast, so she could follow it—at least for a while. *Not that I plan to empty my waterskin in one go.* It held more than the canteen she'd taken when she'd fled Danuil, and as she hefted its newly filled bulk, she was thankful she'd left the other behind. Nissa squinted into the light again as she stepped further into the crowning day, wishing for all the world that when she had left the Singed Keep, her travel plans would have also allowed her to steal a horse.

The sun climbed slowly that day, and she was thankful when it finally positioned itself behind her. Despite the cover of the trees, the light had brutalized Nissa's eyes, and she had given herself a headache from squinting all morning. As afternoon collapsed into evening, an animal scent crept toward her from beyond the next rise of the forest floor. Nissa froze, listening intently, as the sound of hooves and wagon wheels squealed faintly from the same direction. *A road?* She wondered. There was only one way to find out. Nissa had foregone her traveling cloak in the heat of the day, but now, she pulled the black length from her pack and gave it a good shake before throwing it around her and fastening the button at her throat. Her skin prickled in protest as sweat beaded on her flesh, but Nissa ignored it as she pulled the hood over her hair and tucked the flyaway pieces beneath it. A road meant civilization, and civilization meant a greater chance of someone recognizing her.

She crept forward through the trees, focusing on minimizing the rustling noise that betrayed her footsteps across the forest floor. Over the next rise, a cleared expanse of land revealed the road that she had known she would meet. Indeed, there were horses and wagons traveling in both directions, but there were plenty of groups traveling on foot as well. She let out a breath of relief that her traveling status would not draw undue attention her way. Nissa stepped down toward the road, making sure to stay alongside the edges as she inhaled deeply and wrinkled her nose at the smell of horses and close quarters. *Smells like a city is on the horizon.*

"Come on now, we're nearly there. Once we get to town, you can rest," a mother soothed her child, who pulled obstinately at her hand.

"I'd hardly call Domogién a *town*, Iryne." A man who Nissa assumed was her husband frowned down at her. The woman rolled her eyes good-naturedly, but Nissa missed what was said as the woman swung her child up into the man's arms and they continued moving.

"I guess that answers that question," Nissa muttered to herself. She turned to follow them and took another deep breath. *You're almost there,* she soothed herself, and she allowed herself to melt into the crowd of her fellow travelers.

Domogién was like nowhere Nissa had ever been before. While her home in Danuil had a decently-sized population, the chill that filled the air around the city deterred most residents from spending unnecessary time wandering the streets. Domogién, it seemed, had the opposite problem. Beyond the iron-wright gates, artfully crafted in a design that mimicked flickering flames, the heat was blistering, but no one seemed in a hurry to escape indoors.

A melody floated on the air to meet her ears, and Nissa found herself stepping in time and resisting the urge to skip with the lively tune it carried. *Musicians! There are musicians performing out here.* At home, music was a more somber affair, exclusive to theaters and scheduled performances. To see it displayed here so casually felt almost sacrilegious. She loved every moment of it.

Like the Singed Keep, most of the buildings seemed crafted of stone, but the colors varied widely from sun kissed auburn to soft grays, rather than the gradient gray and black of the keep. *Lovely.* The cacophony of colors somehow made sense in Nissa's mind, and she found herself enamored with her first look and itching to explore. *First things first, though,* she reminded herself. Lodgings were at the top of her to-do list; if she was going to stay in Domogién, she didn't want to do it as a beggar, exposed to the elements and the whims of anyone who might stumble across her with ill intent. Nissa still had the small cache of coins that her mother had tucked within her pack, and she had to hope that it would be enough to help her find a place here, however brief that stay might be. *Better still to have a home base in case it's longer than expected.* Exploration could wait. First, she needed to orient herself and take care of the necessities.

Nissa tore her eyes from the lively streets that beckoned her with music and turned instead to the quieter side-streets. A few held skulking figures in their midst, and she found herself turning away from the trouble before it could begin. Another, emptier path caught her attention, and she found herself moving away from the city's gate as though beckoned.

The small street was quiet, but the sound of water echoing beyond what Nissa could see drew her in as the sounds of the more crowded city faded behind her. As it grew louder, she realized that the sound stemmed from a fountain. The artful carvings were like nothing she had seen before, with elegant twists etched into polished stone that seemed to glow with its own inner light. The water that trickled through the deeply carved facets of stone added to the effect, rippling the water that formed a shining black pool against the stone basin at the bottom. Nissa's breath caught in her chest as she stopped and stared, wondering how the few passersby were not likewise overcome. She swallowed thickly as she turned away, wondering how a hunk of twisted stone could make her feel so overcome.

As she tore her eyes from the fountain, Nissa caught sight of a small, unassuming building behind the fountain, built of soft-gray stone. It was a quiet building, and its weathered sign named it as an inn in shining bronze text. She was drawn to the building like a moth to a flame. Perhaps she should have sought out something busier, where she could fade into a crowd of other nameless travelers, but something about the building called to her, and before she knew it, she had entered.

She looked up as she stepped over the scarred threshold to where beams spiderwebbed across a ceiling that was higher than she would have expected from her vantage point outside. Thick, wavy glass glowed translucent against the unforgiving light of the city beyond, and a few glittering specks of dust floated through the air as she blinked to allow her eyes to adjust to the changed light. The room Nissa had entered was spacious, with a bar at one end beneath a lofted space that she assumed led to the rented rooms. The space around the bar itself was deserted, and if it was not for the presence of the few stools being carelessly shoved back from the bar, she would have thought that it was always so. A few tables scattered themselves on the half of the room that bore the bar, but there was no sort of direction in sight. Despite the flecks of sparkling dust in the air, the room seemed clean, and Nissa decided that she was content to wait for service. The thick, dark planks of wood that made up the floor creaked softly as she crossed over to the bar, where she settled herself on one of the stools in the center and decided to wait. Nissa was only seconds into her silent vigil when she got the sense that she was being watched, and she spun on the stool as casually as she could, leaning on one elbow as she angled her body so that she could see the room.

"Can I help you?" a gravelly voice asked near the ear that was nearest to the wall. Nissa yelped in surprise as she lunged off the stool, spinning to face the man who had spoken. She squinted at the man; he was roughly her height, silver-haired with a receding hairline and a long mustache to match—which was presently twitching with the same amusement that deepened the lines around his eyes. She swallowed heavily as she rubbed a spot on her forearm that throbbed; she must have pushed off the edge of the bar. Nissa cleared her throat uncomfortably.

"I was hoping to rent a room," she said once her thundering heartbeats had returned to their normal pace. He sized her up briefly, and his mustache stilled.

"We're a bit far from the center of town here," he said after a measured silence. "Are you sure you won't want to find something closer to the action?" He tilted his head to one side as though evaluating her, and she fought the urge to swallow again.

"The quiet suits me just fine," Nissa said. "Light sleeper," she added with a quick flash of teeth. She held her breath carefully for another moment as he considered her.

"It's just as well. We don't get as much trouble out our way," he said finally, and Nissa felt herself relax.

"I'm definitely not looking for trouble," she said lightly.

"How long will you be wanting to stay?" he asked, raising an eyebrow at her. She felt her cheeks heat slightly at the question; she didn't have an answer to that. Tryamon had told her to lay low for a while, but Nissa had no idea how long it would take for everything to blow over with Ward. A moment passed while she considered, doing nothing to alleviate the nervous heat that spread through the rest of her body. *Say something. Anything.* She released some of her tension with what she hoped was a nonchalant shrug.

"Not sure. Could I go week to week?" she asked. The man grunted, and Nissa thrust her hand into her bag, fishing out her coin purse and counting out pewter and bronze coins carefully.

"You'll need at least one gold for a week's stay," he interjected, and she froze, teeth catching on the inside of her cheek as she stared into the purse that had been rather light to begin with. Nissa had been hoping to save more for the next leg of her journey.

"Oh," she managed.

"It *is* the capital city," he said kindly. Nissa chewed thoughtfully on her lip as she glanced up at him. His brown eyes had softened slightly.

"Just the week for now, then." She dropped the coin—one of her only gold coins— reluctantly into his hand and tried not to look too longingly after it as he turned it over and over between his fingers.

"Tell you what," his eyes met hers, "you help me keep the bar clean after hours, and we'll call it three bronze for the week." Nissa blinked at him for a moment, taken aback.

"Why?" The word shot out of her before she could stop it.

"I may not look busy, girl, but it's just me here at the

moment. The extra help would be welcome," he said grudgingly.

"Oh," she said again. The man extended the gold coin back to Nissa, and she took it, replacing it quickly in her pouch, dropping the bronze coins in his outstretched palm to replace it.

"From one quiet-natured person to another," he said with a twitch of his mouth. "I'm Aegon Dornamir, the owner." She nodded at him.

"Ni—" Nissa froze for a half-second. "Nice to meet you," she amended. One of his thick eyebrows twitched upward at her stammer, but he didn't comment on it. To her relief, he also didn't push for her to share her name.

"Up the stairs and to the left. Second door. The key will be in the lock." He nodded at her as though to affirm the instructions before turning his back and sauntering back through a subtly placed door beside the bar. *How did I not notice that before*? Nissa stared at it for a few moments before shaking her head and glancing across the room at the sturdy-looking staircase. *Might as well get settled in.*

19

———

Each day that Nissa spent in the city set her more at ease. It was as simple as Tryamon had said it would be to fade into blissful anonymity of Domogién. Each street was a melting pot of personalities and professions. Fire Realm citizens were, of course, the most auspicious presence, but Nissa had stumbled across a visitor from the Air Realm quite by accident as well, watching from afar as the man had summoned a breeze on a particularly muggy day. This had been met with applause from those near enough to him to notice, and Nissa had found herself smiling in response.

She hadn't spent much time on the streets of Danuil, despite it being so close to her family home. Her father was fiercely protective of all of his children—rather, fiercely controlling, as she was coming to see it now—so Nissa had been allowed to explore the city only on special occasions, in pre-approved locations, and always with an escort intimidating enough to keep many from getting too close. She wasn't sure if Domogién was comparatively unique or if it was her freedom in being able to explore on her own terms that made it appeal to her so much. Either way, Nissa enjoyed the process of becoming acquainted with the life-teeming paths that she took the liberty of investigating at her own pace. She still shied away from exchanging much more than passing remarks to the vendors in the market who recognized her as a frequent visitor, but she thrived on the sense of adventure that came with each new discovery she made.

The nights spent wiping the bar and sweeping the inn floor were made more worth it when she discovered the city library. Nissa stumbled across it accidentally, when she took a wrong turn and found herself gazing up at an impressive building the color of sand. Its rising columns and a regal staircase of the same material took her breath away. She had been drawn to the front door like a moth to a flame, and upon stepping inside, she had discovered a universe of worlds inside its walls. Since Nissa was not a citizen of the Fire Realm, she wasn't allowed to leave with any of the materials, but she had spent several days inside the cavernous hall, thumbing through book after book to pass the time, leaving only for meals or when her eyes started to blur. One tome in particular, a tale of faeries and assassins, had kept her there for the entirety of a day when she found it impossible to put down. It had been a long time since an escape into fiction had made her forget a meal. Reading, while she hadn't spent much time on the hobby back home, was proving to be a welcome escape from the peak of the hotter days and a way to break up her patterns of travel. Even as she became more comfortable on the city streets, Nissa knew that it would not serve her to have her movements become too predictable. Still, she stayed out as often as she could manage to, mostly to prevent prying questions from the innkeeper as her first two weeks at his establishment drew to a close. Thankfully, he did not seem to be the talkative type—or maybe he just knew somehow that Nissa couldn't be. So far, they'd built a system that worked between the two of them. So far, that meant that she was safe to stay in place, at least for the time being.

Despite Nissa's intrigue with the lively streets at the center of Domogién, she was comfortable in her lodgings off the beaten track. The quaint room was equipped simply with a wood-framed bed, iron tub, and small sink. Through some method that she assumed to be a trick of Fire Realm power, the water in the tub was heated where it came through the pipes, and she had enjoyed the luxury of a warm soak on several occasions. Despite the iron of the tub, Nissa never saw any evidence of rust. Beyond the luxurious plumbing and the curious properties of the tub, it was a simple room, but a part of Nissa craved stability that it brought to the close of each day. There was some sense of foreboding deep in her gut that told her to enjoy it while it lasted.

It was the pursuit of that enjoyment that empowered her to finally venture down to the Artist's Quarter on one especially clear night. The stars twinkled down at Nissa from their own frolicking merriment as the sound of the rambunctious celebration in the quarter grew louder. She stepped in time as the dancing notes of a fiddle rose above the din. Nissa skipped to the tune, toes scuffing slightly as the strings held a singing note. Laughter punctuated the melody, and her lips parted in a smile as she drew closer and saw figures of all ages leaping through the air in dance.

"First time in the Quarter?" A voice reached her ears from the right, and Nissa jumped to see a tall, lean silhouette lift an arm in toast. His brassy-toned goblet glinted in the light as he took a swig of his drink. She fought the heat that rose to her cheeks at being caught in a moment of unawareness as she nodded.

"It is."

"Welcome to paradise. There's nowhere like it." His dark eyes surveyed Nissa over the rim of his glass.

"Thank you," she said stiffly, stepping away from the man. A hand caught her forearm, and she stiffened.

"Slow down! What's your name? What brings you to our fair city?" he asked, face smooth and unreadable as he surveyed her.

"Freedom," Nissa said vaguely, wrenching her arm away. He raised his glass again, and this time, he was close enough for Nissa to scent the faint notes of fruit that rose from his wine.

"To freedom, then," he smirked. Nissa whirled around, casting a wary glance behind her as she twisted between dancing pairs. She felt the man's eyes on her back until she was all the way across the space. As the musical number came to a close, Nissa thought that perhaps she had been too careless in coming to this section of the city at night. She cast her eyes around her, but thankfully, the man had not followed her further, and the weight of Nissa's dread lightened as the fiddler struck up another lively tune. She found a vantage point on a wall and let her toes wiggle in time within her shoes, smiling as she nodded along.

"Do you dance much?" a woman to her left smiled. Splatters of paint coated her tunic and flecked her face, although her hands remained clean. Nissa smiled in reply and shook her head politely.

"Not in some time," she said.

"Go one if you want to. Nobody'll mind," the woman said with a lilt. Nissa shook her head softly.

"Not this time." Her smile turned apologetic, and the woman hummed a response, seeming to understand. Nissa's eyes glanced over the dancers again, and as the melody climbed to sing a high note, she closed her eyes and let it wash over her. *Beautiful.* It was a magic all of its own, and she wondered again if other cities shared it. When Nissa reopened her eyes, she gazed over the others like her, who were soaking in the scene from the shadows of the wall. It lightened her heart to see that what she felt was a shared experience, if the naked joy on the faces of those observing the dancers was any indication.

A jerking movement, at odds with the fluidity of the dance, caught her attention from one far corner of the crowd, and Nissa's eyes strained through the shadows to follow it. A broad-shouldered figure was pushing his way through the crowd, which parted just enough for him to pass before closing around. She fought a scowl as she squinted at the offender. *Who wouldn't be enjoying this?* She rolled her eyes at her own reaction. *Not worth wasting time to judge.* She turned back to face the music as a cellist stepped forward, hefting his instrument to join the fiddler. Nissa settled back against the wall with a smile and enjoyed the show.

20

———

When she had reached the end of her third week in Domogién, Nissa finally felt comfortable enough not to check around every corner as she wandered the streets. She was still on her guard of course, and she knew that she would have to be until enough time had passed that she could move on, but Nissa was no longer jumping into a defensive position at every shifting shadow or tensing at each body that came too close to hers on the bustling city streets. And it was, she had to admit, a bustling city.

The Fire Realm's capital felt like a secret gem, with streets bright and busy and lined with vendors. Against her better judgment, Nissa had made a habit of meandering down one street in particular, where a sequence of market stalls boasted of wares and cuisine from across the realms. Of course, few of the booths were manned by those from the realms whose wares they handled so enthusiastically, but the site of such metropolitan enthusiasm had her feeling a bit nostalgic for home and wistful for exploration all at once. *And none of it is out of reach now that you're out from under your father's thumb.* The crowd faded into a dull hum in her ears as she studied the fresh wares. They seemed to change every couple of days, although whether the changes were to add variety or because the booths were so popular, Nissa hadn't yet figured it out. She lingered in front of one stall, and she was studying a woven basket that claimed to be from an Earth Realm artisan when a body plowed into hers. She exhaled sharply as an elbow slammed the wind from her lungs in a whirl of deep blue, and she fought for breath. Nissa glanced up from her nearly doubled-over position at a cry from the one who had run into her.

"I'm so sorry," a dismayed, feminine voice cried, reaching a steadying hand from beneath a midnight blue cloak and pressing it against her arm, "I was trying to get out of someone's way, and I just... I just smacked straight into you."

"It's okay," she managed, still gasping slightly. "I should have been paying more attention." *Again.* She fought for breath as quietly as possible as fluid pooled in her eyes from the lack of air. When Nissa finally straightened, her eyes fell on a slim-boned, oval face that drained of color as her unusually pale green eyes met hers. The woman took a step backward and bumped against another patron.

"You." The woman's words were nearly a hiss as shock widened her eyes, and she didn't bother to apologize to the other patron. The man in question grunted a warning and side-stepped as she took another step back. Nissa blinked, startled.

"Do I know you?" Nissa asked, a chilling dread further inhibiting the air that fought toward her lungs. Those green eyes only widened further as the woman took another away. Nissa reached out a hand of her own in what she intended to be a calming gesture, but she was shoved roughly backward as a broad-shouldered man slammed between them, pulling a plump, laughing woman by the hand behind him. When they had passed, the other woman was gone.

Someone knows who I am. There it was, that thundering, racing, *skittering* series of heartbeats that always came to warn

Nissa when things were about to change. Her eyes scanned the crowd ahead, her vision swimming between the shifting bodies as she fought to catch sight of that unusual, blue cloak. *There!* Halfway up the street and slipping around a corner, she caught a flash of that midnight color again, and ignoring the annoyed protests of those she pushed past, Nissa hastened to follow it.

Despite the woman's head start, it didn't take Nissa long to have her within her sights again. Calling on every tracking instinct Nissa prayed she possessed, she followed at a distance. The woman's pace slowed after she twisted through three or four more streets, and Nissa nearly lost her once more before she stopped in front of a loud tavern. Nissa squinted at the aged wooden sign, swinging in an unfelt breeze, as she fought to make out the name of the establishment, but she was too far away. Raucous laughter poured from the open windows, and the woman danced from foot-to-foot as she hesitated, glancing around her uncertainly as though she was reluctant to enter. As though she had reached a decision, she squared her shoulders. With a surprising swiftness, the woman seized the carved handle of the heavy-looking doors, flung one open, and slipped inside. A few patrons slipped outside to replace her on the stoop, their hoods pulled low over their brow as they glanced both ways across the street before peeling off in opposite directions.

Nissa glanced down at her own worn traveling cloak, thankful that she had put it on instead of leaving it in her room at the inn, studying the dusty, gray fabric. *It's not unique enough to attract attention.* Still, as she found herself in front of the tavern door, staring up at the sign that said, "The Greasy Sow." Nissa pulled her hood up, hoping that the shadow it cast over her face would be enough to avoid unwanted attention. Her long braid fought against the pressure of the hood, but with a snap of her head, Nissa shook it loose as she took a deep breath and slid inside after her target.

Nissa blinked at the assault of the dusty room as her eardrums thrummed in protest at the sudden noise. An explosion of laughter sounded from one corner as the door slammed shut behind her, and she jumped as the roar rolled across the room. Nissa couldn't pick out the source of the din in the shadowy light. The room was illuminated by torchlight, and she could only hope that the dingy appearance of the room was only a result of the dim lighting. As her boot sloshed in a puddle and foul tendrils of stench rose to burn her nostrils, however, Nissa knew her hopes were in vain.

Focus, Nissa. She scolded herself as her eyes roamed the room again, straining for any glimpse of the woman or her cloak. She cursed as a boot stomped on her foot, and as the boot's owner stumbled in front of her, she fought the urge to shove him roughly out of the way. *There are too many people in this gods-forsaken room, and I'm never going to*—she left the thought unfinished as she caught sight of her target, sitting in one of the far corners of the room with her head bent in what appeared to be an intense conversation with two much-larger men. From the way that she gestured madly with her hands and the way the shoulders of one of the men shook with laughter, Nissa knew that at least one of them wasn't taking her seriously. Despite herself, one corner of Nissa's mouth lifted in ironic solidarity. *Been there.* The expression dropped as Nissa realized that she was probably trying to tell them about their run-in.

Nissa willed herself to melt into the shadows as she stepped against one of the more dimly-lit walls and crept closer, straining her ears to hear any indication of who this woman was and why she had seemed afraid of her. She picked up snippets of conversation from the tables as she slid past.

"...plans when they hear about Aella..." Her ears picked up the name of the Air Realm's heir spoken so casually, and she almost tripped over her feet. *Why would they be talking about the*

Air Realm's governing family in the Fire Realm? Nissa shook her head at her own distractibility. The House of Makani was none of her concern. What *was* Nissa's concern was finding out if this woman wanted her dead or not.

"...Telling you that I saw *her*. It was as plain as day." The woman's indignant voice finally reached her, and she sat down hard, forcing a drunken sway, at a half-abandoned table. The other half was occupied by a group of wiry, nervous-looking women, who took one look at the shadows beneath her hood and paled, vacating instantly. Nissa busied her hands with picking up one of their discarded glasses, and she made a show of pretending to sip on the lukewarm amber liquid that remained.

"You're telling me that you saw Nissa Chantara in Domogién. I get that. What I don't get is what she would be doing here, wandering a busy city street in the heart of the Fire Realm, when she's supposedly on the run," one of the men said with a self-satisfied belch.

"I don't know or care what she's doing here. What I care about is that her brother doesn't find out that *I* am here," the woman hissed. Nissa jerked her shoulders involuntarily. *What does my brother—either of them—have to do with this woman?*

"Come on now, Pippa. You've only ever seen her from a distance anyway. How can you be sure that it was her?" Her other companion asked, and his tone told Nissa that he had a steadier head than his friend. She tilted her body slightly to see him narrowing his eyes thoughtfully at the woman across from him, the expression shadowed beneath bushy gray eyebrows that contrasted with the shining bald of his head. Her other companion rocked slightly, running a hand through his mop of shaggily-cut brown hair as he shot her a roguish grin. *Pippa...* Nissa searched her memories for any trace of the name, but there was none to be found. Pippa's eyes spat fire as she raked a hot glare across both men before her expression hardened.

Nissa leaned forward slightly as her voice lowered, struggling to catch her next words as she pushed herself to rise.

"I know what I saw. I thought you two might be interested in the payout I hear comes with delivering such a valuable target. But maybe I'll just find someone else who can..." Pippa's eyes flickered up to Nissa's face, and her dark braid fell across one shoulder as her mouth twisted into a triumphant smile. "Or you can turn around and see for yourself."

21

———

Nissa only froze for a moment before she leaped to her feet. Gone was the frightened young woman she had followed into a strange tavern. Present was a very real threat with an unknown motive, and that threat currently had two formidable-looking men looking hard at Nissa with the light of a hunt in their eyes. Nissa made her next decision in an instant: she bolted.

Shouts rose up around her as she pushed the other nameless, faceless patrons out of the way and fought toward the exit. It was stupid to have followed Pippa; it was even more stupid to have gotten so close. Nissa should have followed Pippa's example and fled the scene of their first encounter, rather than offering herself up as easy prey. The dark wood of the door rose in front of her, growing closer inch by painstakingly slow inch. *If I can just*—a rough hand closed around Nissa's wrist, yanking her backward with a jerk that wrenched her shoulder and left her biting down on a cry of pain. She twisted around to see that it was the bald man who had caught her, who was staring down at her face with an appraising expression. His brows furrowed further into each other as he ripped the hood of her cloak back with his free hand.

"Well, well, well. She certainly *does* match the description." She couldn't read the tone of his voice as he tossed the words over his shoulder to his companion.

"I have no quarrel with you; let me go," Nissa ordered. She gritted her teeth as her attempts to wrench her arm away sent another jolt of pain through her shoulder.

"And miss out on such a lucrative payout?" There was no malice in the response, only calculated appraisal as he looked Nissa over once again.

"There are a lot of people looking for you, girl. People who would pay very well if we handed you in." His companion chimed in with a half-smile as he lurched forward. The hand that wasn't still wrapped around a glass of ale ran itself through his sloppy hair. Behind him, the girl—Pippa—rolled her eyes and she tossed her braid back before fixing Nissa with a dagger-like look. The tavern's general air of casual rancor had already returned, and no one paid them any attention as Nissa glanced around futilely, trying to catch someone, anyone's eye for aid. She fixed her eyes upon Pippa instead.

"How do you know my brother?" Nissa asked, and the other woman flinched, her hands twitching to grasp herself around the middle as she took a step back. It was as though Nissa had physically struck her.

"That's none of anyone's concern," she snapped. Nissa glanced around again, but their only company was the abandoned, half-empty glasses that were scattered on top of the nearby tables.

"I have no desire to speak to Ward about anything or anybody," Nissa tried again, but Pippa shook her head violently.

"I'd rather have certainty and coin than rely on the word of a Chantara." Her eyes hardened. "Take her now, and you can keep a larger share," Pippa barked at the men who flanked Nissa.

"And why should we give you any at all?" The drunken one leered at Pippa. Her eyes flared with temper.

"I don't care what you give me or don't; just get *her* far away from me."

"Who *are* you? Whatever Ward did to you, whatever he is, I'm not him, and I have no idea who you even are!" The cry escaped Nissa without her consent, and Pippa turned that scalding look on her.

"Take her and be done with it," she said coldly, without acknowledging the question. As the second man moved to seize Nissa's other arm, she spun wildly, ignoring the sharp pop of pain as she wrenched her shoulder anew. Desperately, Nissa flung out her free arm toward the glasses of half-drunk ale before hurling all of her ire at the two men.

They screamed as amber fluid burned at their eyes, and the bald man dropped Nissa's wrist, rubbing furiously at his eyes as the alcohol stung its way home. She backed up several steps, barely feeling the drain on her power as she watched in horri-fied fascination what her call to her power had wrought. *Water into wine or water into ale; I suppose it's all the same.* Nissa snorted for a moment before remembering where she was and what hung in the balance. She turned to flee through the crowd, pushing between the stinking, sweaty bodies like a fish swim-ming upstream.

She cried out again in alarm as a whip of water cracked against her wrist like the snapping jaw of a dog, and instinc-tively, she twisted her own powers against it to shatter the stream into a small puddle beneath her feet. *She's a wielder.* And she was from the Water Realm. And somehow, she thought that Nissa was her enemy. Cursing Ward, Nissa shot forward again, relief coursing through her when the door loomed before her. That relief hardened into alarm when a tall, dark figure stepped in front of her. Nissa twisted to avoid colliding with the man, barely keeping her footing.

"Well, well, well. What do we have here?" a voice asked softly. Nissa's eyes shot up to his face in shock as they took in the dark hair and familiar armor. *Cyril?* The thought zapped through her before she focused in on the face. *No, not Cyril.* But from the way that he was smirking down at her with crossed arms, she didn't want to find out who he really was. *This is bad; this is so bad.* Nissa didn't know much about Tryamon's city, but if he was in a place like this, that meant that she needed to get far, far away.

"She's our catch." The bald man appeared at Nissa's shoulder, slightly breathless. Moisture had pooled beneath his eyes from where tears had tried to flush out the alcohol. One of the man's arched eyebrows rose in question.

"Oh? Seems as though she's your escapee," the dark-haired man said with a condescending twist of his mouth. Nissa's head snapped back and forth between the two, considering the semi-known evil and the complete unknown. The man's lip curled so that he nearly snarled at the shorter man, and as he took a step forward, Nissa saw her opening. She dove for it. Her heart thundered in time with the shouts and footsteps behind her as she leaped away from the pair, slinging the doors of the tavern open with a bang as she fled up the still-crowded street.

She chanced a glance behind her and saw the dark-haired man weaving through the hordes of people who stepped to the side to make way for him, and she urged her feet to carry her faster. *Always running, never free.* The reminder powered Nissa's feet as she slipped between people and ducked behind market stalls. Her chest tightened as she hurtled sideways into another street, and she prayed that her lungs would hold out against her embarrassingly low stamina as she pushed her legs to lengthen their stride again.

Her lungs held for only a few more minutes before they

gave in to a wheezing rasp, and she slowed to a trot before lurching to stop on a quiet, off-track, alley-like street. Nissa cast an anxious glance behind her, but no one followed as she crept through the alley, picking her way around the piles of rubbish that occupied each side. It was a roundabout way of returning to the inn, but it would be a better option for losing a tail than following the more-predictable path. *Should I even go back to the inn?* The fact that four people now knew that Nissa was in the city made her question the wisdom, but all of her belongings and the supplies she had purchased during her stay were still there. Armed as she was with only her cloak and the clothes that she wore, returning to the inn was a risk that Nissa would have to take; she simply had to hope that the false name she had eventually given to Aegon held up to scrutiny if any of her pursuers came calling.

Her breathing steadied as she traversed the next several streets and navigated across blocks to reach her quiet destination, and she paused for a moment to bask in her relief as she beheld the soft-gray stone that encompassed the inn's exterior walls. Her eyes darted from side to side along the street, but she beheld nothing out of the ordinary aside from a stray cat, and so, with a deep breath, she crossed the street, holding her head high as she entered the establishment. The main room and bar were mercifully empty, and Nissa let her shoulders drop as she crossed the room and pushed open the swinging door to reveal the stairs that led to the rooms above. The wood creaked in protest as Nissa ascended the stairs, each sound like a knife to the brain as she rolled her neck from side to side to release the tension gathered there. The narrow hallway at the top was dim, the torches on the wall burning low, and she made a note to herself to refill their oil after her shift—if she decided that it was safe to stay, of course. Nissa paused in front of the aged, splitting wood of her door and took a deep breath. *I made it.*

The door swung open to reveal a figure reclined against the

headboard with boots kicked up on the bed and crossed at the ankle. Nissa raked her eyes up the figure to take in crossed arms and broad shoulders before registering the startling cheekbones, amber eyes, and grim expression that made up the face of Tryamon Brandell.

"I thought I told you to lay low once you got here," he said.

22

———

Nissa snapped the door shut behind her as she stepped forward, feeling for any trace of power that could be useful. If Trey had found her here, then others could, which meant that she hadn't been careful enough after all. As though sensing her horror, Trey shot her a lopsided grin.

"None of that now, Nissa. I'll start thinking you aren't happy to see me," he said with a smirk.

"How did you find me?" she demanded, narrowing her eyes. She may have owed him for her escape, but he had a long way to go for her to trust him on sight.

"Word travels fast here in Domogién. It travels even faster if you've got friends in the right places," he flashed a smile. "Pippa says hello!" Her blood ran cold. *They know each other?*

"I'm sure she does," Nissa replied coolly. "Were you the one who put the price on my head, or do I have my darling brother to thank for that one?" she asked. His smile faded.

"She told me about that too," he said.

"She's the one who tried to turn me over for it!" Nissa's voice rose angrily, and Tryamon's lips tightened.

"She won't do so again," he said tightly. Her eyebrows met skeptically as she stared at him.

"Meaning?" she asked. "How did she have time to notify you anyhow? I literally just left the tavern." He swung his legs off the bed and rose so that Nissa had to look up slightly to meet his eyes. She scowled up at him; no part of this made sense.

"It's a small city," he shrugged, ignoring her disbelief as he continued, "and I filled her in on the essentials."

"Which were?" Nissa pressed, crossing her arms as her weight shifted to one hip.

"That you and I aren't enemies, which means that you aren't hers either," he said with a tone of finality. He twisted his back from side to side, and the crackle of pressure release that rose in his spine made the hair on the back of her neck stand up. Her scowl deepened.

"That didn't answer the question of how she had time to notify you or how you had time to get here."

"It's my city. I can make any part of it my business," His mouth tightened, and Nissa shook her head mutinously. He hadn't answered her question. *Fine, keep your secrets.*

"So, it's just Ward she hates now? What a quick turn around," Nissa said.

"Ward's habits don't inspire alliances," he answered abruptly, his expression darkening into a scowl of his own.

"How did you know where to find me?" Nissa asked. A small smile played on his lips. It barely reached his eyes before an impassive expression dropped over his face again.

"As I said, it's my city." he said, lowering himself to recline again. The weight of Nissa's vulnerability left her feeling chilled and exposed, as though she had been tied to the peak of a mountain in the middle of a snowstorm. She shook it off, forcing herself to stride across the room and settle herself in the chair that stood near the bed. She twisted to toss her cloak over the back of the chair before she faced him again.

"And the purpose of this visit?" Nissa asked with what little dignity she could muster. *At least I didn't leave the room a complete mess.* She stared hard at the rumpled bedding that she'd haphazardly thrown over the mattress that morning. It wasn't her finest display, but it wasn't a complete disaster. *A man you barely know shows up in your room without notice or explanation, and you're worried about cleanliness.* She could have shaken herself by the shoulders for the foolish thought. Instead, she crossed her legs, clad as they were in leggings that still bore the dust of the street and leaned back. Trey lounged on the bed, resting his weight on his hands as he surveyed her again. His expression smoothed.

"Mostly just to see if you made it. It's not every day I help a damsel in distress," he said, a small smirk playing on his lips again. She shot to her feet.

"I was *not*—" she began hotly.

"In distress? I beg to differ." His smile broadened.

"A damsel," Nissa muttered before sitting again.

"Your brother wasn't happy to wake up to find that you were gone," he said.

"I can imagine," she replied with a shudder. A shadow dropped over Tryamon's face again, and Nissa wondered if she had said too much.

"His charming display of temper was cut short. It made me wonder if you've ever been taught to defend yourself, given his temperament." Beneath the lightness of his tone, Nissa sensed the very real undertone of concern. She looked at the ground, embarrassed at Ward's overt lack of control. She fought the heat that crept up the column of her throat, and Trey cleared his throat before he continued. "My parents summoned me here shortly after your brother left, and here I've been," he said with a twisted almost-smile. That dark look remained in his eyes, though, and she found the contrast disconcerting. *Did they punish him for helping me?* The question sprang to her lips, but she forced it back. His eyes searched her face, as though expecting to find the answer to some unspoken query.

"And you're just now wondering if I've made it? How flattering." She ignored his commentary on her brother, but the teasing fell flat.

"They've kept me busy here. They have plans," he answered gruffly, dropping his gaze.

"Anything worth sharing?" She didn't know why she asked or cared, but the words were out before she could stop them. *Anything to avoid talking about Ward.*

"Not with you," he answered too quickly, his voice suddenly harsh. Nissa blinked at the sudden change in his tone, her jaw tightening with displeasure. *Serves you right for being forward,* her inner voice chided, and her mood darkened. A muscle twitched in his cheek as he stared hard at the uneven planks of the floor.

"You sought *me* out," she reminded him, annoyance prickling at her.

"You're right. I have other things to do." He pushed off the bed, which creaked in protest at the sudden shift of weight. He was almost to the door when Nissa realized that she should say something. Despite his mood swing, he had made a point to make sure that she was alright in this place, and that had to count for something. She took a deep breath, swallowing the lump of pride that threatened to choke her.

"Trey," she said quietly. He looked back at her, and the storm brewing in his eyes had Nissa resisting the urge to balk. She swallowed again.

"Hmm?" he asked.

"Thank you for checking in on me. If nobody else knows I'm here—where I'm staying at least—I think I'm alright," she said hesitantly. A bit of the tension eased from his shoulders as he nodded. His eyes hardened in the next moment.

"Keep your head down, and don't do anything stupid," he said, and then he was gone.

TREY HUFFED in annoyance as he strode toward the Great Hall of the castle that had been his family home for the past five generations. Three days had passed since his confrontation with Nissa, and the interaction still irked him. He had stuck his neck out to get her out of the Singed Keep under Ward's nose, and all he had asked was that she lay low when she got to the city. Somehow, she had already managed to be spotted by bounty hunters and attract attention. He let out a low growl of frustration. The whole point had been to avoid detection, not to serve her up on a platter for his parents. He wanted to keep her away from them as much as he had Ward; as volatile as Ward was, his parents could be just as ruthless. It had been a fight to remain calm when Pippa had stumbled into his office above the tavern, white as a sheet as she told him what had happened. He normally liked holding the space when he was in the city; nobody bothered him there... until they did.

"Nissa Chantara is *here*," she'd spat at him with the ferocity of one of the wild cats that roamed the Midlands. He had glanced at her over the financial records for the Singed Keep that had engrossed him for the past hour, trying to mask his shock that she had already been found out before he replied.

"I know," he answered mildly, fighting to keep his face neutral. *Is that woman incapable of self-preservation?*

"You *know?*" Pippa snarled, her hand jumping to rest on the swell of her abdomen. "You know that Ward Chantara's *sister* is in Domogién, and you didn't think to tell me?" Betrayal spasmed across her face as her breath hitched, and Trey took a deep breath.

"She's not here for you. She's running from her brother just as much as you are," he answered, shuffling the papers as he fought to keep his tone even.

"*Nobody* is running from Ward as much as I am," she'd hissed. Trey closed his eyes for a moment, taking another measured breath before he fixed them on Pippa's still-pale face.

"She's not your enemy, Pippa. She's fighting her own battles with her family, and I'm the one who helped her run. How did you find her?" he asked carefully. Pippa's pale, green eyes narrowed into slits.

"I ran into her in the market. I *apologized* to her before I saw who she was," the disgust dripped from her tongue, "and then I slipped away when I realized. She followed me here." Trey set down the papers abruptly as his knuckles clenched and crumpled them.

"Here? Why would you come *here*?" he'd asked.

"Because Randall and Gendrick were here," she answered unflinchingly.

"You set bounty hunters on her?" he demanded, shoving his chair back as he stood. Pippa winced at the scrape of the chair legs across the wooden floor and recoiled, and he fought to take another steadying breath as his temper flared.

"Don't worry, she got away," Pippa muttered darkly. Trey forced himself to drop his shoulders, but the movement did nothing to release the tension in them.

"Why would you not come to me?" he asked, barely leashing his temper.

"I found them first," she retorted. He shook his head, his mouth twisting with displeasure as he remembered his disappointment with her. He had ordered her from his office then, pushing past her and taking a chance on the inn he thought would have caught her eye upon her arrival in town. To his relief, he had found her in one piece. He scowled, *despite her best efforts.*

Now, he rubbed his temples wearily as he prepared to greet his parents. It was hard enough being home and having to deal with his mother and her ideas about his future; now he had to worry about Nissa stirring up problems for him too. He shook off his agitation as he shoved open the heavy, iron and wood doors that led to the Hall and scowled at the sight of his parents sitting in their thrones on a dais near the head of the room. He had always found the idea of thrones obnoxious, even for a governing family, and he had made no secret of his disdain over the years. His father, red-haired and fair, leaned over to whisper to his mother, who swept a lock of her shining, dark hair out of her bronzed face as she narrowed her dark eyes at him. He held her gaze, the muscle in his jaw ticking.

"You're late," her voice rang out. His father's warm, brown eyes found Trey's face and landed there, softer and more approving where his mother's were hardened to stone.

"I was busy," he said rudely, ignoring the hiss of displeasure as his mother's expression soured.

"The Makani family has finally responded to our proposal," she said coldly. Tryamon felt his heart still in his chest as he waved a hand dismissively.

"And?" he fought to keep his voice disinterested.

"They accept." He gritted his teeth.

"Funny, I don't remember doing that myself," he drawled, and his mother's face pressed into harsh lines.

"I don't remember you getting a say. When something is for the betterment of the House, you do it," she snarled. Trey fought the urge to recoil from her venom as his father laid a calming hand on her shoulder.

"Aithne," he said quietly. Her eyes softened as she turned to her husband.

"It's time he faced reality, Edris. Given his...," she waved a hand vaguely, an echo of his earlier gesture. "This is the best option." Trey felt his face harden. *Deficient in her eyes as always.* His lip curled as he surveyed his parents.

"As long as you get what you want, right? Everyone else can just go to Hell?" he demanded. Any warmth that flickered in her face when she turned to his father died as she faced her son again.

"Tryamon, show some respect for your mother," his father warned, an edge to his voice now.

"Where's hers for me? I'm not a child anymore," he snapped.

"No, you're a Brandell," she said snidely, "and that means you have to do what it takes to support our cause."

"At whatever cost?" he snapped. His mother settled back into her chair as her eyes flashed again.

"I'm glad we finally understand each other," she said, folding her hands in her lap. The words echoed through the empty room with a clang, and suddenly, Trey felt the walls closing in on him, suffocating him where he stood. He turned on his heel and stalked from the room, feeling the eyes of his parents boring into his back as he made his exit. Nobody stopped him.

It was all he could do to keep himself from storming from the castle and back out into the city. Too swift of an exit would leave people talking, and fueling gossip was the last thing he needed. He rubbed at his eyes again, letting out a low sound of frustration before wrenching himself into a turn and stalking down the hall to his left.

23

―――――

Nissa kept her head down for the next few days by sticking close to the inn; the only exception she allowed herself was when she ventured out to the library. She'd immersed herself in a history of the last armed conflict between the Water Realm and the Fire Realm. It had been over half a century since it had ended in a stalemate, and she'd thought herself familiar with the conflict before she'd stumbled across this account. Traditionally, the victors wrote the histories—or rewrote, depending on what they chose to do with the finer details. In this account, the details of the conflict had been recorded so differently that it might have been two different events altogether.

The musty smell on the book and the brittle nature of the pages told Nissa that it had been a long time since anyone had explored this particular volume. To back up her assumption was the odd look on the face of the staff member who had received her request. She had chosen to ignore the unspoken question on his face as she'd taken the heavy tome from his hands and settled herself in one of the nearby armchairs to begin reading.

The minutes blurred into hours before Nissa felt a prickling on the back of her neck that told her she was being watched. She whirled around to tell whoever was behind her to mind their own business, but she stopped short as she met a pair of clear, amber eyes. Trey had claimed an armchair of his own and was watching her with folded arms as he settled back into the wings, his deep charcoal tunic growing taut across the shoulders as it shifted with the movement. The figures that scuttled around him to complete their own tasks gave both of them a wide berth. Even without the intricate, traditional dress of a ruling family, he was a recognizable figure. Nissa narrowed her eyes at him as she looked down at her own book again. With a sigh, she closed it gently and rested the volume on her lap. When she glanced up at him again, Trey half-waved with one hand, and Nissa lifted her chin in acknowledgement. Apparently, he took that as an invitation, because he rose from his seat and ended his silent vigil a moment later.

"How long have you been following me?" Nissa asked pointedly as he approached and stood near her shoulder.

"I only just arrived. You have good instincts," he complimented awkwardly.

"Thank you, Lord Tryamon. You do me a kindness with your words," she answered flatly. He winced at her formality and after a moment, he dropped into the seat beside her, looking warily around them before he spoke.

"Come on, Nissa, aren't we—" Nissa set her book on the table in front of her with a thud.

"What do you want?" she asked, cutting cleanly across whatever he had been about to say.

"You never answered my question the other day, so I was making sure you—"

"You didn't ask me a question," she interrupted again. Nissa watched the annoyance heat in his eyes before his chest rose with a deep breath of his own. Satisfaction at his irritation flickered in her chest before she shoved it away.

"No, I came to make sure you were safe. What I *hinted* at was whether or not you'd been taught to defend yourself. Your brother was—is—explosive. And now you're traveling alone." He lifted a dark eyebrow.

"I know some things. I've spent a month in this city alone and been fine." Nissa shrugged. She hadn't had more than a handful of uncomfortable encounters—with the exception of meeting Pippa, who hadn't resurfaced—but he didn't need the specifics.

"I know, I just—" he looked at the ground, jaw tight. "You're in Domogién. I'm in Domogién. Unfortunately, Cyril is now in Domogién, and he's not the worst thing out there. It feels like my responsibility to make sure you're safe here." She blinked once and cut her eyes at him.

"I'm not your obligation, *Tryamon*. We barely know each other," she answered stiffly.

"That's not what I'm saying," he huffed in exasperation, and she felt herself soften.

"Look, I appreciate the thought and that you helped me get away from the Singed Keep, but I'm just laying low until the smoke clears. Then I'll be out of your city. Hell, I'll probably be out of your realm. Either way, I'll be gone for good." Nissa shrugged again, unable to meet his eyes. His mouth tightened and twisted slightly to one side.

"I'd feel better knowing that you're prepared for whatever's out there," he said.

"And would you be the one preparing me?" she asked sweetly. He snorted at the tone.

"If it kept me away from being lectured by my parents and out of their house, I'd spend my days shoveling manure," he said. Nissa's shoulders shook slightly as she repressed a chuckle.

"Always the best compliments from you. I'm sure the women in this city fall to pieces over your silver tongue," she teased. He lifted his eyebrows at her words, and as she caught the unintended innuendo, Nissa's ears warmed, and she pressed her lips together as she fought back a flush.

"You know what I mean," he said, cutting across her embarrassment before it could fully take hold. Nissa rose, letting out a long-suffering sigh as she lifted her book and leaned toward him, taking care to keep her voice low when she spoke again.

"If you're really concerned and want to help me, I have an idea," she suggested, looking up at him beneath her lashes. He leaned toward Nissa, curiosity lightening his eyes.

"What's that?" he asked cautiously.

"Stop approaching me in public when I'm supposed to be laying low," she answered, letting an edge sharpen her voice again. Without waiting for a response, Nissa spun around and stalked away, dropping the heavy book on the return desk. She didn't look back as she left the library, but the bark of laughter that followed her could only have come from one person.

THE KNOCK at her door early the next morning had Nissa grumbling as she roused herself and rubbed the sleep-filled crusts from her eyes. She'd collapsed into bed after a sloppy wipe-down of the bar, and she felt sure that she would be scolded for it. Nissa snagged her fingers on her cloak, still draped over the chair where she had discarded it the night before. She blinked at the pale dawn that fought through the mist-fogged glass of her small window as she pulled the cloak around herself to shield her nightclothes. The split in the cloak didn't do much to hide her bare legs, but it at least covered the thin fabric that overlayed her chest. Nissa seized the handle of the door and pulled, apologies for her sloppy cleaning job leaping to her lips, when she stopped short. Tryamon stood before her, arms crossed in front of him as he took in her haphazard attire with a wolfish grin. He was clad in black leathers and a traveling cloak that she recognized from her time at the Keep.

"What are you doing here?" Nissa pulled the edges of her own cloak more tightly around herself.

"I told you; I'd feel better knowing you're prepared for what's out there," he said. Nissa rolled her eyes.

"So, you're what, training me now?" she asked. In a fluid movement, he pulled a folded bundle of cloth from an interior pocket of his cloak, tossing it in Nissa's direction. She narrowly caught it, the edges of her cloak fluttering as she lunged for it.

"Get dressed. Let's see just how prepared you are."

24

———

The clothes Trey had brought her fit surprisingly well. The long-sleeved black top was fitted enough not to be cumbersome without being too hot. The same could be said of the lightweight, olive-green pants. She was thankful for the easy weight of the clothing when Trey led the way down the city streets at a run. Her hair, braided back tightly, thumped along her back as she set her pace. In the early morning, the streets were still, and they saw no one as he led her in a merry chase throughout the more-deserted city streets, many of which she hadn't ventured down before. She ignored the pull of the muscles in her legs as she forced her stride to lengthen and match Tryamon's; he hadn't given her enough time to stretch, and the whole bed-to-run immediacy was not helping her warmup. Still, Nissa gritted her teeth against her complaints; she was determined not to show weakness. She didn't need his help; she had made it a month in *his* city and only had one major run-in. That had to speak for something if things were as dangerous as he seemed to think.

Nissa nearly smacked into his back when Trey lurched to a stop in front of a short, dark building with no windows. Clumps of rough grass grew haphazardly through cracks in the stone leading up to the worn door, and a tendril of vine climbed one wall. She pressed her lips together skeptically as she stepped backward, surveying their destination with her hands on her hips and fought to settle her breathing. *If he hears you wheezing, you'll never live it down,* something inside her warned.

"Is this the part where you tie me up and send ransom notes to my family?" she asked, ignoring the warning as she fought to keep her voice light. He turned back toward her with a twinkle in his eye.

"Are you into that sort of thing?" He lifted his dark eyebrows, and Nissa scowled.

"You're in a mood this morning," she grumbled. He laughed lightly, and the sound bounced around the empty street.

"I had to pick a place where we wouldn't draw attention. No one ever comes here," he explained, striding up to the door and seizing the handle with a firm grip. Nissa wiped a bead of sweat from her brow as he pulled it open; the pressure of the muggy air already threatened to smother her like a blanket. Trey disappeared through the dark opening, and she stood outside alone, shifting uncertainly from foot to foot as she sized up the building again. Abandoned buildings and moody men with unknown motives were usually a recipe for disaster. Still, he'd had his chance to harm her at the Singed Keep, and he'd let her go. And it was, as he'd so eloquently pointed out, *his city*. The truth of the matter was that she could be at his mercy in an instant. Nissa shrugged off the thought. She lifted one foot to take a step just as his head popped outside once more.

"Coming, Chantara?" he asked with a smirk. Nissa ignored him as she swept past him through the door and came face-to-face with a thick, black curtain. She lurched back, stumbling as she really did smack into Tryamon this time. His hands grasped her elbows as he steadied her, and she whirled around to face him indignantly.

"You could have warned me it was there," she snapped. He snickered, and Nissa fought back a glare.

"Where's the fun in that?" he asked. He led the way around the curtain to a room that, despite the appearance of gloom from the outside, was spacious and well-lit. She stopped short when they rounded the curtain, taking in the mat that took up the center of the room, the weighted plates in the far corner, and the man-shaped target that stood in another with an array of weapons stacked on a rack behind it.

"Where are we?" she asked warily.

"The one place in Domogién where no one will bother me." He crossed to the mat and turned to face her, his arms crossed sternly again as he looked her skeptically up and down. "Now, are you going to prove to me that you can defend yourself, or are you going to stand around gawking all day?" Nissa narrowed her eyes at him before she joined him, positioning herself in the far corner of the mat. The fingers of one of the hands at her side curled and uncurled as she beckoned any ounce of her power that would listen. Tryamon's smirk widened, and after a futile moment of trying and failing to summon her abilities, Nissa rounded on him.

"What?" she hissed.

"You can't wield in here," he said.

"I got that, thanks," she grumbled. He took a step toward her, a challenge in his eyes, and she lifted her face to meet it.

In the next breath, he shot forward with an arm extended to grab her. Nissa ducked and twisted, dancing three steps to the side, and his hand closed on open air as she stepped toward the other end of the mat. He glanced at her with a flicker of surprise and a soft smile that she couldn't help returning. In a flash, Tryamon leaped toward Nissa again, this time moving to grab her around the middle, and she spun away with her arms locked against her body, shifting just as his fingertips grazed the fabric of her shirt. He turned back toward her with his teeth bared in a fierce smile, and Nissa jerked her chin up as she bounced on the balls of her feet. He stepped toward her again, and she crossed one foot over the other as she matched his footsteps, barely noticing the fabric of her pant legs rustling against each other where they brushed. They prowled around each other for several heartbeats, circling like wolves.

"You're quick," he admitted. She jerked a nod without breaking her focus on his movements.

"Usually," she agreed.

"What happens when you're not?" he asked. Her smile broadened before she narrowed her eyes mischievously.

"I rarely find out," Nissa crowed. She had learned from a young age to be swift on her feet in any confrontation. Speed was her best weapon in a fight with any larger opponent, and as men, they often were larger than she was. Ward had always been. The thought of her brother sent a twist through her stomach that she forced herself to ignore. Her strategy had evolved over the years: tire them out until they're off-balance and then run for the hills. The results of her few training sessions with Faris had only supported that strategy: for the most part, it had worked. When it didn't, Nissa had to think smarter, like she had in the tavern with the ale. She tried not to think about what would happen if her resourcefulness ever failed her.

Her eyes dropped to study the movement of Trey's hips as his weight shifted suddenly, and she shifted a half-second behind to make up for the unexpected movement. She looked up just as Tryamon shot forward with an open palm, and she twisted slightly off balance as he shoved against her shoulder. He clicked his tongue as she bounced back several steps to put space between them again.

"You dropped your eyes for too long," he chided, and she scoffed.

"The hips give away the movements," she argued. He shrugged.

"Sometimes the eyes show just as much," he replied before shooting forward again. This time, Nissa wasn't quick enough as he grabbed her and spun her roughly around, one arm wrapped around her torso even as his other forearm pressed against her throat. He bent his head so that she felt hot breath tickle her ear. "You got distracted."

"Don't flatter yourself," she snarled.

She shoved roughly back against the hard plane of his leather-clad body, feeling the shift of his weight as he adjusted his feet. Her chin tucked inward as she fought to bring it to her chest, and she let out a growl of frustration as his forearm remained locked in place. His grip tightened, and Nissa shoved backward again, gaging his movement as he accommodated the change.

"Hurry, Nissa. What are you going to do?" he said in a low voice. She closed her eyes to brace herself as she took a deep, slow breath. Nissa slammed backward into him again, narrowly avoiding bashing his face with the back of her head. He yelped in surprise as she hooked her foot around one of his ankles and tugged when he shifted his weight. In the next moment, they had collapsed on the floor, and Nissa was scrambling out from under his weight. She clawed toward her freedom on all fours, huffing when he grabbed her again and wrenched her back. This time, Nissa didn't wait.

She threw her weight into one elbow and flung into a roll, grunting with the effort as she made contact with one cheek and his head snapped to the side. She thrashed again, fighting for escape, but she only succeeded in spinning to face him before his grip clamped down on her again. He looked down into her face with glittering eyes and the grim sort of smile that asked, *now what?* She smiled sweetly at him for a moment, and the expression staggered. As his arms loosened slightly, Nissa took advantage of his momentary lapse and brought her knee up toward his groin. He grunted and twisted his hips so that she made contact with the outside of his thigh, and in the next moment, she was falling, pressed against the ground as he pinned her against the mat. She fought for breath as his larger weight threatened to force the air from her lungs, and she glared up at him as something in his expression turned smug.

"Asshole," she muttered, tensing to try and thrust herself up unseat him, but before she could strike, his weight disappeared, and he had retreated several steps. Nissa pushed herself to sit, straightening her shirt as she rose to her feet.

"Not bad. You have good instincts," he commented as his golden eyes roved up and down her body appraisingly. Her cheeks heated as a retort sizzled against her tongue. "You're out of practice, though." The critique stopped her temper in its tracks.

"You had the weight advantage," she muttered, glowering at him.

"And with a bit more muscle behind your strikes, you might have gotten out of the hold anyway," he answered. She considered this for a moment. She had always been slim, but the past several months of strain were taking a toll on her body. She was verging on thinness now; Trey's criticism was valid.

"Hmm," she answered begrudgingly. They stared at each other for a moment, silent, before he spoke again.

"You're better than I thought," he said grudgingly. Nissa tossed her now-sloppy braid over one shoulder.

"I usually am," she said, and he snorted with a shake of his head. She dropped the smug mask a moment later. "Why are you doing this?" He looked at her for a long moment before his chest rose on a breath.

"I got involved at the Keep, and maybe I shouldn't have, but now you're in my city. There's a lot at stake for both of us, and I just..." he paused. "You should make it out alright." Nissa considered the non-answer silently before taking a deep breath of her own.

"No ulterior motives?" she asked. His eyebrows shot up, and he opened his mouth to speak, but she laughed before he could object. He twisted his mouth in a reluctant smirk.

"My reputation would take a hit if I was linked to someone, helped them, and then they wound up back where they started," he said.

"Your ego, you mean?" Nissa fired back, and he tossed his head back in a surprisingly open laugh. He positioned himself on the mat again, raising and lowering his eyebrows in invitation.

"Round two?" he invited innocently. Nissa rolled her shoulders and tilted her neck to one side, shuddering at the pop that reverberated through her body as the pressure released. Then, she stepped toward the mat with a smile of her own.

THE CHANTARA GIRL was better than he expected, Tryamon had to give her credit where credit was due. Round after round of sparring had sent her splattering to the mat in the end, but she had gotten in some good hits. He winced as he turned at the waist, the edge of his leathers pressing against a bruise that bloomed on his ribs from a kick he had taken to the side. He studied her as she took her stance again, weariness lining the face that wore an expression of determination that he hadn't seen before. *Stubbornness is more like it.* He snorted at the thought. He had come to enjoy seeing Nissa every few days; their training sessions were a welcome escape from the dull, aching pressures of life in his family's home.

She had tied her hair back into a braid before they had begun, and now it stuck out in tufts where it had come loose. A crest of hair stuck above the rest from where it had pulled when she had spun on the mat, and a small smile played on his lips at the sight. She was strong for her size, thankfully, since her size wasn't much. He wasn't sure if it was the traveling she had done or whatever she had endured in Danuil, but he could tell that some of her muscle had atrophied, leaving her hips and elbows bony. Her ferocity would still take an opponent by surprise, but once they overcame that initial shock, it wouldn't be hard for a seasoned fighter to pin her.

He was still assessing her when she launched herself at him again, landing heavily on her knees when he turned to avoid the impact. Tryamon snapped back to face her as she sprang to her feet again and rounded on him. Her eyes were narrowed with laser focus on his left knee, and he took advantage of the insight to dodge right when she threw herself at his legs. As he sidestepped, she kicked out a foot, tripping him and throwing him off-balance. He let out a huff of surprise as he fought to maintain his balance, but quick as a flash, she shoved him to the ground, his arms wheeling wildly as he sank to a knee. He fought a smile as she attacked again, and when she left herself open, he ripped her against him by one arm and wrapped himself around her, effectively locking her in place. This was what he had needed to blow off steam.

She thrashed against him, spitting her annoyance, and he had a sudden awareness of how close they were as she wriggled against him. The thought loosened his grip, and he ignored the cold caress of air as it swept in and replaced the warmth where her body had been. He dropped his smile as she spun to face him again, her frustration evident as her hazel eyes, looking very green in this light, narrowed at him appraisingly.

"I told you, the eyes can give things away too," he said, running a hand nonchalantly through his dark, damp hair. The fact that he had anticipated her movements hadn't kept him from working up a sweat. She huffed out a breath.

"I still knocked you off-balance," she said, her eyes bright above cheeks flushed with exertion. It was the liveliest he'd ever seen her, and he fought the urge to smile again.

"That's true," he admitted with a shrug. "But I still pinned you in the end."

"Again, you're bigger than me. You have the advantage in hand-to-hand," she said, obviously disgruntled.

"Excuses won't win you any fights," he warned, not missing the way her eyes flashed at the words.

"Neither will ignoring someone else's advantage," she snapped. He inclined his head.

"That's true," he agreed. She blinked, seeming surprised at the admission. "What would you do to counteract that?" he asked.

"Carry a knife, for one," she said quickly.

"Why?" he raised an eyebrow.

"It's easily concealed, for starters," she pointed out. He motioned for her to continue. "For another, I'm practiced at using one, and I'm fast enough that it would be easy to slip it in between your ribs." He stilled as a chill ran through him at the words. There was little emotion in her matter-of-factness.

"Let's hope our sparring sessions won't come to that," he managed dryly. She flashed him a wicked grin as her eyes brightened again. He glanced toward the door; a windowless space made it hard to gauge the time of the day, but he knew that he needed to head back to the castle by dinner. His parents had one of their famous announcements to make. When he turned to Nissa again, her expression had dimmed, as though she knew what he was going to say before he had a chance to get the words out.

"You have to go," she offered. It wasn't a question. He nodded stiffly, feeling the armor of his position drop around him. He sighed.

"I do. Thanks for the sparring," he said, the formal tone feeling foreign in his mouth.

"Not like I had a choice," she muttered at the ground. He snorted softly in amusement.

"Use this place any time," he offered, surprising even himself. She looked back up at him, eyes widening slightly with surprise. She watched him for a moment, as though expecting him to say something else, but when he stayed silent, she simply nodded.

"Thank you. I need to get stronger." The admission surprised him even more than his offer, but he chose not to comment on it.

"Until next time, then," he said. The corner of her mouth lifted as she nodded.

"Until next time."

25

———

Nissa became a frequent visitor to Tryamon's hidden gem of a gym; he'd invited her to use it whenever she wanted, and slowly, over the next several weeks, she found herself finally building muscle. She hadn't realized how much of it had atrophied over the weeks of neglect. She often trained alone, although Trey would occasionally join her for a sparring session. She grew stronger, faster, and more confident. The night that Nissa pinned him to the mat for the first time, he suggested that they switch to sparring with weapons, and it was once again her turn to be the disarmed party.

Nissa cursed as she dropped the makeshift sword with a clang, grabbing her wrist and glaring as laughter spread across Tryamon's face. The impact had reverberated up her arm, leaving a kind of tingling numbness in its wake, and she wiggled her fingers experimentally before gently rotating her wrist.

"Give a girl some warning," she said gruffly.

"What's the matter, Nissa? Never held a sword before?" She couldn't bring herself to meet his eyes. She had, of course, *held* a sword—she just hadn't actually wielded one. She didn't think that the semantics were important.

"Don't you have better ways to spend your time than tormenting me?" Nissa asked. His smile dropped slightly, the way it always did when she brought up the outside world, but the amusement didn't completely fade from Trey's eyes as he leaned back on his heels and crossed his arms.

"Are you stalling, Chantara?" he asked.

"Never," she shook her head, reaching for the hilt of her weapon.

"Then on your guard. Let's see how fast you really are." Then, they were whirling again, a blur of leather and steel until another hit sent her sword clattering to the floor.

"Not fast enough, apparently," she huffed, reaching for it again. A boot pressed the sword into the floor, and she looked up to see Trey leaning over her, his face mere inches from her own.

"That's enough for today," he said.

"We barely started!" she complained. He snorted, shaking his head and backing up a step.

"I know you got a full set in before I got here," he said, jerking his chin toward the weights that she hadn't had time to put away. "Plus, we were on the mat before this. Don't push it too hard." Nissa ignored him, hefting the sword into the air and catching it by the hilt.

"Scared, Brandell?" she teased. He rolled his eyes and shook his head with a half-smile.

"You are *relentless,*" he said.

"You're the one who said I was out of practice," she pointed out, taking a stance. He grimaced.

"A woman using my own words against me. Why am I not surprised?" he asked in a long-suffering tone. Nissa smacked his arm with the flat side of her sword, and he yelped, rubbing the spot.

"And what a strong warrior to withstand such a mighty blow," she crooned. He narrowed his eyes at her in a contemplative sort of way, and she took a half-step back, unable to read him. As his mouth opened again, the door clamored open, and Nissa spun around in time to see a cloaked figure step from behind the curtain. A gloved hand, impractical in the heat, reached to pull back the hood of the cloak to reveal the widened eyes of Pippa Woodrose. Dark spirals of hair framed her oval face, as she studied Nissa appraisingly, her gaze flicking from her to Trey.

"I'm sorry; I didn't realize you had company," she said quietly. Nissa took a step further from Tryamon as he shook his head.

"No, I'm sorry. I forgot about our meeting. Let me just—" he gestured vaguely in the direction of one corner, and then stepped away, leaving Nissa and Pippa eyeing each other in mutual distrust.

"Tryamon says that you can be trusted. At least, he says you're not like your brother." Pippa said the words hesitantly, and Nissa tilted her head slightly as she studied her. Pippa's tongue flicked out nervously to moisten her lips as she clasped her hands in front of her. Nissa raised an eyebrow.

"Can you? Should I expect bounty hunters to come bursting in to capture me in the next few minutes? If so, I should stretch first," she said pointedly, and Pippa's cheeks flushed.

"I may have reacted hastily before," she admitted. Nissa scoffed.

"You may have," she agreed.

"If you knew what—" Pippa cut herself off, taking a deep breath before she continued, "look, I reacted on instinct, and—"

"I'm not my brother," Nissa said coldly, crossing her arms. Pippa's flush deepened.

"I know that now," she answered, her voice betraying nothing. Nissa looked hard at her, and she met the gaze evenly, the pale green of her eyes unwavering despite the slight trembling of her lips.

"What did he do to you?" Nissa whispered. Pippa leaned forward to catch the words, brushing one curl out of her face as it fell. The trembling in her lips grew to a tremor, and she pressed them together into a firm line.

"I can't—" she broke off again.

"He's a monster," Nissa said firmly. "That's not a secret to me. Whatever it was, I'm sorry. On behalf of myself and my family." *Not that I have any business apologizing on their behalf when I've fled too.* Pippa's eyes dropped, and Nissa knew she had said the wrong thing.

"It's not yours to bear," Pippa said softly. Nissa studied her, looking for clues between the lines in her face. She revealed none.

"Here it is," Trey's voice jolted Nissa out of her concentration. A jangling coin purse dangled from his fingers as he passed it to Pippa. The woman extended a gloved hand to take it, the movement sending the edges of her cloak fluttering open. Nissa's eyes dropped at the movement to where the other woman's abdomen swelled beneath her dress. Her breath caught in her throat, and Nissa looked up into Pippa's face again, searching once more for answers as Trey stiffened beside her.

"Did he—" In Nissa's horror, she couldn't find the words. Pippa shook her head.

"Not what you're thinking." Her voice had evened again, and her eyes had cleared. Nissa glanced back toward Trey, edging away from him again.

"Is it—" she began again, looking between them.

"No!" Tryamon interjected roughly. Nissa glanced at Pippa

for confirmation, and she shook her head with a light huff of laughter.

"Definitely not," she affirmed.

"Then why?" She gestured vaguely at the purse.

"Pippa came to our city for refuge after she left the Water Realm," Trey's words were careful, questioning, and he looked at the other woman as he began the tale. Pippa held up a hand.

"Things ended poorly with your brother, and I chose to leave the realm. I ended up here. I met one of Lord Tryamon's friends in a tavern one night, and he learned I was good with horses. Tryamon found me some work, and in exchange, I keep him apprised of the dealings of some of the horse traders who work across the realms. I found out about this," she gestured to her midsection, "after. It's proven a lucrative friendship for both of us," she hefted the coin purse with a fast grin. A chill ran through Nissa as she considered what it meant to have dealings with her brother end poorly. In light of the dark images the thought brought to mind, she decided not to press.

"I—" Nissa stammered out, and Pippa's responding smile didn't quite snuff out the sadness that still filled her eyes. She pressed a hand to her swelling stomach.

"I should go. I'm sorry for misjudging you. I hope we meet again, Nissa," she said. She pulled her hood back over her head, and then, in a twist of midnight blue, she disappeared behind the curtain and the closing of the door signaled her exit. Nissa stared after her silently for a moment before turning to Trey, who was watching her with a curious expression.

"What did Ward do to her?" she asked, not meeting his eyes.

"I told you before, that's her story if she wants to tell you," he said. His voice was surprisingly soft, but she knew the matter was closed. Nissa unleashed a sigh, trotting back to the mat to pick up her training sword. Her thoughts were whirling, and she needed to *move* to take her mind off of them.

"Another round?" she asked without looking at Trey's face, "Or are you too scared to go again?" Tryamon's laughter was her only response as he reclaimed his sword and joined her on the mat.

26

"You're late. *Again*." Tryamon tried not to flinch as the sound of his mother's cold disapproval cut through his flesh like a winter wind.

"I was delayed." He offered no further explanation; he'd begun to chaff under their constant demands to his presence, and they deserved none. It never mattered what time he arrived anyway. In his mother's eyes, he was always late, always deficient, always less than deserving. "What was so urgent?" He forced himself to lift his eyes and lock them with Aithne's. He saw no mother's love there, no real emotion, just that same hardened disapproval that had followed him his whole life.

"It seems that there are rumors floating around Galarmos, Tryamon. Rumors about you." He stiffened imperceptibly, trying not to let his alarm break through. Slowly, he let his eyes roam to the seat that his father usually occupied. If this went badly, Edris would be the one to reign in his wife's temper. It was empty; he'd have no help in this.

"There are always rumors. You raised me to pay them no mind. The powerful never need to make excuses for themselves. Isn't that what you've always preached?" he asked. His mother's lip curled, half cold amusement and half disgust. *You've never been powerful enough*, her eyes said. He braced himself for the cutting words.

"When they make our family the subject of ridicule by our enemies, the strategy changes," she said instead. He cocked his head slightly, confused, and his mother lifted one fine hand to wave to the guards he knew were stationed at the edges of the room. He winced at the thunderous noise that the blackened doors made as they slammed into the walls. The clanking of chains punctuated the banging with an ominous sort of harmony as whomever they held was dragged to judgment. He fixed a look of careful indifference on his face as he turned toward the luckless captive, blinking as he found himself face-to-face with two captives. One, he didn't recognize. The other, beneath the grime and strings of filth that had been soft, brown hair only weeks before, was Shae, the servant from the Keep. The look in her wide eyes was pleading, and his heart twisted. His expression, he could not change, although he couldn't stop his nose from wrinkling at the harsh, sickening taint of singed flesh. *She's burned them.* Lines of horror prickled beneath his shirt, imprinting themselves in the flesh of his memory. He turned back toward his mother with a raised eyebrow.

"What's this?" he asked as mildly as he could. She threw back her head in a clanging laugh that made the hair of his neck stand on end.

"As if you don't know. Even you ought to recognize a traitor by now." He blinked, surprised for the first time. Shae had been a newcomer, but in their brief acquaintance, she'd never struck him as a traitor.

"The girl served in the Keep. I don't recognize her companion." Out of the corner of his eye, Trey saw Shae flinch at the reference to herself. He was treading on dangerous ground. Aithne's lips parted as though she was about to speak, but before she could, the hall doors opened again, and another figure swept in. Trey's knees nearly buckled with relief as he saw his father stride forward, a cape of black and gold billowing from his shoulders with each powerful step. When Aithne spoke again, her voice had risen to address them all.

"I'll allow Lord Edris to explain. After all, executing final judgments is his role as Governing Lord. I defer to his wisdom," Aithne said, leaning back in her chair as her fingers laced together. *A performance, all of it.* His mother had never shown such deference in all of Trey's years. They had an end goal, something they were trying to find out.

"I apologize for my tardiness," Edris said, inclining his head to his wife.

"Think nothing of it, my Lord," Aithne said sweetly, and Trey felt bile rise in his throat. He felt Shae's eyes hard upon him, but there was nothing he could do, nothing he could say to save her. He'd seen too many performances in his parents' court to doubt where this one was leading. Edris inclined his head to his wife as he settled into his seat before sweeping his cold gaze across the captives. There was nothing of Trey's warm, affectionate father in his expression now.

"I wish we could have met each other on better terms. Each citizen of our realm is dear to me. Yet, it seems that you do not feel the same about the realm?" Trey held his breath as he waited for the response. When there was none, Edris turned his gaze upon him. "If you will join us, my son." He barely noticed as his feet carried him toward the dais, to his spot at his father's right hand. He barely saw the scene in front of him. The only thing about the room that felt real was that same, sickly stench of burning flesh.

"Please, my Lord," Trey closed his eyes as Shae's wobbly voice interjected, "I never meant to betray anyone. I'm as loyal as they come, and I always have been."

"Then why were we not notified at once when a valuable

visitor from another realm went missing while under your care?" Aithne's voice cracked like a whip, and Shae whimpered.

"My Lady," she began again, "I thought that Lord Tryamon—"

"*Silence!*" Aithne hissed, and Shae broke off again with a squeak. Tryamon fixed his eyes upon the quaking slip of a girl, watching as one sleeve threatened to slip from her shoulder. Why would his parents have expected to hear from her? He knew the answer as soon as the question flashed through his mind. *She was a spy*, he answered himself dully. They almost always were.

"You don't recognize her companion, I presume?" Edris posed the next question to Tryamon, and he shook his head irritably.

"I'm afraid I've not seen him before."

"And you wouldn't," he said. "This man was captured not far from the Keep, where he'd been hidden in wait." Trey blinked.

"In wait for what?"

"Why don't you ask him?" Tryamon turned and posed the question. The man's dark eyes, bright beneath layers of filth and oozing wounds, stared defiantly up at him.

"Your silence won't help you here," Trey said agitatedly. In the next heartbeat, a glob of spit landed by his feet and the man's head snapped backward as one of his guards landed a blow to his jaw. Shae cried out, flinching away, only to be wrenched back into place by her own captor.

"It appears the Water Realm has eyes everywhere. You weren't as subtle as you might have been," Edris chastised his son, and Trey closed his eyes again, steeling himself with a breath.

"I swear I didn't know him until we were both taken. I would never betray you, Lord Tryamon." Shae staggered forward with broken sobs and fell to her knees.

"Foolish girl, your loyalties were never to be to him. We made that quite clear when we last spoke," Aithne said coldly. She rested her elbow on the armrest of her chair, sending sparks dancing and winding between her fingers, and the girl cringed away. "But the heart is fickle, isn't it Tryamon?" Trey forced himself to meet his mother's eyes again. They had narrowed into snake-like slits as her lips twisted into a cruel smile.

"I'm not sure I—" She broke him off with a wave of her hand.

"Don't bother. The man here has given us the full story." She motioned for him to step forward, and at the twist of her wrist, he pitched toward them with a shove from his guard. "Speak."

"I am Linden Farsee of the—"

"We don't care about that," Aithne interrupted sharply. "Get on with it. What did you see?"

"I saw Tryamon Brandell arrive to the Singed Keep with Nissa Chantara in tow."

"And then?"

"I saw Ward Chantara arrive to claim her."

"A mess that we had to orchestrate cleaning up," Edris interjected with uncharacteristic coldness. Trey couldn't bring himself to face his father. "Go on."

"And then I—" The man broke off on a cough, crying out as the roughness of the motion split open one of the many wounds that littered his face. The ooze spilled a trail through the grime on his flesh, and Trey felt his stomach churn. The man lifted a hand to the wound, a lone ring on his finger the only bright point on his black and filthy skin before lowering it again.

"Continue," Edris said unfeelingly.

"And then I saw Lord Tryamon assist Lady Nissa in her escape." The hall was silent, the only sound the crackling and popping from the torches that rested carelessly in sconces on the walls as the words sank in. Trey's heart pitched. He'd been seen.

"And how did she escape?" Edris's voice was soft, dangerous.

"By boat. East."

"I wonder where she could have been going." Aithne's gleeful statement was not a question, and Tryamon's blood ran cold. "Where would my son, our *heir*, send the daughter of another governing family?" His mind whirled as he thought of a lie, a deflection, any words to say to absolve them all.

"It's not my business where she wound up. She was no threat to us."

"That wasn't your decision to make." It was his father's snapping voice, this time, that stopped him in his tracks. Trey inclined his head respectfully.

"The girl can hardly wield," he tried, but he was again waved to silence. The sparks pulsed dangerously between his mother's fingers. He tried not to look at them, tried not to remember the pain they could inflict as a bones-deep fear prickled the flesh of his back once more.

"All the more reason to retain her. Pity is a weakness, Tryamon," Edris said.

"And now others must bear the consequences. How fortunate that we now know the truth of the matter," Aithne added silkily. The sparks in her fingers ignited to flame in her palm.

"What is it you want from me?" Tryamon asked carefully.

"It's time you did your part for the family, Tryamon, as any dutiful son would do." His father's words struck him, and his chest tightened. He didn't have to ask for clarification. He knew what it meant.

"Your judgment, my love?" Aithne asked quietly, the flames casting shadows on her lethal beauty. Looking suddenly tired, Edris waved a hand.

"There is no room for traitors in the realm. Nor spies. You may execute my judgment. I have other matters to attend to." Edris rose suddenly, sweeping an apathetic gaze across Shae and her companion before striding away. Tryamon moved to follow him, but his mother's free hand locked on him, and he turned to see that she had risen from her seat.

"Oh, no, son. You stay and watch. And as you watch, remember." And then the screaming began, the stench of charred flesh choking the air from his lungs.

27

Their training sessions had shifted from chance encounters to a startling regularity, and Nissa had come to anticipate the opportunity to try her luck at besting an opponent. More to the point, she now looked forward to the challenge of besting Tryamon. Each of their meetings brought new challenges; Trey was never at a loss for ideas when it came to putting her through new exercises, and while she still wasn't at a level of training where she felt she would confidently best an expert fighter, she slowly came to understand what he was giving her was a fighting chance to get away. Whether he fully realized the gift he was giving her or not, her awareness of that fact sparked something in Nissa's chest. No one, other than Faris with his basics of self-defense, had ever cared enough to give her that. When they both flopped to the mat, sweating and swearing sorely after beating each other senseless with staffs, she had a renewed sense of gratitude as she turned and found Trey studying her carefully, his expression inscrutable. Nissa brushed an errant strand of her brown hair from her face, reaching behind her head to tuck it into her haphazard braid.

"Can I ask you something?" The question was soft and cautious, at odds with Tryamon's usual tone. She flashed back to the last time he had spoken to her that way, when he had given her an escape at the Singed Keep, and a sense of foreboding loomed over her in shadow.

"Yes," she answered hesitantly.

"Why was your family so intent on you marrying a Pallinor?" Nissa started, turning to face him with an eyebrow raised.

"That's what you wanted to ask me?" she asked, threads of surprise and relief weaving together within her.

"Is that a problem?" he asked warily. She shook her head, waving a hand.

"No, it's just... I didn't expect it. It's fine." Her mind whirred as she fought to find a space in the walls that threatened to rise around her. For all that they had become comfortable with one another, he was still of another realm, another house. Nissa inhaled deeply, feeling her chest rise and fall with the motion of the breath.

"Then why?" Trey asked again, studying her carefully.

"Do you know why your parents married?" she asked cautiously. It would make more sense to start with what he knew of power mingling.

"Of course. My parents both come from strong wielding lines. Their families felt that coming together would consolidate that power," he said, making a sour face that she couldn't quite understand.

"Right," she continued, taking another breath. "Well, my parents married for the same reason. Water Wielders can manifest two sides of their power, as I'm sure you've heard. My father can wield ice. My mother works with flowing water. Both lines are powerful in their own right." Trey nodded as though he understood.

"So, they married for a similar reason, and they wanted you to do the same?" he pressed. She tilted her head back and forth for a moment, debating on how to continue before she spoke again.

"Sort of. When they united their houses, there was a theory that their offspring would have the chance of having both sets of abilities. In a way, they were right. My brother wields ice, and I inherited my mother's abilities," she sighed wearily.

"Okay?" he said, studying her. She sighed again, her heart fluttering nervously in her chest. She had never shared any of this with an outsider before. That old, ingrained loyalty to her realm was hard to overcome, even if she owed it none.

"They're hoping my younger brother manifests both." She held her breath as she waited for him to respond; her parents had guarded the secret carefully for years. His eyes only narrowed in confusion.

"Both?" he repeated.

"Torian is a cousin on my father's side. He shares his power," she emphasized vaguely. It was hard for her to get the words out; the specifics of her explanation felt as though they were choking her where they caught in her throat.

"So, they, what? They want to see if *your* children will have both?" he asked, his eyes widening in horror as Nissa nodded and the gravity of her situation clicked into place.

"Something like that. I guess they want to see what happens with a little more ice in the line," she said softly.

"They're forcing you into marriage for an experiment?" he asked incredulously. Nissa nodded her confirmation again.

"Essentially," she said with a shrug, turning away. A strand of hair fell into her face again, and Nissa twirled it around her fingers before tucking it to join the other errant strands twisted back. The braid suddenly felt heavy as it pulled on her scalp. The sudden urge to rip out the braid and adjust the updo seized her, and Nissa lifted her hands, her fingers curling into claws as they prepared to dig into the tangled mess.

"I guess ambition transcends the realms. It's the one thing

they must all have in common," he muttered darkly. Nissa's hands dropped as something in her stomach pitched.

"What do you mean?" she asked.

"I need to tell you something," he said finally. She felt her heartbeat fall into a now-familiar cantering pattern as she took a fortifying breath.

"Okay?" Nissa waved a hand for him to continue, willing her face to remain carefully neutral.

"I'm leaving." The words fell like a blow, but she did not allow her expression to change.

"Ah," she replied in a half-strangled voice.

"As much as I like to be away from Domogién," he made a face, "it's not because I want to this time. My parents are sending me out of the realm. To the Air Realm." Nissa arched an eyebrow. Trey rarely mentioned his parents; in fact, he steered all conversations as far away from the subject as possible. For him to bring them up at all meant that what he was telling her was important.

"For?" Nissa asked nonchalantly, relaxing her stance.

"It's a matter of some secrecy," he forced out, sounding a bit strangled himself. She bit the inside of her cheek with a nod, trying not to let her annoyance show. *Of course it is, but so was what I told you.* He fell silent then, waiting for her to say something.

"When will you be going?" Nissa ventured, still reeling from the sudden subject change.

"Three days." Each syllable was a blow. For all that she had thrived with freedom and solitude, Nissa had enjoyed the sense of loose camaraderie that they had developed over the past weeks.

"Ah," she said again, "I just wanted to know when I'd have this place to myself." Nissa flicked a piece of lint off of her training clothes, a set of charcoal leathers that she had purchased for herself at the market on a whim. It wouldn't be as effective as full armor, but it would protect her more than what she had worn before.

"I think you should come." The silence roared between Nissa and Trey as she blinked at him. She had to have misheard him. Nissa raised an eyebrow, rolling her staff experimentally against the mat.

"You don't think that would draw undue attention?" she asked. "The daughter of the Water Realm's Governing Lord traveling with the heir to the Fire Realm?" His lips flattened into a line.

"I have it on good authority that your father has not made your bid for freedom public knowledge beyond our two realms," he said warily.

"Yet," Nissa corrected.

"Yet," he agreed. "But more to the point, I don't want you in the city when I'm not here." She flicked her eyebrows, palming her staff for a moment before her fingers closed around it.

"You sent me here by myself," Nissa pointed out, squeezing the staff.

"That was when Cyril wasn't here and before my parents had their suspicions that you were within reach," he said darkly. She repressed a flicker of unease; *Aithne and Edris know I'm here?*

"He's not going with you, then." It wasn't a question.

"No."

"What a shame you won't get the pleasure of his company when you leave the city," Nissa said sarcastically.

"He knows you're in the city after your little run-in with Pippa. He'll be looking for you," he snapped, eyes flashing suddenly.

"And yet I've gone weeks without seeing him anywhere," Nissa fired back.

"Why do you think that is?" Tryamon's voice rose. Nissa curled her lip. "I keep him on a tight leash when he's under my direct orders, Nissa, and he doesn't openly challenge me when we're here. You'll get no such promises from my parents when they decide to come looking."

"When?" Her eyebrows lifted again.

"He won't hesitate if it gets him what he wants," Trey growled, ignoring her question.

"And you don't think the Makanis will think it's a little strange that you're traveling with a woman from the Water Realm?" She posed the question with a shake of her head. "Once you leave, I'm not your problem anymore. I would think you'd be glad to be rid of me."

"You're not staying here," he ordered flatly. His eyes flashed again as Nissa opened her mouth to argue.

"I can find my own way out," she snapped. His mouth twisted into a sardonic grin.

"Strength in numbers, Chantara. Don't be stupid enough to turn down an escort." With a scoff, Nissa rose, spinning around to toss her staff into a nearby bin before she stalked from the gym. He was right; it would be stupid to turn down an offer of an escort to leave the Fire Realm, and if what he said really was true and her parents hadn't extended their search... Nissa heaved a breath, and as she opened the door to the city street, the tension in her shoulders dropped. She turned on a whim, annoyance sparking through her as she considered the offer again.

"I guess I don't have anything to gain by staying," she replied. Trey's light laugh followed her into the open air as the door swung shut behind her.

28

───────

Sweat poured from Nissa's brow as she forced her stride to lengthen, ignoring the whining protest from her hamstrings as she pushed herself to run faster. She soared over a puddle with an extra push on the balls of her feet before landing with a grace that surprised her. The uneven stones that cobbled together to form the street might as well have been paved smooth for all that she noticed the difference in texture, and terrain that had once snapped at her ankles like a starving dog gave her no fight as she continued her run. It was the last that she would take in Domogién.

She had one night left in her rooms–if she was set to leave the city with Trey– and that meant one more night of wiping down the bar at the inn. She wondered what Aegon would do without her help; they'd grown used to each other over the past few weeks. As she slowed and steadied her pace for her next interval, Nissa fought the sense of grief that threatened to swallow her whole. Tonight would be her last chance to hear the revelry of the Artist's Quarter from afar. She hadn't gone back into the crowd after her first and only venture there, and she wasn't going to tempt fate by doing so again so close to her departure from the city.

Aegon had seemed unsurprised at her announcement that she would be leaving his establishment. He had only nodded along and stroked the ends of his mustache thoughtfully. They still never spoke much beyond the necessary pleasantries that the laws of politeness commanded, but Nissa felt that they had gotten used to each other. She wasn't looking forward to the change; he'd been kind.

She slowed to a walk for her last block of cool-down, her chest rising and falling heavily as she tried to ease her breathing. Running regularly was something Nissa had decided to try to balance out the muscle that she was building in Trey's gym. It still didn't come easily to her, but she was making progress. *How much progress will you make when you're traveling again?* Nissa ignored the flash of doubt that accompanied the thought. She still had little idea of what awaited her on the upcoming journey. She didn't know if they would be traveling alone or in the company of others. Nissa assumed the latter because of his position, but she was in no state to pretend that she knew the answer, and she hadn't seen him since the day that he had effectively ordered her to come with him. The sting of that order still rankled; he may be the heir to the Fire Realm, but he had no lordship over her. Still, his proposal made sense, and Nissa hadn't changed her mind in the days since.

As she approached the fountain, gleaming in the fading light, Nissa paused to take in the carvings one final time. Nothing about it had changed, but in all the weeks she had spent in the city, something in it still fascinated her. She felt her fingers reach up to grasp the hunk of obsidian she still wore as a pendant as she approached, staring into the waters that rippled against the inky stone of the basin. Her mother's attempts to scry her—if there had even been more attempts— hadn't bothered her again. Nissa wondered briefly how she and Lorcan were faring, alone beneath her father's roof, and she felt the sudden urge to pull the cord over her head, remove the obsidian, and attempt to scry them herself. Her mother had taught her once, when her powers had first manifested, and Nissa thought that she could still do it. *Maybe, if I want it badly enough.* Her fingers locked around the obsidian, the facets of the stone scratching against her palm as they pressed into her hand. It wouldn't do to tempt fate in this way either. *Maybe once I'm settled elsewhere.* Reluctantly, Nissa let her hand drop and rested her arm by her side, peering at her reflection in the pool.

She'd filled out in the weeks since her escape from Danuil. Her face did not appear so hollow, and the muscles of her arms and in her core had visibly developed over the past few weeks. The change might not be obvious to anyone who hadn't known her before, but Nissa felt stronger. It had taken one day at a time, but change was finally coming. She glanced down at the fitted, gray shirt and olive pants she had donned for the run, briefly thankful for the stretchy fabric, before squinting before she looked hard at her reflection in the pool. Somehow, the slick fabric was unmarred by the moisture that should have drenched it. Wispy strands of hair stuck out from the crown of Nissa's head where her braid had come loose, and she tucked them down into the twisted pieces, grimacing at the slick sweat that coated her scalp. Maybe wherever she was going would be less humid.

"Are you finished admiring yourself?" A sardonic voice called out from behind her. Her heart hammered against her throat as she spun to see Trey leaning up against the wall of the inn, his arms crossed as he stared hard at her with an inscrutable expression. She silently cursed her lack of attention to her surroundings.

"What do you want? We aren't meant to leave here until tomorrow?" she asked.

"Change of plans," he said, pushing himself off of the wall with a shrug. "We're going now." Nissa blinked at him.

"What?" The edges of his eyes crinkled with what might have been amusement, but his lips remained pressed into a firm line.

"Now, we're going." Nissa scoffed, rolling her eyes as she turned away from the pool.

"You don't have to rearrange the words; I understand the concept. I meant *why?*" she emphasized. He shrugged his powerful shoulders again, his muscles taut beneath the now-familiar leather armor.

"I have my reasons. Namely among them that my mother has *ideas*," he spat the word, "about appearances when we enter the Air Realm. I don't want to be paraded like a show pony." His eyes snapped with annoyance.

"Couldn't you just say no?" The twin points of amber hardened and went cold.

"You don't say no to Aithne Brandell," he answered ominously, and Nissa knew that the matter was closed.

"Do I get a say in this?" She crossed her arms. With a face of stone, he bent his head to stare hard at her.

"No." She stumbled, slightly off-balance as he thrust a pack into her arms, laden with what Nissa assumed were all of her belongings.

"You went through my stuff?" she demanded. He crossed his arms again.

"We don't have time for this," he growled.

"It's an invasion of privacy," Nissa said.

"There are worse things," he retorted. She huffed before tossing the pack onto her back, pulling the strap over her head and cinching it tightly across her body.

"I don't even get to bathe before we leave?" she asked, wiping another trickle of sweat from her forehead.

"Like I said, there are worse things," he said. He bent his

head suddenly, nostrils flaring as he took a whiff. "Not by much, though," he added, making a face. Nissa swatted at him in annoyance, but he stepped out of reach.

"Are you leaving so soon, Nissa? You've only just started getting to know the city." Nissa's blood ran cold as Cyril's silky voice reached out from the shadows in a sickening caress. She forced herself to turn slowly, determined not to give any evidence of the hairs that rose along her neck at his appearance.

"I've been here awhile, Cyril; it's time for a change of scenery. I'm getting bored." She faked a yawn behind one hand, resisting the urge to step back as Trey stiffened beside her.

"What are you doing here?" he demanded. Cyril let out a low laugh, and Nissa clenched her teeth to stop from shuddering as he looked her up and down.

"I live here too, cousin. We returned together, remember?" He smirked.

"You know what I meant," Tryamon spat, drawing himself up to his full height as he fixed his stormy gaze at Cyril. It did nothing to deter his cousin from moving closer. One of Cyril's dark eyebrows lifted as he nodded in mock-respect.

"Just wishing our sweet Lady Nissa safe travels on her adventure. I assume you're doing the same. After all, it wouldn't do to meet with your fiancée and her family under any kind of suspicion. I'd hate for them to get the wrong idea." *Fiancée?* Nissa stiffened.

"It's none of your business," Trey thundered, and Nissa edged away a step. The movement was not lost on Cyril.

"Ah, so he didn't tell you that his parents are using him for ties with the Makani girl to better their position. What was her name?" he furrowed his brow in thought, "Aella, isn't it?" Trey let out a low growl.

"That's not public information," he said coldly.

"But I'm *family*," Cyril drew the word out slowly. "And

power gained for one member of the family helps us all, isn't that right? I'd hate for any kind of doubt as to your intentions to mess that up." Nissa wasn't quite sure what Cyril was getting at, but if what he was saying was true, then Trey wasn't on an ordinary visit to the Air Realm. She felt Trey's eyes flicker toward her before he locked eyes with his cousin again.

"I'm an escort to the border for her, nothing more. Keep your filthy thoughts to yourself," he snarled again. Nissa flinched at the tone, but her expression was fierce as she glared up at him.

"And here I was thinking that you helping me to the border was to be kept between *us*," she hissed. Trey turned to face her, the cool concern on his face like a balm against the fiery sense of betrayal that coursed through her veins. It did nothing to soften Nissa's expression, and only a heartbeat passed before his eyes hardened again.

"Where you go after is your own business," he answered coldly.

"As *I've* said," she retorted, lifting her chin. Cyril let out a snort of amusement, and when Nissa turned to face him again, he was grinning with glee.

"I've learned more than enough. Safe travels, Nissa. Good luck to you," he said, bowing with a flourish. She knew that Trey's eyes were on her as Cyril turned and melded in with the street's shadows in the fading light, but she refused to meet them.

"We were leaving?" she asked acidly. And so, they did.

29

Nissa and Trey met no resistance as they snuck out of the city gates, not that she expected any. Trey would have been careful enough to ensure that they weren't caught. Only the faintest hint of music trailed them as they slipped beyond the great, stone pillars that announced the city's entrance, and it seemed to whisper *farewell* as the breeze carried it to their backs. As the sun set, the clouds moved in, and it turned into an overcast night—lonely without the stars smiling down on them, but better for avoiding detection. Nissa followed Trey in a kind of trance, not questioning where he was leading as he turned northward toward where the brightest of the stars normally hung on the horizon at this hour.

She kept her eyes on his pack, which was about the same size as hers but somehow seemed so much smaller nestled in between his wide shoulders. His deep black armor made him hard to pick out in the gloom but for the small, brass-colored buckles that held his leather armor in place. Tryamon's movements were surprisingly feline, and as he brushed back a strand of his dark hair with one hand, Nissa was impressed by the fluidity with which he moved. He knew his body; it was evident with every movement that took them closer to his future—*to his fiancée*, she corrected. The thought made Nissa uneasy, not because it was a surprise to her—given her own father's goals of marrying her off, she didn't underestimate any Governing Family—but because he hadn't told her himself.

"So, as my escort to the border, how long does that keep us in each other's company?" Nissa whispered ahead of her. Trey stiffened and ran a hand through his hair again.

"Until our paths take us in different directions, I suppose," came the non-answer. Nissa cut her eyes at the back of his head.

"What kind of philosophical horseshit is *that* supposed to be?" she snorted. *I should drag him to the Midlands Archives instead. The scholars would eat him alive.* Trey's laughter trickled back to meet her ears, and she smiled in spite of herself.

"My *intention*," he emphasized when the laughter faded, "was for you to accompany me to Sel'veren."

"Where you'll be meeting with Aella Makani. Your fiancée?" she pointed out. He shrugged, remorseless.

"I've made no agreements," he said, "and it would be easy enough to say that you were a stranded traveler I offered my protection." He waved his hand casually, and Nissa shot him a disbelieving look.

"Yes, oh great one," she bowed mockingly, making a show of looking around at the lack of accompanying reinforcements. "Such defenses you offer! Anyone who comes across us will surely quake in terror." Trey raised his eyebrows, a movement that she barely caught in the fading light.

"Are you done?" he asked. Nissa made a show of bowing again.

"As you will it, my Lord," she said dramatically. He rolled his eyes, the whites catching in what little light glowed between the clouds. When he started walking again, she moved to walk beside him.

"We're getting a head start on our 'reinforcements,' as you call them. A guard force is accompanying us, or they were supposed to be. They're set to leave tomorrow." Nissa allowed herself a wry smile.

"So you just wanted to get a head start?" she asked.

"I like my privacy," he grunted in response.

"And when Cyril goes back and lets them know you've already left?" she asked, cocking her head.

"He won't," came the instant response.

"You sound very sure," Nissa began hesitantly.

"I know my cousin. He won't have anything easy to gain by telling them, so he won't," he doubled down confidently, and she let it go with a shrug.

"If you say so." A few minutes later, another thought occurred to her. "Wouldn't he have something to gain by turning *me* in?" Tryamon was silent for a moment before he shook his head.

"No, not now that he knows we've left. He's too close to it; he'd have to explain his involvement in all the rest." He waved a hand, as though swatting at a gnat. "You heard him, 'power for one member of the family helps us all,' and all that. He won't do anything that could tarnish his name. He'd have to explain why he knew that you were in the city for so long without acting. Not to mention the fact that he let you leave," he explained with a shrug. Nissa wasn't convinced, but she nodded all the same.

"So we're in the clear?" she asked, silently jeering at her own hopefulness.

"For now," he said. "I'm sure he's biding his time, but you'll be long gone by the time he decides to act, I'm sure." Nissa considered that for a moment, chewing on her lip as they continued northward.

She repressed her surprise as Tryamon continued north in relative silence. Traveling this way would involve a water passage at the border. Nissa, of course, didn't mind this, but for the Fire Realm's prodigal son, it could be another story. There was another way, if she remembered correctly, that took a trade route through the eastern mountains, but it was longer. *That's what I'd do if I was stalling*, but Nissa kept her doubts to herself as she wondered silently how he would expect for them to cross the famed lake that separated his territory from that of the Air Realm.

Maybe that's the real reason he brought you along. Nissa scowled at the thought. *What, would he expect me to part the lake and provide his highness with a dry path?* She shook her head impatiently, and the scowl faded into thoughtfulness. Trey hadn't so much as mentioned her wielding since she'd come to Domogién. He wouldn't have relied on it for a journey, not when he didn't even know the scope of her abilities. Her scowl returned; *I don't even know that scope myself.* Whatever power she had summoned at the river, Nissa had never accessed anything like that before, and she hadn't been able to replicate it—not that she'd really had the chance to try while she was laying low in Domogién.

For the first time in a while, she thought back to her home and those who remained. Nissa had seen her mother, of course, and her father, when Marin had scried her, but that experience had been such a brief flash of time, she couldn't be sure what had been real and what had been a figment of her imagination. She fingered the obsidian that hung around her neck. She wondered briefly if it would keep her from scrying in the same way that it had thwarted any attempts for her to be seen by other Seers, and before she could think on it further, she posed the question to Trey, forgetting her earlier annoyance. He stopped walking and stared at her for a moment, head tilted thoughtfully to the side before he answered.

"I don't know," he said, sounding intrigued at the thought. There was an invitation in his voice, and Nissa knew that he was thinking along the same lines that she was: *there's only one way to find out.* She made a noncommittal noise, and to her relief, Trey didn't press the issue. In fact, he didn't really press conversation on any point as they trudged along, their footsteps growing more sluggish with the passing of the hours. They stopped only for water and to relieve themselves when the call of nature refused to be ignored, and they fell into a comfortable sort of silence that made it easy for Nissa to soak in the landscape. They veered slightly east after the sun rose along the horizon, and Nissa sent up silent prayers of gratitude that it had risen beyond the point of searing her eyes. The sun hung low in the midafternoon sky at their backs when Trey announced that they would stop and make camp where they were. Nissa glanced skeptically at the lack of cover that the rocks around them provided, but her aching feet, unrested since before her run, gave her no room for argument.

"Here?" Short of a few clumps of coarse grass and spindly trees, the space was quite exposed.

"It's not the most comfortable, but we need to rest." Nissa pressed her lips together without argument. Her bones-deep weariness had been screaming for a reprieve for hours.

"I won't argue. Does one of us need to keep watch?" she asked, dropping her pack onto the earth with a thud. She rolled the ache from her shoulders—or at least tried to—before she slumped to sit beside it. Her spine crackled as her posture shifted, and she shivered at the sudden release between her shoulder blades. A thunk sounded beside her, and she jumped as a bedroll landed near her feet. Without looking at her, Trey had turned to pull his own from where it was strapped to the bottom of his pack. Nissa stared at it for a moment before her eyes flickered up to his face.

"No, no one will see us here. Set up camp," he said without meeting her eyes. "We'll rest for a few hours and then move again." Nissa scrambled to her knees and fumbled with the buckles and leather straps that held the bedroll together. When she had her bedding laid out on the flattest piece of earth she could find nearby, Nissa crawled inside, glancing back toward where Trey was laying in his own, unmoving except for the faint rise and fall that told her he was breathing; he was already asleep, and she wasn't long to join him.

30

Night had fallen by the time that Nissa's eyes snapped open again. A sudden coolness in the air had made her stir, and dread prickled through her as she frowned at the sky. Clouds darkened the horizon, blotting out the stars that lingered there. The ones overhead still twinkled rebelliously in place. *It feels like rain.* She glanced toward Trey's still form and at the sparse landscape around them. There was no shelter nearby, nothing to shield them from any downpour that might erupt over them. She sighed, studying the moon as it struggled to edge out from behind the clouds. They needed to move if they wanted to avoid being soaked.

She peeled back the layer of covers that blanketed her and stifled a groan as her stiff joints protested the movement. At the rustling noise she made, Trey shot straight up, eyes wild as the moonlight flashed against the whites. They probed the darkness that surrounded them, relaxing when he seemed to realize that they weren't being ambushed.

"It looks like rain," she said in a sleepy rasp. She cleared her throat. "We should probably find better cover," she added more clearly. He nodded abruptly and rose without comment, so

Nissa turned her attention to rolling and resecuring her bedroll. She frowned at the strap that was meant to fasten it at the bottom of her pack, squinting into the darkness as she fought to pull it around the bundle and fix it in place. When she finally stood, Trey was watching her carefully.

"I have room for that in mine," he said, nodding at the bedroll dangling from her pack. Nissa shook her head, feeling a flush rise in her throat. The last thing she needed was for him to think she couldn't pull her own weight.

"You carried it this far; I can get it from here." Her muscles whined as she shouldered the bag, but she fixed a close-lipped smile on Trey, choosing to ignore the skeptical lift of his brows.

"If you're sure. But I have room," he said again. Nissa shrugged, repressing a wince at the twinge of pain in her shoulders, and shook her head. One corner of his mouth twitched, pressing a line into his cheek before it smoothed again.

"Thank you, by the way," Nissa said belatedly. He turned back to her, brows lifted in surprise.

"For what?" he asked. Nissa gestured at her pack.

"This was much more comfortable than the rocks would have been," she said, wrinkling her nose at the rocks beneath her feet. He snorted in response.

"We should get moving," he said, studying the moon as it finally edged above the growing clouds. They stood silently for another moment, watching its progress.

"Into the storm, I suppose," Nissa said dully.

"Would you expect anything else?" That flicker of a smile flashed again.

"Not with my track record," she muttered.

"We're not far from another stopping point. There'll be more shelter there." She narrowed her eyes at him.

"*If* we make it in time," she clarified.

"If we make it in time," he echoed. Her chest heaved in a sigh as she looked tiredly up at the still-growing clouds.

"Lead the way, then," she said, as resigned as always to her fate. Tryamon started down the rocks, and she tailed him, stepping cautiously in the dark. To her relief, she didn't lose her footing as they picked their way down the gentle slope. Her calves nearly gave out in relief as it eventually flattened again. *Just keep moving,* she commanded herself, nearly stumbling as her toes scuffed against the earth.

She smelled the tang of rain in the air before it hit in gentle flecks of water that danced across her cheeks. Lightning crackled on the horizon, and she inhaled the sharp taste of it as the first bout of ominous thunder rolled across them. When the sprinkle rose to a drizzle, Nissa clenched her teeth against the stinging blows, trying not to think about the fact that every possession she still had was getting drenched.

"We're getting closer," Trey's voice rose hoarsely over the din, muffled by another peal of thunder. Nissa squinted as the wind swept across them again, sending the rain sideways. She threw out her hands on instinct as a spiraling thread of her power rose, sending the next torrent careening to the side. She gasped at the sudden draw on her power and at the flashing burn that seared her flesh where the obsidian pendant pressed against it. She lurched to a stop, fishing out the pendant and flinching as she brushed against the welt that stood out against where it had rested. Her fingers bit against the cord as she ripped the stone from her neck.

"What the hell is this?" Strands of Nissa's hair plastered to her face as she dangled it in one hand and Trey turned to face her. The question in his eyes melted into horror as she pulled back the neck of her shirt to reveal the waxy burn.

"You tried to wield?" he demanded. Nissa narrowed her eyes at him, flinging the pendant at his head. It flashed against the night as another bolt of lightning tunneled for the earth, and he lunged to catch it, horror and fascination at war on his face. She curled her lip in a snarl as she threw her hands up again, leaving the rain streaming around her as she manipulated its flow away from her.

"What the hell, Trey?" Nissa stalked up to him, and he flinched at the extra water that now cascaded off of her protective bubble and directly toward him.

"I didn't know it would do that." He raised his hands in innocence as he took a step back. Another torrent of wind sent the rain roaring around them, and Nissa growled in frustration as she widened her arms and took several steps forward to meet him. Her bubble of dry air now encompassed them both. Nissa glared at him, ignoring the water that dripped from her body.

"You didn't know it would repress my abilities?" she snapped accusingly. His lips twitched as though he was searching for the right words to say.

"I didn't know it would burn you," he clarified. She snarled in response and turned away. He yelped as the dry pocket of protection slid away from him and he was drenched anew. She barely heard it. It was a violation to interfere with someone's abilities, especially an ally's, and her wielding, however paltry it might have been considered within her family, had always been the one thing that no one could take away from her.

"You had no right," she muttered darkly, turning back. Remorse replaced the uncertainty on his face as, once again under her protection, he blinked the rain from his eyes and inhaled the drier air.

"I wasn't trying to *repress* you, Nissa! The scrying is drawn to the magic of its object, and the obsidian shields from your kind of power. Wearing it cloaked you and made you invisible," he explained.

"It also *crippled me* while I was wearing it, if this is any indication," she snapped, gesturing forcefully at the blooming welt.

"Not entirely," he argued. Nissa thought back to the tavern, to the ale she had splashed in the faces of those bounty hunters to help secure her escape. *It didn't burn me then.*

"How does it work?" she demanded, crossing her arms over her chest and hating the way the fabric clung to her skin. It would dry quickly, but the knowledge did nothing to stop the goosebumps that erupted across her flesh. The effort of wielding without channeling through her hands tugged on her, and Nissa's muscles fought to sag in fatigue, but she lifted her chin in defiance. *I will not show weakness.* The shield stayed up, and the rain continued pouring around them.

"I don't know exactly. I just knew that it would keep you hidden." Nissa chewed on the inside of her cheek skeptically, but she let the rebuttal that sprang to her lips go unsaid. She was effectively lost without Trey as a guide; she had no idea where they were, and for all that she wanted to turn tail and leave him in the storm, she knew that it would be foolish to go alone into the tempest.

"We should get to whatever shelter you think we can make it to. I can't keep this up forever," she said shortly. His grasp tightened on the necklace, and he flicked his eyes between Nissa and the storm outside. Trey nodded, a quick, jerky motion, and turned, continuing in the direction they had been traveling without comment. Three paces behind him, Nissa raised her arms again, feeling the strain of the power ease as she channeled it again from behind him. *What else is he keeping from me?*

31

———

They sheltered on the edge a lake that looked as dark as rippling ink beneath the lightning-threaded tempest that burned above. A few gnarled trees, hunched by wind-bent trunks, dangled their fronds over the water as though tempting whatever creatures lurked beneath the surface. The branches danced in the wind, but as Nissa and Trey ducked beneath the tendrils, only the faintest trickle of water brushed against her wielded water-shield. She dropped her hands unsteadily, swaying slightly as the power tugged at her, even in release. She fought through the haze to remember when she had last wielded for so long, but her efforts to punch through the clouds of thought were futile. Tryamon eyed her as she swayed again, leaning forward with a hand half-extended when she sat down hard against a root. The thick twist of wood formed a kind of seat beneath her knees as she slumped in place, and as she settled, his hand retreated.

"What?" Nissa snapped bad-temperedly as the pressure of fatigue throbbed against the edges of her eyes.

"You should wear this." He pulled the pendant from his

pocket and dangled it in front of her face. She stared past the polished obsidian to focus on his face, unamused.

"And if I need to wield?" she asked coldly.

"You can always pull it off again," he offered. Nissa shook her head, shivering slightly as damp strands of her hair dragged against her neck.

"You don't even know how it works; I'm not sure I want to tempt that again," she said. His mouth twisted in disagreement.

"If you go into one of those trances right now, I don't know what it'll do to you with you so drained. They're debilitating when you're at full strength," he pointed out. She bit her lip to keep from snapping a retort. He wasn't wrong. With a huff, she held out her hand and wiggled her fingers. With a grim expression, he dropped the necklace into her hand, and Nissa draped it over her hair, wincing as it settled against the spot where it had burned her chest.

The wound on her chest had already scabbed over as it started to mend itself, and despite the itch, she was fascinated by the rapid progression of its healing. *Must be something with the magic it's connected to,* she reasoned. She plucked the dark shirt from her chest and held aloft; the rubbing of the fabric wasn't helping the itch. She needed to change. More to the point, she needed to bathe. Nissa hadn't had the chance to wash her body since before they'd left Domogién, and in light of the prickling scab blooming beneath her clothes, she needed a good scrub down. She looked glumly into the still-present storm, at the edge of that ominously rippling lake, and sighed.

"You should wait until morning," Tryamon said, as though he was reading her thoughts. She ignored him as she rose to her feet.

"Why don't you use that famous Brandell magic to start a fire so we don't freeze," Nissa said without looking at him. She eyed a place where the bank dipped and water lapped more lazily against it. Between the dip and the shadows, she would be hidden from sight if she exposed herself. She pulled a damp blanket from her pack before tossing the pack to the ground. It bounced haphazardly against the stones wrapped around one of the massive roots before she parted the branches and stepped back out into the storm.

Nissa ignored the rain pounding against her now; she was about to get wet anyway. She clenched her teeth to stop their chatter as a finger of water trickled down her spine. Tossing the blanket to the earth beneath another, sad-looking tree, she squinted her eyes shut as she peeled her sodden clothes from her body and tossed them onto the ground near the shore. She took a deep breath and wrinkled her nose with displeasure as she stepped into the frigid waters, rinsing the sweat from her body and soaking herself through.

She was unable to stop the trembling of her jaw as she finished and wrapped the blanket around herself, wrinkling her nose again at the squelching noise of her steps. The rain had lightened slightly, but it was still coming down, and her already bone-deep exhaustion prevented her from shielding herself any further. The blanket was a pitiful barrier from the icy drops, but it was better than nothing. Nissa shouldered her way through the fronds as another shiver rattled against her teeth, and she focused on the glow of the fire that Trey had apparently built in her absence. She waddled toward it, settling down on her root again with the blanket wrapped around her as she huddled against the earth. He'd placed the fire far enough away from the roots and branches that they wouldn't have to worry about the tree igniting, but thankfully, it was still close enough for the sear of the flames to pour into her tired joints.

"Do you want me to...." She turned her face toward where Trey sat, leaned against another trunk with his boots off, ankles crossed as he warmed the soles of his feet. He pointed his finger in the air and twisted his wrist to mime turning around. Nissa's cheeks heated at her renewed awareness that she was still unclothed beneath her blanket. The corners of his mouth twitched as though he, too, was trying not to think about it

"Sure," she said, looking anywhere but at his face. A rustle came from his general direction as he obliged, and in the next heartbeat, Nissa dove for her pack, feeling for the fabric that felt the driest. When she ripped out a pair of lightweight pants and a loose-fitting tunic of rich maroon, she frowned at the color. *These aren't mine.* A gust of wind fluttered against the fronds of the tree, and in the next moment, she had pulled on her underclothes and the pants and tunic—unfamiliar colors the furthest thing from her mind. She took up the blanket again, debating wrapping it around her shoulders, but as the dampness pressed against her hands, Nissa spread it near the fire to dry instead.

"Done," she said quietly. Trey turned and looked at her with the hint of a smile.

"Nice colors," he nodded at the tunic. Nissa looked down and scowled.

"Outfitting me in Fire Realm colors was a nice touch," she muttered, the mystery solved.

"Seemed less obvious than what you had." He shrugged. Admittedly, her traveling clothes from home were looking more than a little threadbare.

"You're probably right," she allowed. Trey lifted his eyebrows, but he otherwise masked his surprise at the admission.

"Your bedding's laid out over there." He jerked his chin past a tumble of stones on the far side of the fire, and Nissa looked to see that both bedrolls were, in fact, ready and waiting. She shot him a look that was equal parts wary and grateful.

"Thanks," she said carefully. Still shivering slightly, Nissa turned to face the bedding and made her way over to her set-up. She climbed inside and pulled the cover over herself. Leaving Trey reclined against the trunk of his tree, she slept.

32

"There's a place close by where we can cross," Tryamon decided aloud, surveying the expanse of the lake with a hand held up to shield his eyes from the sun. They had made quick work of packing up their makeshift camp, and after dousing the embers from last night's fire, there was nothing left holding them to this side of the border.

"And then we'll be in the Air Realm," Nissa muttered, mostly to herself. Somehow, she had never thought she would make it this far across the expanse of Galarmos; it was not a small continent.

"We will. We can meet up with the guard once we cross, but we should get our story straight before then," Trey said, not quite meeting her eyes.

"What, you don't want it going around that I'm a Chantara?" she asked sarcastically.

"As much as I know we both love complications, I'd have to say that's a no," he snorted. The ghost of a smile flickered on Nissa's face before it dropped. Joking aside, if she wanted to avoid being shipped home— *to my parents' home*, Nissa corrected silently— then she needed to come up with something.

"So what, I'm to be some helpless female you came across while traveling?" she asked with a sigh of resignation. Trey shrugged as a smile played on his lips.

"If you want to be," he said with a wink, earning a scowl from Nissa.

"So, we found each other after you crossed the border, and you offered me your protection?" She wrinkled her nose in displeasure at the thought, and Trey's smile broadened.

"Making me out to be the hero? How refreshing," he said. Nissa rolled her eyes, unamused.

"Anything's possible when you're making up a story," she fired back, earning another snort from Tryamon.

"What about a name?" he asked. She stared at the roots thoughtfully as she considered her options. Nissa was an uncommon name, but it wasn't unheard of. Her family had been private during her upbringing, outside of Ward's exploits; Nissa doubted anyone beyond the Water Realm would associate it with her. She bent to pick up a smooth stone that caught her eye, brushing her thumb over it when she lifted it. It had a surprising weight to it as she hefted it.

"Give me whatever surname you'd like," she said finally. "I'll figure out a first name." A wicked sort of grin spread over his face.

"How about 'Brandell?'" he asked innocently. Nissa sent the stone flying for his head, and he ducked to the side with a peal of delighted laughter.

"That'll hardly help your alliance," she pointed out dryly, ignoring the prickling heat that crept up her throat. He tipped his head back and only laughed harder.

They reached the place where Trey decided they could cross the lake without incident, and she gazed over the water, wondering briefly if he expected them to swim to the other side. She shuddered at the thought; Nissa loved her element, but she did not relish the thought of getting soaked to the skin again. She had barely shaken off her chill from the storm.

"There's a boat," Tryamon answered the unspoken question. Nissa jerked her eyes up as he nodded in the direction of the bank that twisted off to their side. She squinted at it until she noticed the wooden dinghy that rested upside down on the lake's edge.

"How long has it been stored like that?" she asked cautiously, glancing up at the rising sun. Sun could wreak havoc on unprotected wood if it was neglected for long enough.

"Not long enough to damage it," Trey said confidently. Nissa side-eyed him and moved closer to examine the vessel for herself. *He's not wrong,* she allowed. The wood was unblemished and well-kept, if a little dusty from where it had been dragged through the mud along the bank and stored on the shore. She rapped her knuckles on a structural point on the hull, and the sound thunked through the sturdy wood.

"Fine," she said, turning to face him and ignoring the smug expression that dashed across his face. To his credit, he didn't gloat as he grasped the edge of the dingy and flipped it over. Nissa winced as the hull clattered against the earth. A set of oars rested in the dirt the boat had covered, centered between two gouges in the earth from where the oarlocks had dug into the ground. She leaned forward and grasped the shafts of the paddles in her hands before setting them in the craft with slightly more delicacy than Trey had managed.

"It's not made of glass, Nissa," he said, rolling his eyes.

"You should take better care of your boats," she chided.

"It's replaceable," he said, and Nissa scowled at him.

"It won't need to be replaced as soon if you take care of it," she said. He ignored her, and she bristled as he shoved the boat into the lake without response.

"Want to do one of your tricks with the current to get us

across the lake?" he asked, gesturing for her to get in. Nissa's scowl deepened. She hadn't realized he'd been watching as she'd drifted from the Singed Keep. *Of course he had.*

"The real reason you brought me along, I'm guessing?" she raised an eyebrow, and Trey lifted his hands.

"You've caught me. The truth always comes out," he said sarcastically. She rolled her eyes again.

"I'm wearing this, remember?" she reminded him, pulling her obsidian pendant from beneath her clothes and letting it hang in her fingers. "I'd rather not get burned again so soon."

"Singed, really," he corrected with a devilish sort of smile. Nissa huffed and clambered into the boat, dropping her pack into the center of the hull as she fixed the oars in place.

"Get in," she ordered.

"I'm not letting you row us across the lake," Trey crossed his arms, fixing her with a stare. Nissa looked skyward in exasperation.

"Get in the boat, Tryamon," she said in a huff. His amber eyes darkened, but he didn't argue. One of her cheeks dimpled, and she turned to face the water to hide it.

"We can trade off when you get tired," Trey muttered, and Nissa masked her laugh behind a cough as she began rowing them out to the water.

"I'll take that as a challenge." She smirked, settling into the familiar burn of her muscles as she heaved them out and across the open water.

"This feels wrong," Trey complained after several minutes of silence. Nissa snorted and shook her head as she rowed, reveling in the power as the boat surged with every stroke. She waited until her shoulders were screaming from the effort to finally yield the oars to Trey, and when they traded places, she lounged against the boat, watching him as he tried to find his rhythm. One of the oars popped out of the oarlock, and Nissa smirked, biting her lip to keep from commenting at his expense. He shoved it back into place and tried again, and she was grudgingly impressed to see that he kept control once their momentum picked up again. Nissa occupied herself with staring out across the lake, at the trail of ripples that they left in their wake as Trey pulled them toward the opposite shore. He had good rowing form, for a fire wielder. His powerful shoulders rippled as the muscles worked to haul them closer and closer to their destination. His eyes fixed over Nissa's head on the shore they had left. She shook her head imperceptibly. What was the heir to the Fire Realm doing pulling himself across the Air Realm border with a rowboat? As she watched the dance of his muscles under his clothes, Nissa didn't notice at first when his eyes, glinting gold against his sweat-studded brow, dropped to her face. A lazy smile played on his lips, and she looked away, her mouth suddenly dry. *Great,* she thought, *let's add to that famous Brandell arrogance.* At least she wouldn't be around for long to suffer through it. With a pang, she realized that once they reached the shore, they could go their separate ways. Trey had seen her to the border out of obligation, but once they crossed it, their agreement was over. She bit into her cheek thoughtfully as her eyes found Trey's again; his expression had darkened, as though he had reached the same realization. They were only a few hundred boat lengths from the shore when Tryamon pulled up the oars and crossed them over his lap. Nissa looked past him, eyes wide with confusion as she tilted her head in question.

"What are you doing?" she asked. He scrutinized her face, and she resisted the urge to squirm.

"You don't have to leave at the border, you know. I meant what I said about seeing you to Sel'veren." *Where his fiancée and his responsibilities to his realm wait.* Nissa blinked at him in disbelief before turning back out toward the water.

"You've more than met whatever obligation you feel," she

said roughly. She had left home to get away from Realm politics. The last thing she needed was to become tied up in Trey's.

"It'll be easier to travel elsewhere once you reach the city. You need to resupply anyway," he reasoned with a shrug. She glanced back at him, but he didn't meet her eyes. Nissa studied his face for a moment, trying to see past the mask to whatever angle he had.

"Won't that complicate things for you? Cyril was right; traveling with me could jeopardize...," she waved one hand as she tried to find the words, "whatever it is you're doing here."

"It won't." He flashed a confident grin that didn't convince her.

"I don't know." She looked past his shoulders and to the open, sandy shore that waited.

"Come on, Nissa. They'll never even know; they aren't supposed to meet me until after we arrive in the city. It makes sense to stick together," he pressed. Nissa grimaced, unconvinced despite the flutter that rose in her stomach at his last words.

"It doesn't for you," she pointed out. He frowned, the expression casting harsh lines on his face. Nissa held his gaze, unyielding, until his shoulders dropped and he sighed.

"Look, living like this, traveling with company but without a guard force... it's been an unexpected freedom. I don't want it to end yet," he admitted, and Nissa could hear his hesitation in every sense of the word. *He doesn't want to do this, this engagement to Aella.* The feeling was all too-familiar, and she felt bile rise in her throat. She bit back her response, that his freedom didn't have to be sacrificed. She had fled; he could too.

Even as she had the thought, she discounted it. Trey was Edris and Aithne's heir, and she had never been her father's. Their pursuit would be relentless; she couldn't dangle that risk in front of him, however much she might want to. Worry creased her forehead as she considered her options. She could leave once they reached the border and travel through unfamiliar lands toward an unknown destination with only the vaguest sense of direction, or she could let Tryamon take the risk and travel with him to the city, where she could bide her time until she was comfortable enough to make a move again. She sighed once more, and triumph flashed across his face, as though he knew her answer before she spoke.

"Alright," she said. If this would be his final act of rebellion before a lifetime of commitment to the Brandell cause, well, she wouldn't deny it of him. She would have wanted someone to do the same for her. Relief, clear and reckless, flickered through his normally-shadowed eyes, and she thought that she must be imagining the hint of fear that lurked beneath it. Without another word to either confirm or deny her suspicions, Trey picked up the oars and rowed them the rest of the way to shore.

33

Nissa stiffened at the sound of thundering hooves, and she turned slowly from the boat to face them as Trey placed the oars in the dinghy and slung on his pack. It was hard not to remember what had happened the last time she had crossed a new realm's border, and she fought to steady her breathing as it hitched at the thought of being confronted again. Trey raised his hand to block out the sun as he peered toward where the riders were approaching. His motionless calm was at odds with the alarm that swelled in Nissa's midsection, and she wondered what she was missing. She squinted at the figures of the horses herself; there were three of them, one of them riderless, although they were still too far away for her to make out their faces or even the colors they wore. Tryamon, it seemed, had no such difficulty identifying them.

"They're right on schedule," he observed with a casual shrug. She stared at him incredulously.

"You know them?" He shrugged again.

"I told you I was supposed to travel with guards. I expected they'd meet us here," he answered, a small smile playing on his lips. She shook her head.

"And to think that we could have had horses all this time." She clicked her tongue reprovingly, and the smile widened. It faltered, however, as the riders drew near. Her eyes darted nervously between her companion and the approaching men.

"What's wrong?" she asked quietly. He shook his head, the movement stiff and jerky.

"Trey," a mid-tone voice greeted, "we were wondering when we would catch up to you." A wiry man dismounted, blond hair brushing across his forehead as he dipped his head in greeting.

"You two get more predictable by the day," Tryamon replied with a smile that Nissa didn't fully believe.

"I could say the same. Is this who I think it is?" the man asked with a friendly smile. The dark-haired rider behind him, still mounted, rolled his eyes.

"Nissa Chantara," Trey said, gesturing to her. Nissa stiffened as he used her full name. These were strangers; she had no clue who they were or if they could be trusted, and now... She took a breath. Trey shot her a concerned glance, seeming to notice her tension, but she forced a tight-lipped smile onto her face as she nodded at the pair.

"And how did you come to be in our beloved lord's company?" the dark-haired man drawled, his dark eyes scanning over the maroon tunic and leggings that she wore. She shifted uncomfortably under his gaze, and Nissa wished for all the world that she had thought to don her leathers.

"The story we're telling is that she was traveling to the Sel'veren when we crossed paths. I offered her protection for her journey until we reach the city," Trey interjected, and Nissa sent up a prayer of gratitude that she wouldn't have to come up with a story on the spot.

"How noble of you," the dark-haired one said with a smirk. "I'm Baloriel. This is Tanyl. By the way that you're staring at us like we're about to pounce on you, I take it Trey didn't tell you about us." She glanced between the men,

noting the way that a faint smile played on the blond man—
Tanyl's— lips.

"I'm afraid he neglected to mention it," she said stiffly. Baloriel let out a low laugh as he turned back to Trey, and Nissa
slumped forward as his eyes released her.

"Tanyl and Baloriel are accompanying us." Trey waved a
hand at the guards behind him. "There, introduction done."
Tanyl's smile widened as Baloriel snorted, dismounting from
his horse and striding forward to extend a hand. She took it and
shook once before letting her arm swing back to her side.

"Nice to meet you, Nissa. Officially, that is." She shot
Tryamon a look from the corner of her eye, noticing the way
that he winced and shook his head.

"Officially?" She raised a brow, racking her brain for when
she might have seen the man before.

"We bumped into each other in the Artist's Quarter," he
clarified. She squinted at him, still not placing him. "We were
on assignment," he said.

"Assignment, hmm?" she asked, eyebrow lifting further as
she turned toward Trey. A suspicion dawned on her as he
pressed his lips together. He met her eye for only a moment
before he turned away with a light wave of his hand.

"I told you, Domogién is my city." Fire shot through her
veins as a retort sprang to her lips. Tanyl shifted again, and
conscious of the audience, she gritted her teeth, nodding
shortly. *We'll discuss it later.*

"I'm surprised we both got clearance. Your mother was
surprisingly easy to convince," Tanyl said, changing the subject.
Nissa didn't miss the way that Trey shot him a grateful look.

"You nearly got stuck with Vulred," Baloriel said, and Trey
grimaced.

"Who's Vulred?" Nissa asked.

"My mother's lapdog. Consider yourself lucky that you
don't know." Trey's eyes flickered with something dark.

"He's barking after other prey," Baloriel interjected with a smirk. Beside him, Tanyl snorted, shaking his head with an expression of reluctant amusement. His mouth twisted to one side as he glanced at Nissa, and she resisted the urge to look down at her travel-worn clothes.

"What did you do?" Trey asked. Baloriel chuckled to himself.

"Gave him a new scent."

"I only brought the one horse," Tanyl observed mildly, breaking the conversation. "I didn't know for sure she'd be with you, and I thought they'd find it suspicious if I took two." He considered her with a curious tilt of his head, and Nissa felt her cheeks heat. She fixed her eyes ahead, determinedly avoiding Trey's eye. In doing so, however, she caught a glimpse of Baloriel's expression, and the twitching corners of his mouth did nothing to ease her embarrassment.

"She can ride with me." He stepped forward a step, moving around his friends without so much as a glance at her as he moved toward the unclaimed horse behind them. Metal clanked as Trey checked and adjusted the straps fixing the saddle. Nissa craned her neck to get a view of the mount and recognized Tryamon's horse, Hagan, by the mottled pattern on his flank as she caught a glimpse. She smiled in spite of herself at the sight of the familiar creature. *At least that's one welcome face.*

"Apologies for not readying your saddle for you, Lord Tryamon." Baloriel's eyes danced as he mocked his lord. Nissa's eyes flashed with a glare that he didn't see. Trey snorted, and she stopped bristling, realizing that this must be normal for them. *What must that be like, that easy kind of friendship?* Nobody spoke again until he returned to her side, and suddenly, she found herself unable to meet his eyes. She focused instead in the vicinity of his mouth.

"Front or back?" he asked her, his lips pressed in a line. She stared at him in confusion for a moment until he gestured toward Hagan.

"Oh. It doesn't matter much to me." Nissa kept her tone soft, adopting the manner she'd maintained for years in her father's house. Trey may trust these men, but she didn't know them. Until she figured them out, she wasn't sure that she wanted them to know her either. Trey turned away without a reply, and Nissa followed him wordlessly as he made his way over to Hagan.

"Hello, boy," he whispered, stroking Hagan's neck as he leaned close. He turned to Nissa. "Up you go," he said, jerking his chin toward the saddle. She complied, placing her foot in the stirrup to swing her leg over Hagan's back. A moment later, Trey settled into the saddle behind her, and Nissa kept her eyes fixed on the ground in front of Hagan as he twisted toward the guards.

"Off we go, then," Baloriel said, amusement glimmering in his voice. Trey flashed a smile at the man, and his gelding leaped at a silent command, streaking ahead of their companions in a canter that collapsed into a gallop. A shout erupted behind them, and Nissa turned her head to catch a glimpse of Baloriel and Tanyl close behind. Eyes streaming at the sudden wind in her face, she ducked her head as she faced the front, conscious of Trey's body quaking with laughter where it pressed behind her. It was going to be a long afternoon.

34

Tanyl had a fire going within minutes of them stopping to set up camp for the night. Nissa watched, transfixed, as he pressed his hand against the small pile of wood that they had foraged from nearby. The branches beneath his hand glowed and sparked before they erupted in cheerful flame. The male rocked back on his heels, brushing a strand of his sandy brown hair off of his forehead with a self-satisfied smile. Tryamon had disappeared for a few moments while he worked, returning shortly with a bundle of leafy plants in his hands.

"How did you *both* manage to end up here?" Tryamon asked Baloriel, so low that Nissa's ears barely caught it. Tanyl swept his hand up the length of the fire again, and it grew in response to his motion. Only the slightest twitch at the corner of his jaw betrayed the effort.

"It was last minute. Tanyl and I were supposed to be sent elsewhere. Lady Aithne—your mother ordered us to find you once she realized that you had already left. Something about us knowing your patterns best." Baloriel shrugged, and Nissa flicked her eyes between him and Tanyl as Trey swore again.

"She must think you're getting predictable." The man's eyes gleamed mischievously, but from the set of Trey's jaw, he was unamused. She felt herself begin to stiffen, and she ordered the tension from her limbs. These were men that Trey trusted; they were his friends.

"To us, at least," Tanyl added with a shrug of his own, leaving the merrily crackling fire at long last.

Trey muttered something that Nissa didn't quite catch, and she found herself leaning forward, as though she could snatch the words from the air. She stilled as Tanyl's eyes found her, and his head cocked to one side as a knowing smile spread across his face. She stiffened again at the open curiosity of his stare.

"They're friends," Trey reinforced, shooting a firm look at Baloriel as the man disguised a chuckle behind a cough. "They've known about you since I returned to the city." Nissa studied him for a second, weighing the matter as Tanyl's lips covered his teeth and his smile softened.

"Domogién may be the capital city, but it's not that big," he explained. "Trey asked us to keep an ear out for trouble... *before* he returned," Tanyl corrected. She narrowed her eyes at Tryamon, who smiled tightly.

"I hadn't gotten around to sharing that part yet, Tanyl."

"I thought there was going to *be* trouble in the Artist's Quarter the other night," Baloriel said, reclining with his head cradled in his hands. Tryamon looked sharply at his friend, who shrugged in place, the shift of his hands ruffling his dark hair. "She made quick work of fading into the crowd. I wasn't needed. Good thing too; it would have been a damned unfortunate way to ruin the music." Nissa's eyes widened at Baloriel, and he smirked.

"You *were* there?" she asked. He shrugged again, raising an open, cupped hand in mock-salute.

"To freedom," he toasted, and Nissa blinked at the memory

of the man from the quarter. He had grabbed her arm, had been pushy in conversation, but overall, it had been nothing. Baloriel had been following her that night? She fell silent at the reminder of that night, remembering the way the music had skipped off of the walls lining the streets. Would she ever hear music like that again? Tryamon glanced sideways at her, and she narrowly kept herself from stumbling on her thoughts and getting lost in them.

"In light of your brother's tenacity, I thought additional eyes might be wise," Trey said quietly. "I sent a messenger after you left the Keep." Nissa nodded slowly as the pieces fell into place.

"Thanks for looking out," she managed, turning to look squarely at the other males. "All of you."

"I'll be right back," Baloriel said to no one in particular, and a moment later, the night swallowed him. They were silent then, aside from the crackling fire. Nissa watched the sparks take flight as a log popped against one of its brothers, training her eyes on the shower of them until they faded into the sky. She lost track of how many heartbeats, minutes, or hours passed before Baloriel returned, dangling two, brown-feathered birds by the feet. He tossed them onto the ground, jerking his chin at the bundle of leaves Trey had rested on a flat stone.

"Well, at least we won't starve now," he said with a smirk. Trey lifted his shoulders and dropped them again.

"A side dish," he offered, crossing his arms. Baloriel scoffed, shaking his head.

"A contribution worthy of the Fire Realm's mighty heir!" Nissa sucked in a breath, glancing between the men nervously. Another second passed, and then Tryamon's lips curled into a smile.

"Your ego would never survive if I gave it a *real* effort," he said. Baloriel's eyes danced again as he glanced at Nissa, and his lips parted as though he had a ready retort. Trey fixed him with an unflinching look, and his mouth closed as he apparently rethought whatever it was he'd been about to say.

Conversation was stunted as the birds cooked over the fire. Tanyl stepped around the perimeter to make adjustments to the flame as the now-featherless game birds rotated slowly on a spit. Despite the ugliness of the cleaning process, Nissa's mouth watered as the aroma of cooking meat painted the air. She and Trey had moved too quickly to hunt, and they had been surviving on foraged goods and bread rolls for days. When the meat was cooked and portioned, she sank her teeth into a leg, stripping a juicy chunk of meat from the bone and savoring the surprisingly mild flavor. It wasn't bad for cooking without spices... or maybe she was just that hungry. She swallowed and studied the leg contemplatively before diving in again to devour it. Baloriel and Tanyl glanced at her periodically as they took their meal in silence. She did her best to ignore their open curiosity as she focused on her meal, and she called it an early night before they could pepper her with questions.

The air grew arid throughout the next morning, growing drier still the further they rode from the lake and the coast. The horses seemed to soar over the dusty earth, the pace feeling like a gallop despite the trot, and Nissa became aware with each hoofbeat that she was drawing closer to the next leg of her new life. The landscape of the Air Realm was like nothing she had ever seen before. The soil was sandy and rockier than she had become accustomed to at home, and hardy shrubs and thick tufts of grass stood like leaved fortresses against the cross breezes that swooped to stir them. They made frequent stops in those next two days, watering the horses whenever they could, although the streams were few and far between on this side of the lake. Nissa made a conscious effort to pull from her own waterskin whenever she could; once or twice, she had thought she had seen a whirl of dust, rather like a tornado, shadowed on the horizon and she stayed on edge, looking to the sky for any evidence of turning weather. She found none.

Despite the fact that she wasn't relying on it for her wielding, Nissa breathed a sigh of relief on the third day as the shining surface of a small lake glimmered in the distance, flanked on one side by a few thin trees. As they drew closer, a floral aroma tickled her nose, and once they arrived, she blinked into the stunningly-bright orange and pink-speckled flowers that stuck out against pale green shrubs as the scent's origin. She had never seen anything like it. Tanyl caught her eye from a few feet away and grinned.

"The plants in the Air Realm are something else," he observed. Nissa felt herself nod.

"I've never seen anything like it." Her home had been lush with green and full of traditional pastels in the spring—when her father allowed anything other than ice to reach Danuil, that is—but the combination here was one of a kind. She turned her head to take in another blossom of deep purple, which bloomed at the head of a prickly type of cactus. It was marvelous. She glanced sideways at where Trey stood, studying her with an impassable expression.

"You're not impressed by the flowers?" she asked with a flash of a smile.

"I've seen them before," he said heavily. Nissa's smile fell as she studied them again. His words were a reminder of all that lay ahead of them. For her, it was freedom and a new life. For him, it was a continued existence as a puppet on a proverbial string.

"I'll water Hagan," she said softly, leaving him to his thoughts as she led their mount down a gently sloped path toward the pool of water.

"He's got a lot on his mind." She jumped as Baloriel materialized at her side. They both stared hard at the horse as he drank his fill.

"Is it always this hard for him?" she asked cautiously. Baloriel turned to her, eyes fixing on hers contemplatively before he shrugged.

"Would it be hard for you?" She bit back her response, that it already had been, but the details of her old life were more than she was ready to share with him.

"Why are they doing this?" Nissa asked instead. Baloriel arched a dark eyebrow as he turned back to where Trey stood, arms crossed over his chest as Tanyl occupied him in conversation. He shifted his weight before sighing wearily.

"Fire needs air to thrive. That's the theory, anyway." Nissa shook her head, disgusted. Her parents, Trey's parents, they were the same.

"You would think," she said with a hint of an edge, "that the Brandells were admitting a weakness." Baloriel shifted again, averting his eyes.

"I can't speak for them," he said.

"If their ancient bloodlines are as powerful as they've claimed across the continent, they shouldn't need to look elsewhere for support. The blood of their heir should be enough to withstand anything else," she pointed out. Baloriel shrugged noncommittally, staring out at the water again as Hagan lifted his head and studied them.

"I can't speak for them," he repeated. "And I don't pretend to understand Aithne and Edris." She blinked at his casual use of their names, but Baloriel didn't seem to notice. He glanced back toward Trey, and Nissa turned to see that he was watching them now, his face shadowed by the angle of the sun. It didn't make sense to her. The House of Brandell had always been a proud bunch, and from what her father had said of Lady Aithne, her House had been much the same. Tales of their abilities had reached even the far reaches of Danuil over the years. Why, then, were they seeking an alliance outside of their realm? Why would Tryamon's fire need air to thrive? If the rumors were true, he was just as powerful as his parents, perhaps more powerful, since he had unified their bloodlines. Nissa shook her head. These were questions for Trey, and they were none of her business. They would reach Sel'veren, and she would be on her way. That was their agreement, and that was what he had wanted.

"Ready to continue?" Trey asked when she and Baloriel returned to the group with Hagan in tow. His eyes flicked between Nissa and the guard, as though probing for any hint of what they had been discussing. Nissa kept her face carefully neutral as she raised her newly filled waterskin and took a sip, meeting his scrutiny with clear, calm eyes.

"Whenever you're ready." She hadn't meant it as a slight, but his eyes narrowed slightly. Before she could explain, he turned, grabbing his waterskin and moving to stow it. Nissa turned to do the same when Tryamon's hand closed over Hagan's reins and he leaned in.

"Were you two talking about anything interesting?" His voice was so low that she had to lean toward him to catch his words.

"Small talk, really," she breathed back. He let out a low, short noise that told Nissa he didn't believe her as he motioned for her to move into the saddle. Moments later, he was seated behind her, settling his own weight on Hagan's back. The horse shifted on his hooves, and Nissa leaned forward, murmuring soothingly as she rubbed a hand against his neck.

"Does it hurt him... having both of us on his back?" she asked curiously.

"No." She felt Trey's chest rumble behind her. "He comes from a southern bloodline that's bred for it." She stroked Hagan's neck again thoughtfully. When he settled, she leaned back again, and Trey nudged Hagan back in the direction they'd been traveling. As they turned, she caught sight of another whirl of sand and stone to the west, and the hair on the back of her neck rose again. This time, she knew she hadn't imagined it.

35

A cloud of dust rose on the horizon. Nissa shielded her eyes from the sun as she surveyed it up ahead. It wasn't shaped like the spirals of dust that she had begun to notice a few times each day. This was a true cloud, the kind that rose up behind them when they had spurred their horses into a gallop. The telltale rumble of hooves that clattered toward their ears as the cloud drew closer verified her suspicions. Someone was approaching from the direction of Sel'veren. Behind her, Trey had stiffened, his knuckles whitening on Hagan's reins, and she dropped her arm, knowing that he had reached the same conclusion.

"Nobody was supposed to escort us until we reached the city." His voice was strangled, and with the guards distracted by frowning toward the approaching riders, Nissa laid a steadying hand on his arm, the muscles of his forearm taut with high alert. Hagan's hooves danced across the rocky soil as he trampled across the scrubby grass. The desert-like sand had yielded to sparse grassland that resembled a moor the closer they drew to their destination.

"Maybe they changed their mind," she offered. She felt a brush against her hair as Trey shook his head.

"Raenon doesn't change his mind," he said tightly. She removed her hand; if it was a Makani force, it would do Trey no favors for them to see that kind of familiarity.

"I don't recognize their colors," Baloriel called back to Tryamon from several horse lengths ahead. Nissa cocked her head in wonder; how could he see through the haze? Ahead of them, Tanyl dismounted his horse cleanly, and Baloriel followed without a backward glance. They would wait, then. She moved to do the same, and Trey pressed a hand against her side to stop her. She sucked in a breath at his touch against her ribs.

"Not yet," he said. She glanced back at him in confusion, but his eyes were fixed firmly on the newcomers. The figures in the distance had materialized with more substance, and she made out four riders now, approaching as though they were galloping on the wind.

"Well, well, well. What brings your little troupe this close to our city." The hair on the back of Nissa's neck stood on end as an oily voice assaulted her ears. She whipped her head around as Trey yanked on Hagan's reins. The horse's eyes rolled in protest as he danced backward. The figure in front of them was stooped, cloaked in a dusty, hooded robe. *Where did he come from?* It was as though he had materialized from the sand itself.

"We have business with the House of Makani. We're expected." Trey's voice was cold, sharp, lethal. It was a voice she hadn't heard since the Singed Keep. Nissa resisted the urge to call out a warning as the figure stepped closer and Trey dismounted, gripping the hilt of his sword.

"Perhaps *some* of you are. I doubt Lord Raenon will care what happens to *her*." Nissa stilled at the inflection.

"Ride for the city." Trey addressed her without looking at her, and Nissa grabbed the reins, nudging Hagan back another few steps as the figure slid forward. There was only one man, and there were three of them. Why would he ask her to—

She blinked as five more figures spun into existence in quick succession, surrounding them. Hagan let out another nervous sound as his eyes rolled again.

"And let your pretty guest miss out on all the fun?" The first man spoke again, and she heard a low laugh.

"Now," Trey ordered roughly, and she lifted a hand to the obsidian that rested beneath her clothes. With just one quick motion, she could dispose of it and be in full possession of her abilities. *You'd be more of a liability if they have any sort of training.* The niggling voice of doubt taunted her from within her own mind. She raised her chin defiantly as she stared hard at each of the figures in turn.

"I'm not going anywhere," she said firmly, and he let out a noise that was somewhere between exasperation and annoyance. Nissa pressed her hand against the space beneath her tunic where two knives were strapped to her thigh and tensed in wait. Should she let them make the first move, or should she wait for them to strike? She didn't want to chance having to react to their attack, but if she moved first and moved wrongly, she'd be without one of her weapons. *Two knives and four of us against seven men. Impressive odds.* Or impossible ones, but she wouldn't even grace the possibility with a thought.

On the edge of her line of sight, something shifted, and she rounded to see one of the other figures moving toward her. Baloriel intercepted the clear shot he'd have at her, unsheathing his own blade as he shifted into a stance.

"Wouldn't do that if I were you," he warned. His tone was mild enough, but the threat in his words was clear. Apparently, the hooded figure agreed, because in the next moment, the circle erupted.

Nissa clutched tightly onto Hagan's reins as sand and stones swirled up into her face, stinging her eyes and her flesh with their jagged edges. Hagan tap-danced across the earth, spooked, and when he lunged forward, she swung off of him, landing in a crouch in spite of the unexpected motion. She lurched forward as her knees fought to absorb the impact, gritting her teeth against the howling wind that was broken only by the clang of steel and shouts of the men fighting. She pushed to stand, staggering as she fought the tug of the wind. She forced her eyes to open into slits, wishing for all the world that she could spin the wind herself. Nissa flinched backward as heat blazed against her face, orange and red against the tan of the earth around her, and she ripped the obsidian off of her heck, crushing the cord in her fist as she shoved it through the straps belting her daggers to her thighs before swinging the stone through its own loop and leaving it to swing at her side. The heat slammed into her and she dove away from it on instinct as panic shot through her bones, propelling her out of the literal line of fire. Some thread of power sang to the surface, and she clung to it like a lifeline as her hands began to tickle, the sensation prickling against the flesh of her face as she held on.

"Hello there." A voice she didn't recognize curdled the contents of her stomach, and she lashed out with the whiplike thread half-blindly against the spinning grit around her. A bark of pain emanated from the voice's general direction, and she knew that her magic must have found its mark. She called it back, fumbling for one of her daggers as she gripped the hilt. It was one of her throwing knives, but she wouldn't dare chance flinging it away, not in this wind.

Won't do you a bit of good against a stronger blade, a thought snaked through her mind, and she shoved it away before the fear it brought could latch on.

"You're fast; use that," Nissa muttered to herself. Something rumbled in the distance, and she dove after the thread of power she'd grasped as it threatened to slip from her grip again. A gloved hand grabbed roughly at the back of her neck, spinning her around to face one of the hooded figures.

"Little bitch," he swore roughly, and she caught a glimpse of moon-white skin, streaked red from where her power had struck, beneath his hood before he slapped her across the face. The blow sent her reeling, as the man had intended with his insult. She scrambled to her feet as he stepped toward her, looming mockingly as the wind spun around him.

"What do you want?" she demanded, clutching her blade. The air around them stilled, and she blinked the grit from her eyes as she focused on the man. "Who are you?"

"I'm here to right the wrong." She couldn't see his face anymore as he stepped menacingly forward, but the sneer was plain in his voice.

"Did my brother send you? Or was my father bold enough to do his own dirty work?" she snarled with a confidence she didn't feel. She twisted the knife, adjusting her grip against her fingers. The man tilted his head back, and she saw his lip curl against yellowed teeth.

"We would not sully ourselves with the House of Chantara." Nissa swallowed heavily, stunned for only a moment before she forced a cool indifference onto her face.

"More's the pity." She flung the knife from her grasp, watching with wide eyes as it spun for its target at an agonizingly slow pace. The man seemed frozen as it spun closer and closer, pulled toward the base of his throat as though it was being drawn by a thread. A gust of air whipped through the space, and the blade veered, slicing through the sleeve of the man's robe and leaving the gaping mouth of the fabric flapping in the wind.

"Throwing knives at an air wielder. They really don't teach you anything in Danuil." She barely had a chance to register the insult before he lunged for her again. She dropped, barely slipping out of the way as his blade *snicked* past her cheek. She sprang upward as he stepped backward, forcing her shoulder into his chest, and he grabbed her as he lurched off balance, bringing her with him when he hit the ground. Warning flared in her chest as Nissa leapt away, only to be yanked backward by a firm, long-fingered jerk on her ankle. She collapsed into the earth, scrabbling madly as she thrashed and fought while he reeled her toward him, his mocking laughter echoing in her ears. She lashed out with a thread of magic, flinging it wildly against him. A whiplike crack told her that her blow had hit its target, and she scrambled out of reach, flicking her tongue against lips that were now painfully dry. She winced; she had drawn the water from herself.

She braced herself as he lunged for her again and again, ducking out of the way. The wild thought raced through her that if she could just dodge enough, tire him out enough, then maybe he would make a mistake. As the pair danced, Nissa began to stumble, her steps growing clumsy with fatigue as her muscles cried out in protest, and she quickly disposed of the hope. She needed to strike, and quickly. Her opportunity appeared a moment later.

He slipped again, only for a moment, but it caught him off balance, and Nissa sprang forward on instinct. Her sweat-stained fingers fumbled with her second blade, and for one, heart-stopping moment, she thought she'd lost her grip. In the next moment, however, she had buried it in the hollow at the base of the man's throat, and it was the pulsing of his blood that made her fingers finally slip away. She staggered backward as he collapsed to his knees and fell forward, an awful, sucking noise splitting the air between them as he clutched at the blade and made to yank it out.

"It won't matter if you do or you don't. Your fate is sealed." Her voice was cold, detached, and sounded startlingly unlike her own. His hood fell back slightly, revealing cheeks that hadn't yet hollowed with age; he couldn't be that much older than her. The pale gray of his eyes gleamed with hatred as he clawed the earth with his other hand, and still that terrible, choking sound did not cease. She stepped forward, ripping her blade from his neck. A moment later, he was still, leaving scarlet bubbling at his lips, and as he died, the pocket around them dissipated, sending the sand and stone swirling around her once more.

36

The howling tempest returned with a vengeance, spitting against her skin and burning where it lashed against her face. Nissa held up an arm, pressing herself into the wind as it tried to toss her this way and that. How could she follow the shouts when the wind kept whipping them around her at random? Still, to remain in place was to provide an easy target, and that was the last thing she needed. She clenched her teeth and pressed through the spiral of air and grit, following the dull flashes of yellow and orange that told her a fire-wielder was near.

A slash of heat seared the air next to her, and with a muffled curse, Nissa flattened herself to the ground to avoid being singed. She waited until the sensation had passed before she pushed herself onto all fours, shielding her face with one hand as she squinted into the storm. Her heart plummeted as she saw a broad-shouldered silhouette take a blow and slump. She jerked herself to her feet and took one staggering step after another, willing her legs to move faster and faster. She broke into a sprint as the figure raised his blade.

With a howl, she barreled into the robed figure, knocking

him off-balance as she slammed her shoulder into his side. She yanked her body to one side as he stumbled, twisting to avoid landing within his reach. She sprang to her feet, not daring to look toward the figure who could have been any one of her companions. A low snarl edged out from under the figure's hood.

"This isn't your fight," a male voice rasped. She felt her lip curl.

"Your companion seemed to think otherwise." She fingered her remaining dagger, feeling within her for that thrum of power that had come to her aid before. Her tongue flicked out to wet her cracking lips, and she winced as the sting intensified. *You can't afford to pull from yourself again.* With a sharp noise, the man plunged forward, his steel arcing toward her and flashing through the sandy gloom. She tensed, preparing to spring out of the way.

A strangled cry emanated from the man's throat as he froze in place, and her eyes widened despite the storm around her as she looked down at the blade that had sprouted from her chest. She stumbled back a step as he fell, collapsing as though he'd been shoved roughly aside.

"Nissa!" Her face jerked up as she examined the sword's owner, and she felt her knees weaken in relief as she recognized Trey.

"I'm here," she answered. "The others?" She looked toward the body that had fallen, and he followed her gaze for a moment.

"Baloriel," he identified. "Have you seen—" His question cut off as the air froze around them, and she blinked as he was thrown into sharp relief. He wheeled around, stepping protectively in front of her as he raised his sword. Nissa peered around him to see that three of their assailants remained standing, and locked between two of them was Tanyl, blood streaming from a cut on his forehead as he leaned away from the sharpened point of the dagger pressed against his throat.

"It's over, Lord Tryamon. Concede, or we'll slit his throat where he stands." Nissa recognized the same, oily voice of the first man who had accosted them.

"What do you want?" she demanded sharply, ignoring a warning hiss from Tryamon. The leader of the trio threw back his hood, revealing golden skin, weathered by the sun and marred by a jagged scar that ripped through one cheek. His pale eyes fixed on her, and she felt pinned in place, unable to break the hold that his gaze had on her.

"To right the wrong." He echoed the man who had assailed her earlier.

"What's wrong?" she asked, voice raising.

"The Prince of Flames would fetch a mighty price," came the non-answer. Nissa glanced toward Baloriel, still prone on the ground as she wracked her brain furiously.

"This is for ransom?" she asked incredulously.

"This is for all of those who belong. Not the abomination who threatens to usurp us," the man hissed, stained teeth flashing with the words.

"What are you—" her words broke off in a cry as the world upended again. Three pillars of sand and stone swirled before them, throwing up slicing chunks of the earth as they spun into existence. Nissa threw herself out of the way as a large rock catapulted toward her head, and when she looked up, Trey had disappeared within the storm. She plunged forward, ignoring the slicing blows of wind and grime that clawed at her as she fought her way through. Then, she stumbled as, as quickly as it had begun, the tempest cleared. She fell to her knees at the sight of the three robed men, collapsed against the earth as their exposed eyes stared sightlessly at the sky. Tanyl stood in their midst, his face colorless behind the scarlet of the blood that still pulsed from his wound. Some distance away, Baloriel was getting gingerly to his feet, fingers prodding at a discolored lump on his head as Tryamon helped him up.

Three figures remained shrouded by the dust that pushed forward from behind them stood, surveying their work. Two stocky forms held back silently, crossing their arms as a tall, lean man stepped forward.

"Lord Tryamon," a deep voice greeted. The tall, lean man turned toward the remnants of their attackers, his deep black skin shining in the sun as the dust cleared. Trey stiffened as he surveyed the man, at the pale blue and yellow crest on his tunic, and he took a half-step back toward Nissa as his eyes roved over the similarly clad trio of guards behind him. She watched as he silently calculated the distance, and she held her chin high as she stared down the newcomer when he turned toward her. Her heart thundered up into her throat; they may outnumber the trio, but they were in no shape for continued violence.

"I wasn't expecting an escort until I reached Sel'veren," Trey said evenly. The man's full lips parted to reveal bright white teeth as he turned back toward Tryamon and inclined his head.

"The House of Makani felt that, given the nature of your arrangement with them, an earlier escort may be fitting. I am Lord Elrand Waera of the East Wing. I was sent to collect you. Would you care to introduce your companions?" The man's voice was pleasant and smooth as it slid over them, and Nissa felt her body relax in spite of itself. Despite the easing tension of her body, her mind swirled. Their attackers had known who she was, and it had put them in danger.

"Guards from my House, Tanyl and Baloriel. Both of Domogién." Trey waved a hand to indicate each of the men who accompanied them. He flicked his eyes toward Nissa, and she saw a flash of nervousness before it vanished. He dropped a mask of formality in its place as he turned to face Waera.

"Elyssa Broffet, Lord Waera," Nissa introduced smoothly,

stepping forward and extending a hand. The man grasped it, bringing it to his full lips as he pressed a greeting kiss there, his eyebrows climbing toward his hairline in surprise. His eyes sharpened with interest as they met hers.

"We were expecting only Lord Tryamon. How did we come to enjoy the pleasure of your company, my lady?" he asked without missing a beat. Could he sense the lie? She held his gaze unflinchingly.

"We came across Miss Broffet shortly before we crossed your border," Trey interceded on her behalf, and Nissa felt a flutter of gratitude. "I offered her my realm's protection until we reached Sel'veren."

"A pleasure to meet you, Miss Broffet. I am happy to continue the offer of Lord Tryamon's protection." Waera's smile was genuine as he dipped his head to her politely. Nissa nodded in response.

"Call me Elyssa, please," she murmured, casting her eyes downward to give herself the opportunity to think. Traveling under the supervision of Air Realm guards hadn't been part of the plan, nor had being associated with Trey once they reached Sel'veren. This was supposed to be her fresh start, an untraceable beginning to her new life. If the Air Guard could link her back to Tryamon, they could link her back to her old life, and the thought of that link hardened in her stomach as she raised her eyes to Waera's kind smile again. She returned it with a wavering smile of her own, and she had to resist the urge to slump with relief when the tall man finally shifted his eyes to their companions. *At least they don't know the truth.* She thanked the heavens that she had followed her instincts to use the false name when they had joined the trip.

"Well, then. Shall we continue? We're less than a day's ride from Sel'veren. If we ride now, we may make it before nightfall," Waera posed the questions to her male companions, and Trey nodded assertively. Nissa's head was spinning; she would reach a new city at nightfall and have no time to accrue resources or lodging before the darkness enveloped the city. It was a less than ideal situation. Some of her concern must have shown on her face, because Waera smiled kindly at her again.

"I'm certain the Makani family will welcome you into the city. Their good favor can earn you a lot in Sel'veren." Nissa barely resisted the urge to flinch at the unspoken threat in his words. However kindly meant, the meaning was clear. Their displeasure would have consequences. Tryamon stiffened again and turned away from Waera to busy himself with adjusting the saddle on his horse, but Nissa noticed the way that his eyes flashed as his expression darkened. He clearly had not missed Waera's meaning either. The men made small talk with each other as they mounted their horses, with Nissa swinging into the saddle in front of Trey. For all of her earlier complaints and continued discomfort, she was growing accustomed to tandem riding, and the motion was natural as she wrapped her hands around the saddle's horn and she settled in front of him. Waera watched them with lifted brows before he swung into his own saddle, and Nissa frowned as she lifted a hand and patted Hagan's mottled hair absently. Waera's eyes were shrewd as they surveyed the pair, and Nissa could almost see the wheels turning in his mind. Still, the Air Lord didn't speak as he nudged his own mount with his calves, spurring the creature into a trot as he tugged the reins to face Sel'veren.

The Air Guard kept a steady pace once they hit the open road, and Nissa felt Trey shift in the saddle behind her as he urged Hagan into a canter. The space between their bodies was warm, and although the air turned drier as they drew closer to Sel'veren, she could feel sweat beading along her spine where their bodies brushed.

"What do you think he's up to?" Trey's low voice tickled her ear as he leaned forward, and she twitched in the saddle.

"Who, Waera?" she breathed in response. They were out of earshot from the others, but Nissa kept her voice low.

"Or his friends," Tryamon offered. She repressed a shiver at his closeness, at the breath in her ear again, resisting the urge to wriggle forward.

"No idea," she muttered back, "but I don't trust him." Those eyes that saw too much unnerved her. Trey gave a noncommittal grunt as he settled back into the saddle, and despite the warmth of the day, the space where he had been pressed against her felt cool in the absence of his body. Nissa tried not to focus on that fact and instead focused her attention on Waera and his trio of guards, none of whom had so much as glanced her way since they had begun their ride.

They stopped only to water the horses and themselves, and Nissa took advantage of the opportunity to stretch her legs, twisting and bending to ease the tension in her muscles. Trey did not stray too far from her side whenever they stopped, and when he did, Nissa noticed quickly that either Tanyl or Baloriel stepped in with a watchful eye. Their arrangement did not escape Waera's notice either, if the knowing glint and unreadable smile on his face were anything to judge by. Nissa felt a prickle of discomfort each time his dark eyes rested on her; it felt as though he could see her every thought, and she did not like feeling so exposed.

It was with a mix of foreboding and relief that Nissa caught sight of the distant walls of the Air Realm's ancient capital city. Sel'veren predated the separation of the realms. The weathered, sandstone blocks that encircled the city stuck out against the intermingled stone and grass of the moor. Nissa knew from her studies as a child that the stone had been harvested from the center of Galarmos centuries before, and that— while the city had changed with time— the walls had remained stoically the same. Her breath caught in her throat as their horses thundered closer, revealing the true size and scope of the ancient city. She felt Trey lean in slightly, and she allowed her back to press against his chest as she took another breath to gather herself. The city was within their sights, and that meant that it was nearly time for them to go their separate ways. *And there's not time or the space for a proper goodbye.* Nissa frowned, wishing that she had expressed her gratitude to him when they had been alone. Trey had taken a chance on her, freeing her from her brother at the Singed Keep, and then another by meeting with her to make sure she could defend herself. Nobody else— let alone a stranger from a rival realm— had ever given her that kind of consideration, and now, they were going to continue their respective journeys alone, and in all likelihood, she would never see him again. The thought caught in her chest, and she swallowed roughly, surprised at the raw emptiness that swelled the space around it. *Sometimes, the price of freedom is loneliness.*

37

The city gate was bound in iron, dark against the sandy brightness of the wall. Nissa thought privately that it looked like a yawning mouth, ready to devour anyone who dared to enter the city. Lord Waera turned, a glint in his eyes as he gestured for Trey to step forward with him, and Nissa felt the breeze of his movement as he complied. Her mouth twitched as she swallowed; the emptiness beside her felt like a void after the days of closeness on the road. As though sensing her discomfort, Tanyl stepped forward to fill the space, and she glanced at him from the corner of her eye to see his eyes fixed mildly on the gate, even as his hand rested on the hilt of the sword on his hip.

"Stay close to us," he said softly. Nissa shifted her feet as she nodded her reply, her eyes locked back on Waera and Trey ahead. She focused on the door ahead of them, at the iron that threatened to swallow them whole, and she repressed a tremor as Waera stepped to the left side of the door and knocked on a barely-visible panel there. The sound echoed in Nissa's ears as the panel slid open a sliver.

"State your business," a thin, reedy sort of voice ordered.

"Vaughn, you know that it's me," Waera said impatiently. "I've returned with Lord Tryamon and his companions." The panel snapped shut, and Waera stepped back as the gate creaked open. He turned, flashing a wide smile as he motioned for them to follow him. Nissa glanced at Tanyl uncertainly before she fixed her eyes again upon Tryamon's back. His shoulders had tightened, and he held his head high as he followed Waera without looking back, the ends of his dark hair twisting in a cross breeze. Something in Nissa's chest pitched slightly as he disappeared through the gate, and she took a deep breath as she followed, Tanyl matching her steps as they moved into the shadow of the gate. The iron gate clanged shut behind them.

A small, wiry sort of young man met them on the other side. Nissa blinked at him; he was clearly younger than she was, and his youth was even more evident as he flashed a sheepish smile at Waera, clasping his hands behind him as he inclined his head. As though compelled to do so, the two nameless guards who had accompanied Waera turned on their heel and strode away. Nissa's eyes followed them until they rounded a corner and disappeared from sight.

"I'm glad to see you're taking your new duties seriously," Waera's voice was laden with amusement, and relief flashed across the guard's face.

"I apologize, Lord Elrand," Vaughn inclined his head again, and the older man laughed as he clapped a hand on his shoulder.

"No apologies needed," he said with a chuckle, dropping his hand as he led his horse forward. "Send word to the House of Makani that we've arrived. And find someone to take care of our horses; we can continue on foot," he ordered more seriously. Nissa's eyes roved the streets in front of them. Towering structures of that same sandy stone rose above them, the layers of age evident where they had been added to over the centuries.

"Yes sir," the youth bobbed again and turned, disappearing through a door beside the gate, presumably to follow the order. Nissa's eyes found Trey again. He had turned to survey the city streets, his jaw tight. Still, he did not look at her. She shifted her weight from one foot to the other as she looked out at the streets that twisted behind the towering structures, wondering what secrets lurked behind them.

"Thank you, for the escort to Sel'veren, Lord Tryamon," Nissa ventured, stepping forward. His eyes snapped to meet hers, hard against the planes of his face, and she narrowed her eyes in concern.

"I'm pleased we could assist you, Elyssa," he replied distantly. Waera glanced between the two, his brows drawing close as he considered them.

"You may accompany us to the center of the city, Miss Broffet," he offered in a tone that told her it wasn't really an offer at all, but an order. She blinked at him in surprise, and he raised his eyebrows as though daring her to respond with anything other than agreement.

"I—I thank you for your consideration," Nissa lifted her chin to meet his dark eyes. A muscle in Trey's cheek began to twitch. She did not know what Waera's offer meant, but a swell of foreboding crashed against her stomach, twisting it in knots. Was Sel'veren so dangerous that their protection extended into the city's limits as well? Nissa knew that the ancient city was large, that much was obvious from the expanse of wall they had seen outside of the gate, but she didn't know what that meant for her. As Waera turned away, she stared hard at Tryamon again, but his face had descended into that impenetrable mask, and there was no reaching him.

"It won't take us long to reach our destination," Waera said more conversationally, nodding toward where the sun had begun to descend toward the horizon. "We should reach it by sundown." Nissa did not reply, but a glance toward Tanyl yielded a wary expression that was a mirror of her own feelings. The realization did nothing to ease the knot in her stomach; they hadn't expected this either. She flinched as Baloriel stepped forward to flank her other side.

"Stay calm," he breathed, and she replied with the slightest nod.

"I take it this isn't a good sign?" she whispered. From the corner of her eye, Nissa saw his mouth tighten.

"It's an unexpected one." She huffed; she had already gathered that.

"It could be exactly what it seems," Tanyl said from her other side.

"It could be." Baloriel didn't sound convinced. The conversation ceased as a pack of boys approached, clad in the now-familiar blue and yellow colors of the city.

"We are here to collect your horses, my lord." The boy who spoke was clearly the oldest, and his voice crackled with the changes of puberty as he dipped his head to Waera. The older man nodded, his eyes softening as he met the brown-skinned boy's surprisingly light eyes.

"We thank you." Nissa glanced at him in surprise; the gratitude seemed out of character for him. Clearly, the boy did not think so; his eyes lit up as he smiled and inclined his head again. They yielded their horses to them, and Waera turned to them again.

"After me, then." He turned without waiting for a response and stepped toward one of the twisting streets, Trey matching pace beside him.

Sel'veren was a maze. The streets intertwined and crossed over each other with no sense of rhyme or reason—at least, not one that Nissa could figure out, and she wondered at the ease and confidence with which Waera led them through the tangled web. She understood quickly why they had left the horses behind; the streets were cluttered with foot traffic, and they were narrow enough that the bodies clogged their path frequently, although most parted when Waera cut through the crowd. The sight of the crowds yielding before him did nothing to abate the looming sense of dread that clouded over her; this was a man with influence, who knew that she was in the city. Where could she go within Sel'veren that wouldn't be under his watchful eye, now that he knew that she had traveled with Trey? She frowned at the thought; for all of their efforts, she was in the same situation she had been hiding from in Domogién, although admittedly without the threat of Cyril looming over her.

As large as the structures lining the city streets were, the Makani house—if one could even call the structure a house— shadowed over them all. Nissa sucked in a breath, her eyes widening as she craned her neck to see the top of the towers that rose over the city. Openings arched against the smooth stone that had seamlessly melded across time as columns rose to support the balconies that peppered the different levels. A great dome shone bronze as the sunset streaked across the sky, bridging between the towers that spiraled from each of the corners. This was no house; this was a palace. She cleared her throat as they approached the gate that barred them from the interior. Waera lurched to a stop, turning to survey her with one eyebrow arched in question. She cleared her throat again.

"I thank you for the escort," she began again. "The house is a thing of beauty." Waera smiled at her without showing his teeth.

"I'm glad that you appreciate it," he replied, teeth flashing white against his skin as he spoke. The hair on the back of her neck prickled as she took an instinctive step back.

"I can take my leave of you. I should find lodging before night falls. Lord Tryamon," she directed her voice at Trey again, and his eyes shot up to meet hers, the hardness in them softening only slightly as she addressed him. "Thank you again for your protection," she managed. He nodded once, holding her eyes for a moment before that same, impenetrable mask rose over his eyes once more. Waera studied their exchange with a widening smile. She turned to face the streets behind them, and she lifted her foot to take her first steps toward freedom when a strong, warm hand locked on her upper arm, pulling her back.

"Don't put yourself out, *Elyssa*." His voice was soft as he emphasized the name she had given him. "The Makanis welcome you as their guest." Nissa twisted, trying to break his grip as behind him, naked panic flashed across Trey's face. Tanyl and Baloriel stepped forward, reaching with twin grasps toward their swords. They froze as guards stepped to the gate, their own weapons drawn.

"That's kind of them, but I would hate to impose," Nissa said, not faking the quiver in her voice. She had been close, so close to that taste of freedom. The false promise of it soured on her tongue.

"You don't say no to the House of Makani," Waera replied, an edge to his voice now. "Open the gate," his voice rose to an order that those behind the gate leaped to obey. Without taking his hand from her arm, Waera shoved her through the opening as it appeared, with Trey, Baloriel, and Tanyl snapping at his heels.

38

———————

The only thing that rivaled the outrage threatening to split open Trey's chest was the fear that speared through him. Nissa flashed terrified eyes at him before she was led away, down one of the twisting hallways of the house. There were any number of rooms that they might have taken her to; he was thankful that the hallway that they had disappeared through did not lead to the dungeons. Beside him, Waera stood with an impassable expression. He rounded on the taller man, who studied him with steady eyes.

"It was foolish to bring her here," he said, the condemnation rumbling in his voice.

"I was just her escort to the city, Waera. She doesn't have to be here," Trey snapped, gesturing wildly to the room around them. He didn't think he was imagining the flash of pity that brightened in Waera's eyes, but it was gone too quickly for him to know for sure.

"That's not how Lord Raenon sees it." The mention of the Makani patriarch had Trey's eyes shuttering.

"And how," he practically spat the accusation, "would Lord

Raenon have come to learn of her presence at all?" Waera's deep eyes narrowed to study him.

"You should consider yourself lucky that the family is still unaware of her identity," he said steadily. Tryamon jerked his chin in challenge. How had the man known?

"She's just some girl that I met and tried to help," he snapped, meeting the other man's eyes with a glare. Waera just shook his head with a low laugh.

"You're a fool," he said. Trey felt the first sparks of rage shock in his chest, and he knew that he needed to rein in his temper. He tugged on that internal leash, banking it like an untamed stallion as his teeth gritted with the effort. He took a step toward the older man, and in the next moment, he found himself pinned against the wall, Waera's face close to his own as he gripped his chin in a hand and forced Trey to look into his face.

"I could incinerate you where you stand," Trey snarled. Waera's eyes narrowed.

"We both know *that* isn't the case," Waera said smoothly. Tryamon jerked against him, but a sharp blade prodded against his ribs, freezing him in place. "I see no reason for Lord Raenon to learn of Lady Nissa's identity while she is here. This alliance isn't her mess. But remember, boy, my loyalty is to the House of Makani, and I will do *whatever* it takes to protect their interests." Trey let out another wordless snarl at the threat, taking a step back as Waera suddenly released him and sheathed his knife.

"Some loyalty you have, to conceal her identity in the first place," Trey challenged, suddenly reckless. An answering gust of wind slapped across his cheek in answer as Waera's eyes glittered with dark power.

"Don't test me. Even my patience has limits," he met the challenge coldly. "Get to the throne room. They want to see you." Without so much as a backward glance, Waera swept up one of the staircases to the right, the steps shining as the last rays of sun met the stone.

With a low growl of frustration, Trey whirled around and stalked in the direction of the large, carved doors that he knew would open to the Makani throne room. Disgust curled in his gut as he studied the carved design of the door, which looked as though it had been designed from the twisting caresses of the wind. It was a thing of beauty, but in that moment, he hated it, hated everything that that door and all that waited behind it symbolized. He placed one broad palm on the door and shoved.

Despite the darkness that snaked in from the high, vaulted windows, the room was softly lit by candle-flame. The stone tiles that made up the floor were patterned with shades of interspersed blue and yellow that overlapped as they led to the elevated dais at the far end of the room. Centered at that level were two, wooden thrones, designed in the same fashion as the carvings on the door. Two figures, dark skinned with rich hair that gleamed with lavender and gold jewels in the candlelight leveled him with matching, silver stares of silent observation. Two guards flanked each side of the dais, staring blankly ahead as Tryamon approached the Makani rulers with echoing footsteps.

"Lord Tryamon," The man in the larger throne rose, regal robes of golden yellow shimmering against his shining skin. "You are very welcome here." Despite the words, the man's tone was cold, appraising. It was not hard to sense the presence of the tempest lurking beneath. Trey stopped as he reached the edge of the dais and inclined his head in a shallow bow.

"Lord Raenon. I'm honored to have returned to Sel'veren." The words were hollow in his throat. Raenon raised a hand, his muscled arm unwavering as he held it in place, and a cutting wind sliced across Trey's cheek as it swooped for the door behind him. The door slammed shut, and the sound rocked Trey's core.

"I'm sure you are." Trey tried not to bristle at the easy confidence in his voice. "You may rise." He forced his face to remain neutral and disinterested as he surveyed the Governing Lord of the Air Realm. It would be impossible to guess his age; his face was miraculously unlined, despite years in power, there were no streaks of silver that looked out of place. Much like the city he occupied, Lord Raenon was timeless.

"You wanted to see me?" Trey asked mildly. Raenon's expression did not falter.

"I'm certain you remember my daughter, Lady Aella." There was a knowing glint in the lord's eyes as he turned to beckon to the other figure who remained shrouded in shadow on the adjacent throne. Tryamon plastered an obligingly polite smile on his face as she rose, the thin fabric of her lavender gown all but glowing against her deep black skin. Her hair was wound into an intricate web of braids, twisting up but for one ringlet that curved brightly against one sharp cheekbone. She did not smile.

"We are pleased you have returned, Lord Tryamon." Her voice was cold as she raised her chin against his scrutiny, baring the slim throat that rose in a column above her gown.

"It was kind of you to greet me," he matched her formality, and one of her eyebrows lifted.

"And what of your companion?" Raenon rumbled again, "how does she like our fair city?" Alarm blazed in his chest at the mention of Nissa, but he fought to maintain an even expression as he tilted his head appraisingly to one side.

"I'm sure she finds it quite impressive. I'm afraid she was removed from my presence before I had the chance to ask her," he said with a cold smile. Despite his best efforts, something must have shown on his face, because Aella shot him a sharp look. "She did not anticipate being welcomed into your home,

Lord Raenon. I merely offered her protection as she traveled to the city."

"So we have been informed," Raenon answered mildly. "Since she was your companion for so many days, we thought it fitting to give her a proper welcome." Trey's blood ran cold as Raenon's face yielded nothing of what a proper greeting entailed. Aella tilted her head to one side as she surveyed him.

"I shall enjoy getting to know her," she said finally in a voice that was as smooth as silk.

"I'm sure Miss Broffet will be honored," he replied, inclining his head to his fiancée again as his mind reeled. She nodded at him, and the faintest glimmer of hope broke through the chill in his veins.

"Go rest and recover from your travels, Prince of Flames," Trey bristled at the title as Raenon spoke again. "We will see you for breakfast in the morning."

39

The rooms Nissa was given were surprisingly nice. Open and airy, the pale stone arched and rose high above her, and the two windows that rested in one gave her a nice view of the city beyond it—the city where she might have been free. Nissa sighed as she surveyed the expanse, smoothing out a ripple in the light, floaty fabric of the dress she had been lent. The ivory cloth was lovely. This was a gilded cage, but it was still a cage.

A knock at the door stumbled her out of her weary thoughts, and she turned, the skirts of the fabric dancing upon the air with the movement. She pulled open the door to reveal a pale, thin woman who looked to be only a few years older than her. The woman's large, dark eyes rounded as they took each other in for a few moments.

"Miss... Broffet?" the woman asked uncertainly. She was clad in a dress of the same floaty material as Nissa's, although hers was a pale blue. Something about her was familiar, but Nissa could not put her finger on what it was.

"Yes?" she asked, fixing what she hoped was a pleasant smile on her face. The woman brushed a lock of white-blonde hair out of her face and smiled in return, although the expression didn't fully reach her eyes.

"My name is Liana. I'm a guest here as well. I thought you might like some company." Recognition roared through her at the introduction. This was Liana Noor. They had met before, years ago. She masked her shock and horror as she inclined her head with a wider smile.

"It's a pleasure to meet you. Call me Elyssa," she said, inwardly reeling. The last time she had seen Liana had been at one of the few summits between the realms, when she had been presented to their neighbors after the manifestation of her powers. Liana had been there, alongside her fair-featured mother. She had been quiet, but she had been kind. While Calanis Noor had been a guest at in Danuil occasionally in the years since, Nissa had not seen Liana again... until now. For her to be in Sel'veren, Nissa knew that it meant she was beginning to shoulder other responsibilities as her mother's heir. It was preparation for the responsibilities she would have in the years to come; the Light Realm maintained a friendly relationship with all of the others. That was no guarantee that Liana would be an ally to Nissa personally.

"It's so nice to meet you, Elyssa," Liana's smile widened, reaching her eyes this time. "Have you eaten yet?" Nissa shook her head.

"Not yet; I wasn't quite sure where to go for breakfast," she admitted. They had left Nissa alone after bringing her to her rooms, and no one had come back. "I'm not even sure if I'm allowed to leave."

"Nonsense," Liana stepped forward and linked her arm with Nissa's. "You're a guest here just as much as I am." Nissa felt herself relax; Liana hadn't recognized her.

"How did you come to be in Sel'veren?" Nissa chanced to ask the question as they made their way down yet another twisting hallway. Liana let out a musical laugh.

"Family business. My mother is… she has business with the Governing Lord, and she sent me to oversee it this time. Part of her trying to pass the torch one of these days." She shrugged, and Nissa stared.

"That sounds like a lot of responsibility. Where are you from?" Nissa asked, feigning ignorance. Liana waved a hand.

"Nerafell," she answered, making a face.

"The Light Realm is a long way to travel on business," Nissa said cautiously. Liana shrugged again.

"That's what I told my mother, but she said that travel was the cost of doing business," she sighed, gesturing at the walls around them. "At least it's pretty here. Last month, she had me traipsing all over the Midlands, and they weren't nearly as accommodating." Nissa blinked at her candor, at the naked openness of someone who didn't have anything to lose.

"It *is* beautiful," she admitted.

"So, how'd you come to be traveling with Tryamon Brandell?" Liana wiggled her eyebrows at her, and Nissa stiffened. *Ah, so that's the reason she came. At least she gets directly to the point.*

"He was my escort. We were both traveling to Sel'veren, and he offered me protection since I was by myself." That was the story, and Nissa was determined to stick to it. She half-expected the other woman to express her doubts, but there was no suspicion in Liana's face as they entered what Nissa assumed was a hall for dining.

"You're lucky!" Liana said. Nissa wrinkled her nose in confusion, and Liana must have noticed, because in the next moment she said, "I've never known Tryamon Brandell to do anything for anybody that he didn't have to." Nissa looked away, shrugging. The sentiment was not a surprise; she had thought the same thing before.

"I was surprised, but maybe I misjudged him."

"Maybe we both did," Liana allowed. Nissa glanced around

the spacious room, at the tables striped the floor in long rows, leading up to a spectacular table of shining, polished stone that rested upon a dais. Four chairs of equal sheen rested behind it, looking down upon the rest of the room. Mercifully, they were empty.

"That must be a nightmare to clean," she muttered to herself. A peal of laughter rang from the woman beside her, and Nissa turned to see Liana had doubled over, face split by a wide smile as her eyes squinted in mirth.

"You're funny. I think we're going to be fast friends." Nissa found herself smiling in return. She followed Liana's lead as the other woman found them seats at one of the tables and placed a polite order with the servant who rushed forward to attend them. Across the room, she caught a glimpse of Tanyl and Baloriel with heads bent in discussion. Tanyl caught her eye and nudged Baloriel, who nodded at her in acknowledgment before returning to their conversation. Their food materialized in front of them in what felt like minutes, carried by additional servants who had seemingly been waiting in the wings. Nissa blinked down at the breakfast feast in front of her. Whatever the Makanis were as rulers of a rival realm, they ran an efficient house. She dug in, chatting with Liana between bites and listening to the dull hum of breakfast conversation as more people trickled into the hall, laughing as Liana descriptively introduced each one with stories that she knew had to be embellished. She was still chuckling at one of her more lewd comments when a silence swept the room. Liana's eyes rounded as she stared at something behind Nissa's shoulder, and she turned slowly to face it as the back of her neck prickled beneath the cord of the obsidian pendant.

Facing her now was a tall, leanly muscled woman in a dress the color of a pale, yellow dawn. The floating material offset against her gleaming, black skin, drawing Nissa's eyes upward to where silver eyes shone from beneath dark brows. The woman's tightly coiled curls were bound at the nape of her neck, framing angular cheekbones as she stared down at Nissa with a contemplative expression. Nissa found herself rising. This could only be one woman, Lady Aella. The Air Realm's prodigal daughter was two years younger than her, and as a result, Nissa had never seen her, since her father had not allowed her to attend the summit when Aella's abilities manifested. The air of quiet authority left little chance of her being anyone else. Nissa dipped into a shallow curtsy, bending respectfully at the neck.

"Lady Aella, good morning!" Liana chirped from beside her. "I was just getting to know your new guest." Aella's silver eyes flicked over to Liana and warmed slightly before they refocused on Nissa and her expression dropped by several degrees.

"Thank you for your hospitality, Lady Aella." Nissa hated the deference she had to force into her tone. If they had met as equals, both daughters to governing lords, there would have been none. As Elyssa Broffet, however, she had no such rank. Aella inclined her head.

"You are welcome here. Lord Tryamon was kind to offer you protection during your journey. We are pleased to be an extension of his kindness." There was no emotion in the flat formality of her response.

"You are kind," Nissa said, because there was really no other way to respond to that. Aella considered her a moment more before she swept away, trailing her shimmering skirts behind her. Nissa released the breath that she had held.

"That went well," Liana commented, popping a small, round fruit into her mouth.

"Is she always so...?" Nissa trailed off. Liana let out a light laugh as she lowered her voice.

"Yes. If you knew her father, you'd understand." Nissa winced. She knew a thing or two about overbearing fathers. A thought crossed her mind, and Nissa froze. Lord Raenon was

Aella's father. He had been there, all those years ago, when Nissa's powers had manifested, and she was here, staying in his house. If he recognized her— She'd thought to avoid him, but she supposed she'd been foolish to think it was possible in his own house.

"Elyssa?" Liana's concerned voice yanked her from her spiral of thoughts, and she faced the other woman, pushing her plate ahead of her.

"I think I'm finished eating," she said as calmly as she could manage. Liana cocked her head to one side, a lock of her white-blonde hair falling into her deep brown eyes. She brushed it away impatiently.

"Are you alright?"

"Fine. I just wanted to get some air." Nissa said with a reassuring smile.

"There's a courtyard off this level of the house. It has a lovely garden, and it's not ever very crowded if you want some time to yourself," Liana offered, understanding smoothing across the concern on her brow. Nissa nodded gratefully.

"That sounds perfect." She pushed back from the table and rose, nodding a farewell to Liana once the woman gave her directions. She fought to keep her pace leisurely as she moved to exit the room, and she glanced down at her feet as one of her shoes scuffed against an uneven stone. A shadow fell across her path, and when her eyes jerked up to behold the source, they found twin pools of amber gazing down at her.

"Elyssa," Trey greeted, his mouth set into tight, formal lines as he surveyed her. She froze for a moment before she remembered herself, dipping into a quick curtsy.

"Lord Tryamon. I hope you're well this morning." Nissa allowed her voice to carry.

"And you," he answered, his expression darkening as he focused on something behind her. Nissa danced from foot to foot as they stood in silence.

"I was just going to explore the gardens. Lady Liana says they're quite lovely." She hated the dryness of the subject. Trey nodded absently for a moment before his eyes found hers again.

"I hope you can enjoy many hours of peace there," he replied, tilting his head ever so slightly. Her eyes narrowed incrementally, and Trey looked beyond her again. "Enjoy your day." He swept past her, and Nissa did not turn to follow him with her eyes as she continued on her path from the hall. The dizzying weight of countless eyes bored into her back as she kept her head high.

40

Trey swore as he surveyed the apparently-empty garden, the curse at odds with the setting of blossoms and vines that draped across the walls. He'd hoped that Nissa would still be spending time there, but breakfast had run long and Raenon had demanded his attention for longer than expected. Aella had left breakfast shortly after he had arrived, but Vulred had unexpectedly appeared just as the conversation with Raenon was winding down, bearing a message from his mother. The contents of the letter had led to other discussions about the terms of their alliance. He kicked his boot at a nearby bucket, which toppled over with a clang and spun, prepared to leave the garden when a cough sounded from behind him.

"Temper, temper." Nissa stepped out of the garden as he whirled around again and stopped, crossing her tanned arms over her chest as a smile played on her lips. The dress that she wore, a shade just slightly off of white, accented the depth of her sun-kissed complexion, and the motion pulled the fabric against the curve of her silhouette. Trey blinked at her, caught off-guard.

"Have you been here the whole time?" he asked incredulously. She lifted her shoulders in a shrug, the movement shifting the loose waves of brown that fell across her shoulders.

"I don't have much else to do," she said, "and it's peaceful here." Trey glanced around the garden again, at the elegant pastels that poured over from enclaves in the wall. There was no sign of the sort of tropical flowers they had encountered on their journey.

"I'm sorry. I didn't expect them to…" he gestured wildly with one hand. "I shouldn't have suggested we travel together to the city." She shrugged again, not quite meeting his eye.

"I don't blame you for this," she said mildly. "I just don't know what they want with me." Trey ran a hand through his hair with a groan.

"Lord Raenon is a suspicious man," he said. Nissa hissed a warning as she glanced around the gardens. Feeling reckless, Trey stepped closer to her, reveling in the way that her hazel eyes went wide.

"You're not doing yourself any favors by meeting with me here, then." Despite her startled expression, Nissa's voice was even. He felt his lips curve into a smile, and after a flickering pause, one of her own joined it.

"Serves him right for thinking the worst of me," he said.

"The engagement." Her voice flattened as her smile fell again, and regret replaced his amusement.. His mouth twisted as he bit the inside of his cheek and nodded shortly.

"The engagement. They're trying to move it along." He couldn't keep the bitterness from his voice. Nissa recoiled slightly.

"Are they?" she asked.

"When a Noor shows up, that usually means they're trying to make something happen. Otherwise, they wouldn't need an impartial third party." His lip curled at the end of the statement, and he resented the pity and understanding that swelled in Nissa's expression.

"Trey—"

"They're getting impatient. My mother made it clear that they're expecting this to move along." He was still digesting the information.

"What does that mean for you?" she asked, leaning forward slightly. He resisted the urge to lean toward her himself, so he crossed his arms, shrugging.

"All I know now is that they're expecting more visitors. Maybe that'll give me time to stall." He barked out a harsh laugh, and Nissa didn't smile. The sorrowful understanding on her face threatened to undo him, so he took a half-step back.

"You don't care for her, then?" she asked. As the words slipped out, her eyes widened, and a flush rose in her cheeks. Trey smiled in spite of himself at the sight of it.

"I don't know her," he answered quickly, to save her from her own thoughts.

"If there's anything I can do...." She trailed off, as though knowing that the offer was futile. There was nothing that she could do; his lot in life was sealed. He pressed his lips together tightly. She would never know, but the offer, however useless, meant the world.

"The good news is that if things progress, then you'll be free to leave." He changed the subject, ignoring the way that his insides twisted at the thought. To his surprise, she frowned and dropped her arms.

"I wouldn't want my freedom at the cost of your own." The response was so softly said that Trey was half-convinced that he had imagined it. Her eyes flashed as they found something behind him, and he turned to see Tanyl standing a respectful distance away, trying to act as though he wasn't watching them. Trey repressed a flicker of annoyance.

"What?" he asked, wincing at the harshness of his tone. "Is

something wrong?" he asked more kindly. Tanyl was his friend, and he needed every friend that he could get.

"Lady Aella asked for you. She wanted you to be with her when her next guests arrive this afternoon." He offered an apologetic glance as he looked between the pair, and Trey scowled.

"Go ahead. I'll be fine here." He glanced back at Nissa. An emotionless mask had dropped onto her face, leaving no trace of the conversation that they had been having. Behind it, something intangible swam in her eyes. He nodded his farewell before he turned back to Tanyl.

"When do they arrive?" he asked, stepping toward his friend. Tanyl turned and they left the garden, walking shoulder to shoulder as Trey only half-focused on what his friend was saying, conscious that Nissa was still standing there and watching him go.

NISSA LINGERED in the garden for another half-hour or so, enjoying the solitude. She explored the furthest reaches of the space and happened upon a small water feature, trickling through a section of wall that was carved to form a spout. The water fell into the basin below with a musical sort of trickle that mesmerized her as she sat beside it and studied the ripples. Nissa sighed as a dull murmur of voices hovered in the air behind her shoulder, and she knew her solitude had ended. She spared one more glance at the tunneling, black depths that swallowed the space behind the waterfall before she turned away.

She made her way back through the garden's maze of paths, avoiding the areas where the voices grew louder. Her alone time in the garden might have ended, but she was still in no mood for company—or for anyone's curious interrogation, which seemed more likely in the Makani house. Nissa cast a forlorn glance behind her as she slipped away from the garden. It was a taste of the world beyond in a luxurious prison. She would be back.

She wandered the halls aimlessly, not quite sure how to get back to her room. In the confusion of the morning, she hadn't thought to consider how to reach them from the garden; she had paid attention to the path Liana had taken to the dining hall, but in her excitement to find the gardens, the rest had vanished like dust in the wind. Perhaps if she could find her way back to that main entry hall, it would make for an easier time of finding her room. Another wrong turn dead-ended a hallway, and she glowered at the painting that hung there, its figure looking down its nose at her. She glared at it.

"As if you can judge. You've never had to find your way anywhere," she muttered, turning around. With a huff, Nissa retreated up the hallway, flinching away from a closed door when the sound of arguing voices rumbled through the thick wood. She doubled her pace as the creak of a door opening sounded behind her.

"Nissa?" She lurched forward slightly as she froze in place at the sound of the familiar voice. She turned as the door to the hallway clicked shut behind her, her eyes wide as she took in the carefully styled brown hair. It was clipped short above eyebrows that were lifted by the shock in a pair of pale, gray eyes.

"Faris?" The question sounded faint. Nissa felt for a moment like she was watching everything from outside of her body. The space between her ears felt strangely hollow, the sound of her suddenly roaring pulse echoing through her.

"How are you here? I thought you were—" he stopped short as Nissa felt a presence materialize behind her shoulder. She breathed in the now-familiar woodsy scent. *Trey.*

"Care to make an introduction?" Trey's voice was hard and

sharp, and Nissa turned to see him studying Faris with equally hard eyes. Her eyes darted back toward the guard, who was glaring at the Prince of Flames with open hostility.

"Trey, this is Faris. He's one of my oldest friends. He helped me escape," she rushed out all at once. Trey looked the guard up and down, taking in the uniformed tunic.

"You must be one of the new guests I was supposed to meet," he said dismissively, his eyes narrowing with suspicion. "How did a Chantara guard find his way into the House of Makani?" he demanded, lifting his chin. Faris's lips tightened into a thin line, and Nissa's hands trembled as she looked between the two men.

"How did the heir to the Fire Realm come to be traveling with the Chantara's lost daughter?" Faris fired back. Warning flared in Trey's face as his amber eyes flashed, and Nissa stepped between the two men quickly, steadying her hands.

"It's a long story," she interjected, turning pleading eyes upon her friend. "How are you here, Faris? Did you leave too?" Faris's face fell into harsh lines as he barked out a laugh. Given the uniform, she supposed it had been a foolish question.

"Not remotely." Nissa's breath caught in her throat as her stomach lurched.

"Then how are you *here?* Is anyone else—" she broke off as Faris scowled at the stone floor between them.

"I'm here on your father's orders. *Alone,*" he said tersely.

"Are you here because—" she stopped herself. Faris had been surprised to see her; he wouldn't have been if her father had known that she was in the Air Realm. "Are you going to tell me what they are?" Nissa changed course. The space between Faris's eyebrows creased as they knit together, his eyes clouded past her and stared hard at Tryamon, who still stood at her shoulder.

"You're here with *him,*" came the non-answer. Nissa recoiled slightly at the venom in his voice, at the hint of temper that flashed across his face at the word.

"Yes, but—" she began, starting in confusion. Why was he angry?

"Willingly?" he interrupted, raising an eyebrow. His eyes darted between them again as though he was contemplating something dark. Nissa sidestepped to keep both men in her line of sight while Trey growled out a low warning.

"I'm not his prisoner, Faris," she said firmly, willing both males to remain calm—or civil, at the very least.

"So the rumors are true, then." The words echoed between them, each wary line of Faris's face etched in disgust. She tensed at the condemnation in his tone, forcing herself to remain calm as she bristled. Nissa cleared her throat as Trey's shoulders tensed, those amber eyes still fixed unblinkingly on her friend.

"If you're referring to my brother's disgusting accusations, then no. They are not," she corrected coldly.

"Hmph," came the reply. Her temper snapped against its leash, and she steadied it with a breath. Out of the corner of her eye, Nissa watched as Trey took a step forward.

"Ward has his own way of seeing things," she reminded him, edging her way between the two again.

"It seems that you do too," Faris snapped the reply, jerking his chin in Tryamon's direction.

"Careful now. I would hate for a Chantara *guard* to be rude to a guest of the Fire Realm when the relationship between our realms is already so... delicate," Trey lingered on the word, every syllable pronounced with a threat crackling behind it. Faris sneered at him.

"Careful now," he mocked, "I would hate for the Makani family to hear about the types of guests the Fire Realm keeps when they're still negotiating a betrothal. Let alone how they entertain them." Faris sneered at Trey without looking at Nissa. She inhaled sharply, falling back a step in shock.

"Faris," she gasped.

"You're out of line," Tryamon snarled, stepping forward menacingly. Nissa danced nervously from foot to foot as Faris tensed in response, his hand gripping for the sword he wore at his side. She lurched forward to catch Trey's wrist as he lifted his foot to take another step, and the motion stopped him in place. It did nothing to alleviate the dangerous light of battle that threatened to ignite in either set of eyes. Faris ripped his eyes from Trey's and looked down to where Nissa's had gripped his wrist, something in his face hardening again. He removed his hand from the hilt of his weapon, retreating slightly with one measured step.

"I'll be here if you're in search of better company, Nissa," he said before he turned his back on us both and disappeared back up the long, airy hallway. Nissa rounded on Trey, who was still staring hard after Faris long after he disappeared around a corner.

"Why did you pick a fight with him?" she demanded. Trey glanced down at Nissa in surprise before his eyes hardened into stone.

"He was disrespectful," he answered.

"He's my *friend*! He's the reason I'm not shackled to the Pallinors right now," she said. He fixed her with a long look before his eyes dropped to where Nissa's fingers still wrapped around his wrist. She dropped it instantly, taking a large step back to put some space between them.

"All he did was guard a door. You did the rest," he said.

"He put himself at risk to give me a chance, Trey. He's earned the right to be surprised to find me here with—" *with you.* Nissa clamped her mouth shut, but the unspoken words hung in the air. Trey's lips tightened.

"I will not apologize for stepping in when he disrespected the rank of my house," he said.

"Since when did you care about that?" she demanded.

"Since an alliance is on the line," he said, tossing the words around carelessly. Nissa tried to ignore the way that the thought made her stomach pitch. "You are here as my guest in this. If he disrespects you, if he spreads those rumors, he disrespects the standing we have here, which threatens our safety. I won't tolerate it." He met her eyes steadily, coldly, wearing a mask of disinterest. Nissa pressed her lips together and took another step back, looking up at him in careful study.

"Sorry to be a liability." She matched his tone coolly. Without waiting for another word, Nissa shouldered past him and continued up the hallway, ignoring the way that her stomach clenched in discomfort. *What am I doing here?* she wondered. Perhaps it was time for Nissa to see herself out.

41

———

Nissa flipped through one of the books that had been left on the side table of her room. She had requested some reading material from a servant on her way back, and the servant had been too caught off-guard to ask her for specifics—nor had she remembered to give them. The resulting book that had been waiting in her room when she returned was a flowery sort of romance with simpering characters and no plot that did nothing to hold her attention. She skimmed another page and then another, sighing when the characters did nothing more than make small-talk in a garden. She closed the book and set it aside with a thud. Nissa liked novels, when she had the chance to read them, but this was not the one for her.

"Things could be a lot worse for you than reading dull books in a pretty palace," she chided herself aloud, as annoyed by her situation as she was by the irritation that was rippling out of her core. She had passed plenty of days in the Water Realm sitting in rooms like this one, doing nothing more interesting than walking to take a meal before returning to sit on a pretty couch in inaction. Here, in another place that she was forced to remain in against her will, the routine felt all too familiar.

She had avoided Trey since their fight, not wanting the high emotions to further complicate his dealings with Lord Raenon. Liana had been a friendly companion at mealtimes for the past two days, and she had managed to keep up with the small-talk nature of their conversations as more and more guests arrived to the house, but she was, quite frankly, exhausted. Nissa wasn't sure how the days of inaction had exhausted her as thoroughly as her journey to the Air Realm, but somehow, they had managed to leave her with a fatigue that made it hard to leave the room. She had dedicated half a thought to wondering why Lord Raenon was welcoming so many guests into their home, but aside from that, the hours passed slowly, dripping by like an expired spring.

A knock at the door made her lift her head, staring at the shining handle blandly. She could remain silent, and whoever it was—probably Liana—would think that she wasn't in and would probably leave. The servants had, for the most part, left her alone without any questions when she had told them not to bother with her room as part of yesterday's daily cleaning. The gentle knock repeated with more force, a fist pounding against the wood.

"Open up." It was Trey. She chewed on her lip as she remained silent. There was another pause, and she thought for a moment that he might have given up.

"I know you're in there. Let me in." She sighed again but rose to her feet, her shoes scuffing against the floor as she moved to open the door. Trey stepped back as she pulled the door open and crossed her arms. He stared at her without speaking, his amber eyes smoldering a kind of burnished copper as he surveyed her.

"Do you need something?" she asked dryly.

"Can I come in?" She stepped to the side and gestured him in with one hand before she crossed her arms again. He pulled the door shut behind him and strode over to one of the armchairs in front of the fireplace, sitting down without invitation. Nissa stared at him, lifting her chin silently as she waited for him to speak.

"I need to talk to you." She raised an eyebrow at that.

"About?"

"I owe you an apology." The second of her eyebrows rose to join the first.

"For?" His chest rose and fell as he huffed out a breath, casting his eyes to the side as they darkened beneath close-knit brows. A strand of dark hair fell forward from where he had pulled the top half back from his face, and Nissa studied the way that it rested on his wide-sleeved, maroon shirt. He seemed to grapple with himself for a moment before he spoke again.

"I shouldn't have goaded your friend the way that I did. I'm just... I'm not used to being challenged so openly." Nissa cut her eyes at him. *Cyril would be the exception here, I suppose.* She kept the thought to herself.

"That's not an apology." Her response was clipped, and Trey sighed again, rubbing his face with his hand.

"I'm sorry, okay? I didn't know he was your friend at first, and then the way he was looking at you, *talking about you*. It didn't sit right with me, knowing what you'd been through." She tilted her head to one side as she considered what to say.

"He was surprised to see me here. He was surprised to see me with *you*."

"As you said," he said shortly. She fell silent, and they studied each other from across the room before he spoke again.

"The last name that you chose to give. That's his last name." There was no question in his voice.

"Yes," she answered.

"Is there a reason that you chose it?" Nissa frowned at the question.

"I couldn't very well give my own name to Waera." He rubbed his face again, pinching the bridge of his nose.

"You know what I mean, Nissa. Is there a reason you gave *his* name? Is there a reason he should take it personally that you were traveling with me?" Her eyes narrowed in displeasure, but Trey held her gaze steadily.

"Only one of us is betrothed to someone, *Tryamon*, and it's not me," she snapped.

"I know. That doesn't mean he couldn't have a reason to take it personally." She rolled her eyes.

"We grew up together, and he helped me escape. He's the one who taught me how to defend myself. He has an investment in my well-being because he's my *friend*. That is my only obligation to him. Not that it's your business."

"People do reckless things when they feel they've been wronged by someone they see as...," he trailed off. "I wanted to know what I was up against." Nissa bristled at the implication.

"You don't have to be *against* anything," she snapped. "He's my friend, and I was coming to think that you were my friend. That hardly makes you two enemies." Trey huffed out a short laugh that she couldn't quite read as he reclined in the seat, crossing his legs to rest one ankle across his knee.

"Okay, Nissa. We're not enemies." She squinted at him, tightening her crossed arms against her chest as she shifted her weight to one hip. He studied her mildly, and she sighed, dropping her arms as she approached the chair across from him and sat heavily on it.

"How are the negotiations going?" she asked. His eyes hardened as he looked at the wall behind her shoulder.

"My mother will be pleased," he said vaguely.

"I don't know whether to congratulate you or not," she said, earning a shrug from Trey.

"Thanks for the thought," he muttered.

"Lord Raenon seems to be hosting a lot of guests," she tried casually. He grunted.

"I'm coming to realize that Lord Raenon likes having witnesses around," he muttered darkly.

"Meaning?" she pressed, her heart pitching suddenly.

"I don't know. He's made a lot of noise about taking a step to formalize our agreement. I'm not sure what that means yet." The space between his eyebrows creased in worry.

"What could formalize an engagement more than a formal marriage agreement between realms?" Nissa asked cautiously. There were ways of solidifying a marriage alliance in the Water Realm, ways that made them unbreakable—her parents were example enough of that. She shook herself out of the thought. With few exceptions, engagements across Galarmos were almost universally sealed by paper, ink, and pretty words.

"He hasn't thought to share it with me yet." Nissa frowned at the strained tone of his response.

"Has he made you agree to anything new?" she asked carefully.

"Not yet." He took a deep breath before raising his eyes to meet hers again. His lips twitched uncertainly before he continued. "Could we just... could we just sit for a minute and not talk about it?" The words came out in a rush, and Nissa blinked at him for a minute. She nodded, pressing her lips together.

"Of course. Anything you want to talk about instead?" she asked after a moment's hesitation. He shook his head and leaned his head back to rest against the chair.

"Not really. I just... I need a minute." The admission sounded strangled, and Nissa tilted her head to the side as she considered.

"Sure." He let out a sigh of what she assumed was relief as the lines of tension on his face smoothed and he closed his eyes. She watched him, for a moment, as the rise and fall of his chest slowed, and she noticed, for the first time, the fatigue that bagged under his eyes. She wasn't the only one that the House of Makani was taking a toll on. Nissa frowned as she surveyed him again, considering again the number of guests that had been invited to Sel'veren. She shifted in her seat, her eyes settling on Trey's face as she chewed thoughtfully on her bottom lip. She couldn't shake the thoughts of her parents' union, of the Oath they'd had to take. The thought made her heart stutter again as she froze, her mother's tortured face swimming through her memory, forever imprinted on her at the moment Marin had fought to defy her own rite. She shook herself again; the Blood Oath was culturally exclusive to the Water Realm, and the fact that her parents had taken it didn't mean that this arranged marriage, which was wholly different, would invoke it. Then again—she tilted her head in consideration—Lord Raenon was a clever and ambitious man. If he thought that such an oath would solidify his House's power for the next generations. Her gaze settled on Trey's long, dark lashes. *But at what cost?* She shuddered, looking down. She wasn't sure that she knew the full extent of the consequences of such a promise herself.

Nissa knew two things with certainty about the Oath: it was twofold, and it was irreversible. Those who took it— who bound their lives together and invoked the blood magic to make that promise— united their power in such a way that each was able to wield their own abilities with the enhanced strength of their partner. This was then sealed—in her parents' case, by marriage. There were stories, though, from the centuries before the First War, in which the Oath had been sealed with words of fealty. Regardless, those who took it had access to these powers, but if one partner defied it, their abilities were lost, yielded to the one who remained true. It was a heavy price to pay on an uncertain relationship. Nissa sucked in a breath; *if that's why Faris is here, then*—she shook her head again. The Blood Oath was a carefully guarded secret, even within her own Realm. Her father would not relinquish the details of that knowledge to benefit his rivals. Her father was many things; fiercely protective over his family's secrets was one of them.

She fingered the obsidian at her throat as she studied the sleeping heir to the Fire Realm again. Her mother's scrying hadn't bothered her in weeks, and while she detested the fact that it also interfered with her wielding, she knew that Trey's thoughtfulness in gifting her the pendant was to thank for it. What would it be like, she wondered, to see her mother again? The ability was within her grasp. All she had to do was to remove the pendant and use the washbasin in the corner to channel her power. She stared hard at the black stone that housed the yet-untouched water. It would even be an unmuddied channel; she hadn't dirtied this one since it had been brought the previous evening. If nothing else, it could remove all thoughts of the possibility of the Blood Oath from her mind. With another cautious glance at Trey, still sleeping soundly, Nissa rose to her feet, treading as softly as she could over to the basin. With slightly shaking fingers, she curled her hands around the cord holding the pendant and lifted it over her head. She dropped it on the platform attached to the rounded edge of the basin that was meant as a soap dish, and she peered into the water, the movement rippling the water across her face as she studied her reflection. It had been a while since the last time she scried. She met her own eyes in her reflection, staring hard as she focused on the rhythms of her body, on the thrum of blood through her very veins. In, out, up, down, rise, fall. The inner workings of her body swelled with life, its maintenance, its continuity, its fragility. Her chest rose and fell in tempo with her heart as she called to her powers, singing her abilities into action. Her vision swam in and out of focus as her reflection swam and blurred.

Mother, her spirit sang, *show me my mother. Show me Marin Chantara.* The soul-song was an order, an invitation, and a plea all in one, and as the water trembled with a vibration that wasn't physically there, she knew it was working. The water fogged with some intangible, smokey substance as her eyes locked on the surface. It rippled again and again, the wavelets wrinkling the surface in contrasting directions as they crested against each other. She shuddered once, hard, and the smoke cleared, the ridges on the surface clearing to glass. Nissa remained frozen in place, her fingers locked like claws on the basin's edge as the image of her mother came into focus. Her heart lurched in her chest.

Marin Chantara, Lady of the Sea, sat at her vanity, running a brush through her long, blonde hair absently as her mother's gray eyes studied themselves. Dark circles cut the otherwise flawless flesh beneath them, and her cheeks seemed hollowed. Nissa had avoided the feeling of homesickness for all of the weeks she had been gone; now, the sensation hit her nauseatingly and with full force.

"The boy made it, then?" Marin's face did not turn from the mirror as she continued stroking her hair. She tilted her ear to one side for a response that Nissa could not hear.

"I suppose it will only be a matter of time before things are finalized, then." Her mother frowned at the mirror and plucked a piece of lint from her deep blue dressing gown. Nissa clenched her eyes shut again and pulled from that well within her. *My father. Show me Alvar Chantara.* The image in the pool widened again, and Nissa hissed in a breath as her father's shock of black hair came into view. Her eyes narrowed at the slice of cheekbones that sharpened his cold face. There was no such surge of homesickness at the sight of him.

"It was a gamble, sending him. I'm not sure he earned it." Alvar said, scowling.

"He loves her, my lord. He wouldn't have volunteered otherwise" Marin's soft voice reached Nissa's ears again, and her father turned away sharply. In the mirror, Marin's eyes flashed.

"If what Ward said is true.... I just wish we had *proof*," he hissed at the ground. Nissa started. What had her brother told them? None of the ideas that sprang to mind were particularly appealing.

"We have no way of knowing that." Her mother's voice was like a balm against the sting of Alvar's temper. Apparently, the effect was the same on him, because in the next moment, his shoulders relaxed.

"I know," he said. Nissa clenched her teeth as the image swam before her; she was slipping. She relaxed slightly when it stabilized again.

"Are you certain this is what you want?" Marin asked mildly, turning from the mirror to face her father.

"He'll be my eyes and ears if he feels like we know he does. Since your powers have failed us," he answered shortly. The worry on Marin's face was real this time.

"I don't know why I can't sense her anymore," Marin said softly.

"Your powers with mine should have assured it." Alvar's tone was flat; to Nissa's relief, there was no accusation in it.

"I could try again," she offered quietly. Nissa's heart thundered in her chest as the part of her that was there with them in that place reeled and bucked against the vision.

"No," her father's voice had an echoing quality now. "No, there's no sense in expending the energy now. We'll know soon enough." The vision swam again, and then Nissa was gasping at her own reflection once more, gripping the edges of the basin not in a trance, but to steady herself as her chest heaved. She clawed for the obsidian pendant, slinging it around her throat once more as she craned her neck to look at Trey, who was still blissfully asleep in his chair. When she felt steady enough to let go, Nissa rubbed the tension from the joints of her fingers where they throbbed from gripping the basin. She had more questions than answers, and the one lingering the most was what Faris was hiding from her.

42

———

Nissa picked at her lunch absently, her thoughts wandering as her absent stare fixed across the expanse of the hall. She had greeted Tanyl and Baloriel with a head nod as she entered the room, but that was all the greeting she could muster. What she had witnessed while scrying was still at the forefront of her mind.

She had managed to avoid any direct questions from Trey when he had woken from his slumber and rushed out of the room for his meeting, and their paths hadn't crossed in the half-day since. She hadn't mustered up the courage to start questioning Faris either. Their last interaction had been the argument with Trey, and he had kept his distance in the days since.

"And you'll have met Tanyl and Baloriel on your hall, of course. They're from Domogién, and—oh! Have you met Elyssa yet?" Liana's cheerful voice pricked at Nissa's ears, and she turned, ready to feign a pleasant mood of her own if Liana was going to make an introduction. Her expression dropped when she saw that Liana, her blonde hair braided and shining down her back, was facing Faris, gesturing excitedly with her hands as she spoke.

"I haven't had the pleasure," he responded politely. Nissa glanced at the door, calculating what her chances of success would be if she was to attempt an escape and avoid the pair altogether.

"I'm sure you're still getting settled of course; you've only just arrived. Oh, here she is!" Unfortunately, Liana chose that moment to turn and lock eyes on Nissa. Faris's jaw clenched as he followed her gaze and found her. Nissa locked eyes with him and forced an introductory smile on her face as the other woman all but tugged him over.

"I don't think we've had the pleasure," Nissa dared. She practically held her breath as Faris paused for a heartbeat, indecision flickering across his face.

"This is Elyssa Broffet. It's her first time to Sel'veren as well." Liana bridged the silence, waving her hands between the two as she did.

"Elyssa *Broffet*, is it?" Faris asked pointedly. Nissa warmed uncomfortably, but she forced herself to keep an even expression.

"It is."

"Oh, that's right! *Your* last name is Broffet too, isn't it?" Liana looked between them curiously. "Are you two related?" Faris dropped his eyes to her, looking startled.

"Ah, no," he stammered behind a cough. Liana frowned, glancing between them again.

"I suppose there isn't much resemblance anyway. I always forget that some last names crossed realms after the Great War. Fascinating," she observed. "It doesn't happen much in the Light Realm," she added as an awkward afterthought. Nissa forced herself to look away from Faris and smiled at Liana.

"I imagine there are quite a few of us," she offered. "It's a common enough name where I come from." She braced herself in case Faris contradicted her, but her friend only studied her for a moment before shrugging.

"Uncommon enough where I'm from, but not unheard of," he said.

"What part of the Water Realm did you say you were from?" Liana asked.

"Danuil," he answered shortly, the space around his mouth tightening.

"Fascinating. I've never been there before. Have you, Elyssa?" Liana turned to glance at Nissa curiously. She shook her head, staring across the room. Tanyl had his head bent as he poured over a piece of paper, oblivious to Baloriel sprinkling crumbs in his hair behind him.

"I'm afraid I hadn't traveled much before I came here," Nissa answered vaguely. She repressed a smile as Tanyl absentmindedly scratched his head and froze when crumbs fell across the table. He rounded on Baloriel, whose roaring laugh caused Liana and Faris to jump in surprise at the sudden noise. Liana shook her head at the pair before she spoke again.

"I haven't visited the Water Realm either. My mother usually does the traveling if our business takes us that far to the west," Liana said with a shrug. "Maybe one day; I hear it's beautiful."

"It's home," Faris said, looking at Nissa with an arched brow. To her relief, Liana was looking the other way.

"That's how I feel about Nerafell. I've visited most of the realms, but it will always be home," Liana said in a wistful sigh, staring into space across the room. Nissa privately thought that she had never related to anything less. The thought made something catch in her stomach, and she rose suddenly, feeling hollow.

"You two will have to excuse me," she said softly. Liana stared at her with wide eyes as Faris frowned in concern, but she made no further explanation as she turned and, at a pace that was painfully slow, fled from the conversation. Her breaths grew shallow as she reached the hall, and she leaned against a wall as she fought to calm it. This was all too much: the conversations about home, the illusions she had to uphold. How much longer could she keep living a lie? How much longer could she bear being held a finger's length away from freedom? It was within her sights, but she had never felt that it was so far away. Would this be her life now, jumping from one cage to another because of some twisted combination of circumstances beyond her control and bad luck? The sound of voices reached her as a small group rounded the far corner of the hallway, and Nissa forced herself to straighten, plastering on a mask of placidity as she did so. She inclined her head in greeting as they passed, bound for the dining hall, and she turned her head to keep them in her sights as she rounded the corner. Nissa collided with a slim, solid figure who grunted as they fell back a step. Mortified, she lifted her eyes, and the color drained from her face as she realized that she had run straight into Aella Makani.

"My lady, I'm so sorry," she recovered quickly, dropping her eyes as she bent into a curtsy. A strand of her brown hair fell into her face, and she hooked it behind her ear as she kept her face respectfully downcast. When Aella did not respond, she dared to lift her eyes to the other woman's face. Aella surveyed her curiously, her brows arched over those startlingly silver eyes. Her face was otherwise inscrutable, the smooth skin of her face unlined and unblemished as she stared down at the shorter woman.

"Elyssa Broffet, Lord Tryamon's guest," Aella greeted neutrally.

"And yours," Nissa reminded as she inclined her head. Aella's lips tightened slightly, and Nissa felt a flicker of concern that she had been too bold.

"Always a curiosity to meet with the woman who traveled so

far with my fiancé." Aella lingered over the word as her eyes fixed in careful study of Nissa's face. She willed herself to smile blandly.

"He was kind to offer his protection," Nissa answered mildly, repeating the sentiments of their earlier interaction. One of Aella's eyebrows lifted above the other, and something in her eyes twinkled. *She* did *remember, then?*

"From what I've heard lately, kind is not the first word many would use to describe him," Aella replied.

"I can't speak for others, but I hope it is one that you will be able to use throughout your union," Nissa said with a smile, meeting the other woman's gaze clearly. Aella's eyes narrowed a fraction as she considered Nissa further before her lips curved in an answering smile.

"As do I." Without a word of farewell, Aella sidestepped her and continued her journey around the hall's corner. She did not look back. Nissa released a breath as she let her shoulders slump forward. She did not have more than half of a moment before her attention was required again.

"Elyssa!" Nissa tensed as she half-turned to see Faris hurrying toward her, apparently having shaken off Liana's attentions. She inclined her head.

"I'm afraid I didn't catch your rank, sir, when we were introduced earlier," she said, inclining her head and dipping respectfully toward the floor. Faris pressed his lips together in a tight line.

"Captain now," he said tersely. She blinked at him.

"Quite a promotion," she murmured, too softly for her voice to carry beyond Faris. What had he done to earn it in the few weeks since she had left Danuil? Her voice returned to a normal level. "You must have met Lord Waera when you arrived. He seems to have some dealings with the guard force here." The line of his lips tightened further as frustration flashed in his eyes. Nissa was stalling with the exchange of pleasantries, and she knew that Faris knew it too.

"Yes, Lord Waera has been quite welcoming. As have all in the House," he answered impatiently. He reached for Nissa's wrist and tugged her forward to close the distance between them. "I need to talk to you."

"Would you care for a walk in the gardens, *sir*?" she asked, wrenching her arm from his grasp as she stepped pointedly back. Her eyes blazed with steel, and she felt a prickle of satisfaction when Faris flinched. The feeling was almost immediately drowned by a surge of guilt; Faris was her friend. She softened slightly.

"I'd like that," he said quietly. She nodded, still unsmiling, not speaking until they were well within the maze of climbing roses that took up one side of the garden. Nissa sat on one of the benches that dotted the path, crossing one of her legs over the other as she looked expectantly up at Faris.

"You wanted to speak with me?" she asked, arranging her features into a carefully cultivated kind of neutrality. He sat hard beside her.

"Well, first, I know I was over the line before. It's just... seeing you with *him*. His family have been out to get our realm for years, and you just chose to be here with him?" He turned a questioning face on Nissa, and she sighed wearily. "I know you wanted to get out of Danuil, and I understand why you needed to, but Tryamon Brandell... His family is no better than yours, and you know that." She fought the urge to flinch.

"I didn't choose to be here. He and his cousin found me when I crossed the border into the Fire Realm. They detained me, and then they took me back to the Singed Keep." Faris sucked in a breath, but Nissa continued without pause. "Then Ward somehow found out I was there, and he showed up." Faris's eyes widened. "Trey—Lord Tryamon helped smuggle me out of the Keep. He helped me get to Domogién so I was out of reach. I thought I'd stay there for a while, but then things got complicated..." she trailed off, shaking her head. Faris stiffened, his jaw tightening.

"Complicated how?"

"Just... complicated." She waved one hand to dismiss it. "So he offered to escort me to Sel'veren. He said I would be safer here, and we were supposed to go our separate ways when we reached the city." She took a deep breath. "Somehow, Lord Raenon found out we were traveling together and sent Waera to escort him to the city. Once we arrived in Sel'veren, we were informed that the Makani family expected me to stay as a guest. I couldn't say no. Now, I'm here," she finished with another sigh, glancing at Faris as he absorbed what she had said.

"Aella is a jealous woman, I take it?" Nissa winced and shook her head.

"I don't think that's it. She seems curious about me, but that's it. I can't say I blame her." She drummed her fingers on one knee.

"I don't trust the Makanis," Faris said gruffly. Nissa rounded on him.

"Do you trust *anyone*?" she demanded, exasperated. Not that she trusted them herself. He blinked at her slowly.

"I trust you," he answered.

"Do you? Because I just explained the whole situation to you, and you're still somehow casting it in a different light," she snapped.

"I'm just saying that *Aella* probably—" Nissa rose to her feet, cutting him off.

"You said you needed to tell me something." Her voice was cold as she crossed her arms. Faris took a shaky breath, and there was a sincere concern in his eyes when he spoke again.

"I can't tell you exactly what it is, but Lord Raenon is planning something. You need to leave here, to get out of Sel'veren before it happens so you aren't collateral damage." She narrowed her eyes at him.

"You want me to risk my neck fleeing somewhere *again*, and you aren't going to tell me why?" she demanded incredulously. Faris flinched, dropping his eyes to the floor between them.

"I *can't*." There was true desperation in his eyes as he met Nissa's eyes again, but she shook her head, stepping away in disgust.

"So you just want me to disappear on some vague non-explanation?" she asked. Her hands curled as her power thrummed against her palm. The obsidian at her throat flared in warning.

"You can't be here when it happens," he said. She glared at him.

"So I'm just supposed to leave Trey to deal with whatever it is? After all he's done to help me?" she fired back. Temper flared across Faris's face at her casual use of Tryamon's name, but fear reclaimed his expression quickly as he met her gaze with earnest eyes.

"Please, Nissa. You don't know the risk you'd take by staying," he pleaded softly. She took another step back, shaking her head.

"I was honest with you out of respect for our friendship. It's a shame you can't do the same for me." Faris flinched again as her words struck home, but she did not stay to see the fallout. Nissa turned on her heel and broke into a run before she rounded the first corner. Any plot that required interference from a realm that was wholly uninvolved couldn't be a good sign. Her earlier suspicions came crashing down around her, threatening to drown her. She had to find Trey and warn him before the tidal wave secrets swept him away too.

43

———————

T rey cast a sidelong glance toward the window across from the heavy door, allowing himself a glimpse of the star-studded sky before he turned and knocked, taking a deep breath. The door swung open instantly, and he blinked at the small crowd of people who gathered around the long, dark table, staring solemnly at Trey as the flickering candlelight cast unforgiving shadows on their face. Raenon sat at the head of the table, as he usually did for these meetings, staring hard at Tryamon from beneath the gleaming gold circlet that rested on his brow. Aella sat beside him, stunning in a gown of soft purple that accented her magnificent eyes. She did not look up as Trey entered the room; she simply stared down at the hands that folded in her lap. These were familiar faces in these meetings. It was the presence of the others that caught Trey off-guard.

His jaw tightened as he caught sight of Faris lurking in the shadows of one corner. He had not seemed to notice or care about Trey's arrival; his stormy gaze was fixed out the nearby window. Liana lifted a hand to flutter her fingers in greeting from her place beside a man he didn't recognize. The man was handsome in a casual sort of way, with blond hair that reminded Trey of Tanyl's. It rested, featherlike, against arching brows that rose above piercingly blue eyes and sparked a contrast to his mild expression in the candlelight. Something in Trey's chest roared that something was wrong, that he should turn and flee into the deserted corridor behind him. Instead, he stepped forward and allowed the door to snap shut behind him.

"Quite a crowd for this meeting, Lord Raenon," he said drolly, striding toward the Air Realm's governing lord, who seemed amused by his appraisal. Raenon lifted a dark hand, fluttering a scrap of paper as Trey took a seat at the table.

"You can thank your dear mother for that." Trey's heart stuttered as he fixed an arrogant smile on his face.

"And what news from home? The weather in Domogién is lovely this time of year." Raenon smiled, leaning forward as a figure stepped from the shadows.

"It was. A shame I had to miss it; this is my favorite time of the year." Tryamon froze as the dim light threw the harsh lines of Vulred's angular face into startling relief. His mother's lapdog smiled coldly. "Hello, Lord Tryamon."

"Vulred," he greeted. "A pity indeed." Vulred's smile flickered before he sat hard in one of the chairs across from Trey.

"Now that we've all gathered," Raenon boomed, "we can proceed." Trey raised an eyebrow at the governing lord. From the corner of his vision, he watched as Faris pushed himself away from the window and sat at the far end of the table, as though trying to put the greatest possible distance between him and the others. The man beside Liana rose with a somber expression.

"Welcome, all. Thank you for being willing to bear witness so late in the evening." His voice was like silk, and as his eyes flickered over those gathered, Trey had the notion that his silver tongue could inspire entire armies to fall upon their own swords.

"Bear witness?" he asked. Faris shifted slightly in his seat.

"Yes, Lord Tryamon," Liana beamed at him. "Don't look so surprised. We've been planning it for *weeks*." Her smile faltered. "We're just a little ahead of schedule now." He glanced toward Aella and saw lines forming around her mouth from the way her lips pressed firmly together. It was the only indication that she was as confused as he was.

"A little small for a wedding between two heirs, isn't it?" he said as lightly as he dared. Lord Raenon leaned forward, his silver eyes glittering.

"Don't worry, Tryamon. Your family will have their ceremony. But in light of..." he trailed off, "recent developments, we've decided that some assurances are in order." Faris shifted again, and when Trey glanced at him, the other man's eyes were wide. Aella, too, looked hard at her father, and her brows rose.

"I don't recall giving you any reasons to doubt me—or my family, for that matter," he said coolly as conflicting thoughts hammered against his skull. What kind of assurances could he possibly offer at short notice? From the way that Vulred's smile curved slowly against his teeth, he knew that the man had some notion of what was to come.

"The presence of Miss Broffet seems to indicate otherwise," Raenon said. Trey's eyes narrowed a fraction.

"She planned to depart when we arrived in Sel'veren, Lord Raenon. She is here because you invited her to stay." Raenon's eyes sparked in delight.

"Yes, we've found her presence enlightening." Faris stiffened across the table, and Trey looked between the faces around the table, grasping for any insight.

"Miss Broffet has kept to herself for the most part from what I've noticed, father." Aella's forehead wrinkled with confusion as she spoke.

"It's always enlightening to have a guest from the Water Realm." Raenon inclined his head toward Faris, who blanched. Trey glanced at the water wielder sharply.

"Lord Raenon, respectfully, I don't know what I've—"

"Were you planning to share with everyone that we were hosting Lord Alvar's daughter in our midst in addition to yourself?" Faris's face went paler than Tryamon would have thought possible, and something sour pitched in his stomach. *They know.* Aella stiffened.

"Nissa Chantara is here?" Aella asked. Liana's eyes sparkled as she leaned forward.

"What an honor to have a Chantara visiting another realm. You know how they keep to themselves." She flashed a grin in Faris's direction, and the colors in his face mottled into an ugly flush.

"Yes, our visitor has been masquerading in our midst." Raenon clicked his tongue. "It's a shame; we could have given her a proper welcome." He shrugged, his silver eyes snapping with cold fire. Tryamon's heart lurched. *They* know. Raenon motioned toward Liana's companion again as he fixed an attentive smile on his face. "Master Kairon, if you'd be kind enough to continue." Kairon's somber expression did not falter as he surveyed the group once more.

"Witnesses," he began, "you have been gathered here to form a quorum of the Realms and witness a sacred rite. I, Kairon of the Midlands, will serve as Agent in this matter." He paused to clear his throat as his eyes swept across their faces, freezing Tryamon's veins when they came to a rest on him. What rite? Faris's hands curled into fists where they rested on the table, and Trey snapped his head to stare at the guard. "Representatives, please rise." Liana bounced to her feet as Raenon rose more slowly, gazing at each of them in turn with a dignified tilt of his head. Vulred joined them a moment later. Faris remained stubbornly in his seat.

"Captain Broffet, you are serving as the representative from your realm in this matter." Raenon's voice boomed. Faris met his eyes evenly.

"I will not. I can't condone this, and I'm certain that my governing lord would not wish for me to represent him in this without his knowledge." Raenon's eyes narrowed as he considered the guard, and they stared at each other, eye to eye, for several minutes before he spoke again.

"Lord Alvar was made aware of the developments. He supports us in this." Panic shocked through Trey's core, shattering the ice that froze him in place. Nissa's father knew that she was in Sel'veren? How much had they told him?

"I'm supposed to take your word for it?" Faris raised an eyebrow as he set his jaw. Raenon's eyes flashed, and the water wielder inclined his head toward Aella. "Respectfully, of course."

"I suppose the alternative is informing the governing lord of his daughter's timely arrival in our home." Trey held his breath as he looked between the two. Torment battled against his control as he waited for Faris's response. "I wonder who he'd send to retrieve her?" Raenon said wickedly. The space between Faris's eyebrows creased as he fixed his gaze on Aella. Placing his palms on the table, he rose. Raenon smiled. "Much better." He waved a hand, motioning for Kairon to continue.

"The Blood Oath is the most ancient of pacts in our fair land, set out by the first of our ancestors to strengthen the bonds between the deserving. You have been gathered here to serve as witnesses in this matter as we bind Aella of House Makani to Tryamon of House Brandell." Kairon lifted his chin. "The binding of their blood will be our strength."

"The binding of their blood will be our strength," Liana, Raenon, and Faris echoed the man in unison.

"Will those to be bloodsworn please rise?" Trey sat stoically as Aella stood, shaking slightly as her eyes flickered between him and her father.

"I'm not swearing anything for you," he spat at Raenon. Amusement danced across the Air Lord's face, baiting his temper.

"Take care not to insult my daughter, Lord Tryamon. You would not find a more worthy partner in this." Trey's face tightened as every muscle in his body stiffened.

"I will not have this sprung on me, and I refuse to swear an oath I know nothing about," he said. Raenon's eyebrows lifted at the challenge, but he simply turned to the Oath's Agent again.

"By all means, Master Kairon, please enlighten the Prince of Flames." Kairon inclined his head, the strands of his hair sweeping across his brow.

"The Oath binds your magic with Lady Aella's. By binding yourself to her with blood, your fire will also be bound to her air. The Oath ensures that each of you strengthens yourselves individually, even as you prepare to come together as one through the bonds of your marriage." One of Tryamon's eyes twitched as he rounded on Vulred.

"Surely you wouldn't support me binding myself to someone from another realm without consulting Lady Aithne, Vulred." The man sneered.

"You know as well as I do that I am here at your mother's behest." Trey's hand fisted; he wanted nothing more than to wipe the smug look off of the man's face.

"And if I refuse?" Trey turned his back on his mother's witness and leveled a stare at Raenon. The man's eyes glittered ruthlessly.

"Then I suppose we'd have to hold Lady Nissa responsible for the inconvenience." Trey's mouth ran dry as a throbbing sensation pounded in his temple. "Of course," Raenon went on with a widening smile, "I might be willing to overlook the insult if matters proceed tonight." Tryamon glanced wildly around the table for any flicker of support, at the impassive face of the Oath's agent, the fluttering nervousness of Liana, the downcast discomfort of Aella's face. Only Faris seemed to feel his outrage; his face was flushed again with barely-concealed anger. They were caught, trapped and outmaneuvered by Lord Raenon, and to refuse him now would mean that every experience he had shared with Nissa, from accosting her at their border to escorting her to Sel'veren for her safety, would have rendered her escape from Danuil useless. He was backed into a corner, and as Raenon lifted his eyebrows, Trey knew that the Air Lord knew it. There was no bluff to call; Raenon's ruthlessness was nearly unrivaled in Galarmos, second to only Trey's own mother, and he knew that a refusal meant that Nissa would die. *Or worse; there's always worse.* His blood chilled despite his anger.

"Alright," Tryamon said hoarsely. Faris jerked his eyes up to stare at him, and Trey nodded at him stiffly. "I'll do it." There was an unspoken promise in the words, and Faris's eyes flickered in recognition of their shared interest before Trey turned to meet the governing lord's gaze again.

"Then rise." Raenon ordered coldly before turning to Kairon. "Proceed, Master." Kairon glanced between Aella and Trey for one uncertain moment before turning toward each witness in turn. After receiving a final nod from Liana, who now rested her hands daintily on her lap, he cleared his throat again.

"If those to be bloodsworn will please rise." He said again. Trey felt detached from his legs as they pushed him to stand, and a moment later, Aella rose to join him, her eyes still fixed on the table in front of them. Kairon looked at each of them in turn as he swept his arms apart, tilting his chin up so that his face turned toward the ceiling as his eyes closed. He opened his mouth, and unfamiliar words poured from his lips, spoken in some long-dead language that Trey could not decipher or recognize. A breath of wind swept the room, stuttering the candle flame as the lights dimmed and then surged to engulf the tips of their tapers. Goosebumps erupted on Trey's arms, and as he cast a glance around the table once more, he saw that the others looked similarly unsettled. Faris had gone ashen. Only Liana seemed unphased, still arranged daintily in her seat. He wondered briefly if—between her travels and those of her mother—she had seen it before.

"You may step together." Kairon spoke, his voice a rasp, and when Trey's eyes jumped to his face once more, he saw that the man's pupils had all but vanished into the blue irises that now gleamed silvery-white. Tryamon glanced uncertainly at Aella, whose forehead had crinkled in worry, but the woman did not hesitate as she stepped back from her table and took several paces to join him. He stepped from behind his chair carefully, resisting the urge to rub the prickle of goosebumps from his arms. He cast a glance to the side at Kairon, who stared at them sightlessly, and he motioned for them to step together and take each other's hands.

Aella's hands were icy against his own, and the smooth skin of her palms felt too soft against the calluses of his own. He met her eyes evenly, and the normally-clear silver was fogged with fear. He squeezed her fingers slightly in a way that he hoped was reassuring. Neither of them were alone. They both flinched as Kairon's voice bellowed those strange, dark-sounding words toward the sky once more, and Trey clenched his teeth against the next wave of air that swept the room. He fought to keep his eyes on Aella as the world around him seemed to tilt and spin, and he barely felt it when someone—shrouded in shadow—lifted one of his hands and placed it palm-up in her hands, doing the same to her hand on the other side. Muted and swirling around them, a chant began, and still, the only thing sharp in his vision was Aella's face, unusually pale behind her frightened silver gaze.

"Saenguis klamant, Saenguis klamant..." Trey didn't know who was speaking or where the voices had originated as his pulse raced to a sprint and his heart began to pound. A knife flashed like harsh, white moonlight, rippling with some strange material that he didn't recognize. He fought to free his feet, to open his mouth into a scream as the strange metal glimmered closer and closer, but he could not move. He was forced to watch in horror as the metal drew across his palm, splitting the skin cleanly as the chanting continued.

"Saenguis klamant, dülyo énum. Saenguis klamant, dülyo énum." The knife speared across their hands, where the hilt was grasped by another dark form. Blood spurted across Aella's smooth skin as her palm was opened with a wound to match his. Still, they did not move. The chanting increased in tempo and volume as his heart thundered to match it. Rough hands grasped the hand that lay beneath Aella's upturned palm, and he watched in horror as his upward-facing hand was lifted by a force that did the same to hers. An explosion of agony wrenched through his body as the wounds were slapped together, their fingers manhandled as they were crushed and intertwined, and still, Tryamon could not move. His mind screamed with an unescaped scream of agony as it rang through him again and again, ebbing and flowing in a way that the chant around him seemed to rise and fall with it. A rough voice clawed against his skull, raking down the bone like sharpened talons.

"Say the words, Tryamon. Say the words." He fought to howl that he couldn't speak, he couldn't move, before he felt his lips part and move in time with Aella's own. Her eyes widened slightly, the only sign that she, too, was not in control of her own body.

"Maeum dülum." They repeated the words thrice, and with each repetition, a new wave coerced through his body, spearing through the wounds that fixed their palms together. Then, as suddenly as the ceremony had begun, the sensation of being frozen in place vanished, leaving both Tryamon and Aella quaking where they stood as the room around them faded to light and the candle flames settled on their pillars once more. The waves of pain shook through him, burning with fire and ice and stone and wind as they rippled through his body, and he lurched away from Aella desperately, praying that the removal of their hands would stop this, this—whatever this was. It was a fool's dream. He stumbled against the table, and a glancing blow against his hip sent a different kind of pain rocking through him, so different from the kind that was ransacking him beneath his skin. His breath quickened as desperation and panic warred for purchase in his chest. He couldn't stop the pain. There was nothing he could do. *Get out. Get out!* Something instinctive demanded that he flee somewhere, anywhere safe.

He stumbled sightlessly from the room, barely aware of the alarmed cries around as the pressure in his skull flooded the edges of his vision with a tempting, rippling blackness. Still, nobody stopped him as he fell to his knees in the hallway, sending a new kind of agony cracking through his legs. He pushed himself to stand again as he staggered up the hall, glancing off of objects and leaning heavily on the walls when a new wave of rippling pain threatened to collapse his body in on itself. He fought with ragged breaths, each one broken between dry sobs as he followed some unknown sense, and when his legs finally failed him, he crawled.

44

———

The uneven tempo of a knock at her door jolted Nissa from her sleep that evening. She yanked the covers to the throat, covering the thin shift as she got her bearings. The room was silent except for the sound of her ragged breathing, and she wondered if she had imagined it before the knock sounded again, this time punctuated with a groan. She leaped to her feet and dashed to the door. Something in the back of her mind told her that she should slow down; nothing good would bring anyone knocking on her door in the dead of night. The reckless side of her won out as she seized the handle and yanked inward.

Tryamon was swaying on his feet in front of the open door, his face startlingly pale as the lack of color threw freckles she'd never noticed before into startling relief. She stepped to catch him around his ribs as he lurched sideways dangerously, grunting under his weight as she half-dragged him into the room.

"What happened?" she managed, rasping under the strain. Her answer was another groan. She felt a wetness leech into the fabric of her nightgown as she hauled him across the room and set him in the nearest chair. As she hurried to shut the door, she glanced down, and her heart pitched. It was blood.

She rushed back and fell to her knees, scanning Trey's body as she checked the black-and-gold fabric for any deeper circle of color that would tell her where the blood had come from. Finding none, she cursed. How had she ever believed him when he'd said they would be safe in Sel'veren? Her eyes dropped to his slightly-curved hand as something dripped from it. Nissa grasped his arm around the wrist gently and turned so that his palm faced upward, and he flinched. Her eyes flew wide with shock as she hissed in a breath.

An angry slice split the skin on his palm, the flesh around it pink and gaping up at her. Blood oozed from the wound, pooling in the lines of his hand, and she searched frantically for anything to help staunch the flow of bleeding. Finding nothing within reach, she set his hand across his lap and tugged at the hem of her nightgown, grimacing at the sound of the shredding fabric as she pulled a strip from it. Gently, she lifted his hand and wrapped the strip of linen across his palm, winding it as tightly as she dared before securing it. She looked up at his still-pale face again. Something else was wrong; the slice on his palm was deep, but it wasn't something that would incapacitate him.

"Trey," she said softly. His eyes sought hers, the normally clear amber clouded with fatigue and pain. "What happened?" He swallowed heavily, his lips dry and cracked.

"They made me," he whispered hoarsely. The hair on her body stood on end as a chill ripped through her body.

"Made you what?" she asked quietly. "Should I get some-one...? Baloriel or Tanyl?" He shook his head violently, wincing as the movement disturbed the hand that was still resting palm-up on his lap. A horrified suspicion colored the chill in her blood as she stared at the wound on his palm again. It was something she had only heard about back home, and she had never seen it done in person. She looked up to see him watching her as she put the pieces together.

"I didn't have a choice," he protested weakly, as though reading her face. She recoiled from him, rising quickly as she stalked across the room. She turned again to face him as regret carved lines to frame his mouth.

"Nissa, I didn't have a choice." The words slurred as his body spasmed, and she shoved away her horror as she rushed back to his side and fell to his knees. The magic rippled through him as it wracked his body, sending visible waves of power through his torso and out through his limbs. She grasped his forearm, holding it tightly as she gritted her teeth against the burn of magic she felt beneath her palms.

"You're okay. You'll make it through this; the magic just has to run its course." Her voice echoed in her ears as memories swam to the surface of her mind.

"You'll be expected to take the Oath yourself one day, Lady Nissa. You would do well to pay attention." The exasperated voice of her childhood tutor clanged strangely in her memory as she remembered her lesson, the horror she'd felt as she'd realized what a rite of that magnitude entailed. She'd protested then, just as Trey's body was crying out a protest now, thrashing against the bonds of magic that lashed against each other.

"The Oath is made by blood and then sealed with an Oath of Fealty..." She had shuddered then, already bucking the idea of tying herself to someone in that way, and now, she shuddered as she watched it happen to Trey before her very eyes.

Vine-like tendrils snaked under his usually-tan skin, and he writhed in his chair, sucking in a breath of pain as they wrapped around his limbs, constricting his bones as the magic merged with every part of him. She felt a heat behind her eyes as she rubbed a thumb over his arm.

"It will be alright. I'm here, and it will be over soon. You're okay, and you're not alone. It's all going to be okay." The words spilled from her helpless lips as she watched him tense and spasm. He panted as the twitches receded from his limbs and each breath he took shuddered through him. The space between convulsions lengthened imperceptibly. She rose to her knees and brushed a hand softly across his forehead, where the dark hair had plastered across his face.

"You're not alone; it's almost over," she repeated, ordering her voice to steady as her lips trembled. His eyes fixed on the wall across from him, unblinking as they shone with a feverish sort of light. His skin grew hot to the touch as the final sealing magic burned through him, and he thrashed again as his breathing grew shallow. Nissa clenched her eyes shut as he howled once; every Oath was different, and there was no telling when it would be over for him. She forced them open again and brushed a hand across his forehead again, and a part of him seemed to relax at the touch. She lost track of how long they sat there, with her stroking his hair as the waves under his skin rippled through him, rising and falling in rapid succession before they finally began to slow. When they finally steadied out, the shuddering waves through his body turned to shivering, and the feverish heat beneath her hands receded. His eyes snapped to meet hers, and she felt the heat build behind them again.

"I didn't want to." His voice shook at the admission. "I didn't want to, but I didn't have a choice."

"I know. I know, and it's okay," Nissa soothed, brushing both hands down his face to get the hair out of his eyes. She pressed her thumbs against his temples and massaged lightly, pressing the tension from his body as his shivering became more violent.

"I didn't have a choice," he repeated, his voice a whisper once more. Nissa glanced around as she massaged his temples for a blanket or something to cover him. Her eyes landed on the bed, and she wondered if she should step away to grab a blanket. If her lessons had been correct, and so far they had, he would need to sleep off the last touches of magic and their hangover to let the process lock into his body. She got to her feet and lightened her touch to move away, but before she could, his hands locked on her wrists, holding them in place as his wild eyes found hers again.

"I'm just getting a blanket; you're freezing," she said calmly. The wild light of panic rose in his eyes again.

"Don't go. Please don't go." She stared at him for a moment; she had never seen anyone this vulnerable, this undone, let alone someone like Trey, who had always held himself somewhat apart. She battled with herself for a moment.

"You need to rest," she said softly. The pressure of his fingers only tightened, even as he winced in pain.

"Don't go." It was a plea, and she softened further at the desperation on his face.

"Do you think you can stand up?" she asked gently. His teeth still chattered as he gave a short, violent nod. "Okay," she added, "I'm going to help you up, but you have to let go of my hands." The icy lock of his fingers loosened and then released entirely as he shivered. She ducked under his shoulder and guided him as together, they took a staggering step toward the bed, then another, then another. Nissa barely ducked from under his weight as he crashed against the mattress with a moan, spent from the combined effort of moving and the toll of magic on his body. She put her hands on her hips as she looked critically at his booted feet. With a sigh, she bent down to untie the laces and pull them off. The second boot was bound more tightly to his leg, and she had to pull hard to get it to budge. When it finally parted with his foot, she fell onto her backside with a grunt.

"Don't ever say I never did anything for you," she muttered softly, and his answering groan sent a flash of remorse through her. With another sigh, Nissa lifted his legs again and pulled them around to rest on the bed before surveying her handiwork. A quilt was folded at the foot of the bed, and she pulled it out from under his legs, fluffing it once before she placed it over his still-shivering body. *It's not much, but it'll have to do.*

She glanced toward the armchair Trey had just vacated. There was a flush of heat in her face from the effort of moving him, but she knew that in just her nightgown, it wouldn't take long for the cold to return to her. She glanced toward where her clothes were laid out in preparation for the next day and then back to the other side of the bed. Trey's breathing had relaxed, but he was watching her again. *Don't go.* His expression said the words that his mouth was too exhausted to form now. She sighed again, glancing at the door.

"I'll be right back," she said, striding over toward the door. She flinched at the grating noise that scraped across the floor as she dragged a chair with her. She tilted it onto its back legs, tucking it up underneath the door handle. She dusted her hands off as she stepped back. It wouldn't withstand anyone who *really* wanted to get into the room, but it would have to do. She made her way back toward the bed and crawled onto the other side of the mattress beside Trey's tense form, burrowing down into the layers of the blankets she had left with a shiver of her own. She lifted a hand on instinct and brushed it down his hair, and his eyes closed against her touch. His breathing hitched and smoothed in expanding intervals as his eyes shuttered closed, and she continued stroking long after his breathing had deepened into sleep.

45

When Nissa woke again, sunlight was streaming through the window of her room, and she was curled tightly against a warm body. Her lips parted in a small smile as she snuggled more closely against the figure and her eyes fluttered closed again. They snapped open a moment later as the memories of the night came flooding back. She shot up, the blanket pooling at her waist as she turned to survey Tryamon, who still slumbered peacefully beside her, the lines of strain from the previous evening smoothed in sleep.

There was no doubt in her mind as to what had transpired. He had taken the Blood Oath. She hadn't warned him in time, and he had taken the Blood Oath. Her stomach pitched as she scanned his face, searching for any residual damage that the oath might have left on him. His flesh was unmarked, aside from the shining scar that was already forming where he had cut his palm. It was already healing as the Oath sealed within his body. *Magic.* She spat the thought like a curse. Their abilities were a gift, but the corruption of that force... She shook her head in disgust. Aside from the scar that remained on his palm and the slight bags that had formed under his eyes, Trey looked more or less the same. She breathed a sigh of relief as she sat back against the pillows.

He'd said he didn't have a choice. The memory made her stiffen again. What had they done to him so that he felt that he had to do something as drastic as the Oath? Another thought made her freeze. *This is what Faris was keeping from you.* She barely repressed a hiss of rage as she stared down at Tryamon again. The Blood Oath was a Water Realm tradition. Faris, as an emissary of her father, would have known exactly what it was and what it entailed. Her blood ran cold as she considered an alternative; perhaps he had been the one to put the thought in Lord Raenon's mind. She curled her lip in a soundless snarl. Surely he wouldn't be that *stupid.*

Trey stirred in the bed beside her, and Nissa froze, scanning him anxiously for any sign of ongoing pain. The memory of his renewed tremors throughout the night, punctuated by sickening moans as he pleaded for a reprieve, turned her stomach, and she forced herself to focus on the clear, unburdened expression that now occupied his sleeping face. His eyelids fluttered, and she scooted a half-inch toward the edge of the bed, suddenly self-conscious as she pulled the blanket up further into her lap again. How much would he remember? How much would be hazy from the pain of the Oath meshing with his magic?

Trey's eyes fluttered open, and his lips curved with a small smile of his own as they found her face. The expression dropped an instant later as he took in her state of relative undress and the bed on which they were laying. He scrambled into a sitting position, shooting to the far side of the mattress as his hair floated around him, staticky from rubbing against the pillow through the night. He winced with the motion, flexing his arms and legs in turn to gage the soreness. Nissa gave what she hoped was a reassuring smile.

"How are you feeling?" she asked cautiously, her face heating slightly as he stared at her nightgown again.

"What—" he began as a flush crept into his cheeks. It did nothing to ease the heat in her own as it spread traitorously through her body.

"Nothing happened. I mean, you showed up here, and then you got really cold, and I just thought you'd be more comfortable over here," she babbled hurriedly. He glanced over at his boots, neatly side-by-side at the foot of the bed.

"I feel like shit."

"I would expect you would, after taking the Blood Oath," she ventured. His head snapped up so that he stared hard at her again, eyes round and bright with horror.

"How do you—" She waved a hand to silence him.

"I'm a Chantara, Tryamon," she said sourly. "I know all about the Blood Oath." He studied her appraisingly, a nervous flicker crossing his face before it disappeared into his familiar mask.

"I didn't—"

"I know, you didn't want to. I can't imagine why anyone ever would." She let out a humorless laugh and then quieted when he flinched. "What happened last night? You said that you didn't have a choice." Something like longing flashed in his eyes before it disappeared to join the nervousness that had come before it. Trey looked away darkly.

"I can't tell you," he said, his voice suddenly cold.

"You came to my room in the middle of the night while you were having an absolute fit from all of the magic you just dumped into your body. I think I've earned the right to know why," she snapped. He flinched, but his jaw set stubbornly.

"I can't." He looked up and met Nissa's eyes, and sorrow swelled there, reminding her of the naked vulnerability of his terror throughout the night. "I wish I could, Nissa, but I just can't." She narrowed her eyes at him before swinging her feet off the bed and rising to her feet.

"Do you know what the Blood Oath is?" she asked quietly. She listened with her back turned as his breath caught.

"Yes. They explained it to me. But this doesn't change who I am, Nissa. I'll still be me. I'm still—" She rounded on him, furious.

"It sounds like they didn't explain it, then. This changes *everything*, Trey. The oath is woven into the fabric of who you are now; it's bound through your magic. To defy it is to lose your power forever. Did they explain *that*?" she spat. Something flashed in Tryamon's eyes, too quick for her to identify it, before he took a deep breath and fixed her with a steadying look.

"I can't wield fire, Nissa. They can't control what I don't have." Her heartbeat thundered in her ears, and for the first time, she was at a loss for words.

"You—*what*?"

"I can't wield fire. That's why my parents orchestrated this whole arrangement." He waved a hand. "They thought that what my abilities needed, what my future offspring needed, was a little more air to fan the flame," he spat the words with obvious disgust, and Nissa flinched. She thought back to all of the times they had traveled together, the nights that they had spent in front of a fire. It dawned on her that she had never seen him spark one. It had always been built while she was away, or someone else had breathed it into existence once Baloriel and Tanyl had joined them. *No powers. No wielding.* She sat down hard on the edge of the bed. For a Brandell, that was likely to be a nearly disinheritable offense.

"I-I didn't know."

"Most don't." He looked away. "They can't manipulate me with powers that I don't have."

"Did they know?" she asked. There was no need for him to ask who "they" were.

"Not at first. I don't know what my mother will tell them now." He took a deep breath, meeting her eyes again. Nissa was reeling. What had the magic bound to?

"How did you become blood-sworn without wielding?" she asked. "I saw it bind to something." She narrowed her eyes at him, and he looked away.

"I don't know," he answered shortly. "All I know is that the whole oath was bound through something that I don't have."

"It can still compel you," Nissa said. Trey frowned.

"I don't see how. I don't feel anything different." His confident smile didn't reach his eyes. Nissa shuddered as she remembered the way he looked writhing in agony mere hours before. There could be no doubting it.

"It's there. Even if it's not bound to fire wielding. It's there." She was certain.

"It doesn't change anything about me. I'm still myself." Nissa closed her eyes for a moment, taking a deep breath before opening them again. She fixed them on his face, her lips trembling with the words she was about to say.

"You're not." Each syllable fell like a blow.

"You don't know that." Trey glared.

"I do. You think my mother just stayed with someone like my father of her own free will? You think she just sat by while he treated her daughter like she was only worth as much as the person who bought her?" Nissa couldn't help it, her voice rose.

"Of course she didn't want that life, Nissa. Nobody would. But if she was too weak or afraid to run—" Nissa leapt to her feet in fury, the edges of her vision reddening.

"You have no idea what you're talking about. It cost *everything* for her to help me leave. She had to fight it every breath she took, and it still almost wasn't enough." Her chest rose and fell with heaving breaths, but Trey met her spark of temper with burning coals of his own.

"The fact that she couldn't hang on to her sense of self doesn't mean that I can't," he spat.

"Did you swear fealty?" Nissa's voice was dangerously quiet.

"What?"

"Did you swear fealty? Or take any vows?" she hissed. He stared at her, and she held her breath while she waited for his response.

"Would it matter if I did?" The words stabbed into her like a physical blow.

"You have no clue what you've just done," she whispered, knees wobbling as she fought the urge to sink to the floor.

"It's not *your* problem," he snarled at her. Her mouth fell open as she looked at him, stunned. How could these eyes, blazing with anger, be the same that were glazed in terror only hours before as he'd begged her not to leave him. Something deep in her chest slammed shut as her blood chilled.

"Get out," she whispered, holding his eyes as her temper pooled beneath her flesh and threatened to spill over. He took a half-step forward.

"Nissa," he began.

"Get *out!*" Her voice rose to a shout. Taken aback by her sudden change in tone, he fumbled for his boots and then staggered toward the door with Nissa on his heels as the first tear of rage threatened to spill. He turned as he stepped over the threshold, eyes brimming with regret as he took her in again.

"Nissa," he tried again.

"Don't worry, Lord Tryamon. I'm not your problem either." Furious with herself, she slammed the door in his still-stunned face. As she turned from it with disgust, the tears fell.

46

———

Several hours had passed when a gentle knock at the door jolted Nissa from her thoughts. Again and again, she had poured over the memory of the previous night, replaying every detail. She hadn't tried to leave the room. Each time the thought entered her head, a constricting, binding sensation twisted around her chest, holding her in place. So she continued to sit in the room, in the gilded cage that had defined her time in Sel'veren. She ignored the knock. What was the point in answering? It would either be Trey, who was woefully ignorant of the consequences of his actions, or it would be Liana, trying to keep her company. Nissa wasn't in the mood for either. The knock sounded again, and she glowered at the door, willing whoever it was to take the hint and leave. Instead, the latch rattled as someone tugged at the knob.

"Come on, Nissa. I know you're in there. Let me in." She blinked at the door. It was Faris. Her eyes narrowed at the realization. What could he possibly want with her? Their last interaction hadn't exactly been friendly. She sighed as the knock sounded again, pushing herself to her feet as she shuffled across the floor. Her fingers wrapped around the handle of the door and tugged lightly, cracking the door, and she let her arm drop as she returned to her chair. The scuff of boots on the ground behind her told Nissa that Faris had followed.

"What do you want?" she asked dryly as she settled herself in her seat and stared at him. Faris's gray eyes were dark, stormy with concern, and he held his hands behind his back.

"I wanted to check on you."

"Why?" He flinched at her question.

"Because I'm your friend." She lifted her eyebrows.

"Are you?"

"I always have been." He pulled his arm from behind his back, a gleaming bottle shining in his hand. "You look like you need a drink." Nissa shot him a look from the corner of her eye as he set the bottle down on the nearest side table—with it, two glasses that he had somehow conjured from his other hand—and settled himself in the seat. She let out an emotionless laugh.

"I suppose you know what happened last night?" she asked pointedly. Faris cleared his throat as he reached for the bottle, uncorking it.

"I think we both need a drink," he amended his earlier statement. A quick, flashing smile leaped to her lips before it disappeared again. Nissa leaned back in her chair, drumming the fingers of one hand on the arm as he poured the wine. She took hers without protest, wrapping her hands around the glass despite the fact that her touch would warm the drink.

"So, do you want to tell me how Lord Raenon found out about the Blood Oath?" Faris choked on the swig of wine, coughing as he inhaled the drink.

"Not from me," he managed between coughs. Nissa rolled her eyes.

"Not from the one other person who's here from the Water Realm?" she asked skeptically. "Not from the person who's been openly hostile to Trey since arriving?" Faris reddened and took another dignified sip of his wine.

"My feelings about Brandell have nothing to do with this," he answered stiffly.

"How very convincing." Nissa took a sip from her own glass, rolling the liquid across her tongue as she savored it. She blinked in surprise at its sweetness; she hadn't expected it to be a port. She lifted her glass in mock salute, and amusement glimmered in Faris's eyes as he lifted his own.

"What are we toasting to?" he asked with a tentative smile.

"To really good wine on a really awful day," she answered with a smile of her own and took another mid-sized sip.

"Did he at least tell you himself?" Faris asked, not meeting her eyes as he posed the question. She glanced sharply at him, but there was no sign of any ill will on his face.

"He came here last night when the magic was binding to him. It was... It was awful." She shuddered, taking another sip. Faris hummed and nodded. She considered her next words for a moment, but considering how much he already seemed to know, she felt there was no harm in asking. "Have you ever seen one done before?" she asked, studying him carefully. He shrugged, taking a swig of his own.

"Once, a long time ago. It's not done often anymore... As you know."

"Which begs the question of how Lord Raenon came to know about it." Nissa tilted her head back to look at the ceiling. "My parents took one."

"I know."

"My mother stopped being her own person because of it."

"She still helped you."

"At a cost." Nissa sat up again, fixing Faris with a hard look. "What will the cost be for Trey? The Fire Realm can't want their heir to be sworn to another realm; it will imbalance their power. What was the goal here?" Faris shrugged again.

"I wish I knew." He took another drink. Nissa studied her glass for a second, tilting it so that the light fell across the rim and played where it was stained with the dark liquid. It was entrancing watching the liquid dance in the glass. She twisted her wrist forward and back, rotating it so that the wine raced along the smooth surface.

"Do you know where they got the idea?" she asked quietly.

"I don't know." The response came so quickly that Nissa's eyes snapped up to meet Faris's, but there was nothing dishonest about the way he was looking at her. She brought the rim of the glass to her mouth again and drank, ignoring the tingling in her nose as she took two gulps before lowering it again.

"You never told me how you earned your promotion—congrats, by the way," she added as an afterthought.

"There was a lot of confusion that night. Your mother—Lady Marin started screaming when you left, and then I was caught having replaced the man who was supposed to be on duty. The former captain accused me of being involved, but Lady Marin stepped in and said that I had been her escort to your rooms. That was what she told Lord Alvar too. It wasn't technically a lie." He looked at Nissa pointedly as he said it.

"Because a lie told to an Oath-bound partner will always be found out, I assume?" she asked half-heartedly. It wasn't something that she remembered from her lessons, but it didn't surprise her either.

"I don't know if it's that or just the way things are between them..." He shrugged as he trailed off. "In any case, your father got it into his head that the old captain was trying to use me as a scapegoat since you and I are friends, and..." He trailed off again, his face dropping as guilt carved tense lines across his forehead.

"I can only imagine," Nissa murmured, absolving him of finishing the thought. The creases of his forehead seemed to swim and dance against his skin, and she had the strangest sensation that she was staring off into space as her eyes locked on them.

"Nissa?" Faris's voice suddenly sounded far away as he said her name and she lifted the glass to her lips again, taking another swig as her gaze passed to the wall behind him. The sharp edges that marked out the stones of the wall seemed to dance too. Her eyes fell to Faris's face again, and his eyes seemed particularly bright, almost blinding as they too locked in place.

"Do you think we'll ever make it out of all of this?" she asked as she lurched, the words slurring together. She glanced down at her wineglass in a confused sort of stupor. This must have been one hell of a brew to have affected her so quickly with so little. When Faris didn't answer, she looked at him again, and his eyes had gone glassy as he stared at her.

"Far-his?" she slurred, swaying wildly in her chair. Her friend seemed frozen in place, silent aside from the sound of his breathing as color rose in his cheeks. Her vision swam and she toppled to the edge of the chair, pain lancing belatedly through her upper arm as it collided with the wooden accent of the chair arm. She fought to straighten up, but her bones seemed to have turned fluid themselves. The wine slid from her grasp as her body slithered to the floor and the edges of her vision went dark. She could barely make out Faris now, still slightly swaying in his chair, but otherwise immobile.

"What did you do?" she tried to ask, but the words were intelligible. She pressed her suddenly swollen-feeling tongue against her teeth as she tried to remember how she had trained it to speak, but then that, too, slid from her mind as the edges of darkness merged together and the world went black.

47

———

Trey arched his back as he stretched in bed, blinking into the sunlight streaming through the glass of his thinly arched window. With a groan, he pushed himself to sit up, taking a deep breath before he tossed the covers back and braced against the cool rush of morning air. Goosebumps erupted on his bare chest, and he scanned the room to find a clean tunic. The events of the previous day came rushing back, and some of the weariness he had tried to sleep off poured back into his joints as he groaned.

After his argument with Nissa, he'd been boxed into meetings with Raenon for the majority of the day to finalize the terms of their alliance. Aella and Liana had claimed his attention in the evening to discuss wedding plans, and by the time he had shaken them off, it had been too late to apologize. Aella, observant as she was, had taken the hint early enough, but Liana... Trey shook his head. She was relentless. With a sigh, he reminded himself not to alienate the Light Realm; they were an important ally to most of the realms. Still, if she started talking about cake toppers again, he thought that he might explode. He recognized a piece of maroon and gold fabric poking out from beneath a pair of pants and he jerked it out, bringing it to his nose to take a sniff. *Clean.* He paused as he lowered the shirt, wondering when he had gotten to the point of sniffing clothes to determine whether or not they were suitable. With a shrug, he discarded the thought and pulled the shirt over his head, lifting his hair from where it was trapped beneath the collar once it settled on his shoulders. Trey tied it back loosely and yanked on his pants before he made for the door. If he could move quickly, he would have time to see to Nissa and make amends before he was expected at breakfast.

Trey winced as the door slammed shut behind him; he had forgotten to muffle the sound. He didn't let himself pause to look back as he hurried up the hallway, nodding unsmilingly to a servant as she pressed against the wall to let him pass. Her eyes were wide, frightened. He lingered on the thought of that for a moment; was there something about him that made her afraid? Then, as quickly as it had come on, the thought vanished, and he had only his destination in mind.

"Lord Tryamon!" Trey stiffened at the sound of Faris Broffet's voice colliding with his back. He considered continuing down the stairs and slipping through a side door, but something in the other man's voice made him pause. He curled his lip against his displeasure before huffing out a breath and spinning to face him. Faris nearly collided with him, reeling backwards to avoid smacking into him.

"What do you want?" he asked coldly, studying the Water Realm captain through narrowed eyes. He hadn't seen Faris since his Blood Oath, and now, it was all that he could do to stem the flood of bile that churned in his stomach.

"Have you seen Nissa?" he asked. Trey narrowed his eyes, confused.

"Not since yesterday morning." He squinted further. "Why?"

"I can't find her," Faris said. Trey huffed out a breath and shook his head, moving to turn away.

"Maybe she's avoiding you. I don't have time for this." He took a step before Faris gripped him on the shoulder and spun him around. "Take your hands off of me," he ordered. Trey's eyes flashed with cold fire as he surveyed the man. Faris dropped his hand and stepped back, nostrils flaring.

"Something's happened to her. She doesn't have a friend in Sel'veren, except for you and me. If neither of us have seen her—"

"And Tanyl and Baloriel. Have you checked in with Liana?" Trey crossed his arms. "Look, I really don't have time for this. If she wants you to find her, then she'll let you. For now—"

"We were drinking," Faris blurted, color rising to his cheeks. Trey's heart dropped a fraction as he fixed Faris with a stare.

"You were drinking?" he prompted slowly. The color in Faris's face deepened as he shifted his weight between his feet, fidgeting with the sleeve of his tunic.

"We were drinking. She was upset after, well..." he trailed off, waving his hand. Trey had the sudden desire to snap it at the wrist as his stomach tightened with dread. He pressed his lips into a tight line as he crossed his arms.

"Yes, she was upset. Out with it," he huffed.

"She was upset about the Oath, and I understand why. Where we're from..." Faris shuddered. "It's a serious thing, and..." He trailed off again, and Trey fisted his hands in his shirt to keep himself from wrapping one of them around Faris's throat and shoving him into the wall. "There was wine. We were drinking, and neither of us had enough to..." Faris took a deep breath. "Look, I knew she was upset, so I brought her a drink. We had a few, and then the room started spinning. I know it must have been for her too, because she fell over." Faris's eyes fixed at a point near Trey's shoulder, as though he was reliving the memory. The dread was shifting, ice-cold, into his chest as the first darts of fear threatened to puncture his heart. He took a deep breath, hoping that his hunch was wrong.

"Were you drugged?" he asked shortly, closing his eyes as he awaited the answer.

"I don't know. I just woke up in her room, and she's gone." Something in Trey ruptured. He turned on his heel and stalked for the stairs, taking them two at a time as he plunged down through the hearthstone of Sel'veren. He was conscious of two things as he made his descent: Faris's footsteps behind him and the roaring of his own pulse in his ears. He gritted his teeth as he fought to leash his rage, his fear.

"Where are you going?" Faris's voice sounded miles away behind him, as he stalked toward the hallway where he knew the guards stayed. He slammed open the third door on the right, and the impact of it hitting the wall shook around him as he stepped over the threshold.

"Trey, what's wrong?" Tanyl was on his feet in an instant, his light eyes wide with worry.

"We're leaving," he snarled, as the waves of rage and fear crashed into each other within him. He took a deep breath to staunch the surge as it threatened to overpower him like a tidal wave. Tanyl's eyes fixed on someone behind him, and Trey repressed a growl of annoyance.

"What happened?" he asked.

"Nissa's gone," Faris said, his voice suddenly clear. Trey rounded on him, and the other man backed up a step.

"You couldn't have led with that?"

"I tried. You didn't have time, remember?" Temper sparked in Faris's eyes as he met the challenge. Tanyl shouldered his way in between them, shoving them apart.

"This isn't helping," he snapped.

"He gave her drugged wine, and when he woke up, she was gone." Every instinct howled within him to tear the house apart, stone by stone to find whoever was responsible.

"I didn't give her drugged wine; I was drugged too," Faris snapped.

"Semantics," Trey said nastily.

"That's enough," Tanyl snarled, fixing both of them with a threatening stare. In a twitch of movement, a dagger appeared in each hand, procured from some hidden place. With a rough sound of frustration, Trey tore himself away and stalked across the room.

"Where's Baloriel?" he demanded.

"Out on a patrol. Raenon wanted him to help plan perimeter security for the wed—" Trey stiffened as another surge of wrath threatened to wash over him, and he closed his eyes to steady himself.

"Don't say it," he warned with a growl.

"He's not here," Tanyl amended.

"I'm coming with you," Faris said. "I'll be your third." Sparks winked at him within the roiling sea of his rage, and Trey took another breath. It wouldn't take much for him to lose control completely. To his surprise, it was Tanyl who protested.

"Not a chance," Tanyl's eyes narrowed as he turned to face Faris, both daggers gleaming. "I haven't forgotten your role in the Blood Oath." Faris fell back a step, looking stricken.

"I didn't know that's why I was here. I was a pawn in that as much as either of you." Trey barked out a noise halfway between a snarl and a mirthless laugh.

"And the drugged wine?" he pointed out. Twin spots of color appeared on his cheeks.

"Drugged me too. My fault, but not my doing." Something in that admission stemmed the next riptide of temper that threatened to drag him away, and Tryamon paused, considering the man again.

"Fine," he snapped. "But you're coming with me to talk to Aella." Tanyl blinked at Trey in surprise.

"Too scared to ask your fiancée for permission by yourself?"

Faris sneered. Tanyl took a threatening step forward, lofting the one of the daggers again. The raging tide within Tryamon froze as he looked down at the other man, whose chest rose and fell with rapid breath.

"This is your mess. You get to help explain why we need to clean it up." He shoved past him, not knowing or caring how close the other two men were behind him.

48

As they neared Aella's chambers, Trey gave the order for Tanyl to get the horses ready. He had lingered only for a moment, glancing distrustfully at Faris, before he followed the command, hunching his shoulders with every step he took away. Faris, to his credit, had no response to the dirty look. In fact, he swallowed nervously as Trey raised a fist and pounded on his fiancée's double doors. The latch between them clicked faintly as they opened inward, and it was only Faris's hand on his upper arm that kept Trey from launching forward and knocking over Aella herself as she answered. He inhaled sharply at a thought. Would Liana be inside already, tittering about invite lists and the political capital of one guest or another? As Aella glanced between Trey and Faris, however, only silence poured from the room. She arched a pale brow delicately over one silver eyes, her dark skin seeming deeper and richer in the shadow of the door. Trey swallowed heavily.

"Good morning," he began. "We were—" He stopped short as she turned and took a step back, beckoning them into the room.

"Come in," she invited before saying lower, "it doesn't do to have sensitive conversations where other ears can hear." Tryamon cast a wary glance around the seemingly empty hallway before stepping wordlessly in to join her. She stepped away as Faris slipped in after him and turned to shut the door, looking him up and down with a suspicious look of her own.

"Why is he here?" Her normally low voice rose with the question as her eyebrows climbed across her forehead, and Trey cast a dismissive glance back at Faris before shaking his head impatiently.

"Consider him our chaperone." He let out a breath. "Look —" She held up a hand, her eyebrows bridging together in question.

"You think we need a chaperone?" she asked incredulously. He blinked at her. Gone was the careful, deliberate voice he had become used to hearing in meetings with her father. He winced as he took a step back from her.

"That's not what I meant, Aella. I just—"

"What *did* you mean? You think you're so charming that you could just knock on my door and I would—" Faris stepped forward as Trey fell back another step with wide eyes.

"Look, with all due respect, that's not why he's here. I'm sure you'll have plenty of time to discuss what you'd do alone in a room together once you're married. For now, we have other things to worry about." He looked sharply between Trey and Aella, whose jaw hung open for a moment before she collected herself. She drew herself up to her full height.

"You dare to—" Faris let out a short laugh, the color high on his cheeks.

"Yes, I dare. I'm going to cut to the chase to save you both the misunderstanding. Lord Tryamon is not here to make any sort of advance on you or discuss your upcoming nuptials. Lord Tryamon, Aella has no interest in sleeping with you right now, so don't flatter yourself by trying. Does that about cover it?"

Their eyes were wide as they stared at Faris, and Trey knew that he should say something to defend himself, to defend his fiancée. He took a deep breath to run interference, but a choking sound from beside him had Trey wheeling around in alarm. Aella had one hand pressed to her abdomen and the other across her mouth as she twitched back in forth, her knees threatening to buckle. Another choking sound escaped her, and he knew that he should—wait! She was laughing? As though his realization had severed the last of her control, Aella buckled forward, rocking with mirth as she glanced between the men with howls.

"No one has ever... spoken to me with... that kind of candor... before..." she said between bursts of mirth. Trey stared at her. Who was this? The Aella he knew was quiet and serious and soft-spoken. This woman, with glee glistening in her eyes, was a stranger.

"Happy to oblige," Faris said with a wry sort of grin. Trey exchanged a glance with him and the grin dropped. When they turned back to Aella, her laughter had faded into concern.

"What is it?" she asked cautiously, eyeing them both. Trey swallowed the lump in his throat as he fumbled for the right words to explain their predicament.

"It's Nissa," Faris chimed in, ignoring the glare that Trey shot him. Tryamon did not miss the way that Aella stiffened at the name.

"Nissa as in the woman you brought here trying to pass off as Elyssa Broffet?" she asked with another raised brow. Trey squinted at her.

"You knew before the Oath?" he asked in disbelief.

"Liana knew. She passed along the information." Aella said with a lift of her chin. "She recognized her from a summit."

"You didn't say anything." Trey's mouth was suddenly dry.

"I assumed you had your reasons. I hope they aren't what

her family is convinced they are." Trey groaned, putting his face in his hands as he rubbed his eyes.

"Does your father really believe all that nonsense, or was he bluffing earlier?" he asked. Aella snorted.

"He would have to pay attention to something beyond his own plans to notice something like that. It was a bluff." Her amusement faded again. "What about Nissa? What happened?"

"She's gone," Trey said.

"Disappeared," Faris clarified. Trey raised an eyebrow at him and the other man stepped back, lifting his hands apologetically.

"And this involves you because..." Aella trailed off. Trey closed his eyes and took a deep breath, forcing himself to steady before he opened his eyes again. It was a gamble, but he would have to trust her.

"It's my fault she's here." Aella's full lips pressed into a skeptical line, and he shook his head. "No, let me finish. She was in a bad situation back home. She left the Water Realm before she even met me. I caught her crossing the Fire Realm border... with Cyril," he paused. Her mouth twisted slightly, but she motioned for him to continue. "We ended up taking her to the Singed Keep. Ward found out she was there, and—well— you've seen or heard how Ward Chantara is, I imagine." She nodded, so he continued, "I couldn't let him drag her back there after hearing how he talked to her, and it was my fault that she wasn't already long gone. So, I helped her escape to Domogién." He raised his eyes to meet Aella's, expecting judgment, but what he found next was understanding.

"Then you brought her to Sel'veren?" she asked pointedly, although not unkindly. He fidgeted slightly as Faris's head swung between them, waiting for him to continue.

"I didn't trust Cyril. There were incidents in Domogién. Close calls. I felt like it wasn't safe for her to stay there once I left, so I offered to bring her to the Air Realm. We were planning to go our separate ways once we reached the city," he offered weakly. Hearing it all laid out like that really made it clear just how much of this mess was his fault. She'd been so close to a new life, and he'd gotten in her way at every turn. It was all he could do to keep from hanging his head in shame. Aella nodded slowly as though the pieces were falling into place.

"And then Elrand Waera met you outside the walls," she finished for him, her mouth twisting into a wry kind of smile.

"I think she's been taken back to the Water Realm." The words escaped Trey, and he could have sworn at himself. There were more diplomatic ways to make his request. Aella's smile faltered.

"You know we can't interfere in another realm's business. Not like that," she said, the space between her brows creasing worriedly.

"They came into your home and took her, Aella. They threatened your hospitality and your father's. What will their actions say about your family's might? About their ability to protect their guests?" He held his breath once the last question slipped out, and her eyes hardened.

"Everyone should know not to question the strength of my house." Her voice dropped dangerously as her eyes narrowed at him.

"More so if they know that you can protect those within your walls." He held her gaze evenly, meeting her challenge as Faris hissed in a warning breath. Aella tilted her head slightly as she beheld him, and Trey felt the first wings of hope flutter in his chest. *She isn't saying no.*

"What do you want from me?" she asked finally.

"We want to go retrieve her." She raised an eyebrow.

"We?" she asked. Trey cleared his throat.

"Tanyl, Faris," he made a face, "and myself." Her mouth twisted slightly as she considered.

"Why you?" she asked, watching him closely. He swallowed heavily as several responses battled to be the one that leaped from his tongue.

"This is my mess. I'm the reason she was found at all, and at the end of the day, I'm the reason she was in Sel'veren. I owe it to her to fix my mistakes." Aella's eyes sharpened.

"You see your interactions with her as a mistake?" she asked, tilting her head again. Beside him, Faris crossed his arms and raised an eyebrow, but he mercifully remained quiet as Tryamon shook his head.

"No. I don't." The admission lifted a weight from him that he hadn't known he was carrying. Of course he didn't regret meeting Nissa. He regretted that it ruined her escape from her realm, but how could he regret meeting her? She was the first one to challenge him, the first one to make him laugh for as long as he could remember. She understood his plight with his engagement better than anyone should. He'd sought her out after he'd taken the Blood Oath because she was the one place that he knew without a doubt that he would be safe. Regret his interactions with her? He could sooner regret each breath he'd taken in the weeks since.

Some measure of what he was feeling must have shown on his face, because in the next moment, the carefully-blank mask Aella always wore had slipped over her face once more, and the only sign of the emotions she had worn was the chill that lingered in her eyes. Faris shifted from one foot to the other as they each awaited her response. Trey resisted the urge to count his breaths; the longer they stood here debating it, the greater the danger to Nissa.

"Alright," she said finally. "I'll make a bargain with you." His heart rose hopefully even as something hardened in the pit of his stomach. He felt his own unreadable mask slip into place as he met Aella's contemplative gaze.

"The terms?" he asked.

"You will go to the Water Realm, and you will release Nissa Chantara if she is, in fact, there. But after," he felt his stomach clench, "you will return to Sel'veren, and you will focus on building the alliance between our realms. No more of these split loyalties. We took an Oath, and you need to honor it." He considered for a moment, his heart flying and falling in equal measure. The terms of her bargain were vague, which left them open to interpretation, but her meaning was clear. There would be no more of putting Nissa's safety before his own responsibilities. Trey swallowed heavily. The terms were fair, given that Aella owed them nothing. He put out his hand.

"We have a bargain," he said clearly. She looked hard at him for a second before placing her slim hand in his. They shook once before he released it. She glanced between Trey and Faris for a moment before turning away, squaring her shoulders.

"Go, and return quickly." A sideways glance at Faris showed the other man staring at Aella's back with a curious expression. Trey shifted; he didn't want to give her a chance to change her mind.

"Thank you, Aella." He inclined his head to her turned back, even though she couldn't see the gesture.

"Don't ask me to do this again," she said, her voice raw with some emotion he couldn't read. He sensed that pushing the issue wouldn't help him, so he backed out of the room, shutting the door gently once Faris joined him.

"What are the odds that Tanyl already has the horses ready?" Faris asked. Trey flashed him an annoyed look.

"Knowing him, he's already scrounged together provisions as well. Let's go; we've wasted enough time," he said shortly. In the back of his mind, doubt lingered. He would help Nissa regain her chance at freedom, but he knew that he would never shake the shadow of the door that was closing on his own.

49

Nissa was rising, floating as she climbed up and up and up. Her stomach pitched as she fell, her heart leaping to her throat before she had the sensation of being caught again. It was as though she had become the very sea-foam that glimmers on the crest of the waves as they set a course for the shoreline.

But wait! She knew that didn't make sense. She was in Sel'veren, and she was closer to the center of Galarmos than she was to any coastline. It had been the wine. Something had been wrong with the wine, and she had fallen, fallen out of her chair and landed on the ground. Her arm still throbbed where she had slammed against the arm of the chair. Where was Faris? Faris had given her the wine, and now he was gone. She couldn't hear him or see him anymore. It was all dark, and she was flying and falling, and climbing and swaying, and...

A jolt cracked her head against a hard surface beneath her, and her eyes split open a hair. It was dark there too, with only streaks of light streaking for her eyes, her eyes that preferred the dark. It hurt, the light hurt, and it should all be dark, and she should be rising and falling again. She clamped her eyes shut, focusing on the steadiness of the movement beneath her. Were those voices? A murmur sounded just within earshot, but she couldn't make out any of the words. Wasn't that funny? Her ears couldn't hear the words just like her tongue hadn't remembered how to speak. Maybe she really was seafoam, rising and falling and climbing and swaying in an endless dance. Maybe that was what she'd really been meant to become.

The movement beneath her ceased, and she was suddenly painfully, achingly still. She wasn't sea-foam. She was Nissa Chantara, and something had been wrong with the wine. The wine had made her not herself, and now she was—. She cracked her eyes open again, gritting her teeth as she made out the hazy shapes around her in the faint light. She was in some sort of wagon. Despite the stillness of the platform beneath her, Nissa's vision swam. Somewhere, a faint, almost unintelligible voice crept forward from the back of her mind to warn her. *You've been drugged.* There was something wrong with the wine, and now she didn't know where she was.

Her nostrils flared as she forced herself to inhale deeply. The air smelled different here, wetter somehow. This wasn't Sel'veren. This wasn't anywhere near the Air Realm's capital city. She ordered her body to rise as terror penetrated the haze still trapping her body in its prone position. She clenched her eyes shut as the platform beneath her jolted again. They— whoever they were—were taking her... somewhere? And what about Faris? He had been drinking the wine too; was he locked somewhere too, unable to move, or speak, or do more than mentally scream? A sudden thought made her blood run cold.

Faris was the captain of Lord Alvar's guard now. He had done something to earn that promotion. He'd said it was because he'd been scapegoated, but what if this was what he had done to earn it? After all, he'd given her the wine. He'd been the one to seek her out and lull her into lowering her guard with their conversation. What if, after all this time, he had decided that their friendship wasn't worth the cost after all.

A rustling noise behind her had Nissa craning her neck, trying with all of her might to turn her head to find the source as more light filtered in from behind her. A grunt punctuated the scuff of boots before the light vanished as quickly as it had entered the wagon.

"She's waking up," a rough voice said, the sound muffled by the material between them. A moment later, the light returned, and a waterskin was placed against her lips. Nissa spluttered and tried to thrash against it as the water filled her mouth and throat. Desperate for air, she lashed out with her powers, trying to divert the water away from her lungs, but the only response was a searing protest from the obsidian she still wore around her throat.

"That's enough," a different voice ordered sharply. "Let her breathe." The waterskin disappeared, leaving Nissa gasping as she fought for air. Her eyes streamed against the onslaught as liquid and air battled for control of her lungs. As the liquid cleared her lungs and her breathing settled, she tried to force her eyes open once more; she needed to get her bearings so that she could make a plan. She couldn't stay here, left to whatever fate these strangers decided for her. If she could just open her eyes—but her lids had grown heavy once more, and in spite of her internal protest, she was again set adrift.

She was floating again, although this time, the rising and falling sensation didn't dissipate as clarity sharpened her senses. The rocking sensation shifted so that she was swaying side to side as her spirit rushed back down to join her body, and the room around her creaked with the motion. Wait, she was in a room. Her eyes opened and took in the foggy shapes of stained beams crossed over her head. A rushing sound accompanied the rocking now. A boat! She was on a boat. Where would she be going on a boat? Thoughts hummed in her head like bees, buzzing just out of reach. She was tired, so tired, and her lids sank down again as she blinked slowly. If she could just rest for a while, then—blackness overtook her vision again as she was plunged into another dreamless sleep.

It was cold when Nissa's eyelids fluttered again. They had moved her again. She was shivering against a chill that she could not fully feel; her extremities felt half-numbed as she fought to shift them against the rocking of another wagon. Someone had thrown a rough blanket haphazardly over her prone body, but the thin fabric did nothing to keep out the bite of the wind that cut through the slats of wood around her. She flexed her fingers and they bent slowly, stiff from either the cold or from disuse; she did not know which. The male voices she had heard over the course of their journey were eerily quiet now; the only sound came from the errant squeaks that came from the wheels of the wagon as they rumbled across the uneven terrain. If she could just sit up, then—but no, she was still too weak, and even her fingers stubbornly refused to move again under her command. Her eyes widened as a mutter reached her from beyond the wagon, and she quickly snapped them shut. If they found out that she was waking again, they would drug her again, and she couldn't afford to be helpless for any longer. *Save your strength,* she ordered herself. The road, wherever they were, smoothed, and the gentle sensation of rocking resumed. Nissa let herself relax into the motion as she drifted again. *Soon,* she told herself. She would gather her strength, and then she would figure out how to escape.

50

She was in a bed. That was the first thing that Nissa realized when she came to again. The mattress beneath her was soft, like she imagined it would feel to lay on a cloud, and the blankets around her swaddled her in warmth as she roused herself from the deep slumber. The soft crackling sound of a fire had her lifting her eyelids, and as she inhaled the smoky scent, she caught sight of the small, cheerful fireplace of pale, gray stone welcoming her from across the room. Her eyes traced the walls of the room as she took in the rock that was only a shade darker, resting on the window to her left. Frosty tendrils crackled against the glass, and she watched, frozen, as powdery flakes floated through the air beyond them. She knew this place; she had been here before. She looked down at the white-and-green covers of her bed and certainty clicked into place. Nissa was in the Frosted Keep. Her heart spiraled in free-fall as she swung her legs over the side of the bed. It stalled in relief as she realized that she was still in her own clothes.

She wheeled around wildly, tensed for a fight as the door behind her thundered open. They wouldn't keep her here; they couldn't. She had fought too hard and for too long to escape this fate for her to—. Her thoughts screeched to a halt as her brother filled the doorway. She fell back a half-step as his harsh mouth twisted into a smile that did nothing to relax her. Above it, his pale blue eyes, so like their younger brother, were hard and cold.

"Welcome home, little sister," he said smoothly. Nissa felt her eyes grow wide as she took another half-step back.

"You!" she breathed.

"You led us on quite the chase. For a while, I almost thought you'd had us beaten." He stepped closer, and Nissa resisted the urge to shrink back from his approach. His dark blond hair had been cut short, and his cheekbones cut harshly against his face. Despite this, he had grown considerably broader since she had last seen him. She had no chance of beating him in a hand to hand fight, especially not with her so weak from—how many days had it been since she was in Sel'veren?

"How long?" The words slipped out before she could stop them.

"Not as long as I'm sure you're thinking. Once we cut north, and once we hit the river in the Midlands, we covered a lot of distance quickly," he answered, brushing his eyes across her once. Her stomach clenched, painfully hollow.

"How long?" she repeated with a whisper.

"A little over a week." Nissa reeled backward. That didn't make sense; a week without food? How was she standing so comfortably? Her hands dropped to her torso. She had grown thinner, but not as much as she would have expected. She lifted her eyes to her brother's face, now wearing an amused expression. The amusement did nothing to relax her in his presence.

"You ate plenty on the trip. Don't you remember?" Thinly veiled mockery lifted his voice as his eyes slanted knowingly. She furrowed her brow. Had they fed her while she was drugged? They must have; she only remembered sleeping. Her blood ran cold and she shuddered at a horrified thought. What else had happened that she didn't remember?

"Nobody touched you," he snapped roughly. "I made sure of that." She narrowed her eyes at him, curling her lip.

"How considerate of you," she said with the hint of a snarl. "Where's Faris?" Nissa would have given anything to claw the smirk that followed off of Ward's face.

"He's still in Sel'veren, finishing his job." The words fell like a blow. "Although I'm surprised you care at all, considering where your loyalties currently lie." Ward's voice grew dangerously soft, and Nissa knew she was treading on dangerous ground.

"You made a lot of assumptions. It must be hard to be so mistaken." Ward's responding slap sent her head reeling backward, and she fell back a step to avoid hitting the ground completely. Eyes blazing, she stared at her brother, loathing snapping in them.

"You should learn to watch your mouth." Ward examined his palm, and as he stretched his fingers out, the sting in her cheek throbbed.

"Such a temper," she said in a low, seething voice. "You'd better learn to control it if you don't want to make enemies of the other realms." He jerked his arm as though to strike at her again, and she flinched in spite of herself. Ward's low laugh set her teeth on edge as rage and self-loathing battled for purchase in her chest.

"Starting with your precious Tryamon, I presume?" he mocked.

"He's my friend Ward, no matter what your filthy mind has tried to convince you."

"I'll let you work out explaining it all to your fiancé. I've already seen enough to make up my mind." Her vision blurred as her brother laughed again. He hadn't always been this way, hadn't always been so cruel. It was like he had just woken up one day and snapped.

"What happened to you?" she demanded, regretting the words instantly as her brother went very, very still. He stalked toward her and grabbed her face with a claw-like grip, ripping her toward him as her hands scrabbled uselessly against his arm.

"Never question me," he said in a low snarl. Fear replaced the blood in her veins as he fixed her with a stare of dominance that lasted several, painstaking heartbeats before he flung her away. To her dismay, her knees buckled from the sudden shift in weight, and she hit the ground with a thud, barely catching herself on stinging palms. She stared hard at the floor beneath her hands for a moment before daring to look up again. Ward had turned his back on her and was already striding toward the door without a backward glance. She reached one hand up to grip the cord that held her obsidian pendant. She could rip it off of her neck so easily. Ward's back was turning, and if she could wield again, she could—

The door slammed behind him; she had missed her chance. She sighed as she pushed herself to her knees, shaking her palms before brushing the fingers of one hand against the welt rising on her cheek. It was probably for the best; the last thing she needed was to exhaust her magic while she was still so weak. If she could bide her time, if she could gain her strength, then maybe she would have a fighting chance. She got to her feet, feeling eerily light as she swayed with the motion. It was as if her body had become something other than her own during their journey, as though whatever drug they had used on her had detached it from her spirit. She traced her fingers across the ribs of her torso, half-wanting to reassure herself that she could still feel anything at all. The numbness, the sense of detachment, it was more frightening to Nissa than her brother had ever been.

She sat hard on the mattress, which bounced her for a second before she settled into the seat, facing the window. The vines of frost had bloomed with buds that she hadn't noticed before, and despite the warmth of the room, it showed no sign of melting against the glass. The Frosted Keep had gotten its name for a reason, and while it had its own sort of beauty, she had no interest in calling it home now or ever. She glanced at the promise of comfort that rested in the fold of blankets that she had vacated, but her skin crawled as she remembered that she was still wearing her clothes from Sel'veren. She hadn't bathed in over a week, if what Ward had said was true, and the idea of slumbering in her own filth rendered the bed suddenly unappealing. With a sigh, she glanced toward the small wash basin that stood in one corner of the room. At the very least, she could wash her face. It was better than nothing. She rose and made her way over to it, touching the pendant at her throat again as thoughts of Trey crossed her mind.

She had been taken from the House of Makani, drugged and forced to travel against her will and largely without her knowledge. Was he safe? Had he been hurt on her account? She brushed the pad of one finger against one of the sharp facets of the stone. There was an easy way for her to find out. All she had to do was slip it off and stare into the pool. Surely, she could spare enough of her energy to make sure that he was still safe. Her hair tickled the back of her neck as it clung to her skin, peeling away as she removed the necklace. Nissa set it aside, flexing her fingers experimentally before she stepped closer toward the pool. If she could just access the energy—the door thundered open, derailing her train of thought, and she glanced up, startled, to see the lean figure of her cousin step through the door.

51

Torian hadn't changed much in the several years since she'd last seen him. His hair was still his trademark white-blond, which Nissa had always thought deepened his pensive eyes. Now, they were underlined in shadow, as though they held all the secrets of the universe but none of them were pleasant. He had a smaller frame than Ward did, but what he lacked in height was made up of lean, wiry muscle. The points of his ears had sharpened further in the years since their last meeting, a further testament to the powerful line that Alvar hoped to join with his own. Despite the shadows beneath his eyes, her cousin had grown into a handsome man. He twisted a band around the thumb of one long-fingered hand as he surveyed Nissa wordlessly. The rich brown of the ring seemed at odds with his green-stitched white tunic, and she fixed her eyes on it as he turned it again and again.

"Nissa," he greeted finally, his voice clear and crisp. She blinked at him; his voice always took her by surprise. She always expected him to speak more timidly than he did.

"Torian," she mimicked, tilting her head slightly to one side.

He took her acknowledgment as an invitation to step further into the room.

"I'm pleased you made it safely." He twisted the ring on his thumb again as his eyes bored into her face.

"I don't know that I would call being drugged and unconscious for the majority of the trip 'safe,' personally." She raised her eyebrows. Torian's thin lips tightened imperceptibly, and despite her dire circumstances, she felt a prickle of satisfaction run down her spine.

"I regret that it was deemed necessary," he said shortly. "Ward felt—"

"Ward feeling anything would require him to have a heart or a soul," Nissa cut across him. She narrowed her eyes dangerously, and Torian swallowed.

"I regret that it was deemed necessary," he repeated. Nissa looked skyward and huffed an exasperated sigh.

"What do you want?" she asked, not bothering to mask her annoyance.

"I wondered what you were up to." Nissa bristled.

"*Up to?*" Torian sighed.

"We *are* betrothed; it's natural to be curious about each other." She curled her lip in disgust, looking away.

"I don't want to know *anything* about you." He blinked, studying her with those calm, dark eyes, as though he had expected that to be her response.

"I'm not your enemy, Nissa."

"No, just your father's puppet," she sneered. He flinched, then, his eyes dropping to the floor, and she felt another prickle of satisfaction at landing the blow. His shoulders shook slightly as he took a deep breath before lifting his eyes to hers again.

"I don't want to fight with you. We are, each of us, a victim of this circumstance; I'm simply trying to make the best of it." Torian's voice was unwavering, and her eyes narrowed further as she considered his words.

"You're content to just let your father decide the course of the rest of your life?" His shoulders rounded, laden with some unspoken burden, and the pale gray of his eyes darkened as they dropped to the floor again.

"A union with my cousin would not have been my first choice," he said slowly, seeming to choose his next words carefully. "But this was the hand that I was dealt, and I am learning to accept that." She laughed, a careless, scornful sound.

"You'll have to excuse the fact that I never will." His eyes rose to her face again, the expression in them brimming with emotion.

"I'm not your enemy, Nissa," he repeated before sighing wearily. "I'll come back to see you again when you're more settled. I just wanted to make sure that you were alright." He inclined his head to her before he turned on his heel and retreated, swinging the door curtly shut behind him. A rough cry of frustration ripped from her chest, and she clawed at the nearest pillow, flinging it harmlessly across the room in rage. Of course she wasn't alright. If this was her life, she would never be alright again. Her eyes flashed, white-hot and burning as she stared at the basin again. Nissa willed herself to take deep, steadying breaths as she forced her wrath down to form a molten core within her. She was physically unharmed. What mattered now was making sure that Trey shared that with her. Her magic would be unpredictable if she didn't get her emotions under control, and ensuring his safety was what was important right now. She closed her eyes as her breaths settled, and when she opened them again, the rage was a glittering kernel in her chest, under control and ready for her to release it when she was ready.

She turned and stepped toward the basin once more, leaning over the pool and fixing her eyes upon her reflection as she focused in on Trey. She pictured his dark hair, plastered against his forehead as he weathered the storm of the Blood

Oath. She saw the way that his amber eyes flashed with inter-twined annoyance and amusement as they trained together in Domogién. She saw the suspicion in his eyes slowly give way to grudging trust and respect as she replayed her memories of him over and over again in her mind. The surface of the water rippled as her reflection fogged. She willed it to clear, to give her something tangible, but the fog remained unmoved. She gritted her teeth as she released the flow of magic, stiffening her spine against the slight drain on her energy. The shining hunk of obsidian beside the basin seemed to wink at her, mocking her frustration. Of course, if he had given that to her for protection, he was probably wearing something himself. Nissa cursed at her own stupidity as she turned from the basin and stalked several steps away. She froze when another thought crossed her mind. *Faris.*

Nissa set her mouth grimly as she turned back to the basin. Part of her—a large part—raged against the idea of scrying him. If what Ward had implied was true and he had remained in Sel'veren to finish an assignment, then there was a good chance that part of his assignment had been included in the chain of events that had led to her capture. It was a potential reality, but that didn't mean she wanted to see it up close. She sighed again as her shoulders slumped forward. Her decision made, she returned to the basin, peering into it once more as she reached for that stream of power that lurked within her.

Faris Broffet. She allowed his face to swim into her mind as she closed her eyes. *Captain of the Chantara guard, and...* Nissa hesitated before she completed the thought. *He's my friend.* The smoky haze coated the layers of the water once more as she tensed into the stream of magic, repeating his name and focusing in on his face as she'd known it through the years until the trembling in the basin ceased. She opened her eyes, and he was there.

Faris's gray eyes were slits as he lurched forward and back

in repetition, his brown hair flying errantly around his face as the landscape blurred around him. He bent forward further, over the neck of a splotched horse, and his mouth moved soundlessly as he spurred his mount to go faster. He was riding, then, but no worse for wear than she was. Nissa wrinkled her brow in concentration; this was telling her nothing about his motives in drugging her. He could have been complicit, or he could have been just as much a victim as she was herself. She sucked in a breath as she urged the vision to push outward, to see more about his surroundings, gritting her teeth as she met resistance. The vision wavered for a second before it froze. Cracks splintered through the surface of the water before the vision shattered, leaving shards of ice in its wake. Nissa grasped the edge of the basin, her breaths ragged as she stared down at what she had done. Where rippling water had rested in the basin, now jagged ice remained. She took two staggering steps backward, staring at her trembling hands in horror. What had she done?

52

___

Despite the fact that Nissa was reeling, she didn't have much time to consider what had happened to the water in the basin. She stared down at her hands again; the trembling in them had stopped. She turned them over to scan her palms, as though expecting to see some new line marking them. They were as unremarkable as ever, the creases unchanged. She steadied her breathing as the shock stuttering her heart calmed. The door to her room slammed against the wall as it swung forward, sending her heart racing again.

"You're wanted at dinner," Ward said roughly in greeting. Nissa clenched her hands into fists to stop their tremors as she slowly met her brother's eyes.

"They're not wanted by *me*." Ward's eyes narrowed, and she met his glare.

"You don't get a say, Nissa, not after your behavior for the past few months. I'll drag you there myself and chain you to the table if I have to." Her glare faltered; she had no doubt that Ward would be true to his word.

"Such theatrics," she muttered, moving toward the door. It was as much of an attitude as she dared. Nissa refused to flinch as she swept past him, although she jumped as he slammed the door behind him.

"You *will* behave yourself at dinner." There was steel in Ward's voice, and she fought the urge to roll her eyes, the memory of his claw-like grip on her face still imprinted on her flesh.

"And who all will I have the pleasure of dining with?" she asked coolly, refusing to look at him.

"Torian and I of course. And Lamaris. Círden too." Nissa resisted the urge to groan. Lamaris was a harmless—if dull—boy, but Círden was miserable company. It was a wonder that his sons had turned out as tolerable as they were; Círden's favorite activity was crowing about his own wealth and might.

"Lovely," she muttered. Ward turned and lurched toward her, and she ducked out of his way. He stepped in front of her, and she backed up until she felt the roughness of the wall press against her spine.

"You will not mess this up tonight. You have no idea the trouble you caused running off with the Brandell heir. If you do anything to jeopardize this union further, I will *personally* see to your punishment. Is that clear?" Nissa felt a chill run up her spine, but she forced herself to stare into Ward's pale, unfeeling eyes. She could read the sincerity of the threat in the set of his mouth, in the coldness of his expression. Nissa forced herself to nod.

"I understand." She felt her mouth move as though she was a puppet; the words felt as though they were being spoken by someone else. Ward smiled coldly, the expression doing nothing to ease her discomfort as he stepped backward. She let out a breath and resisted the urge to shudder with relief.

"Good." He motioned for her to resume their pace as though nothing had happened, and Nissa fell into step beside him once more, numb as she stared down the hallway that seemed dark in spite of the light that flickered from fixtures on the wall. When had Ward become so…?

Nissa could remember a time when Ward had been as carefree as any other young boy. *Well,* she amended, *maybe not* quite *as carefree.* He had always been a little on the serious side. This cruelty, this ruthlessness… She wasn't quite sure when it had started, whether it had happened slowly or all at once, but the man who stood beside her, who met her steps with equal strides of his own, was not the brother he could have been. Nissa knew that he would never divulge the reason why, and she wouldn't ever risk his temper by asking. Still, the question of "why" lingered on.

She stared blankly at the door that rose in front of them, at the twin vases that stood on pedestals on either side as she took in the dark green sprigs that sprouted from them. Ward reached to grasp the handle of the door and pulled it open, and she stepped mechanically over the threshold into the dining hall of the Keep. It reminded her of the one at the Singed Keep, and in her detachment, she wondered briefly if one of them had been styled after the other. One long table stood in the center of the room, which was dimly lit by flames that gleamed against brass sconces. An elaborately-candled chandelier dangled from a chain from the high ceiling, and as Nissa glanced at the candles, she wondered briefly if she needed to expect it to rain wax. At the table itself sat the three figures that made up the remaining members of the Pallinor family. Torian's dark eyes fixed hard upon the green-and-white ribbon of cloth that split the table. Across from him, she recognized his younger brother. The features that were so angular in Torian were softened in Lamaris, with the exception of the darker circles that underlined his sunken eyes. Her eyes landed on him with a frown; Lamaris was visibly unwell.

"Welcome, Nissa. We are so pleased that you could join us."

Nissa stiffened as the reedy voice of Círden Pallinor grated against her ears. She lifted her eyes to study her future father-in-law as he rose from his seat to greet her. Círden shared Torian's smaller frame and angular features, but his eyes were a pale, muted blue that reminded Nissa of her father. Unlike his sons, Círden moved with a calculated grace that came with age and cunning. Silence lingered as he waited for her response, and out of the corner of her eye, Nissa noticed Torian twisting the ring on his thumb without looking up.

"Thank you for welcoming us to your table, Lord Pallinor." Ward answered on her behalf, his tone thinly masking a threat as he continued, "You'll have to forgive my sister. She's still recovering from her journey." He guided her forward with a hard nudge in the ribs, hidden behind her back, and Nissa fought the urge to wince as her eyes watered. Círden lifted his goblet to take a swig.

"Forgive me, Lord Pallinor," she said reluctantly, her voice as flat as the spirit that had died in her chest. He lowered his glass, swallowing quickly as he waved his other hand.

"Think nothing of it, my dear. Please, sit down. We left an empty chair beside Torian." Like a sleepwalker, Nissa moved to the far side of the table. The walk seemed to take an eternity before she found herself settled beside her cousin, her eyes fixed on the same table runner that had absorbed his attention. It was a lovely thing, really. Conifers of a deep green were stitched against the white fabric, while subtler woodland creatures peered around them, done in a more muted shade. Across from her, Lamaris coughed.

"Was your journey very taxing, cousin?" Lamaris's voice was as high as his fathers, but it was thinner, somehow. Nissa tore her eyes from the embroidery and her gaze soften as she met his eyes. Sincere innocence shone there; he had no part in his father's schemes.

"I must confess I don't remember most of it. It was a bit of a blur," she said softly. She watched from the corner of her eye as Círden's smile faltered, his dark eyes hardening.

"We're thankful you have finally made it home," he said with a warning tone. Nissa blinked. So, Lamaris didn't know the conditions of the arrangement she had with his brother? In another lifetime, Nissa might have found the prospect of a potential ally interesting. Now, she filed the information away the same way she might a report about the weather.

"I am thankful to have arrived safely," she deflected politely. To that, Círden had no reply, and the group ate in silence for several minutes, the only sound the clinking and scraping of silverware on china. Torian's silverware remained untouched, as his fingers continued to work the ring around his thumb.

"And how have you planned to introduce your fiancée to her new home, Torian?" Círden broke the silence. Torian's hands stilled.

"I hadn't given it much thought yet," he replied mildly, raising an eyebrow. Nissa repressed a snort as Círden glowered at his son. Across the table, Ward worked his jaw furiously.

"A poor welcome so far, then. My apologies for my son, Lady Nissa." Círden's eyes flickered between her face and Ward's.

"What do you like to do, Lady Nissa?" Lamaris tried again, leaning forward to capture her attention. One corner of her mouth lifted.

"I like to read," she shrugged. "I enjoy being outside. I like to do many things," she said quietly. Lamaris's eyes brightened.

"We have a library! Torian, you should show her the library." He turned excitedly to Nissa again. "You should see it! The shelves go all the way up to the ceiling and—"

"I'm sure Lady Nissa would rather see it for herself than have it described to her," Torian cut across his brother. She cut her eyes at him sharply.

"I don't mind." She kept her voice mild as she turned to Lamaris again, but the damage was done.

"Well, you'll see it sometime," he mumbled without meeting her eyes. Nissa set her mouth in a firm line as she picked at her food. She didn't look up again.

53

———

"You're needed for a meeting with Lord Pallinor if you're ready, my lady." Nissa blinked at the man, middle-aged and polite as he inclined his head to her. His quiet knock at the door had intrigued her; it was unlike the demanding pound of her brother, who had been the only one to approach her for the past few days. Torian had steered clear of her outside of dinner, and she hadn't seen or heard Lamaris at all. It was a shame; Lamaris had been the bearable one.

"And the nature of this meeting?" she asked cautiously. It didn't really matter; she knew she wouldn't have a choice in attending. To her surprise, he was apologetic as he spoke again.

"I'm not sure, my lady. They didn't say." He inclined his head again. She sighed, turning to glance at her reflection in the mirror. The dress she'd stuffed herself in had wrinkled, but she didn't really care. She glanced back at Círden's messenger.

"Alright, thank you."

"Do you know where to go?" he asked politely. She considered for a moment; she hadn't sat in on any meetings with

Círden during her stay, but Ward had been meeting with him in the same room each time.

"I think so." She turned away again to step into her shoes. "What's your name?" When she turned back toward the door, the messenger was gone. She sighed again. *Typical.*

Her footsteps echoed as she made her way through the halls, and they seemed particularly loud as the floor opened up when she reached the stairwell. She took a deep breath as her eyes scanned upward before she began her climb. The next floor was more brightly lit, highlighting the marbling of the stone walls. A plush green rug stretched across the narrow hall, muffling her footsteps as the soles of her slippers scuffed across it. She paused in front of the now-familiar door, hesitating for only a moment before she raised her hand and knocked.

"You may enter." Círden's high-pitched voice set her teeth on edge. She shoved at the door with her palm, and opened with surprising suddenness. He stood near the window on the far wall; through it, she could see the frost-coated gardens glimmering in the pale sunlight. Ward sat at the ornately carved round table that occupied the large center of the room, gleaming a polished, deep brown. He assessed Nissa with an unreadable expression. Círden managed a thin smile when he turned to face her.

"Ah, Lady Nissa. So good of you to join us." A scuff jerked her attention to her left, and Nissa glanced over in time to see Torian barely catch a decorative vase. He replaced it on the table in the corner sheepishly before meeting her eyes with a surprised scowl. He clearly hadn't anticipated seeing her.

"I'm afraid I wasn't told the purpose of this meeting," she turned back to his father with what she hoped was a pleasantly placid expression. Being invited to a meeting with Lord Pallinor, particularly one that also included Ward and Torian, didn't seem like a good sign of what was to come.

"Yes, a hasty arrangement. You'll forgive the oversight, I'm sure." The slightest edge to his voice told Nissa that there was no room for her to do otherwise. Her heart stuttered in her chest as her palms dampened. Whatever had brought them together couldn't be good for her.

"Of course, Lord Pallinor." She settled herself in the seat furthest from Ward, ignoring the tense lines that sprang up around his eyes when she sat without invitation. The room was silent except for the fire that burned merrily in the hearth that took up the wall to the right of the door. She sat quietly, hands clasped on the table, and barely managed not to flinch when a loud pop sprang from the burning logs. She shifted in her chair as Círden spoke again.

"Your brother and I have been discussing your impending marriage to my son. We believe," he shot a glance at Ward, who nodded in silent agreement, "that it would be the most prudent to move forward with the arrangements as quickly as possible." The fire cracked again as Nissa's eyes flicked toward Torian. The color had drained from his face, leaving him paler than ever.

"Are you sure that's wise?" Torian whispered hoarsely. Nissa narrowed her eyes as she studied him. Clearly, he had been taken off guard as well. Círden's eyes flashed with warning as he turned to his son, and Nissa tensed.

"You'll do as you're told." His voice lowered to a growl, and the effect on his normally reedy tone lifted the hair on the back of Nissa's neck. Inwardly, she was reeling, part of her gripping the bars of her inner cage as she thrashed back and forth, screaming for release. She roared for her freedom, for vengeance on those who fought to keep her in a cage. She leashed the feeling as her lips curved in a smile.

"When did you have in mind?" she asked placidly. She was aware of Ward watching her closely, but she kept her eyes fixed politely on Círden as she cocked her head slightly with the question.

"Within the fortnight." Her lips trembled slightly, and she hoped that she was seated far enough away from Lord Pallinor that he wouldn't notice.

"So soon," she observed. Ward shot her a warning look.

"Lord Ward," her brother flinched at the title, and Nissa repressed a smirk, "and I have agreed that in light of the rumors that have been circling across the realms, sooner would be better." Lord Pallinor answered.

"I see."

"What rumors?" Torian asked, squinting at her. Círden swung his head around to glare at his son.

"My sister, as you recall, did some traveling—" Ward hesitated over the word, "—before she returned to our realm. Once she crossed the border, she was seen in the company of Tryamon Brandell. I believe she even stayed in his Keep." His eyes glittered dangerously in Nissa's direction. That inner part of her reeled at the challenge, boiling in her stomach and demanding to be allowed to speak. She faced her brother and inclined her head slightly in acknowledgement.

"A tragedy when unfounded lies are allowed to roam free," she said lightly. Ward's expression soured.

"Yes, people tend to draw their own conclusions from things they've seen or heard. Of course, those will fade in time," Círden interjected, rubbing his chin. Torian's eyes narrowed at Nissa in question, but she pretended not to notice.

"All the faster once they find out we've followed through on the engagement," Ward added. Nissa's lips twitched against her urge to argue as she kept her eyes downcast.

"A fortnight could be seen as rushing things to cover something up," Torian offered. Nissa snapped her gaze to him and noticed that some of the color had returned to his cheeks.

"There is more danger in waiting." His father's reply left no room for argument. A sudden queasiness in Nissa's stomach twisted and sank, leaden, and she rose to her feet, drawing the attention of the men.

"If you'll excuse me, my lord," she inclined her head to Círden, who wore an expression of mild concern.

"Are you alright?" She tried to ignore the way that suspicion darkened on her brother's face from the edge of her vision as she inclined her head.

"I am. I just—I'm afraid I'm not feeling well," she said softly. Apparently, something in her face convinced him, because in the next moments, his expression softened.

"You are free to go, my dear. Rest. We have many days of planning ahead." He waved one hand, and Nissa turned, slipping from the room and letting the door click shut behind her before she broke into a run down the hall. Her shoes slapped against the floor as her heels slipped inside them, and she stopped only to remove them before she upped her pace. The twisting sensation in her stomach swelled, and bile rose in her throat.

She almost made it to the door of her room when she doubled over, retching as the contents of her stomach hit the back of her throat. Hot tears streamed down Nissa's cheeks as her stomach clenched again and again, seizing as it rejected its contents. She sank to the floor, splattered with her own vomit as she gasped for air and the tears of strain turned into tears of panic. She had two weeks to escape or be bound to this place, this family with no escape. The sobs wracked her body as she hugged her midsection. She had been so close to tasting a free life, and now it was being ripped from her by the roots of her soul. A few hushed movements rustled at the end of the hallway, but she did not have the strength to feel self-conscious, and they had the decency to move on without coming near her.

Nissa wasn't sure how long she sat there, hugging herself and covered in her own bile, but the spots on her dress had gone cold by the time she managed to control her shuddering body. She brushed her fingertips across her cheeks to wipe away the moisture that lingered there, wincing as they brushed the raw tracks that her tears had left behind. She rose shakily and floated like a ghost to her room, leaving the door cracked as she changed out of her dress and donned leggings and a tunic before she collapsed against her mattress and stared blankly at the wall opposite the door. Frosty vines still twirled their designs on the outside of the glass, and she hated them. They were a false promise of growth and of life in this dead place. Still, she lacked the strength or the desire to turn and face the door—she wasn't sure which—and so she laid there, staring blankly at the frost flowers and hating every twinkling facet as the storm within her raged on.

54

Tryamon tried not to stare as Faris wordlessly grabbed the reins of his horse and, along with his own, led them toward the stream. Tanyl caught his eye from where he was setting up his bedroll, a distance from the crackling fire that he had built, and shrugged. Trey sighed; Faris had barely said three words to him on their journey, but there he was, watering the horses. He glanced over in time to see Faris guiding a ringlet of water, bouncing faintly with the motion, into the lip of his canteen before dunking his water-skin to fill it. He blinked; Trey hadn't seen the other man wield before. *A water wielder, then. Not ice.* He had the same type of power that Nissa did. Trey's grip tightened on his bedroll as he pulled it from the horse's saddlebags. He studied the backs of his hands, and the veins that carved paths beneath tanned skin. What would it be like to use that kind of magic with the same natural ease as breathing? He frowned; that wasn't something that he would ever know.

"He's not so bad." Tanyl appeared beside him, surveying their side of the campfire. Trey grunted as he got his bedding straightened out.

"He'll do."

"He's not what I expected. I owe Baloriel some money." Trey glanced up at him sharply, and Tanyl held up his hands sheepishly. "Bal and I had a bet on how much of a pain in the ass he would be once he realized you and Nissa were in Sel'veren together. He won." Trey snorted.

"He doesn't have a *reason* to be an ass. Nissa and I are...," he paused. *Friends? Allies?* Tanyl shot him a knowing look, and Trey scowled. "He doesn't have a reason to have a problem with me. Beyond politics, that is. Even then, I haven't done anything to him." Tanyl's eyebrow crept further up his forehead. Trey knew he was rambling. "We have the same end goal," he muttered to finish. He pressed his hands to his knees as he heaved himself to his feet and stepped toward Faris's saddlebags. If the other man was going to water the horses, the least he could do would be to set up his bedroll. He reached down and tugged on the edge of the roll. As it slid from the pack, a fluttering flash of pale blue and yellow caught his eye. Trey stiffened, shooting a glance in Faris's direction, but the man's back was turned as he stared across the stream to the other side. Trey bent down to pick it up.

He held up the square of pale blue fabric, studying the embroidered yellow thread that swirled across it. He narrowed his eyes curiously. A souvenir, perhaps? They were Air Realm colors, but he hadn't seen the markings before. Trey cast another curious glance in Faris's direction as he hastily stuffed it back in his bag.

"We should be out of the Midlands by morning," Faris said as he approached. He had tied and blanketed the horses while Trey had cooked over the fire. Tanyl had slipped into the trees to ensure that they wouldn't be interrupted in the night.

"Will we make it to the Water Realm border, you think?" Trey asked neutrally. Faris raised a dark eyebrow.

"Tomorrow, you mean, or in general?" Amusement flickered

in his eyes, and Trey pressed his lips together as they threatened to curve upward. Faris snorted at the motion. "If we follow the river upstream, we can probably reach a crossing point tomorrow evening. We'll need to make a decision after that, though. The shortest route will take us to Danuil, but they're not exactly friendly to Fire Realm lords there." Trey considered what his mother had told him about Alvar Chantara and his temper. Aithne Brandell was ruthless; if something gave her pause, then it was likely a force to be reckoned with.

"I can imagine," he said quietly.

"No, you really can't." Trey went still as his eyes flashed toward Faris. The water-wielder was staring hard at the ground, and his face had darkened. Trey debated with himself for a moment before he asked his next question.

"What was it like for her... there?" Faris's eyes rose to meet his, and the hardness of them took Trey aback.

"She didn't tell you?" he said.

"She told me some." Faris stared hard at him again for another moment as though deciding something before he relaxed and leaned back on his hands.

"She and I grew up together. Did she tell you that?" Trey tried to ignore the feeling that flashed in his stomach at Faris's casual question. He swallowed and forced himself to nod.

"She did."

"I've known her for most of her life. My father was..." Faris waved a hand. "Anyway, I joined the junior guard when I was ten to begin training. Lord Alvar takes his house guard very seriously, so the training was done on-site at his home. We saw quite a bit of each other."

"She said you taught her to defend herself," Trey tilted his head, considering Faris as pride flashed in the other man's eyes.

"If you knew her family, you would have too." Trey chose not to mention their sessions in Domogién as he motioned for Faris to continue. "Anyway, if the whispers are to be believed,

Alvar's been obsessed with this idea of gaining power for most of his adult life. My father told me that's how he came to marry Lady Marin—Nissa's mother. She came from a powerful line of wielders in the south, and when he met her, he made his mind up pretty quickly."

"Nissa told me that they took the Blood Oath," he said quietly. Faris nodded, smiling grimly.

"I'm sure you know better than I do how it works." Trey shrugged, looking at the ground between them.

"Not as much as you'd think." Faris blinked at him for a moment before continuing.

"The Blood Oath is an old tradition among Water Wielders. Nobody really knows where it comes from. All that's really known about it is that it binds the blood between two wielders and that it's a two-fold process. The first step involves binding the magic between partners." Faris inclined his head at Trey, and Trey nodded, his mouth twisting to the side in displeasure. Yes, he knew that part all too well.

"And the second?" He had an idea, but Nissa hadn't had the chance to fully explain it to him. For some reason, he thought that Raenon might not have given him the full picture.

"The second involves fealty. It can be sworn platonically, but it's more powerful alongside a romantic connection or another oath."

"Marriage," Trey suggested. Faris nodded slowly.

"Marriage." Trey's eyes darted back and forth as he considered how to pose his next question. "You didn't swear fealty and complete the second step, Tryamon." Trey's eyes snapped to Faris's face as blood rushed through his body.

"But those words I said—"

"They were just a mechanism to bind your magic with the Old Language. You didn't swear fealty. And obviously, you didn't marry Aella." Trey's heart quickened in his chest as thoughts tumbled through his head. He batted them back as he tried to retrace the thread of their conversation.

"So, Alvar and Marin...," he prompted. Faris blinked as though he'd forgotten what had led them to discussing his Oath.

"Oh, yeah. Well, they sealed theirs with marriage. Lord Alvar wields ice, and Lady Marin wields water like me or like Nissa. He thought that if he took the Oath and married someone with complimentary powers..."

"That their children might have both." Trey finished for him. Faris nodded as his lips pressed together tightly. "Shit," he added. Knowing that part already didn't make it any easier to hear.

"Lord Alvar hoped that one of his children might inherit both sets of powers. Ward inherited his ice-wielding, and then Nissa took after her mother, and Lorcan—he's their younger brother—his powers haven't manifested yet, but Nissa and Ward haven't manifested anything out of the ordinary. On the stronger side, sure. But nothing unexpected."

"I can only imagine how that pressure took its toll." He thought to his own mother, of the disgust that marred her face whenever she looked at him, a consequence of coming of age without manifesting the expected fire wielding ability. He had hardened against it quickly; he could only imagine what it might have done to Nissa—or, he considered for the first time, to her elder brother.

"It got to Ward, I think. He wasn't always so..." He waved a hand again. "But it doesn't matter, since he is now. Nissa never let it break her." There was a note of familiar pride in Faris's voice that made Trey prickle uncomfortably.

"She's brave," he said, and Faris glanced at him in surprise before he nodded.

"Very. She played her part well until her father decided to marry her off to Torian Pallinor. He was worried about what would happen when Lorcan's powers manifested, and he didn't want the experiment to end with his direct offspring." Faris's lip curled on the last word, and Trey had to swallow a wave of disgust as he nodded his understanding.

"So she escaped."

"She escaped," Faris echoed, "and found you. And then Ward found her." Trey swallowed hard at the reminder. She wouldn't be in this position if he'd simply let her go when they'd found her on the border. Self-loathing battered against the cavity of his chest.

"I did try to keep her safe. I didn't want this for her," he said quietly. Faris looked him in the face with a violence that set his teeth on edge.

"If I thought you did, you'd be dead already," he snapped before his face fell into lines of bitterness. "If it's anyone's fault, it's mine. I should have known something was up with that wine. I should have felt it. I should have stopped it." For the first time, Trey felt something like grudging respect for Nissa's friend as the man put words to every feeling Trey had experienced since Nissa had gone missing.

"Neither of us could have known." They were quiet for a moment as they both stared into the fire as it crackled and popped. A question burned at Trey's lips as he glanced at the other man curiously. "Did you two ever...?" Faris fixed Trey with a warning expression that told him he'd crossed a line, but Tryamon held his gaze.

"I thought we might, once. But that's not why I was her friend. And it seems like her path has shifted in a different direction." Trey tried not to let himself think too much on what he meant as the fire burned in front of them. They did not speak again.

55

"Lady Nissa," Torian called, hurrying up the hallway toward her. She closed her eyes in annoyance, taking a deep breath before handing her cloak off to the servant she'd been speaking to. She turned away, making to move away from him before he caught her arm.

"What?"

"I've been looking for you," he said, seeming to stumble over the words.

"Come to discuss more lies?" she asked, narrowing her eyes at him. He dropped her arm and stepped back. She fought the urge to grow the space between them with a step of her own.

"I didn't believe them," he defended weakly. She snorted and shook her head.

"No, but you didn't dispute them. If you defend the Frosted Keep as well as you're willing to defend your fiancée, it's a wonder your family still controls it." She felt a prickle of satisfaction from the way that Torian flinched.

"I didn't come to fight with you," he said. She flipped an errant strand of hair over her shoulder as she leveled a gaze at him.

"What do you want?" she asked. He looked hard at the ground, his fingers finding that familiar ring.

"I thought... I thought you might like to see the library. Lamaris was right. If you like to read, it's something that you should see." She blinked at him, caught off guard. He had paid attention to her response? She narrowed her eyes a fraction more, assessing him carefully. Was there an ulterior motive to this? Did he think he'd win her good will by showing her a handful of bookshelves?

She released the tension from her shoulders on a sigh. She was growing bored of flitting between her room and the dining hall. Since she couldn't venture outside, perhaps the library would offer a more enjoyable change of pace.

"That's... thoughtful of you," she answered haltingly, earning a flash of surprise from Torian. She returned the expression with a tight smile.

"Oh. Good." They stared at each other for a moment more. "Would you like to go now?" he asked. She studied him before shrugging her shoulders.

"If you have the time." Maybe the movement would ease the stunted awkwardness of their conversation. They walked in silence for several minutes before Torian spoke again.

"Did you have a very large library in Danuil?" he asked, keeping his voice distant and polite. Nissa resisted the urge to roll her eyes; she hated small talk.

"I can't vouch for the city; we didn't venture there often." *Weren't allowed there often is more like it.* She sighed before she continued. "The one in our home was a decent size, though." It was nothing compared to the library in Domogién. A sudden surge of homesickness crashed over her, leaving her internally reeling. She felt ridiculous; she had only spent a handful of weeks in the city. She chewed on the inside of her cheek, forcing thoughts of Domogién—and the Fire Realm heir— from her mind. Those days were long gone; there was no going back. Seeming to sense her shift in mood, Torian changed the subject.

"What else do you enjoy? Other than reading, that is." She shrugged.

"Art, traveling. I enjoy any number of things." Very few of them would be accessible to her trapped on the island.

"I like to paint," he offered. She flicked her eyes over to him with a slight nod.

"An entertaining hobby, I'm sure." His flinch was so slight that she almost missed it, and she considered the movement.

"Something like that," he muttered. The realization hit her that he had shared something personal with her, and a flash of guilt replaced her preoccupation. She cringed inwardly; she was alienating one of the only potential allies—or at least, men who wouldn't be an outright enemy—in the Keep.

"If you're willing to share, I'd like to see your work sometime. I appreciate paintings," she ventured. A flicker of surprise crossed his face before he met her eyes.

"Sure," he said after a beat. A hesitant smile graced his features, and she returned it with a small one of her own.

Torian lurched to a stop in front of two dark doors. A strange sense of foreboding gripped Nissa as she scanned the dark, wrought-iron design that clung to the door. Was everything in the Frosted Keep meant to feel dead? Torian turned and seemed to read her thoughts, because a wry smile tugged at his lips.

"My grandfather had a flair for the dramatic," he said, gesturing to the door. She wrinkled her brow.

"Surely the Keep is older than that," she said. Torian shrugged and flicked his brows.

"Doesn't mean we don't like to redecorate every generation or so." She blinked at him. He lingered for a moment before reaching past her to open the doors. As they swung open, Nissa's eyes strained in the gloom for any sign that the room had been used in the past decade. Torian stepped in first, and after a moment of hesitation, Nissa followed him, wrinkling her nose at the musty smell of the room.

"When was the last time someone was in here?" Her voice rang in the dank stillness of the room.

"Not sure. I grabbed something to read a few months ago, maybe?" he replied, sounding further away than she expected. She blinked as Torian lit a torch and placed it back in one of the iron sconces on the wall. "It's not much, but it's better than nothing." He gestured around the room, and Nissa's eyes followed the motion. Several shelves occupied the walls, looming over her and studded with dusty volumes. She stepped toward one of the shelves and blew out a breath to clear the layer of dust, coughing slightly as it blew up into her face. She sensed his eyes upon her back, and when she straightened, she took a step back; he was standing closer than she had expected. Alarm flared in her chest, but when she stared hard at his face, there was only curiosity there.

"Why did you bring me here?" she asked. The light in his eyes flickered uncertainly as he glanced around the room.

"You like books, and..." She narrowed her eyes suspiciously.

"Yes, Lamaris had a good idea. But I thought we made it clear that we weren't going to see eye-to-eye. Why waste the energy?" His lips tightened.

"I'm not your enemy, Nissa." She squinted at him. *You keep saying that.* She bit back the words as her expression cooled.

"You've been acting like it. Allies don't kidnap people and try to force them into marriage. That's not even taking into account the Blood Oath you're expecting me to take." Temper replaced the alarm in her chest as her pulse sounded in her ears. Torian's eyes widened as he took a step back, placing a hand on the shelf as he stumbled over his feet.

"None of this was *my* idea," he argued. She unleashed a humorless laugh.

"But going along with it makes you complicit, doesn't it?" The pads of her fingers tingled. "A couple of bookshelves doesn't change that."

"I told you, I'm trying to make the best of it," he scowled at her, stepping back again. His palm brushed across the shelf, leaving a trail of frost in its wake. As though his wielding was a beacon to her magic, the tingling shot up her arms, settling dizzyingly her chest.

"Why are you so complacent?" she asked.

"Why are you so convinced I'm your enemy? We're family!" She tilted her head back as another laugh escaped her.

"You are *not* my family," she snarled. The power simmering beneath her skin flared out in warning.

"Please, Nissa. We don't have to fight." A plea replaced the warning in his eyes.

"You're content to just go along with it? There's not a part of you at all that wants to be your own person, that wants to be more than just what they think you can offer their bloodline?" she demanded.

"Of course I don't want this. I have my own wants and desires, Nissa, whatever you may think. But your brother..." He trailed off on a shudder, and Nissa fell back a half-step.

"What about my brother?" she asked, narrowing her eyes at him again.

"Your father has allowed him to be forceful."

"And your father." She crossed her arms, glaring at her cousin. Alvar's actions had no defense, but if he was going to pretend that Círden wasn't complicit... Torian took a deep breath and rubbed at his temples.

"Nissa," he said wearily. "I'm not *saying* that he's the only one to blame. But there are things at stake. I would rather have Ward on my team than move against him." Her scowl hardened into a glare.

"You think he'll *ever* be on your team?" she asked. Torian's mouth twitched sideways.

"You're his sister, and after our union—" He broke off as laughter, hard and humorless, erupted from her again. The mirth became a cackle, and he took another step backward in alarm. She thought of Pippa, at the way that she had balked at the mere idea of someone connected with him knowing where she was.

"If you think family means anything to my brother, you're more deluded than I thought. The worst things that Ward does are to the people he claims to love." At the sight of his shocked expression, Nissa launched into peals of laughter again, unable to stop herself even as tears streamed down her cheeks. It wasn't funny; none of this was funny, and yet....

She was still laughing when Torian stormed from the room, leaving the door slamming shut behind him.

56

It was the faint sound of sniffling that stopped Nissa in her tracks as passed the unassuming little door that she had previously assumed had been a kind of hall closet. She happened upon it quite by accident; she'd been driven to exploration as a cure for boredom when she'd sat staring at the walls of her room for what felt like hours. This hallway was off one of the main corridors, which was part of why she had deemed it safe and private; perhaps the crier had chosen it for the same reason. The mystery mourner behind the door loosed a shuddering sigh that told Nissa that whoever it was had reached the end of their stint in the closet. She backed away in alarm, eyes wide as she turned wildly between ends of the hallway to determine which escape would be the quickest. Before she could reach a decision, however, the door clicked open, and familiar, red-rimmed eyes met hers defiantly.

"What are you doing here?" Torian asked, his voice ragged. She backed up a half-step.

"I was just wandering. I'm sorry, I didn't mean to—" the words stuttered to a halt as Torian sniffed slightly, and his red-rimmed eyes hardened as the emotion in his face crumbled to dust.

"Well, now you know that I have a heart, whatever you might've thought before." She winced; her words from their last conversation reverberated in her brain. She took a deep breath, preparing herself for sharp words as she spoke again.

"Are you alright?" It felt like a stupid question, given the fact that Torian was just crying in a closet, but as far as Nissa knew, there was no way to approach something like that other than head on.

"Of course, I'm alright. This has been a garden waltz for me, nothing hard about it. I love being the villain in someone else's story, *especially* when it's because of something I can't control." His eyes narrowed, and she nodded. It was essentially the response she had expected.

"You can control it though." She raised an eyebrow at him, refusing to flinch when the resurgence of anger darkened his eyes.

"You have no idea what's at stake for me." His voice ran cold, and Nissa felt the chill of it in her bones. Still, she did not back down as she crossed her arms over her chest and shifted her weight to one hip.

"And whose fault is that?" she asked. His jaw worked furiously as his eyes flashed again. She repressed a self-satisfied smile; she knew he saw her point.

"I don't know why you think you've earned my secrets," Torian muttered crossly. Nissa scowled, rolling her eyes.

"Well, if they're the reason you're going to force me into a life with you, that makes them my business." He gritted his teeth.

"It's not that simple."

"Enlighten me." She lifted her eyebrows. Torian cast his eyes frustratedly around the hall before lunging forward and seizing her outermost arm. She wrenched back against his grip.

"What're you—" Before she could finish the question, he had pulled her into the darkness of the closet and snapped the door shut behind him.

"You're impossible," he hissed in the darkness.

"So I've been told." She felt her lips curve in a wry smile as she recalled Trey saying almost the exact same thing. Her smile stuttered and dropped as she remembered that there was a good chance she'd never see him again. She squinted as a candle flared to life on the shelf in the back of the closet, blinking as Torian's silhouette came into focus.

"I don't know why you feel entitled to ask those kinds of questions." Nissa huffed.

"I mean, speaking as the person who's supposed to be your *wife...*" The word tasted sour in her mouth, and Torian's nose twitched. Apparently, he felt similarly. His shoulders slumped as the fight went out of him, and Nissa knew that he saw her point.

"His name is Jasper." Nissa froze. "We met a few months ago."

"Okay," she said slowly, trying to put the pieces together. "And Jasper is the reason you feel like you can't do anything to change our arrangement. Do you want to tell me why?" Torian pressed his lips together, and the skin around his eyes tightened before he exhaled deeply.

"I met Jasper in one of the lumberyards. My father had sent me to check on the progress in one of the mills and..." He waved a hand absently. "It doesn't really matter why I was there, I guess. Jasper was a new face, and so I noticed." His eyes stared off into the space beyond Nissa's shoulder, as though he was no longer really seeing her. "I pulled him to the side because I didn't recognize him, and he was reluctant to answer any of my questions. Of course, that only made me more curious."

"Naturally," Nissa said softly.

"I was there for a little over a week, and by the end of it, we'd become friendly. We struck up a correspondence, and he's been keeping me informed on lumber production. More than that, really, he's been my eyes and ears. We've had a few lumber-lords who feel they're entitled to more than the compensation they receive." His voice tightened. "Jasper is the reason we've been able to stay one step ahead of them for so long."

"And you feel that ending our arrangement will somehow jeopardize that?" she asked, not really understanding.

"Jasper is... He left his home for a reason. If my father ever..." He stopped himself. "He's been loyal to us, and so I have kept his secret. But my father knows that he's an informant, and he knows about our friendship. I-I don't have many friends." His eyes flickered at the comment, and Nissa had the sense that he was embarrassed. Torian's eyes hardened again as they met hers. "That puts a target on his back."

"So, you think that your father would harm a valuable informant just to get back at you for refusing a marriage to me?" she asked. It seemed to Nissa that it would be an overreaction, but as his son, Torian knew Lord Círden better than she could hope to. Torian caught his bottom lip between his teeth, and the motion cast strange shadows on his face in the flickering light. The air of the closet ran cold, and Nissa had to repress a shiver at the sudden change.

"I don't want to take that chance. Nobody should be punished for being—I wouldn't want any harm to come to him for my—" he paused. "I can't take that chance," he repeated. Nissa sighed with resignation. It was a sentiment that she knew all too well.

"Torian," she began. He shook his head, and the chill in the air sharpened.

"No, I know what you're going to say. I'll save you the trouble of telling me that I'm choosing a lifelong decision over a chance, but I can't—I mean…" Seeming overcome, Torian's voice broke.

"I understand," Nissa said in a clear voice. Torian's wide eyes found hers again.

"You understand?"

"I understand the fear of collateral damage. It's a big responsibility." She took a deep breath. "But Torian, there are ways to do this that won't implicate you, ways that will keep your name clear and can keep Jasper safe. You don't want to be tied in with my family." The shudder that rippled through her body had nothing to do with the cold. "Ward, he's… Ward would be a greater danger to you than Círden ever could be." Torian's still-swollen eyes narrowed slightly.

"Meaning?" She chewed on the inside of her lip.

"I don't—" His eyes sharpened.

"A secret for a secret, Nissa." She exhaled through her nose, bringing her fingers up to pinch the bridge before she dropped her hand.

"It's not my secret to tell," she said.

"And Jasper's wasn't mine." Temper flared in Torian's eyes, and she gritted her teeth in frustration.

"Ward is volatile. He wasn't always, but something happened, and—" she threw her hands up. "An example, okay. Ward got involved with a woman. Her name—" she paused and took another breath— "her name doesn't matter, but their relationship ended. Badly. He became volatile, and when she fell pregnant, she knew she had to leave. She had to flee the realm to get away from him, and she's *still* on the edge of running from him. If he ever found out where she was, she— anyway, Ward's reach is far. Once he sees you as connected with him, you become an object. Think of the way that he brought me here, drugged and unconscious. And I'm his *sister*." Nissa drew out the word for emphasis. Torian's wide eyes fixed on her face.

"How far did she have to go?" Nissa squinted at him.

"Does it really matter? She had to flee the realm."

"I just... I find it hard to believe Ward's reach extends across continents." She rolled her eyes.

"It extends far enough that he could kidnap me from Sel'veren. It extends far enough that a woman all the way in Domogién is still looking over her shoulder, waiting for the day that he'll come for her too." Torian blanched, and she knew she had made her point. "It's more dangerous to be affiliated with him than it ever will be to stay out of his clutches in the first place. You can predict your father's reactions, and you can plan for them. With Ward, there is no limit to what he is willing to do. The brother of my childhood is gone, Torian. You don't want to be anywhere near the monster when it comes out. What do you think will happen when he finds out he can use Jasper against you, Torian?" Memories washed through her then, stories of the women that Ward had used and discarded like leftover scraps, messy brawls that her father had cleaned up, vengeful fathers who had simply disappeared into silence. It was safer to be as far away from Ward as possible.

"What if he never finds out?"

"You're worried about Círden, and yet you somehow think *Ward* won't find out? Make no mistake, Ward knows more intimate details about his so-called allies than his most formidable enemies. He *will* find out, and all Hell will break loose when he does." Fear clenched in her stomach at the thought.

"And this is Lord Alvar's heir?" Nissa rounded on him in alarm.

"That's what you're concerned about?" she exclaimed. He fell back a step, hands up defensively.

"I mean, it's a valid concern." She tightened her jaw.

"Of course it is, Torian. But it's not something we can fix right now. This? You and me?" She gestured wildly between them. "This we can fix. This we can keep out of his grip. *Jasper*, we can keep out of his grasp if we move before he gets too close." She gripped his shoulders, resisting the urge to shake them. "Torian, we can fight this *if* we move fast enough and work together." She dropped her hands and stepped back to let her words take effect as she held her breath. If he didn't agree with her, if he refused to act before Ward could— He looked up and his eyes met hers again, this time with a steel-set determination flickering in them.

"We leave Jasper out of it," he warned. Nissa's response was instant.

"Of course." He let out a breath.

"Alright. I'll help you. But I want my name clear of it."

"Done."

57

"We're getting closer," Faris called back to Tanyl and Trey over the howl of the wind. Tryamon squinted as it whipped against his face and stung his eyes. The air had grown cold, and his hands were numb where they clutched at his horse's reins. He glanced down at his saddlebags, wondering at the likelihood that he could retrieve a pair of gloves without dropping them, but his fingers, angry and red from the bite of the wind, refused to loosen at his command.

Trey eyed Faris, whose posture was unaffected by the tempest that swirled around them. The haze seemed to swallow him. If this was how the north was, it was no wonder that Nissa had left it. He clenched his teeth against the renewed ache in his joints as the wind buffeted him again. He had thought it a pretty landscape when the russet of the forest had slowly transformed beneath a sparkling cap of snow. Now, away from the shelter of the boughs and trunks, he thought quite the opposite. There was no shelter once the land turned rocky, whipping the spirals of wind against their bodies and echoing its own howls. Faris had advised them to don layers, but Trey had never seen anything like this.

His horse shied away from another blast as a scrubby plant brushed against its legs. Trey leaned forward, murmuring soothing words as Tanyl rode up beside him. His friend's sandy hair was hidden beneath a woolen cap, but his cheeks and nose had reddened.

"We'll have to stop if this keeps up. It's not good for the horses," Tanyl jerked his head at the swirling mists around them.

"You'll have to tell him. He knows the lands here better than us. It might not be safe to break here." It was hard for Trey to admit that someone else was in charge, especially when it was someone he didn't fully trust, but the words came more easily than he had expected. If there was one thing he'd learned about Faris, it was that he really was Nissa's friend. He wouldn't do anything to jeopardize her rescue.

Tanyl squinted ahead into the building storm, cursing under his breath as he spurred his mount forward. Trey looked away as his horse kicked up the earth beneath him before hunching further as he urged his own to follow.

"We'll have to cut west up ahead," Faris was saying to Tanyl. His voice was hoarse as it rose above the wind. "That should help get us toward the edge of this storm and away from Danuil."

"And then how much further?" Trey bellowed to be heard. Faris glanced at him, and Trey scowled as he realized that the man's cheeks were barely pink from the chill.

"If we can get a ship, it won't take us long to get across to the Keep. The sea is narrow where I'm taking us." Tryamon clenched his eyes shut against another cutting sweep of wind.

"And how long until we're out of this storm?" Tanyl asked through gritted teeth. Trey's eyes watered as he opened them.

"I can't control the weather," Faris said baldly. "But I know where we can find shelter if it doesn't pass." Tanyl grunted, his eyes streaming as he matched his horse to the pace of Faris's mount. Trey pulled his horse around to flank him as he drew closer, and with another collective breath, the trio leaped forward into the storm again.

Trey wasn't sure how Faris had found the cave in the raging weather that whipped around them, but within another hour or two, they had found one just big enough to shelter their horses and—in a smaller alcove toward the back—themselves. They had fortunately found a few sticks of wood amongst the debris that had blown into the cave over time, and Tanyl had made quick work of striking up the fire. The three sat in silence, rubbing the aching chill from their swollen fingers as they studied each other.

"It's a bad one, even for here," Faris broke the silence first, with a nudge toward the edge of the cave.

"Have you been here before?" Tanyl tilted his head to indicate the cave around them. The fire popped, and one of the horses stepped away nervously, eyeing the flames.

"Once," Faris said. "I came across it after Nissa left. Her father sent guards after her and notified his soldiers in all the major cities. I was sent toward the coast, since they thought she might head for the sea." He shrugged. "I almost fell into this after nightfall."

"Lucky you did," Trey commented. Faris fixed him with a look.

"Lucky is one word."

"So, how far from the coast then?" He averted his eyes and changed the subject.

"Probably another day's ride if the storm lets up. Two if it doesn't." Faris shrugged, and Tryamon sighed.

"We've ridden hard, Trey. As hard as we've been able," Tanyl reminded him. Trey nodded without looking at him, chewing on the inside of his cheek. "And we can't be that far behind them." Beside him, Faris twitched, and Trey looked sharply at him.

"What?"

"They would have used their wielding to help speed along the process," he said. Trey's eyes narrowed as he fixed the man with a look.

"Meaning?"

"Rivers, the lake. Probably the sea. They would have chosen a route that relied heavily on water travel. It wouldn't be hard to manipulate the current, especially not in the direction they would have traveled." Trey's jaw tightened.

"You sound like you've given it a lot of thought." Faris fixed him with a stare.

"It's a known strategy, Tryamon," he snapped.

"In general, or for this specific case?" Trey asked coldly.

"I hope you're not suggesting what I think you're suggesting." Faris matched his tone, eyes blazing as blue collided with amber. Trey shook his head and dropped his eyes.

"Of course not. You risked your own neck to get her out. What would you gain by helping drag her back?" They sat in silence, then, for several minutes. The fire cracked, sending a shower of sparks dancing against the stone wall of the cave. One of the horses let out a low whinny.

"We should make sure it doesn't grow too much. Don't want to spook them." Faris jerked his chin toward the fire. Tanyl nodded in silent response, not taking his eyes from the flaming sticks. Trey had no clue how he had built something so comfortable with such little kindling, but then again, it had always been part of Tanyl's gift. He repressed a prickle of envy at the ease with which his friend could wield his magic. It was as natural to him as manipulating the water had been to Faris, simply with a different element. He shoved his hands roughly against his knees as he pushed to stand.

"I think I'm going to get some sleep." His companions

nodded wordlessly, and Trey curled up on his bedroll in the alcove a few minutes later, listening to the muffled whistling of the wind around the cave. What would it be like to be able to summon magic without a second thought? The powers that his companions wielded had made them useful on the journey, while he felt sluggish and burdensome in comparison. Trey frowned as he twisted to face the glow of the still-burning fire.

Faris had said that the family holding Nissa were powerful ice-wielders. How could Tryamon expect to hold his own without wielding an element himself? He had no clue what they were up against, and he couldn't expect Tanyl or Faris to step in on his behalf to cover for his handicap. His lip curled as he flipped onto his back, willing sleep to take him. *Useless and disappointing.* His mother's frosty voice penetrated his thoughts, and he scowled into the darkness. How was it that her ire could reach him even realms away? He flipped again, turning back toward the glow of the fire as the sounds of muffled conversation reached him. A flash of curiosity had his ears straining through the cave to make out any words, but the ever present buffeting of the wind drowned out the soft words. He released a sigh as the soft hum merged together in a kind of lullaby, and slowly, the stiffness in his body began to release. There was no room for doubts; not this close to reaching the Frosted Keep. He would have to save them for another time.

58

T orian stared at Ward in stony silence, wearing a scowl that Nissa pretended not to notice as she picked at her food. Without looking up from her plate, she kicked him in the shin, repressing a smirk at the way that he winced. She watched beneath her lashes as Ward shot their cousin a curious look, and the expression was so unlike the malice that he had worn lately that her heart twisted in her chest. Somewhere beneath the monster, she could still recognize flashes of her brother. From his spot at the head of the table, Círden droned on about the recent developments in the island's lumber trade. The sound of his voice grated against the inside of her skull until she finally set her fork down with a clank, arranging her face into a dull smile as she looked at Círden.

"Forgive me, Lord Pallinor. I was just wondering if Lamaris is feeling better? Have you heard?" Her other cousin's place at the table was still empty, and there had been little explanation as to his condition. It was an easy pivot for her to make. The skin around Círden's eyes tightened as Torian shifted uncomfortably beside her, and she knew that she had ventured onto dangerous ground.

"Lamaris is unwell, I'm afraid. Our healer suggested that he keep to his bed for now," Círden replied stiffly.

"I'm sorry to hear that," she murmured the condolences, dropping her gaze respectfully. She felt a prickle along the back of her neck, and when she looked up again, she realized that Ward was studying her carefully.

"I have news," he spoke up. She lifted her face to stare at her brother warily as her thoughts raced. What new torment did he have in store to spring on her?

"Lord Ward," Círden said politely. Ward's mouth stiffened at the title, and Nissa did not quell the prickle of amusement that ran through her. He'd always hated the way the title had sounded with his name. She'd mocked him mercilessly for it as a child. Not that she dared to now. Her smile faded; their days of lighthearted teasing disappeared long ago.

"I have been called to Danuil. My visit will be brief, but I will unfortunately have to leave you for a few days." He stared hard at Nissa as he said it, and she knew it was a warning. He may be leaving, but he'll be back. It sent a chill through her, raising the hair on her arms. She put her hands in her lap as Círden frowned.

"Nothing too troublesome, I hope." Ward pulled his gaze from Nissa to study Círden, a patronizing smile replacing the harshness on his face.

"No, my lord. Just something that requires my attention," he replied as his frosty grin widened. Círden frowned as he surveyed her brother.

"Nothing that will keep you from our upcoming festivities?" he pressed. Ward's lips closed tightly over his smile.

"As my father's proxy, I can't imagine he would allow me to miss it." His answer held the edge of a snarl, and Nissa looked at him incredulously.

"He wasn't planning on coming?" she asked, thunder-struck. Círden's eyes went wide as she looked between the Pallinor lord and her brother. Ward picked up his fork again and took a small bite, chewing thoughtfully before he answered.

"He's occupied with other things," he shrugged. She inhaled deeply and then huffed as she glowered at him, seething.

"You didn't think to tell me?" Ward raised an eyebrow.

"I didn't think you'd care. This is hardly an occasion you've looked forward to." His eyes flicked over to Círden, who flushed. "No offense, Lord Pallinor."

"Unbelievable," she muttered, clenching her hands into fists against her temper. Torian shifted beside her again, this time leaning forward.

"So, father. We were discussing the lumber business?" he said, placing his fork between his teeth with another mouthful. Círden launched into another tirade about prices and working with the other landowners while Nissa chewed her food thoughtfully. What could be so significant in Danuil that her father wanted Ward to handle it? More to the point, if he was gone, would that give her a better chance of slipping away from the Frosted Keep?

When she found herself back in her room after dinner, Nissa laid in bed, staring at the blackness of the ceiling as she considered the opportunity that Ward's absence would present. Círden had no reason to suspect her of being anything but compliant with their wedding plans; she'd played her role well, and she suspected that Ward wouldn't stir up ill will with him by warning him before he left. If she could get Torian on board with the idea, then maybe there was a way out for both of them? She could leave, and then he wouldn't be bound to her anymore. Nissa frowned; it still wouldn't solve his problems, but it would get him away from being forced into a union against his will. If he was serious about wanting an out, this could be their chance.

She sat up, goosebumps erupting against the chill in the air as she slung back the blankets covering her body. Nissa wouldn't be able to rest, not until she had a more concrete plan in place. She changed out of her night clothes and into a more presentable dress; there was only one person who could help her determine whether or not it was possible.

Torian opened his door only seconds after she knocked, blinking the sleepiness from his eyes as his expression sharpened. He opened his mouth to say something, but before he could, she pushed into the room. She didn't trust the blackness of the hallway at night, not when so much was on the line.

"Did something happen?" Torian asked, stifling a yawn. She shook her head.

"I couldn't sleep," she said, and Torian rolled his eyes.

"So what, misery wants company?" he asked, scowling at her. A smile twitched on her lips. If only he knew.

"Were you serious about what you said before?" He blinked at her for a moment, and she tapped her fingers impatiently on the side of her thigh.

"Which part?" he asked. She barely resisted the urge to roll her eyes.

"All of it, but mostly, the part where you offered to help me leave." She raised an eyebrow at him, crossing her arms as she waited for his response. He blinked at her again, all traces of sleep gone from his face. He released a sigh, and she stiffened, expecting the worst. *Uh oh.*

"Of course I wish I could help, Nissa, but—"

"We have an opportunity, Torian. Your father doesn't suspect that I'm anything but willing, however begrudgingly, to play into his plans, and Ward is leaving tomorrow morning. We have a real chance to make it happen... if you're really willing to follow through." She held her breath as she fixed her eyes on him. A series of expressions twitched across his face before he sat down hard in a chair.

"This is all very sudden," he said. Nissa huffed out an exasperated breath.

"So is him leaving. We have to make the most out of what we're given. This is a chance for you too." His chin jerked in a stiff nod as he sighed again.

"It's risky."

"If you meant what you said, then help me. If I get caught, they never have to know you were involved," she pressed. Torian bit the inside of the corner of his mouth as he visibly considered what she had said, and Nissa balled her hands into fists as she fought to stop herself from pacing.

"It'll be dangerous," he said reluctantly. Hope flared in her chest, but she fought to keep her expression neutral.

"So is keeping things as they are. We both deserve better." She held her breath as she waited for his final answer. Resignation and caution warred on his face before he met her eyes again, and she knew his answer before he spoke.

"Fine. I'll help you." She let out the breath she had held, feeling slightly giddy as the old air rushed from her lungs. He looked hard at the ground as a shadow fell across his face.

"Thank you, Torian," she whispered. "I know it won't make it any easier to live the life you want, but at least this way, I won't be one of your obstacles." He looked up at her again, his dark eyes meeting her bright ones, and reflected in them was the unfiltered pain of his separation.

"Don't make me regret it. I'm sticking my neck out, so you'd better make it count," he said tightly. She nodded.

"I won't." Torian sighed, rubbing at his face as he looked through his window and into the darkness that still shrouded the Keep.

"I guess I won't be sleeping anymore tonight." Nissa loosed a small, breathless laugh.

"We'll need to move fast," she agreed. He gestured to the chair across from him.

"Then sit. Let's get this over with."

59

Not a single part of Nissa regretted seeing her brother's form shrink into the distance, bound for the docks. She let out a breath, feeling some of the tension ease from her shoulders and back as the reality of her situation hit her. Ward was really leaving, and in just a few days, when he had put enough distance between himself and the Frosted Keep, Nissa would have her taste of freedom again.

She turned from the window, smiling to herself as she crossed the room. The thought made the idea of finalizing her wedding guests more bearable. She rolled her eyes at the thought of listening to Círden fuss and fret about seating charts and balancing the invitation list. It was a momentous occasion for him, allying his house more directly with a governing family, but she didn't see how it mattered whether Calanis Noor sat beside Círden or on her father's left. *If she's offended by getting the wrong place of honor, maybe she shouldn't be invited.* She snorted; it didn't matter in any case, because the event itself would never come to pass. The reminder lifted her spirits. Just another couple of days, and it would all be over.

She hadn't had the chance to go over the plans with Torian

since they'd finalized them. He'd been kept busy with this task or that, and it had only been a day. If he could forget the details of something in that short of a time frame, then they had bigger problems to worry about. She smiled and nodded to a pair of servants as they passed by, each carrying a bundle of bedding, and they nodded back with wide eyes, seeming startled at the acknowledgement. The thought made Nissa frown; she had never been one to dismiss others based on their position, but here she was, about to leave, and she had never thought to learn their names.

You've been a little preoccupied, she reminded herself, but the excuse felt hollow. She shook herself out of the spiral; in all likelihood, she would never see them again. That realization did nothing to alleviate the prickle of guilt in her stomach. She chewed on her lip thoughtfully as she continued to Círden's office, unable to shake the feeling until he swung open the door at her first knock.

"Thank you for joining me today! We've received word from the Light Realm; Calanis's daughter will be joining us in her stead." Nissa blinked. Liana? Hadn't she said that her mother was the only one who ventured toward the Water Realm. She masked her surprise with a pleasant smile.

"I'm sure it will be an honor to have anyone from the House of Noor in attendance." Círden scratched at his chin without looking at Nissa, nodding thoughtfully.

"Yes, the House of Noor has been a friend to your father. How they manage to keep such friendly relationships across the other realms is beyond me." Nissa thought that it was wise to keep her thoughts to herself. She wondered briefly how Liana would feel about finally venturing into the Water Realm. She sat softly on one of the chairs placed at the round table, nodding and smiling at the appropriate intervals as Lord Pallinor rambled on. She didn't notice he had asked her a question until she glanced up to see him scrutinizing her, silent.

"I'm sorry, Lord Pallinor. I seem to have gotten lost in thought." She fixed a gentle smile on her face, and his eyes softened.

"Think nothing of it, dear girl. You have a lot to think about." Inwardly, she bristled. "I wanted your final opinion on the mingling of our house colors." He held up two swatches of color, one bearing the white and green of the House of Pallinor, and the other the silver and blue Chantara colors. Nissa made a show of examining the samples, holding them up at different angles in the light.

"Shall we go with the silver and green? I'm afraid the blue would distract from the richness of the green." She didn't miss the way that Círden's face brightened in delight at her willingness to make the colors of his house more prominent.

"As it should be, I agree." He turned back to shuffle the papers behind him, and Nissa rolled her eyes. It was too easy to play the role of submissive future daughter-in-law. She chided herself; she should be thankful that he wasn't more suspicious. *Finally, Ward's paranoia works to my benefit.*

"Should I ask Torian for his opinion?" she asked. Círden shook his head without facing her.

"I don't think so. Men don't think of such things." She rolled her eyes again.

"Will Lamaris be well enough to attend?" she ventured. She still hadn't heard any updates on his condition. Pallinor he may be, but he seemed to have a kind heart.

"Hmm? No." Another pause filled the room.

"Have we received a reply from our guests coming from the other realms?" she asked mildly, keeping her tone light. She had been curious to see what would happen with the Houses of Makani and Brandell, given their most recent developments. Seeming to find what he was looking for, Círden turned back to face her, glancing absently up from the page before he refocused on whatever was written there.

"Lord Raenon has sent his regrets; it arrived this morning. He's busy preparing for his own event. I haven't heard from the House of Brandell." From the way that his mouth pressed into a firm line, Nissa knew that he took the nonresponse as a personal affront. She paused, considering. Could they be moving forward with the finalization of Trey and Aella's oath? The thought tasted sour, and bile rose in the back of her throat. She would gain her own freedom if all went according to plan, but that would do nothing for Tryamon's circumstances. She unleashed a quiet sigh. They sat in silence for a few more moments before Círden glanced up at her in surprise, as though he had forgotten that she was still there.

"You may go. I'll send for you if there's anything else to discuss." He arched a thick eyebrow in a clear dismissal, and she inclined her head with that same, colorless smile on her face. When she turned away from him, her expression dropped to a scowl. *Pompous old goat.*

Her feet took her in the direction of the library. Dismal as it was, it was a change of scenery, and the last thing she wanted to do was go sit in her room and count the minutes. The room was bright when she entered, and she blinked at the change it had undergone since she'd visited last. Gone were the inches of dust and grime. Someone had cleaned the shelves and thrown open the heavy curtains so that light streamed into the room. She cocked her head curiously, considering the change. It was still a darkly accented room, but it had lost the stench of neglect. She wondered briefly if Torian was responsible for the change. He had seemed shocked by its condition when he had introduced her to it. She shrugged off the thought; whoever was behind it, she approved of the attention.

Nissa chose a shelf at random and browsed the volumes, picking books on a whim before she found one she thought she could use to distract herself. She cast a wary glance at the cushions in the armchairs; no matter the attention to the shelves, she was skeptical that anyone could clean those thoroughly. A bench near the window caught her eye, and after an appraising scan over the piece, she settled herself on it and flipped through the pages. It wasn't long before she was absorbed in the tome, a fascinating account of the Great War that had established the realms. It was rare to find a volume that included accounts from the time Before, when Galarmos was unified into one mass nation. She shook her head, the idea of the rival realms merged as one, living peaceably among each other, seemed like a fever dream.

She lost track of how long she spent browsing through the volume, but it must have been significant, because when the door clicked open across the room and she glanced at her progress, she had covered a fair amount of ground. She glanced down at the hem of her sleeve and yanked at a loose thread before folding the book over it to mark her place.

"There you are! I was wondering where you'd run off to," Torian said, his voice echoing slightly in the open room.

"Just wanted a change of scenery," she shrugged.

"Find anything interesting?" He approached her bench, glancing curiously down at her choice. She lifted the book so that he could see the title.

"I've never come across anything like this," she said. Torian nodded in understanding.

"Yes, my father got his hands on that on a whim. He said it was a good reminder that the governing lords were once just like everyone else." He snorted, and Nissa's brows flicked upward in amusement.

"He's not wrong," Torian half-smiled.

"But he likes to convince himself he's not as arrogant. Old fool." He sat down hard on her bench, and Nissa lurched as she felt the aged wood shift under her weight.

"Guess that's something they have in common." She glanced down at her book again as Torian laughed.

"I got in touch with Jasper," he said casually. Nissa stiffened and glanced around the room warily, surprised that he would mention his lover's name so openly.

"That was fast," she said cautiously.

"He doesn't live far." She nodded.

"What are his thoughts on this whole debacle?" she asked, waving an errant hand. He glanced at her, seeming surprised that she asked, and she shrugged. "You never said." Torian let out a slow breath.

"I think he'll be glad to see the back of it. This brings us one step closer." She nodded, angling her body toward him as she set the book to the side.

"I hope you'll both see the back of it all soon. You deserve happiness, Torian." She met his eyes evenly, and Torian nodded as he glanced to the side.

"I think so too."

60

Nissa paced across her room, fidgeting with her hands as she wore a track in the thick rug that lay across the floor. Torian was late. She paused to stare out the window, crossing her arms to still her hands. Her fingers drummed rebelliously against her arms, and with a huff, she resumed her pacing.

If things were already veering off course, how would that bode for the remainder of the plans? She paused again, glancing at the door, as she wondered if she had misunderstood the plans for their rendezvous. Or perhaps, with Círden off meeting with the lumber distributors north of the keep, Torian thought that they could be more lax with the schedule. The thought set her teeth on edge. Even with the extra time that Círden's absence afforded, the plan needed to continue seamlessly for it to work. They didn't have time for this. She moved toward the door; casting a glance back toward the pack she'd concealed beneath her bed. They had probably miscommunicated, and Torian was probably waiting for her in his rooms. Still—the door swung open loudly, and Nissa jumped back in surprise as Torian appeared in the opening. She relaxed slightly, offering a wobbly smile as he stepped forward.

"I was wondering where you were. I was about to come searching for you." Torian stared at her with a stone face, and a flicker of doubt flared in her chest. "What's wrong?"

"How long?" he asked hoarsely. She took a step back.

"What?"

"How long have you been planning to use my secrets against me?" She backed up another step as he lurched toward her.

"Torian? What are you talking about?" she asked. He thrust one hand into a tunic pocket, ripping a crumpled sheet of paper from it before he waved it in the air.

"Your brother has an unfortunate sense of timing." Dread joined the doubt and formed a pit in her stomach.

"Unfortunate how?" she asked.

"For you." Torian let loose a laugh, and Nissa flinched as spit speckled her cheeks. She wiped away the droplets.

"Torian," she fought to keep her voice calm, "I really don't know what you're talking about. What did Ward do?" She fixed her eyes on the wrinkled page in his hand, racking her brain. What could Ward have possibly said to get Torian so worked up when he was all the way in Danuil. Torian narrowed his eyes dangerously, and Nissa took another sidestep away from him.

"You're going to pretend that you don't know how he found out about Jasper?" The color drained from Nissa's face at Torian's admission.

"Torian, I had no—" she breathed before he cut across her again.

"Oh, look who's going to play innocent. Is that how you convinced him to leave town? To send him on a wild goose chase to save yourself?" Torian snarled, his complexion turning an ugly, mottled purplish color. She locked her eyes on him as she stepped forward.

"Torian, I did *not* sell you out. What would I have to gain from that?" She stared unblinkingly at him until he dropped his eyes. They rested on her face a moment later as they filled with torment.

"I don't believe you," he said softly. She took several steps back at the admission to put space between them as she glanced toward the door. Would she be able to make it through in time?

"I'm telling you the truth," she said as her eyes flickered toward the door again involuntarily. A harsh, humorless smile twisted Torian's lips as he followed her gaze.

"You're a liar, Nissa. You sold me out, and there will be consequences." She looked wildly around the room as she internally grasped at any thread she could find to make him see reason.

"Why would I go out of my way to hurt someone who's helping me?"

"If you get what you want in the end, what's a little collateral damage?" he snarled. "I trusted you. I thought that helping you was the right thing to do. I guess I should have listened to my father when he told me to never trust a Chantara." She flinched.

"I'm not my father," she said quietly, feeling behind her as she stumbled into a table for anything that she could use as a weapon.

"Maybe I should be more like mine."

"I swear I didn't lie to you! I don't know what else to say to make you believe me." Nissa took a step to the side as she circumvented the table. Torian's dark eyes flashed with fear and regret and something else as he closed the distance between them again.

"Ward's very informative. He knows everything, and he explained everything. It seems that you left out quite a few details when you made our plans." Torian's hand twitched toward the ring on his thumb, but he balled his hands into fists, clenching them by his side. Nissa blinked at him, distressed as she took another step back.

"I don't know what you're talking about, Torian. I told you everything I know! You know who I am." She stepped backward again, stumbling as her knees smacked against the side of her bed. She side-stepped it and edged around the corner, keeping her eyes on her cousin.

"I thought I did. You weren't going to tell me that the Prince of Flames," he said in a snarl, "has taken the Blood Oath to unite his house with the House of Makani?" She bit her lip to keep from biting back a retort as she took a shaky breath.

"That has nothing to do with you or I," she said as calmly as she could.

"Horse shit!" Torian's fists shook at his sides. "You don't think that an enemy realm gaining power that way doesn't change everything?" Nissa narrowed her eyes.

"Trey is *not* our enemy, Torian. He had as little a choice in his betrothal as we did," she bit back the snarl that threatened to creep into her voice.

"Oh, poor little prince, gifted with more power than he deserves," Torian mocked, stepping toward Nissa again. "If you think for one second that we can allow that kind of alliance to go unchecked, then you're a fool, Nissa."

"He didn't want it," she snapped.

"It doesn't matter what he wants," Torian's voice rose angrily.

"You sound like our fathers." Torian faltered at that before anger bloomed on his face once more.

"And in this case, maybe that isn't a bad thing! They're *dangerous*, Nissa. We have to protect our realm. We have to protect ourselves." Panic battered in her chest like the beating of frantic wings as Torian lurched for her, and she swung out of his way.

"What are you doing?" Her voice rose to a shout. She paused to lower it again as she fought to hang on to whatever reason lurked beneath the surface of his fear. "We can still leave, Torian. We can still get out. We can escape this."

"Don't you understand?" he roared, sending a side table tumbling to the floor with a vicious kick. "There's no escaping who I am. Ward made that very clear, and now he knows about Jasper. Turns out that your brother made a stop on his way to Danuil. If I leave now, he's as good as dead, and I'll be hunted for the rest of my life. And with this alliance, we'll be running from the gods-damned Brandells until they stamp us all out."

"You don't know that. We can free him. Find out where Ward's keeping him, and—" she broke off as he kicked at a chair, sending it several scraping feet backward.

"And then what? I'll always be running from something now, and the only way to protect myself is to make sure that I have all of the power in my hands when it comes for me again," he snarled, grasping for her again. Nissa spun again, and Torian stumbled as his hand closed on empty air.

"You'd rather live a lie than take a chance on freedom? What did Ward say to you? What did you *do*?" she asked, her heart hammering against the walls of her chest. The glitter of Torian's darkening eyes was his only response. Nissa's hands curled in preparation for his next lunge, and when he dove for her again, she sent a whip of water racking against his face. Torian yelped and swatted at the fluid tendril, backing away as he assessed the welt that rose on his jaw. His spine stiffened as he straightened, his hands dropping to his sides as his expression turned murderously cold.

"I made a bargain, Nissa. I intend to see the rest of my end through." Nissa jerked as manacles of thick, searing ice formed at her wrists. She thrashed as they pushed her back and back and back until her knees buckled against a chair and she collapsed against the seat.

"Torian, stop! You're not a monster. Don't do this!" She thrashed as her voice broke on the plea, but there was no emotion left in her cousin's eyes as he loomed over her and pulled a knife from his boot.

"It'll be better for you if you don't fight. Be good, little cousin, and you can walk Pippa Woodrose through the Oath when it's her turn."

61

A scream of horror ripped out of her body at Torian's betrayal. Pippa had been the price of Jasper's freedom? Rage washed over her, drowning the horror as Torian's mouth curved into a self-satisfied sneer.

"You *told* him? How could you? She's an innocent!" Nissa thrashed again, the ice around her wrists burning against her flesh as she fought in vain. She lashed out with her feet, and Torian sidestepped the blow, securing her legs in matching bonds of ice with a wave of one hand. He paused as he stared at her for a moment, something like remorse crossing his face before it hardened into that foreign mask once more.

"In this game, there are no innocents. There are only the weak who don't have what it takes to survive." He lurched forward again, and Nissa screamed as the blade of the knife sank into her forearm, the metal practically singing into the dancing streams of blood that poured from the wound and wrapped it in a scarlet embrace. He was going to force her into the Blood Oath. She screamed, twisting like an animal caught in a trap, as rage and terror crashed against her in a rising crescendo. *Out! I have to get out!* She twisted again as another shining flash of the knife sent Torian's blood cascading to join her own on the floor.

"Torian, don't do this. You don't have to do this! This isn't you." She hated him; she hated herself for begging him.

"Who knows? Maybe once Ward's found Pippa, he'll pay Tryamon a little visit. He can remind him what happens when you play with things that don't belong to you." The smile twisted further as he stepped toward her again, sending the knife clattering to the floor as he prepared to press their wounds together to begin the sealing of the Oath. A roaring swept through Nissa, and she closed her eyes as she clenched her teeth against the typhoon. She felt the room spin around her and still, she sensed Torian stepping closer and closer. She raised her face to the sky as her back arched against her bonds, a bellow of rage and pain and fear all mingled into one. A crack splintered through the storm within her, freeing the bonds at her ankles, and she clawed at the arms of the chair to hold as the flood within that threatened to sweep her away.

Another crack echoed through the room, and the pressure of the chair arms beneath her forearms disappeared as Nissa's wrists curved upward, shaking in the wrecked shards of the manacles she had worn. As though some other force was controlling her body, her feet slammed against the ground as her legs pushed her to stand. She opened her eyes, glaring down at the now-cowering form of Torian, who held his arm as blood streaked across his face. She took a step forward, and he skittered backward, slipping on the shards of ice that remained behind him.

"What are you?" he whispered, horror replacing the rage that he had worn as a second skin. She bared her teeth at him.

"I am Nissa Chantara, and you will *never* control me." Her voice echoed with the remnants of power as she raised one arm. Torian yelled as the shards around him tinkled across the floor to reform, binding his wrists and ankles together. Nissa flexed her fingers, and the remaining shards melted, forming another tendril of water as it wrapped around his bound limbs. Her nails bit into her palm as she clamped her fingers against her palm. The rope-like water hardened, a binding of thick ice that burned red welts against his skin. Torian's fear turned into panic as his lips chapped and cracked. Nissa did not pause to consider why as her power plunged deeper, the icy shackles staining red as they gouged past his skin. The scream that tore from him next rose the hairs along her neck, but there was no stopping it.

"Don't kill me. Please don't kill me," he panted as the ice-bonds prevented his body from making even the slightest of movements. Tears trickled freely down his face, hissing as they fell against the ice that wrapped around his chest. She stared down at him with burning eyes, raising her hand again as she felt that thrum of power beg to be released. He gasped out a half-strangled sob as she considered him, and she heard the ice hiss as his blood poured over it. The sight froze her in place as she felt the terrifying grip of her power ease.

"In this game, there are no innocents," she repeated him, the words sounding empty in her ears. "But my hands will remain clean." At her words, the power stalled to a vibration, shaking through her limbs, and she hissed as a burning sensation seared against her arm. Looking down, she stared blankly at the slice on her arm that still poured blood. It seemed as though it belonged to someone else, to another lifetime. She swayed in place as she stared at it for a moment longer before looking at Torian again. She stepped toward him, and his lips trembled in another spasm of terror as a fierce expression slashed across her mouth. She caught a glimpse of her reflection in the mirror that hung across the room. There was nothing beautiful in her smile.

"You will not call an alert until I am gone. You will not come after me. After this, I will never see you or your family again, or

I won't be so lenient next time." Torian nodded violently, and she stepped back. "Good," she replied to the nod with one of her own, that strange emptiness still yawning inside of her like a void. She swept back, brushing him with her skirts as though he was as significant as the dust of a forgotten road, leaving him quivering with cold and fear as she slammed the door to her rooms behind her.

Servants brushed past her with wide eyes and spoke in hushed voices as she passed. In her detachment, she had no fear that they would go and notify guards. She had no fear of anything to fill the hollowness in her stomach. Like a sleep-walker, she lurched down the stairs to the main level. Her knees shook by the time she made it to the entrance of the Keep. Nissa took a deep breath as she placed her palms against the double doors that formed the entrance and shoved, nearly falling to her knees as they swung open. She took a staggering step forward to catch herself as she blinked into the midday sun, her breath fogging in the frosty air. A coat—she'd forgotten to grab a cloak or a coat or any shelter against the chill that lingered in this part of the realm. She set her mouth in a determined line; she wouldn't go back inside; not now that she was this close to freedom. She moved again.

She shivered as a gust of wind blew across her body, taking another step forward. One step closer. The Frosted Keep was a looming figure behind her as she moved toward the coast, where she knew that ships would be tethered in wait for instructions. It would be quick work to clamber aboard and rest. She frowned at her arm; she needed to wrap it. The pressure she had applied against her sleeve had kept her from a dizzy collapse, but when she peeled her hand from her arm to look beneath, a fresh gush of blood from the deepest part of the wound nearly brought the ground spinning to meet her. Cursing in a whisper, she pressed her hand against it once more, biting her tongue to keep herself from crying out. She froze in place as the sound of hoofbeats reached her, each jingling step like a crack against her determined flight.

Nissa turned slowly, keeping her eyes downcast as she calculated the cost of reaching for her well of power again. If Torian had sent someone to pursue her, there would be no mercy for him this time. She lifted her eyes, a blaze of defiance flashing in her eyes as she met the riders. Her vision swam as the lead rider—were there three or was that her eyes playing tricks on her? —reigned his horse to a halt and swung his leg over to dismount. She blinked to clear her swimming vision as the dark-haired man approached her, his amber eyes shining with concern as he took in her trembling form. His hair blew around his face as an icy blast cut around them, baring arched ears and sharp cheekbones, and she pitched forward as one of her legs buckled traitorously.

"T-Trey?" she managed, shivering against another gust of wind. The trace of icy power coursing through her had vanished, leaving her more susceptible to the chill than ever.

"Nissa?" Trey's eyes searched hers before dropping to assess her. They darkened to a deep bronze as they took in the arm she had pressed beneath her hand. "You're hurt." Anger simmered, molten across his face as her shudders grew more violent. Her vision swam again, and then she was sinking, the earth shifting up to meet her. He caught her in strong arms and pulled her to his chest, his torso warm against her icy skin. He turned and barked an order to someone behind him, and a cloak floated over to cover her. She quaked against the fabric, ordering her teeth to stop their defiant chattering.

"Help me," she managed, hating the way that her voice broke on the last word. The simmering anger turned to boiling rage as he looked down at her again.

"Who did this to you?" he demanded, lifting his gaze to the Keep behind her as jagged bolts of wrath sparked in his eyes. In the distance, thunder rumbled, and Nissa shuddered again; she wouldn't survive a storm, not now.

"Tryamon," a male voice behind him warned. *Tanyl.* Trey gritted his teeth, jaw working furiously as he visibly fought for control.

"Please," Nissa asked softly, "please help me leave." The world pitched around her as she swayed in his grip.

"Who did this? I need to make sure they won't follow," he managed, sounding strangled through his clenched teeth. His fingers, clad in the black leather of his gloves, curled as he looked down at the wound on her arm again. He fixed his eyes upon the Frosted Keep behind her, unfiltered wrath blazing across his face.

"They won't, I just..." Trey's fist closed, and with it, a flash appeared in the sky. Nissa jumped as it illuminated the sky, turning to watch in a mix of fear and fascination as it tunneled down toward the Keep.

"Trey," Tanyl warned again.

"A warning." The words muffled against the crack of splitting stone as the bolt struck home sending a statue from the East Wall tumbling to splinter in against the earth. Nissa shifted too quickly to look up at Tryamon again, and she swallowed roughly against the rising tide of nausea. She searched his face for understanding as his amber eyes bathed her prison with a fury that promised to incinerate it. Nissa stared up at Trey as the realization finally dawned on her.

"Lightningbearer," she whispered. Her stomach twisted as the world spun once more. The drain of magic-use and blood-loss seized her consciousness, and the world went dark.

62

———

"Lightningbearer," Nissa whispered. Her voice penetrated through the blind fury that howled through his bones, demanding that he destroy the threat that stood behind her. Trey dropped his eyes to her face in time to see her eyes roll back in her head as she slumped back. Fear jolted though Trey as her head lolled to the side, and he felt another surge of power swell inside him.

"What did you do to her?" Faris demanded crossly, stepping forward to grip his shoulder.

"Don't touch me," Trey ordered through gritted teeth as he fought for control. It was taking everything in him not to blast another bolt of power toward the Frosted Keep; he wasn't convinced that he wouldn't incinerate the other man on contact. Faris scowled, but he took an obliging step back before he crouched beside them.

"It's the only mark on her. They tried to make her take the Oath," he muttered, jerking his chin at the wobbling, crescent-shaped slice on her arm. The observation did nothing to quell the surge of power that still roared in his veins.

"Respectfully, keep your mouth shut." Trey growled as he

fought to leash the urge to destroy. He had kept his well of power buried deep for a long time, too long, and now it didn't want to go back in its cage.

"Maybe you should..." It was Tanyl's calming voice, suddenly hesitant, that made Trey realize the danger that he posed by being so close to her during this internal war. When he was in control, he would never hurt her, but here, teetering so close to that plunging free-fall, there were no guarantees. All of his instincts screamed their protest as he lowered her gently the rest of the way to the ground and retreated several feet away. He closed his eyes, breathing deeply before he steadied slightly and moved a few steps toward them, as close as he dared.

"Can you tell if they succeeded?" he asked Faris shortly. The other man's gray eyes probed him with distrust as he studied the mark on her forearm again. As he brushed his fingers against the edges of the wound, Nissa flinched, and Trey bit down on the urge to roar at the man not to touch her.

"I don't think so," Faris said slowly. "There's no sign of magic binding to her, and there would be." He looked up and met Trey's eyes. "The Pallinors are a powerful family."

"We have to get her away from here," Tanyl said, his normally-clear eyes shadowed with worry. Trey's mouth worked furiously as his eyes darted toward that towering, looming Keep. He should be storming into it, ripping apart the Pallinor line for trying to force Nissa under their control. A low growl of frustration rumbled through him. It would be easy to exact vengeance... so easy.

"There's no time, Tryamon." Faris's voice was clipped, and when Trey dropped his gaze to the other man, he saw rage flicker across his face as well. Clearly, Faris felt much the same. The realization had Trey's wrath flickering to calm itself as he forced it down and down and down. They had come to the Keep to rescue Nissa. She had gotten herself out; now, they needed to finish the job of getting her to safety. He forced himself to repeat the sentiment until his rage was contained enough for him to step forward another step.

"Back to the boat, then?" he managed tightly. Tanyl visibly relaxed at the words, and Faris nodded darkly.

"Back to the boat. I doubt they'll be looking for it yet." Trey didn't doubt him. He had proven he could be trusted, at least as far as Nissa's safety was concerned.

"He's my friend," she had said. Trey had no doubt that the other man felt more than that, but either way, Trey knew that Faris wouldn't put her in harm's way. Nissa stirred as Faris lifted her from the ground with a grunt and turned toward the horses. His eyes flickered toward Trey before glancing again at the three mounts. Nissa's eyes fluttered open and she twisted in Faris's arms, confusion emblazoned across her face.

"She'll ride with me," Tanyl stepped in between them, seeming to sense the unspoken question. Trey opened his mouth to protest, but another glance at the set of Faris's shoulders had him rethinking it. Now was not the time. Nissa twisted again.

"I can walk," she protested in a small voice. Faris rolled his eyes but rested her feet on the ground without argument. She leaned heavily on him for support as they moved slowly toward the horses. Trey stepped wordlessly to her other side, ready to catch her if she needed more support or if—gods forbid—Broffet was to drop her. Tanyl swung his leg over his mount and settled himself in the saddle. Trey braced himself, ready to support Nissa's weight when his friend held up a hand.

"Wrap her arm first," Tanyl said.

"There's no time," Faris interjected. Tanyl's eyes flashed as he looked down at the other man, and through the numbness of Trey's control, he felt a tinge of surprise at his forcefulness.

"Make time," he said. Faris shot Trey a questioning look, and he nodded in response, moving to support Nissa's weight as the other man slipped out from under her arm. He fumbled in his saddlebags for a moment before returning with a clean roll of bandages.

"We'll have to be quick. Hold out your arm, Nissa." She obliged, still shaky but supporting more of her own weight as her friend wrapped the wound.

"Thanks," she answered in a rasp, and Trey frowned. She had lost blood, but she hadn't taken the oath. What had happened to exhaust her so thoroughly? More to the point, how had she gotten away?

He did not have time to pose the question, so without further delay, he and Faris hefted her into Tanyl's saddle before climbing onto their own horses and spurring them back toward the docks. He held his breath as they moved purposefully to board the ship, waiting for someone to call out to them, to question what they were doing with Torian Pallinor's fiancée. His magic bubbled beneath the surface of his skin, ready to jolt to action at the first sign of trouble, but nobody questioned them as they followed Faris with their heads held high. It felt too good to be true when the sloop's sails filled as they headed upwind, pulling them away from the island. The four had not spoken for several minutes before Nissa broke the silence.

"Did you steal this?" she asked, glancing at Faris with raised eyebrows. Trey studied her face as she posed her question, and he breathed a sigh of relief to see that her color was returning to normal. Faris shrugged and ducked his head sheepishly.

"Desperate times. Your father has plenty; he won't miss it." Nissa considered the response thoughtfully before rising to her feet and stepping carefully toward the edge of the boat. Trey's heart lurched as it shifted beneath his feet with the weight change.

"We should go south," she said suddenly.

"South?" Faris echoed.

"To Risadell," she clarified. Faris blinked several times before understanding cleared his expression.

"Ah." Trey glanced between the two. He was missing something.

"What's in Risadell?" he asked.

"My mother may still have friends there. They'll keep our secrets; they hate my father." She said it with so much conviction that he did not question it. She reached up to brush a lock of hair out of her face, and he eyed the white linen that wrapped her arm, feeling a familiar tingle of power rush toward his hands. The hair of his arms stood on end, and he interlocked his fingers, cracking his knuckles to release some tension.

"He tried to make me take the Oath," she said mildly, seeming to notice his attention. He bit the inside of his cheek to put a check on his temper.

"How did you escape?" The question tumbled from his lips, and as her eyes hardened, he wished he could pull it out and bury it. That wasn't the question he'd wanted to ask.

"I almost had him convinced to help me," she said quietly. "But Ward said something that spooked him." She rubbed at the harsh lines of red that encircled her wrists, wincing without looking at them. She looked at him again, her hazel eyes suddenly wide as she leaned forward and gripped his arm in a vice-like hand. Trey stiffened, suddenly on high alert.

"What is it?"

"He knows." She swallowed heavily. "Ward knows about Pippa." She sat down hard, and Trey tensed against the nausea that lurched in his stomach. At the stern, Tanyl jerked his eyes to Trey's face with a dangerous expression. Their friend was still in Domogién, and with the pair and Baloriel gone, she was without protection.

"How did he find out?" he asked carefully. Nissa's expression fell as her eyebrows pressed together in distress.

"It was my fault! I thought I could trust him. I—I made a mistake. He knows what Ward is, and it disgusted him. I never dreamed he would—" she broke off, her eyes filling suddenly. Trey turned to face Tanyl.

"When we make landfall, send word to her. Find a horse and ride straight for the city," he ordered. Tanyl nodded without response, his eyes glittering dangerously. Nissa's hands tightened on his arm, and he turned to face her, fighting to wipe the fear from his face.

"I'm sorry," she whispered. "I'm so sorry. I thought if he knew... He felt so alone. I never thought—" she broke off again as she choked on the words. Trey closed his eyes as he took another deep breath. She had been through enough without him blaming her. He opened his eyes again, and his eyes softened. Trey hesitated for a moment before placing his hand on top of hers, relishing the way that the smooth skin of her fine-boned hand felt beneath his calloused palm.

"We'll keep her safe. And we'll keep you safe." The promise was stilted, but Trey meant every word. Across the ship, he noticed Faris watching the exchange with narrowed eyes. He removed his hand and leaned back against the rail, the space where Nissa's hand had rested a little cold in its absence. He listened to her breathing slow and settle back into an even cadence.

"Are we going to talk about *your* Oath?" she asked softly. Trey tensed again as he looked down, realizing that the angry scar on his palm was facing her. He closed his fist over it, twisting his wrist so that it was hidden once more.

"I don't really know what there is to say about it." His tone was unconvincing, even to himself.

"You said you couldn't wield." There was no accusation in her voice, only curiosity. He braced himself for the fear that would inevitably replace whatever friendship they had, now that he had revealed his secret, but when his eyes met hers, there was only compassion.

"I said I couldn't wield *fire.* I never said anything about..." He waved his hand vaguely as he trailed off. It had been a deception, and he knew it. To his surprise, she didn't ask for an explanation; she only nodded.

"Another secret?" she asked.

"Tanyl and Baloriel know. And now you and Faris." He glanced over at Faris, who had moved to stand by Tanyl and was giving him instruction. Tanyl's sandy brows were furrowed together as he concentrated, and Faris made some quick adjustments to the sail as they adjusted their course.

"Not your parents?" she asked.

"No."

"So, they..." Nissa began hesitantly. He met her eyes again, saw the hesitation in them.

"As far as they are concerned, I am a disappointment to the bloodline," he answered gruffly. "That's part of why they pushed for this match with Aella. After all, a good, strong fire just needs some air, and the kindling is already in our blood." He curled his lip at the last statement. It was something he'd heard repeated hundreds of times, and it felt as though it had been branded into his brain.

"Would it have been different, if you'd told them?" she asked carefully. Trey sighed, his shoulders dropping as he stared at the floor of the ship.

"Maybe. But then I would have been their weapon." He jumped a little at the pressure on his shoulder, but he relaxed as he realized Nissa had rested her head there. It was as much an expression of solidarity as he'd ever gotten, and in that moment, he wished it would last forever. He tilted his head to press his cheek against her hair as the ship bobbed with the waves.

63

____

When Nissa stirred again, Trey had slumped against her. Her head had lolled around the vicinity of his collarbone, and his cheek rested against the top of her head. She listened to the tempo of his deep, even breathing, her lips twitching slightly as the shifting of his breath tickled her hair against her ears. She reached up a hand, careful not to shift too much, and brushed a strand out of her face. Trey grunted slightly, as though sensing the movement, and he rolled his shoulders slightly, leaning back against the side of the ship. Nissa lifted her head and eased herself away as he settled, and she smiled faintly as his nose twitched.

She slid away and rose to her feet, rolling her neck to ease the tension in it as she stretched. Her mouth split open in a yawn as she gazed out over the water around them. They must have caught one of the coastal currents once she'd drifted off; there was no sign of the island that she had escaped. She turned to face the direction of the approaching shore on the other side. It was still a hazy shadow off in the distance; they had a while before it would meet them. She lifted a hand to study the distance, and she barely flinched as a familiar figure approached.

"I owe you an apology," Faris said quietly. Nissa turned to her friend, lifting a dark eyebrow in question as she lowered her friend.

"Do you?" The corner of his mouth tugged downward.

"It was my fault you were taken," he said. She turned away, studying the sea again as different emotions flickered through her. When she had fixed her face into a careful mask once more, she faced him again.

"Did you drug the wine?" she asked pointedly. He started.

"Of course not!"

"Did you know that it was drugged?" He looked away.

"Not at first." She stiffened, and he backtracked, seeming to sense the direction of her thoughts, "I didn't know before we started drinking it, Nissa. I would have never given it to you if I had."

"And you were drinking it yourself," she mused, barely noticing as he nodded.

"Still, I should have been more cautious. It was my lapse." She fixed him with a look.

"You didn't force it down my throat, Faris. I drank it of my own free will," she said firmly.

"And it was handed to you by someone you trusted." Self-loathing carved itself into his face as he stared at her with tortured eyes, and she sighed.

"Trust," she corrected.

"What?"

"You crossed half the continent with Tryamon Brandell, who you've reminded me several times you don't have a high opinion of. That earns you my continued trust, if nothing else," she said. He blinked at her as he processed her words, and Nissa felt a smile tug on the corner of her mouth.

"He's not so bad," Faris said in a strangled kind of voice, as though forcing the admission from his lips. Nissa tilted her head back in a laugh as a bubble of joy burst within her. Faris stared at her for a moment before his own laugh joined it.

"He said something similar about you. I feel like I should be expecting you to declare your undying love for each other any day now," she chuckled, and Faris snorted good-naturedly.

"Let's not get ahead of ourselves." She huffed another laugh. His smile faded as his eyes fell on the bandages that peeked out from under her sleeve. She followed his gaze, her own smile dropping with her eyes as she tugged at her cloak to cover it.

"It'll heal," she said firmly.

"But—"

"It'll heal. There are worse things." He fell silent, and the pair stared out into the waves for what felt like an eternity, watching the approaching land as they crept slowly on. Tanyl called to Faris from the helm, and then Nissa was alone. Eventually, she turned and watched Trey as his head bobbed with the crests and troughs of the waves around them, smiling softly at his blissful slumber. How long had it been since he'd last had a restful sleep? For him to be so thoroughly unconscious, she estimated that it had been a while. She heard Tanyl's footsteps before she turned to see him. Faris had taken over his post at the wheel.

"Aella was kind to let him come," he said without greeting as his eyes retraced the path toward Tryamon that hers had just left. Nissa made a soft, noncommittal noise. She had no desire to think of Aella at all.

"I didn't see her as the villain in this," she replied mildly.

"She's not her father," he said. Nissa's lips tightened into a line.

"That doesn't mean he should be shackled to her if he doesn't want to be. I know that as well as anyone," she said shortly. Tanyl exhaled loudly as he leaned against the rail, still studying his sleeping lord.

"Of course not. What I meant was that she was kind. She didn't ask for this any more than he did. They made a bargain when he wanted to come after you, and she made the terms intentionally vague so that he would have a longer leash." Tanyl plucked a speck of dust from the shoulder of his now-worn, yellow tunic and flicked it away.

"A leash nonetheless," Nissa bit back. Tanyl nodded again.

"A leash nonetheless. But it means that she's not your enemy, and she's not Trey's. How do you think her father reacted to us slipping away in the night? How do you think he reacted to knowing that she's the one who loosened the grip?" Nissa considered for a moment what Lord Raenon's temper might do in the face of her quiet defiance, and her heart softened.

"She's brave," she allowed softly.

"And just as in over her head." He matched her tone. She turned to face him curiously.

"So, what you're saying is, don't come out swinging for Aella when this all comes to a head," she clarified. He lifted both of his eyebrows.

"I'll leave that decision up to you." She rolled her eyes at the response, but before she could reply, Trey stirred across from them. "I'll leave you to it, then." Tanyl nodded toward Tryamon and then rejoined Faris.

It was only a few short hours later—too short, in Nissa's opinion—that they were docking the ship. She stepped onto the weathered wood, looking curiously up at the stone tower that wrapped against the coast, worn and faded from the sun and salt. This was Risadell. This was where her mother had grown up. She nearly toppled over as a burly man shouldered past her, a stinking net of mostly-dead fish slung over his shoulder. Faris caught her and shot the man a glare as she wrinkled her nose. She brushed the wrinkles out of her top, waving her hand to catch Trey's attention as lightning sparked in his eyes.

"It's fine. I was in the way," she said briskly. To her amusement, Trey and Faris exchanged a long-suffering look. She reached a hesitant hand into the folds of her skirt, pulling out the obsidian pendant by the cord. She held her breath as she brushed a finger against her stone, and to her relief, no hidden power burned back at her. Nissa let out a sigh of relief as she brushed the cord over her head and let the pendant rest against her flesh, catching Trey's eyes as it settled in place. Risadell was no place for one of her fits if someone's scrying caught her unawares. She studied the tower again, reveling in the way that the sea-wind swept the hair from the back of her neck. It was as though the sea here recognized her and was calling her home.

64

———

Risadell was a beautiful place. It was as lively and warm as Domogién had been, but without the dust and suffocating heat. It was small too, smaller than Nissa had realized when she was young. She wondered again why her mother hadn't brought her to visit more than the once. Then again, as she stood and faced the sea, perhaps the city was too free for her father's tastes. Better to keep them locked behind the icy barricade than to taste freedom in the salty air. She hadn't found a trace of the friends of her mother's youth, but it had been easy for the alias of Elyssa Broffet, accompanied by her brother and his friend, to make a reappearance, especially once Tanyl had taken off to warn Pippa of Ward's impending pursuit. It had been easier still to find a kindly innkeeper who offered them room and board in exchange for work during their short stay. Nissa had done it all before.

A breeze pushed off of the shore, and she inhaled in deeply, not flinching as Tryamon materialized beside her. Her heart pitched slightly as he said nothing, his own body turned to the open ocean. Out of the corner of her eye, she saw Trey close his eyes and take a deep breath of his own, and she shifted slightly to press their arms against each other. Together, they stood, side by side as they faced the sea.

"You're leaving." The certainty of her words shocked even Nissa. Each syllable fell like a blow.

"I don't really have a choice." There was nothing sharp about Trey's reply.

"What's it like?" she asked, tilting her head to look at him. He faced her with a guarded expression, and she wished she could take the words back.

"I can feel it tugging at me. Aella was generous to let me come after you, but I made a bargain. I have to keep up my end." There was no emotion in his voice, and something in her chest cracked a little.

"You haven't fully sealed it yet, maybe—" He held up a hand to stop her.

"It's done, Nissa. I can already feel it pulling at me. It doesn't matter if we haven't finalized it yet; the magic is already bound in place." His face darkened, and Nissa fell silent for a moment, watching the waves crest and then crash against the shore. On the horizon, clouds gathered.

"You don't think Aella would want out? If there was a way out?" she asked quietly. His shoulders tensed, and out of the corner of her eye, Nissa watched as his jaw worked furiously before he answered.

"She didn't want this any more than I did. We're strangers."

"So, let's just say—" He rounded on her, eyes dark with frustration.

"There's no point. What's done is done. This was the cost of —" he fell silent. "This was what had to happen, Nissa. There's no way out of it. Look at your mother. Don't you think if there was a way out of it, she would have found one by now?" His breathing turned ragged as his eyes blazed into hers. Nissa met his gaze calmly and lifted her chin.

"Hers was fully sealed. Yours is not." He shook his head.

"You are the most stubborn, impossible woman I have ever —" He broke off with an exasperated huff. They were silent for a moment more.

"Why did you take the Oath?" she asked. He blinked at her. "What?"

"You started to say that this was the cost. The cost of what?" He looked away, stepping to the side, and she lunged forward to grab his wrist.

"It doesn't matter," he said roughly. She looked him evenly in the face, a cloud of suspicion rising in her chest.

"Don't you lie to me, Tryamon Brandell. Why did you take the Oath?" He met her eyes again, and this time, sorrow and anger bloomed together in them.

"Raenon said he'd kill you if I didn't." She blinked at him, thunderstruck.

"Trey," she breathed. He shook his head violently and pulled out of her grip.

"Don't. You were only there because of me. You only got mixed up in anyone else's problems because of me. I couldn't let them hurt you, not for something that was my fault." He choked on the last word, and she felt heat build behind her eyes. He had sold himself for a lifetime to make sure she had freedom during hers. A tear slid down her cheek, and without thinking, she yanked his arm again, catching him off balance so he faced her. She stared hard at his face for a moment before lurching forward and wrapping her arms around his waist, pressing her face against his chest. He stiffened in surprise, before his hands twitched up to press against her back. She turned her face to the side, staring out at the sea again as he sank into a hug, wrapping her in an equal embrace as he rested his chin on her head. Tears slid freely down her cheeks now, and she fought the urge to bat them away. There was no shame in feeling, not when he had done this for her.

She lost track of the heartbeats as they stood there, their eyes locked on the waves as a heavy weight of resolve settled in her chest. She would find a way to help him. The bond wasn't finalized; there had to be a way to break it, if it had to be sealed with the final step. She would find out how. He had given her her freedom; she would do the same for him. She wouldn't stop, not until she found a way to free him. She tilted her head back to look up into his face, into those amber eyes that blazed gold as they met hers. Nissa opened her mouth to tell him of her plans, and his face softened, as though he already knew what she was going to say.

"Trey!" Faris's frantic voice stiffened his spine again as he looked hard over her shoulder, and he stepped backward, breaking them apart. Nissa shivered at the sudden chill of the ocean breeze, turning to see that their friend was running, and dread froze her heart in place. Someone was dead, she knew it. Had Ward already gotten to Pippa? Had he—

"What is it?" Trey asked, his eyes wide as Faris skidded to a halt in front of them. His cheeks were flushed as he gasped for breath, and Nissa wondered suddenly how far he had run.

"News," he gasped. "From Domogién." Nissa's heart thundered in her chest. If Faris was bearing news from a Fire Realm city—if Ward had gotten to Pippa before Tanyl could warn her, she would never—

"Is Pippa—?" Clearly, Trey was thinking along the same lines. Still gasping, Faris shook his head as he thrust a rolled paper into Trey's hands, putting his hands on his knees as he wheezed. Nissa and Trey exchanged a wary look before he unrolled it slowly. An elegant scrawl marred the smooth surface of the page.

Let it be acknowledged throughout the Realms of Galarmos that from this day, Cyril Brandell, adoptive son of Edris and Aithne Brandell, will be named as heir to the Fire Realm.

The message was dated at the bottom of the page several days prior. It slipped from Trey's grasp, twisting on its fluttering path to the ground as the wind threatened to carry it out to sea. Nissa pressed her foot on top of it to fix it to the earth, bending to grasp it in her hand. Her eyes scanned the page again before they found Trey's face, white with shock and staring sightlessly at where the message had rested beneath her boot.

The thoughts roared in Nissa's head. His parents had wanted an alliance with the Air Realm to secure the bloodline and ensure power for their future grandchildren. They had forced him into a union that required the Blood Oath in order to ensure that their line remained strong, and now, when they had finally gotten what they wanted from him, they were going to replace Trey with *Cyril*?

"This has to be a mistake," she said, rounding on Faris. "Where did you get this?" she demanded. He straightened, his face still flushed.

"They sent out a message to the major cities in the realms. I'm not sure how one came to Risadell—maybe because it's a port town? I don't know, I just stopped by the pub, and it was posted there, and—" A dark look from Nissa quelled his stuttering. She shot a nervous glance at Trey, whose hands had started to shake.

"Trey," she began. He shook his head, the movement so slight she almost missed it. She fell silent, resisting the urge to reach out and touch him, to offer some measure of comfort. He didn't deserve this; he had done everything they had demanded of him. He had sold his life and his power to their plans, and now...

"I suppose they got their perfect heir after all." His voice was quiet, deadly, and as flat as his eyes as he turned toward Faris. "Thank you for passing this along." Nissa looked helplessly at her friend, who ran a hand through his messy, brown hair, regret and helplessness warring for the territory of his face.

"There has to be a mistake," she whispered. The look that Trey fixed on her froze her in place.

"Yeah. I guess it was me." Her heart cracked, splintering at his deadened expression as he turned from the shore and walked slowly away, his shoulders weighted with the invisible burden he carried, his footsteps heavy with the invisible chains he wore. Every part of her screamed for her to follow, to say or do something to ease that load, but she knew that there was nothing she could do. She rounded on Faris, who stared after Tryamon with something like guilt carved into his expression.

"How did this happen?" she hissed. Faris flinched away from her, and she forced herself to leash her roiling emotions. "Why would they do that? He did everything they asked!"

"He's beholden to the Air Realm now," Faris said quietly. Nissa stiffened. Was this their plan all along? Had they planned to harness power for their bloodline and punish Trey for his quiet rebellion at the same time? Rage pulsed through Nissa as she stared at the shrinking silhouette of the retreating Tryamon.

"They can't do this," she hissed. "Not after everything he's sacrificed for them." Faris looked at her with a look that was almost pitying.

"He didn't do it for them," he said quietly. After a pause, he spoke again, "I should follow him. Make sure he doesn't do anything stupid to blow our cover." And then, Nissa was alone. She gritted her teeth as temper flooded through her, burning as it threatened to consume her. They wouldn't get away with it; they wouldn't do to Trey what Nissa's father had tried to do to her. He was more than a bloodline, and there had to be a way out for him. Determination hardened her heart, and she narrowed her eyes as she stared out at the sea, to the endlessness and possibilities that swelled and crested there. The Oath was two-fold for a reason; there had to be a way out of it. The certainty of that fact swept across Nissa's rage, dampening it even as her determination soared. She turned to face the retreating figures in the distance, watching as Faris fell into step beside Trey. She would find a way out for him. He had given her back the chance of a life, *her* life; she owed him the same.

65

———

"Y̲ou're not going." Trey's flat refusal nearly knocked Nissa back a step, but she stood firm, crossing her arms over her chest.

"I missed the part where I was asking your permission," she said pointedly. Off to the side, Faris snorted, and Trey shot him a glare.

"You don't think Sel'veren is the first place they'd look for you?" he asked. She scowled.

"Only if they think I'm an idiot. The logical thing to do would be to get as far away from there as possible." Trey stared at her as though she'd shared something painstakingly obvious. Her cheeks burned. "So obviously, they won't expect me to go back," she pointed out.

"She has a point," Faris piped up, and he held Tryamon's gaze as the lightning bearer shot him a glare.

"Don't encourage her," he warned, and Nissa scowled.

"Remind me, what was the point in fighting to live freely if I don't get to choose what I do with that freedom?" she challenged.

"You'd be putting a target on your back to go back to the Makani house after everything—" Nissa raised an eyebrow.

"Who said anything about going back to their house? Am I barred from the city now?" Trey pressed his lips together in a firm line, and Nissa knew that her point had hit home.

"She won't be alone," Faris interjected, "since I think it's pretty safe to say my career in Lord Alvar's guard is over once they find out I've left my post." Trey cut him another unamused look, and Faris shrugged. "Just saying." Nissa flashed him a grateful look, and he smiled slightly in return.

"Of all the places that you could go, all of the realms that you could travel to, you're picking the Air Realm. You're choosing Sel'veren." Trey shook his head, and a flicker of nervousness batted around in Nissa's chest.

"Careful, Tryamon. I'll start thinking you don't enjoy my company." She lifted an eyebrow, masking the insecurity with bravado. His expression darkened.

"You *know* that's not it, I—" He broke off as Faris coughed pointedly. "I didn't come all this way to get you out of this mess just for you to put yourself in danger again," he grumbled. Her temper flared immediately to meet the challenge.

"I didn't *ask* you to come."

"Well, no, but—"

"It's not like you were the only one who crossed the Realms, Brandell," Faris cut in sharply. Nissa bit back an appreciative smile as Trey rounded on him.

"Will you *please* just—"

"Can you give us a minute?" Nissa cut across him quietly, and Trey's eyes snapped back to her face. Faris's mouth twisted with displeasure as he shifted foot to foot. She shot him a pointed look, and with a sigh of resignation, he turned and departed.

"I don't understand you." Tryamon crossed his arms on the words as she turned and faced him again.

"Don't you?" she asked.

"No."

"What's there to understand?"

"You've been running for as long as I've known you. Any time I've tried to help you has just made things more complicated. Now, you have the opportunity to *live,* Nissa. You can *really* live without complications or other people mucking it up for you, and now you're insisting on coming back to Sel'veren. It doesn't make sense." She threw up her hands.

"You're ridiculous. It makes the same amount of sense as it did for you to cross half of Galarmos to break me out of the Frosted Keep."

"That's different," he argued.

"In what *possible* way is it different?" Her eyes flashed.

"You wouldn't have been taken if I hadn't dragged you to Sel'veren. You wouldn't be conspicuous at all if I hadn't detained you at the border. That was me righting my wrong. *This,*" he gestured between them, "is madness." She took a step toward him, tilting her head back to stare in his face.

"We aren't going over this again. *This* is doing what's right." He opened his mouth to speak again, and she cut across him before he could get the words out. "You've spent months overextending yourself to keep me safe, even when it didn't make sense. Before that, you took a chance on another woman who was fleeing danger. But how many times has someone fought for you, Trey?" She was close enough to him that she could read the stiffness in his muscles and hear the catch of his breath as she spoke. "Let me fight for you." She took another step forward.

"I don't know what you think you can do," he choked out.

"You didn't seal the Oath, not fully. There has to be a reason that it has two parts. Something has to finalize the bond. If you haven't sworn fealty, then it's not over yet." His eyes dropped to hers, hope and torment warring in the twin points of amber.

"You don't know that," he said. The ghost of a smile curved on her face.

"You've called me stubborn, and you've called me impossible. Let me live up to it. Someone out there knows something, and I won't stop looking for the answer until I find it," she said.

"Nissa," he took a deep breath, and she shook her head.

"Nothing you can say is going to convince me otherwise." She paused for a moment. "Unless, of course, you've suddenly fallen madly in love with Aella and *want* to be bloodsworn to her. She is beautiful, after all, and I can see how one might—" Her words muffled as his calloused hand covered her lips, and she laughed against it as their eyes met. She leaned closer, watching in wonder as longing replaced the hopelessness that lined his face as her heart thundered in her chest. He drew closer, leaning over her as his hand slid from her mouth to cup her cheek. His fingers brushed her hair as his hand wandered to the nape of her neck, drawing her closer. Her breath caught in her throat as the heat of his body warmed against her own. Trey pulled away, and she swayed at the sudden absence of his body as he retreated.

"I can't," he said, his breaths suddenly ragged. She stared stupidly for a moment, repressing a shiver as a breeze filled the space his body had just rested before she found her voice.

"The bond. Of course," she said instantly, casting her eyes toward the ground. A hesitant hand reached forward and lifted her chin so that she met his eyes again.

"It's not that I don't..." he trailed off, dropping his hand, and she nodded.

"I get it, Trey. You don't have to explain yourself to me."

"Are you oka—" he broke off as they stared at each other. A smile fought onto her face as she took in the planes of his face, the edge of his jaw. She memorized the way the light refracted against his suddenly bright eyes. In that moment, she knew, beyond any shadow of what she'd thought she understood before. This man, who had fought so hard for the freedom of a stranger, deserved it himself. Tryamon Brandell had crossed realms and defied authorities and put his own position at risk time and time again so that no one met the same fate that he himself was bound for, and he deserved someone who would fight for him too. She would be that person for him. What was the point of gaining her own freedom if she didn't do some good with it? Nissa lifted her chin as the renewed sense of purpose washed over her. The tidal wave swept her away.

ACKNOWLEDGMENTS

This book would not have been possible without the help of so many in my little village of support.

First, to Reid, Cassie, and Kenly, thank you for agreeing to read early versions of this story. Your feedback made this story what it was, and I am endlessly in your debt for reading those early drafts.

To the ever-talented design team at GetCovers Design, thank you for taking my loose idea for a cover and turning it into something incredible.

To my husband, Colten, who probably knows this story better than anyone outside of myself, thank you for listening to my endless, late-night rants about this book (and the series as a whole) as this project developed from a barely-there concept into something tangible. Thank you for always believing in me.

To my daughter, thank you for always being so excited to point out "that's Mama's book" every time you saw me working or caught sight of my cover art. You keep me going every day.

Finally, to you, dear reader, I want to thank you for taking the chance on By Fire and Flood, the Songs of Galarmos series, and all of the magic that comes with them.

ABOUT THE AUTHOR

Sage Kafsky began writing at a young age. She is passionate about puns and the great outdoors. When she's not writing, Sage enjoys spending time out in nature, reading fantasy novels, and going on adventures. She currently lives in Tennessee with her husband, their daughter, and their furry and feathery family members.

ALSO BY SAGE KAFSKY

Songs of Galarmos

By Fire and Flood

By Heavens and Hail

Standalone

Watchdog

Short Stories

Lemons and Liars

Threshold